ALSO BY CAROl

CW01522142

THE RISE OF I

CREEPING SHADOW

BLEEDING SNOW

TURNING TIDE

WEEPING SKY

FAILING LIGHT

THE RISE OF ISAAC NOVELLAS

FALLING FIRE (PART ONE)

FALLING FIRE (PART TWO)

Find the latest information and more at

www.carolinepeckham.com

If you'd like to stay updated about my upcoming
releases then I'd love for you to join my VIP mailing
list. And in return you'll receive Falling Fire Parts 1 & 2
(A Rogan and Quinn Prequel Novella) for **FREE!**

This ebook is copyright material and must not be copied, reproduced, transferred, distributed, leased, licensed or publicly performed or used in any way except as specifically permitted in writing by the author. Any unauthorised distribution or use of this text may be a direct infringement of the author's rights and those responsible may be liable in law accordingly.

Published by Caroline Peckham 2017

Copyright 2017 Caroline Peckham

All rights reserved

Caroline Peckham has asserted her right under the copyright, designs and patents act, 1998, to be identified as the author of this work.

This is a work of fiction. Names, characters, places and incidents either are the product of the author's imagination or are used fictitiously. Any resemblance to actual persons, living or dead, events or locales is entirely coincidental.

ACKNOWLEDGEMENTS

To my parents for always believing in me and supporting me every step of the way on my journey to becoming a full-time indie author.

To my sister for all her hard work, proofreading and picking holes in my stories to make them the best they can be. And for writing your own books so that we will always be the biggest fans of each others work even if no one else reads them!

To the amazing Victoria for mulling over ideas with me and bringing things to this book that wouldn't be there without our conversations.

To the wonderful Kathleen for your unwavering support in everything I do and for putting up with my book ramblings on a regular basis.

To Julius for your continued support as a fellow indie author – we will make it one day!

And to all the fans who have loyally stood by my books as well as all the new ones who decided to take a chance on them. There are no authors without readers and I'll never stop being grateful for your continued support.

V

games

CAROLINE PECKHAM

Preface

I suspected I might die this way, at the hands of another, their eyes full of murder. But I didn't expect him to be so beautiful.

He bared his teeth, his milky fangs glistening at me in the lambent moonlight.

I fell still, my heartbeat slowing. It had only been a matter of time before I ended up here. And a small part of me was relieved. There were worse deaths than this. Much worse.

I tilted my chin up, baring my throat, my rampant pulse no doubt visible to my killer.

"Make it quick," I panted, the adrenaline subsiding from my veins.

I'd put up a good fight. I'd never go out without one. I'd beaten a superior opponent before. But not this time.

As my killer bore down on me, I recalled the last man who had me cowering in this way, at his mercy.

My stepfather.

After everything, here I was again.

Perhaps it was my fate to die this way after all.

Selena

Hands trembling, heart pounding, I placed one hesitant foot in front of the other.

This couldn't be happening.

I clung to the bundle of blankets, plastic cup and plate I'd been handed by a prison guard. Every single possession I'd brought with me had been taken away. I didn't know if I'd see my things again. That's why they'd had to prise the photograph from my clenched fist: the sacred moment of happiness captured between my mother and I all those years ago. How could they take it from me? It was all I had left of us.

Now, the only vision I had of her was one particularly haunting expression burned into my retinas. The one she'd had at the exact moment the judge convicted me – tears rolling down her ashen cheeks, her mouth parted in an endless, silent scream. Nauseous, that was how I felt. And the type of exhausted I imagined only an insomniac knew the taste of.

Despite my sentence being handed to me mere hours ago, it already felt like days. How much longer would it feel after a month? A year? *Ten*?

I could still see the blood, my pale hand clamped around the hilt of the knife, the blade buried in my stepfather's swollen gut.

His expression of shock and dismay. After all my years of submission, he would never in his wildest dreams have expected me to rise up against him.

A burly guard led me down a corridor of cells. The cavernous room was monotone; metal doors ringed the grey walls which rose up to meet an equally dull ceiling. The bleak space before me was broken only by a harsh red railing that surrounded a central space, rising up two levels above me and one below. Prisoners leered at me, muttering to one another, elbowing their friends to draw attention to me.

I could see it in their expressions, what I feared. They were thinking, *fresh meat*.

The guard halted me in front of a cell, his broad form just a shadow in my periphery. As he slid open a hatch in the door, I couldn't draw my eyes from the the dark hole. What would my cellmate be like? I had never worried about it until now. The trial had taken everything out of me, my courage included.

I'd promised I'd remain strong, for my mother's sake. But now I was here and entirely alone. Whoever stood beyond that door would be my regular company from here on out.

"Stand back," the guard barked and, like an idiot, I responded to his words, realising too late that the words weren't meant for me.

The brick-wall of a man didn't spare me a glance, instead rolling his shoulders and rapping a baton against the grey metal door. I was diminished beside him, my head barely grazing the breast pocket of his clean, white shirt. His chest pressed against the inside of it, all muscle. This man could break me in two, as could most of the guards I'd seen so far. What did they think of me?

A voice whispered the answer in my ear, cruel and all-knowing. *Killer. Killer. Killer.*

Through the hatch, I spotted a flash of red hair, then the guard snapped it shut. A harsh buzzing cut through the air and the door opened with a screech of metal.

The guard took my arm, drawing me closer, his mouth hovering by my ear, his breath so hot it left a heated patch on my skin. "Keep your head down in here."

A warning, or a tip? I couldn't be sure. But why would this man help me? Surely he knew what the rest of England saw me as: a vicious little killer.

He guided me inside. Two single beds sat opposite each other in a space perhaps six by eight feet. A girl stood at the foot of her bed in a grey jumper and jogging bottoms: the same clothes I'd been given to wear. Her fiery hair cascaded around her, hanging almost to her waist. Her face was pale and blemish-free, but her eyes were ringed with darkness and flecked with red veins. Guess I wasn't alone in the exhaustion department. I wondered what kept *her* awake at night.

I turned back to the guard for instructions but he gave me none, swiftly exiting the room. The door clunked loudly into place and a chill fled down my spine.

I'm alone in here. No one is going to protect me but me.

"Hi," I muttered, figuring it was best to break the ice as soon as possible. I was going to need allies in here – a prison was no place for actual friendships. This was about survival. And if there was one thing I knew about myself now, in the aftermath of all that had happened, it was that I'd do anything it took to survive.

The girl sauntered past her bed, her olive-green eyes trained on me, scouring, assessing. She was a year or two my senior. At eighteen, I imagined I was amongst the youngest here. If I'd killed my step-dad a year sooner, I could have been looking at juvenile prison and a far reduced sentence. But hell, I never had been one for good timing.

I dropped my eyes, turning to the other bed and placing the bundle of items on the mattress. No doubt playing the submissive in here was a solid move. At least initially, until I worked out the rules. And right then, I was certain being on good terms with my cell mate was a sensible idea. But genuine trust wasn't in my nature any more.

"You shouldn't turn your back on anyone in here," the girl said, making me snap around. Was she threatening me already? Christ, I'd only just walked in the door.

She was sitting on her bed, her long legs folded beneath her as she observed me. There was something cat-like about her; sweet and innocent-looking, but with a twisted look in her eye like she'd happily devour any creature smaller than her.

Blood pounded in my ears.

I perched on the edge of my bed, trying to keep my expression neutral.

Her eyes roamed over me once more. "I know you."

I stiffened as her gaze pierced through me. "I don't think so," I insisted, but doubt trickled into my gut. My trial had been well televised. And from what I'd heard, prisoners were privy to the luxury of the news.

"Yeah...you're the girl who killed her father."

"*Stepfather*," I corrected without thinking.

A satisfied smile pulled at her full lips and I gathered my thick, ebony curls into my hands, avoiding her gaze.

"Selena Grey," she said my name, her upper lip curling back. "I saw you on Sky News."

My heart clawed its way up into my throat. I'd been painted as a monster by the press. The abuse claims were dismissed by the court. Why didn't I go to the police months ago? Why didn't I show someone the bruises?

"I'm not what you think," I insisted, knotting my hands together.

"None of us are." She raised an eyebrow, evidently amused.

Was she mocking me?

I sucked in a slow breath, calming my erratic heartbeat. "What are you in for?"

She released a derisive snort. "Nothing as bad as you."

I ground my teeth, irritated that I wasn't getting anywhere with the girl. Well I wasn't going to waste my time trying to connect with someone who had clearly made up their mind about me.

I stood, firmly turning my back on her as I started making up my bed. If she believed I was some cold-blooded murderer, maybe she wouldn't start anything with me. I had to be stronger. Perhaps I'd be better off letting them believe what everyone else did.

My mother's final words to me ran through my mind. *"Don't ever forget what you are, Selena. You're a hero, baby girl. My hero."*

My chest hollowed out. Mum was the only person in the world who knew what had really happened. But perhaps that was a blessing in disguise now. The other prisoners mustn't think I was weak. Perhaps I was basing my judgement of prison life entirely on Hollywood films and dramatic Netflix shows, but I wasn't going to let my guard down all the same.

"Arson," the girl said and I made the conscious decision to keep my back to her, hoping it would encourage her to keep talking.

"Oh?" I questioned vaguely.

"I'm in for arson. And my name's Cassandra. Or Cass, if you like."

The fiery haired girl was in prison for arson, how fitting. I wasn't sure whether to believe her, but when I turned around, I saw the truth in her eyes. Call it a gift, but I'd always been able to see through someone's lies. Perhaps it was the years of living under a roof with a compulsive liar that had trained me to read people so well.

Why Cass had opened up to me though, was a mystery. Didn't she see me as some vengeful killer? The one who had taken her own stepfather's life out of spite and jealousy? Or so they'd said.

"What did you burn?" I asked, dropping onto the bed and leaning against the wall.

"I'd have burnt down the whole god-damn world if I could have." Light danced in her emerald eyes.

I couldn't fight a laugh at her tone and she surprised me by joining in. Some of the tension ran out of my shoulders.

"Alright, not the whole world. But one person's: my ex's. I wanted to watch his life be devoured by flames. Still do actually."

"Why?" My heart stumbled at her expression; there was a wildness in her I was instinctively wary of.

No friends, I reminded myself. *Just allies.*

The light in her eyes extinguished. "Payback."

I nodded, unsure if I should question her further, but curious to learn more.

She wound a finger around a crimson lock of hair, glancing away. Guess that was all the answers I was getting for now.

The door buzzed harshly and I stood, feeling safer on my feet as I prepared to face whoever was beyond it. Cass watched, clearly amused by me again.

"I better show you the ropes, little killer." She stood, moving to my side.

I muttered my thanks, letting her take the lead as the door

swung open. She was tall, but then I was pretty small myself so everyone seemed tall to me. Her limbs had a litheness to them that seemed almost model-worthy, even her hands belonged to a pianist. How did a girl like this end up in a maximum security prison? Arson alone surely wouldn't have been enough to land her here amongst the worst of womankind?

The other inmates were emptying out of their cells, all filing towards a metal staircase that led to the lower level. The monotonous clang of a hundred footsteps rang through the air as the women descended.

"Where are we going?" I moved closer to Cass. Ally or not, she was the nearest thing I had to one right now.

"Food," she said in explanation, her mouth barely moving. Her eyes were trained on the women ahead of us, specifically one with a short ponytail of ebony hair, as dark as mine. There was a delicate tattoo of a spiderweb on her neck. The group seemed at ease, laughing and chatting together. It reminded me of school, the cool girls banding together, making a scene as they talked loudly, dominating the space. But the problem with popular girls in prison, probably meant they were dangerous too.

One of them glanced over her shoulder, her pale blue eyes falling on me. She was large, nearly three times as wide as I was, her grey hair scraped back into a messy bun.

She nudged the girl with the tattoo who turned to look my way. She was younger than the rest of the group, perhaps a year or so older than me, I'd guess. A single black teardrop was tattooed next to her left eye.

As her amber irises trailed over me, a violent tremor ran down my spine. I knew that look all too well and it made me horribly uneasy. I was being sized up. A lamb assessed by a butcher.

We turned down a staircase, saving me from the girl's probing eyes and leaving me wondering whether I'd made the cut.

"Who is that?" I whispered to Cass.

"Kite. Don't trust her."

"Kite," I echoed, memorising the name. Whether Cass was trustworthy or not, I had no idea. But my instincts told me I'd rather be sharing a cell with her than someone like Kite or her companions. And my instincts had served me well in the past.

"She's boss around here, or likes to think so anyway. Calls herself Top Bitch, which is pretty fitting seeing as she runs around with a pack of mutts." Cass chuckled to herself and perhaps I'd have joined in under any other circumstances. But not then, not on my first day in prison where I was facing what felt like a lifetime under said 'Top Bitch'.

We arrived in a canteen filled with bright blue benches attached to dull grey tables, running the length of the room. The last thing I was at that moment was hungry, but I followed Cass to the queue anyway and grabbed a tray like everyone else. Despite not having been far ahead of us, Kite and her friends were somehow fronting the line. That was no coincidence, so I guessed Cass was right. That lot ran the place, which meant I was probably of interest. They'd want to make sure I wasn't trouble.

My gut twisted as a dark, Netflix-induced thought crawled into my mind. What if they wanted to put me in my place? What if they had some screwed up initiation test to make sure I was under the thumb, like ironing my hands or cutting my hair off? I gathered my raven hair into my fists, pulling it over one shoulder and running my fingers through it.

"Tray," a woman barked at me from behind the counter. She wore a frilly white apron and had more chins than I could count in the few seconds it took me to grab the tray and shuffle along the line.

Another woman ladled gravy over the meat and veg in the largest compartment on my tray. I mumbled a thank you before following Cass across the room.

"There's no place for manners in here," Cass snipped as we took a seat at the back of the room. I sat beside her, taking advantage of the view we had across the canteen.

Kite and her crew took up centre stage, resting their feet on the surrounding benches to make sure no one sat near them – not that I suspected anyone would try.

There seemed to be some unspoken code hanging in the air that everyone was abiding to without question. I was betting my survival banked on me knowing that code, so vowed to learn it. And fast.

Varick

Summer, 1803

"You're a free man now, brother." Jameson slapped me on the shoulder, giving me his usual cocky smile.

It was all well and good to be arrogant in hindsight, but we'd come within an inch of death today. My neck had had a date with a noose – it wasn't the first time I'd diced with death, but it had certainly been the closest I'd come.

Jameson, my first mate and most trusted crewman, took the English sons of bitches by force. Blew them to hell with our Brigantine. Course, it was that very ship I'd stolen from the men who wanted me to dance the hempen jig for it, not to mention the endless list of other accounts they'd arrested me for. In fact, if they hadn't wasted so much time reading my misgivings to the observing crowd, I'd be buried deep in hell right now rather than sailing my smug arse into the sunset.

"Make haste Jameson, they'll be after us within the hour."

"Aye, Captain Varick, what's our heading?" Jameson manned the tiller, his eye set keenly on the horizon.

I breathed in the glorious sea air, tasting the briny tang of freedom on my tongue. "Anywhere that has enough ale and *women to serve the crew with my gratitude. Not every Captain would be as lucky as I to have such honourable men at his back."*

"No, but that might have more to do with the fact you burned the map to Melwick's gold." Jameson ran his tongue over his teeth. He'd been as involved in that idea as I had, and the smirk that pulled at my mouth was soon mirrored on his. We'd made my life invaluable to the crew. For without me, the treasure was lost.

I tapped my temple. "Insurance, James. Only a fool wouldn't have it."

○ ☼ ○

I blinked slowly, my senses sharp as always, bringing back the scent of the sea from my past, dragging it into my nostrils. An empty space sat in my chest, neither expanding nor contracting, appearing like it always did when I recalled that life. The one I truly belonged to. Not here, kept like a guard dog, fed scraps to keep me strong. Only one full body a month. It was no way for a V to live.

There was a time I could have taken humans whenever I wanted, to feast on the sweet nectar of their blood at my own whim. But now...the world had changed. My kind was forced into hiding lest we be hunted to extinction. Not that I particularly cared for the others. We were all damned. We deserved this hellish life one way or another. And I wasn't going to waste a moment feeling remorseful for the way the other Vs were treated. My prerogative was sating my own needs. Blood first and foremost, always.

In a way, life was simpler now. My needs had been reduced to a singular desire. The thirst was cruel but it could be euphoric too. Only when it was quenched, however. The fact I spent half my time starving made sure most of the men in the castle avoided me. A good move, considering how irritable the thirst made me.

Ignus's mother, Katherine, approached me, her lemon-scented locks carrying to me even over the stagnant air of the holding cells. Like all the Helsings, she was blonde, willowy and fair-eyed, her features sharp and strong. She carried an air of grace and refinement, but the Helsings were probably more bloodthirsty than I was. "Varick, Ignus will be accompanying you to shore today. His father wishes for him to learn the ropes."

She reached out a hand and her silver-tipped nails dug into my wrist, singeing my skin like acid. I ground my teeth, my canines aching for the kill. But she had me under lock and key. We both knew it.

Katherine stepped closer; she was twice my age in terms of our appearance, but in reality I had over a hundred years on her. The Helsings lived longer than most humans, but they were yet to achieve true immortality. Of course, to them, Vampirism was an abomination. A disease they'd fought to eradicate for thousands of years. And yet now they abused their victory over our species. I couldn't quite decide if I'd rather they had annihilated us all, instead of manipulating us for their personal uses.

"It's a shame you're a damned creature of hell, Varick." She reached for the shining cross at her throat, stroking her thumb over it in a slow movement. "You must have been such a handsome man once. But I suppose you had a black heart, even then. Only damned souls would have been cursed with an eternity craving the taste of blood." Her slightly upturned nose twitched in disgust and I fought the urge to crush her slim neck. My fingers itched all the same.

"There's more than one way to be evil," I said simply, eyeing the pendant she wore.

Hypocritical little witch.

She moved closer still, her body brushing mine so my overactive senses reeked havoc on me. The sweetness of sugar seeped across my tongue, the flavour of a tea she'd recently drunk. A whisper of lavender soap from the last time she'd washed her hands. But beneath all the sweetness was something bitter and foul. Garlic oil rubbed onto her neck and wrists. It had no other effect on me apart from repelling me from her blood, but the scent was overwhelming and one taste would have spoiled the freshness of the desirable liquid that resided in her veins.

Simply put, when it came to the Helsings, they needed all the repellent they could get from me. Their blood was royal and pure; the first time I'd smelt it, the thirst had nearly driven me mad. For months they'd kept me locked in their cells, designed to contain someone like myself. Starving me into insanity before gifting me blood at long last. I was broken, then trained like a damned animal, and every day since I'd had to fight the sickness in my gut. The torture of being so close to their heavenly scent and yet forced under their thumb, unable to acquire a single taste.

"You'll make sure Ignus returns to Raskdød safely, Varick, do you understand me?" Her tone was stern, her eyes piercing. I had enough strength in my little finger to snap the woman's long neck, but her power over me was absolute.

Dipping my head in agreement, I waited for her to depart. She remained in place, her eyes trailing across my folded arms. "He's my only son, Vampire. You will protect him at your own detriment if needs be." Her eyes burned into mine as she extracted a slim, silver remote control from her pocket. Horror spiked in my chest but, as usual, I didn't show a single sign of fear as her thumb pressed one of the buttons. The metal capsule in my head responded, sending a shot of liquid silver into my veins. I roared in agony, smacking my head back against the wall to try and dislodge the device. I clawed at my long, dark hair, battling the fire in my body.

It always took six minutes to heal fully from a shot. Six minutes too many. That was what kept me in check. That vile contraption which stole my free will, my ability to sink my teeth into Katherine's pale neck and let the blood flow freely over my waiting tongue.

"You'll do as I say," her velvet smooth voice sailed to me.

Every fibre of my being ached to defy her. And one day, I

would. Mark my words. There was years of ancient revenge waiting to be unleashed on the Helsings, pounding through my veins. And perhaps one of the few things I shared with the other Vs, was my infinite desire to destroy every last one of them.

The war between Vampires and Hunters ended long ago, culminating in the creation of this hellish island. The atrocities committed here on not only Vampires, but humans too, were barbaric. Although I knew that, I never felt the guilt weigh heavily on me. I guessed I must have been a black-hearted man, but it was hard to connect with my past to now, to recall who I'd once been. The Vampire curse had amplified my cruelty, my desire for pain and suffering. I'd experienced the victory of a kill in my human life, man against man, sword against sword. But now, all that blood spilt by my hand swam in my dreams, surrounding me, reminding me of how much of it was wasted to the sea.

I licked my lips, the hunger rising like acid in my throat. It'd soon be time for me to feed. But I had work to do before I'd be given such a reward. The damn Helsings had me right where they wanted me. Not quite hungry enough to lose my mind, but desperate enough that I did as they said without question. All in the hopes of being fed.

At last, my vision refocused and my body fought off the silver. I was on my knees, my gaze landing on the red high heels before me. Probing fingers slid into my hair. The bitch was petting me like a dog.

I ground my teeth, inhaling slowly. "One day, Katherine, I'll rip your little blonde head off. I'll drain the blood from your neck, then I'll hunt down your family and suck the life from them too." I glanced up and she extracted her hand from my hair, her eyes haunted. "Every. Last. Drop."

"Get out," she hissed, recoiling from me.

Regaining my feet, I gazed down at her trembling hands. She tried to hide her fear, but I could smell the sweat sliding down her neck, I could hear the quickening of her frantic heartbeat. My eyes slid to the slim control clamped in her hand. "One day you'll be careless. Just one, fleeting moment and I'll have you. All I need to do is be patient." I smirked at her and she turned swiftly on her heel, hurrying away from me.

A soft groan sounded from one of the cells. The girls were growing weak; it was almost time for the first game of the season. They were cattle to the slaughter, each possessing a value that only paid out in their deaths. I searched for the guilt again, but it didn't come.

As I headed up the spiral staircase, I discovered a man in a suit waiting half way up. He was anxious, jittery, wringing his clammy hands together. His scent made my throat constrict: fear caused the cortisol levels to rise in his veins. A human's flavour was at its best when their body was calm, their heart beating slow and steady. But sometimes the only way to achieve that was through my Charm. Blinking slowly, I locked my eyes on the balding man and spoke, "Calm," I commanded and his pale, green eyes become unfocused, his breathing slowing.

A bead of sweat travelled from his forehead, following the arc of his long face, down to his chin before dripping to the floor. My ears rang as it dropped onto the metal, my senses flooded with the vile secretions of this bony human.

"Speak," I demanded, though I suspected I knew what it was he wanted. It was what all the spectators wanted, the men who visited the island to watch the games.

"Which women are the most desirable to you?" he asked.

He didn't mean sexually, though more than one of these men had tried to pay me off to get close to the girls.

They may have been marked for death, but that didn't mean I'd allow their abuse beforehand. Even a cretin like me had *some* morals. Not that the girls showed any appreciation for it.

"I can offer you something more than money," he breathed, the sheen on his forehead diminishing as my Charm took effect.

"I'm not to be bribed," I said simply, bored of this conversation already.

"Blood. Human Blood," he insisted and my spine straightened.

"Blood?" I questioned and he nodded blankly. "Where would you acquire such a thing?"

"I had a gallon brought with me."

"You've visited the island before," I stated, my eyes roaming over him. Yes, I knew this man. He had attended the games more than once, though he'd never approached me directly before now.

"Yes. I'm aware you have no interest in money. But I'm also

aware that the Helsings keep you starved, to keep you in line."
His words flowed freely. No lies could be told under my Charm, despite the fact his words were practically blasphemy against the Helsing family. No one who came here should undermine their power. At the very least they would have this man banned from the island if they found out, and perhaps even...

My eyes slid to his neck. They'd had me put men to death before, only once or twice in all these years, but for crimes worse than this. Should I risk the deal or simply confess this man's sins to Abraham in the hopes he'd bid me to carry out an execution?

I tasted my lips, listening to the steady beat of his heart. *Tha-thump, tha-thump, tha-thump*. It was mouthwatering, my instincts urging me to feed.

I released him from my Charm and he inhaled sharply, the fear flooding back into his body. I regarded him with disappointment. I'd rather my next meal was someone cleaner than this. And bottled blood wasn't worth betraying the Helsings for.

Sighing, I shouldered past him, knocking him to the ground as I continued my path upstairs. If there was one thing my time under the Helsings' rule had taught me, it was self control. I wasn't like my brothers and sisters out in the game: starved, craving blood, even feeding on each other in their desperation for nourishment.

My skin crawled at the image of them in my mind: haggard, emaciated, their features skewed and animal-like. They were a solid reminder of what I would become if I were left without food for long enough. More monster than man. And the Helsings wouldn't hesitate to throw me into the games if I ever outgrew my usefulness to them.

Selena

I suspected Kite would approach me sooner or later, but not so soon as the second day of my sentence. She cornered me in the laundry room, surrounded by three of her meatier crew. Sheets hung around us like ghosts, draped on row upon row of racks.

I eyed the security camera in the corner of the room. Was anyone watching? Would someone come to my aid if I was under attack?

"Hey, Daddy Killer," Kite said with a sneer. She might have been pretty if she wasn't always grimacing. Her face was make-up free like all of us, but she had the kind of flawless skin that meant it didn't matter. The teardrop beneath her eye was her only blemish, marking her as a killer. Like me.

"*Step*-daddy," I corrected, continuing to fold the freshly dried pillow cases. Why couldn't anyone get that right?

The faint smell of honeysuckle surrounded me from the washing. Hardly enough powder was used to clean the laundry; it was some non-bio, non-lethal, barely-scented crap that basically screamed 'you can swallow it all you like, but it won't kill you'.

"Whatever," spat one of the larger women amongst the group. Her belly stretched out the over-sized grey jumper she was wearing and the way her hair stuck out on either side of head gave her the appearance of an enormous owl.

Kite approached the table I was working at, resting her hands on the pillowcase I was trying to fold. I glanced up, fear spiking through my chest. I tried to hide it, keeping my jaw set and my gaze even. You'd think having killed someone, I might have been fearless. But I didn't feel any braver, or stronger.

"Something you wanted?" I asked, keeping my voice level.

Kite tugged off her jumper and threw it at me. The rest of her clothes swiftly followed, until she was standing in front of me in the tasteless skin-coloured underwear we'd all been given to wear. Tattoos ran over her skin, covering her arms.

"Bring them to me when they're clean," she demanded, strutting away from me with her barely-concealed body on show. A tattoo of her spine ran all the way down her back, like someone had unzipped her skin and left her bones exposed.

The Owl cracked her meaty knuckles, folding her arms as she waited for me to make my next move.

It was crunch time. I either bowed down to Kite or fought back. Logic told me to bow, but my instincts flared up, taking control.

"No," I said, just before Kite exited the room.

She snapped around, her dark choppy locks swinging about her shoulders. "What was that?" Her amber eyes narrowed to slits. "Wanna try again, puppy?"

My hands balled into fists as I struggled to remain calm. "I said no. And I'm not your *puppy*."

The girl with a pixie cut and extremely long legs, placed her hands on her hips. "The new pup's got attitude, Kite. Can we drown it?"

I stiffened as the girls surveyed me, feeling every inch of my body being assessed. Why had I taken the whole group on? Not even Cass was here to back me up.

"Hold the door," Kite barked at the Owl and the last of her pack of mutts. The final girl was tall and Grecian looking with thin eyebrows.

As Kite approached me, I glanced once more toward the cameras, the hairs standing up on the back of my neck. Surely someone was watching? They'd arrive at any moment. They had to.

My fingernails cut into my sweaty palms. Kite was half naked and yet she acted like she had the upper hand on me.

"Let's see how hard you can bite, little pup." Kite launched forward, slashing at me with her nails.

I managed to gather a fistful of her hair as she collided with me and yanked backwards, ducking her claws.

I shoved her back and she hit the table, screeching her fury.

Before she could launch at me again, a harsh buzzing filled the air and everyone froze.

"It's a bloody inspection," Kite hissed, snatching up her clothes and dragging them on.

I pressed against one of the washing machines, my heart racing like mad. "Inspection?" I questioned but I didn't know who I expected an explanation from.

Kite hacked up bile and spat on the clean washing I'd been folding. "This isn't over, pup. Watch your back. Or you might wake up with a knife in it."

The door slammed as they exited and I sagged against the machine, trying to slow my racing heart.

When my hands had finally stopped trembling, I gathered myself together, hurrying from the room. The way that Kite and the others had reacted, meant an inspection was important. But I had no idea why.

As I sprinted up the metal staircase toward level 3, I found the place practically empty. If I was late, I'd be in trouble, I was certain. And after just two days in prison, that was hardly the impression I wanted to make.

When I reached the first level of cells, I discovered the prisoners lining up around the balcony. Eyes followed me as I ran flat out to the next level, panting as I hurried down the line of girls to where Cass was standing outside our cell. She shot me an anxious glance as I joined her. One of the guards jotted down a note as she eyed me.

I hung my head low, desperate to catch my breath as the guards moved methodically down the line, checking our cells one by one. Presumably, contraband was their target, so I knew I was safe. The only possessions I'd brought still hadn't been returned to me. So even if I *wanted* to hide something, I couldn't.

Cass was jittery as the guards grew closer, shifting from foot to foot.

"Something up?" I breathed, trying to move my lips as little as possible.

Her mouth twitched, but she said nothing.

"Cass?" I narrowed my eyes as a bead of sweat slid down her forehead.

"I'm on my last strike," she hissed. "One more and they'll send me to isolation for god knows how long."

My heart rate spiked once more. "What? Why?"

"Shh!" a guard hushed us and Cass hung her head.

I leant back against the rail, hiding from the guard before speaking again. "Have you got something in the cell?"

Ever-so-slightly, Cass nodded.

My mouth dried out as two guards barged into our cell, turning stuff over with very little care for our things. My heart did little backflips as I waited for them to finish the search.

"What is it?" I pressed, but Cass shook her head, her lips clamped together.

My veins rushed with heat as I considered the consequences of them finding something incriminating. If she was taken away to isolation, would that mean I'd get a new cellmate? And what if that cellmate happened to be one of Kite's lapdogs?

My breathing grew ragged as a guard reappeared, his hand clamped around something. "Which one of you owns this?" He unfurled his fist, revealing a sharpened flint.

My heart sank as I glanced at Cass. Her expression grew

distant as she released a small sigh, preparing to own up.

"It's mine," I blurted, making a snap decision.

Cass's eyes grew to saucers as she turned to me.

"Yours, Grey?" the guard confirmed, looking doubtful then lowered his voice, "Causing trouble already?"

I nodded, my hands beginning to tremble. "I picked it up in the yard. I didn't know a rock was banned?" I tried out an innocent expression. The same one I'd used on the stand when being tried for my stepfather's murder. My lawyer had told me to act remorseful, but it was near impossible. That was the single time I'd tried to shirk the blame from myself. But truth be told, I wanted the blame. I was proud of it. I'd defeated the monster who had hurt me and my mother.

"Come with me." The guard took my arm, leading me away from the shell-shocked Cass who seemed desperate to say something.

I thrust up my chin as I passed by Kite and her cellmate. At least this would win me some 'don't mess with her' points.

The guard pulled me closer as we stepped through a security door. "Sorry, Grey. But rules are rules. You'll only be in isolation for a couple of days."

I glanced up at him, eyeing his youthful face and soft hazel eyes. "Why are you being nice to me?"

He stole a glance at a camera as we passed through another door. "Because I believe what you said in court."

My heart lifted as I looked at him. "You do?"

We turned into a corridor of thick metal doors; the air was stifling and oppressive. My heart rate immediately increased.

"Pretty girl like you wouldn't harm someone intentionally."

My heart sunk a little at his words. I thought he'd been on my side for some deeper reason, but my trust in men failed once again.

He unlocked one of the cells, swinging it open and gesturing for me to enter. I took a hasty glance inside the coffin-like room and resigned myself to its grimy walls and grey-green tones, stepping inside.

"I'll be right here," he said with a wink, pushing the door shut with a loud thunk.

I sunk down onto the bed, glaring at the door, my fingers growing itchy. The cell was colder than the one I shared with Cass. I could see why people might go mad in a place like this. Four walls and your thoughts. For a criminal, that had to be hell.

My mother's voice sailed into my mind, something she'd said to me a few days ago, that was now making a strange sort of sense, *"Never stop relying on your gut feelings. They'll always get you right where you're supposed to be."*

An ache sat in my chest as I thought about leaving her behind, all alone in our little town house in Kent. Would she sell the place now?

I tried not to dwell on it. That part of my life had crumbled into dust before my eyes. *This* was my life now. I had to move forward. But how could I, when time seemed to be frozen? Five years, ten, twenty, in this place. No matter how much time passed, I was always going to walk out of here as a killer. Nothing would ever change that.

○ ☼ ○

It was three days before I was allowed to return to the main prison. My act of loyalty to Cass had earned me some respect, at least. A girl who hid contraband just two days after being sent to prison wasn't someone to be messed with. And Cass was now a fully fledged ally. So, despite the icy cell and dreary endless days I'd spent alone, it was probably worth it.

The second I walked back into my cell, Cass hugged me. It was the first hug I'd received since my mother's goodbye, and that did strange things to my head. I wasn't a 'touchy-feely' type of person, but I embraced her briefly, wanting to solidify this bond between us.

I knew for sure she had my back when, several days later, she caught one of Kite's lackies slipping a razor blade into my mashed potato.

"You wanna keep it?" Cass passed the blade to me under the table.

"I'd rather not go back to isolation, thanks." I gently wrapped the blade into a tissue, eyeing Kite and her sour-faced group across the room. "Which one of them was it?"

"That one." She gestured with her chin to the largest woman amongst Kite's gang. Someone who must have weighed three times as much as me and looked like she could crush me like a grape.

"I think I'll let this one slide." I picked at my mash potato, pulling it apart with my fork in case it was hiding any other sharp objects. I couldn't fight the fear at knowing I'd been targeted like that. And for what purpose?

"They like to test the newbies," Cass said, reading my thoughts. "When I came here last year, they replaced my coffee with vinegar every day for a week."

"What did you do?"

"Drank it with a smile on my face." She laughed and there was that crazed look in her eye again. I wondered if there was anything about my appearance that labelled me as a killer.

The weeks became monotonous, slipping by, day and night merging into one. How did anyone find anything to live for in this place?

I lay one night, gazing up at the grey ceiling, wondering what kind of person I would be when I left prison in twenty five years. I'd be forty three, I realised. Which made me silently sob into my pillow for about an hour before I managed to calm down.

Just as I was drifting off at last, resigned to the empty future that awaited me, a harsh buzzing filled my ears. I sprang to my feet in alarm.

Cass rolled out of bed in a daze as the door clunked open.

"I think we have to get out," I said as she rubbed her eyes, yawning broadly.

We headed out of our cell where the lights blinded me, blazing against my retinas. The other prisoners were lining up around the railing as if waiting for an inspection. We joined them, blinking heavily to try and gain our senses.

"Cass, what's going on?" I breathed.

She shook her head, clearly as confused as I was.

"Inspection! Arms behind your backs!" the warden barked, her sharp voice ringing off the metal doors. She was tall with scraped-back, red hair and a pointed nose; something about her always made my spine tingle.

My thoughts were muddled. Why were they doing an inspection in the middle of the night?

My heart beat harder as I came to my senses, my gut telling me something was wrong.

The thrum of heavy footfalls approached down the walkway.

I leant forward a fraction, gazing past the row of girls toward the single man who seemed to be inspecting *us* – not our cells.

My stomach constricted. He was breathtaking, his skin golden and perfect, his eyes two endless mossy pits. His hair was overly long and twisted at the nape of his neck, a thin, black bandanna holding it in place. His broad shoulders tapered down to a firm stomach that met with slim hips; the press of cotton against his body hinted at the muscle that lay beneath.

His heavy leather coat flapped open as he walked with swift

grace in my direction. Whoever the man was, he didn't belong here.

He eyed the girls, seemingly searching for something. Breathing in deeply through his nose, his nostrils flared as he reached me. He halted, turning on his heel, his eyes snapping to mine.

I froze in place, taking in his sharp cheek bones, the stubble on his jaw, tracing every line of his chiselled perfection. He was unlike any man I'd ever seen, near-ethereal, almost inhuman.

His eyes were trained on me like I was the only girl in the room and, for a heartbeat, I felt that I was.

I could barely hold his burning gaze, my heart thumping hard against my ribcage. My instincts told me to run. This man was dangerous, I knew that from the rattling in my bones.

He finally drew his eyes from mine and I released a shaky breath I hadn't realised I'd been holding.

"Name?" he asked the guard who was standing nearby.

"Selena Grey," I answered for him, my voice ringing out in the quiet space.

The inspector's eyes snapped back to mine and my throat tightened. His gaze trailed over me like he was weighing up a cut of meat at the butcher.

"What are you in for, Selena?" he asked in a low purr.

I sensed Cass stiffen beside me, her hand slipping behind my back. I clutched her fingers as they reached mine. She could sense it too. Whoever this guy was, he wanted to hurt us.

I nearly couldn't find my voice, but when I did, it was strangled, "Murder."

A smile tugged at his lips. "You don't look like a killer."

In that moment, he reminded me of my stepfather: sneering, belittling me. It made me stronger. "Looks can be deceptive," I retorted, louder than I'd intended.

His eyes flashed, full of something like lust. But it wasn't that, it wasn't desire. Not in the way I knew it anyway.

He licked his lips, stepping closer, breathing in again. "That they can, Selena." There was a hint in his words of something I already suspected: he was no inspector. This guy had some other agenda. But *what*?

"She kills the men that hurt her," Cass spat and I glanced at her in horror. What was she *doing*?

Cass had that wild look in her eyes again, playing with fire even now.

The inspector's lake-green gaze slid onto her, roaming over her form as if seeing her for the first time. "Does she now? And what do *you* do to the men that hurt you?"

Cass jutted out her chin. "Burn them," she breathed.

He chuckled darkly and I seized the moment of distraction to glance over his shoulder, looking for the warden. I filled my gaze with a silent plea but the woman's eyes were glazed, seeming almost bored. Didn't she care what was happening here? Why were we being inspected by this strange man in the middle of the night?

A sinister smile remained on the inspector's lips. "I'll be seeing you two again." His eyes flitted to me, darting to my neck then up to my lips. "Very soon."

He continued walking and my shoulders dropped in relief as the weight of his oppressive presence lifted.

"Who is he?" I muttered to Cass, releasing her hand, finding mine slick with sweat.

"Trouble," she whispered.

I tried to see who else he spoke with, but he was too far down the line to tell.

After the inspection was over, I was wide awake, lying in bed with fear trickling through my blood.

It made me want to call my mother, pathetic as that was. I just wanted to lose myself in the comfort of her voice, the way I used to when I was a child. When Elijah would come home drunk and shout at us, tell us to get out of his sight. Mum would lie next to me in my bed, cradling me until he came and took her away.

Cass and I lay in our cell in silence, the only sound the thrumming of my heartbeat like the wings of a hummingbird in my ears. But I was sure she was as wide awake as I was.

◐ ☼ ◐

I woke to the sound of sloshing water, my body rocking back and forth. I thought I must be sick, my head spinning. Was I swaying, or was it in my mind?

A briny scent filled my nostrils, sharp and fresh like seawater.

Something wasn't right.

I jolted awake, icy air enveloping my body in a wave. My hands were bound before me. I lay on my back, the cold press of floorboards flush against my spine as I rocked from side to side. It was endlessly dark.

"*Hello?*" I shouted, panic sweeping through me.

I struggled to my knees, the floor swaying and making me stumble sideways. What was going on? Where the hell was I?

"Cass?!" I tried, desperate.

I lay my bound wrists on the wooden floor beneath me, feeling my way as I moved.

As my eyes adjusted, I spotted a faint light above, perhaps ten feet ahead. Moving towards it, I squinted, trying to work out what it was.

My knees knocked into something soft and I reached down, pressing my knuckles into it. A body. Someone was there.

I shook them as best I could. "Hello?" I whispered, prodding them harder.

Cold washed over me as a thought entered my mind. *Perhaps whoever it was, was dead.*

I slid my hands over them, searching for skin. My hand met a warm cheek and I relaxed in a wave.

"Wake up." I prodded them again, but got no response.

Moving awkwardly over them, I scrambled to my feet, still

crouching low . I felt almost drunk as I walked, the floor beneath me rocking precariously. A light swept over me and I found myself gazing up a staircase toward the sky, the glow of a crescent moon shimmering on my skin.

I clambered up the steps, peering out of the hatch, my breath stolen by the view beyond it.

I must have been dreaming.

I was on a boat, a yacht I guessed. Its sails were stark white above me, the wind pushing hard against them, making them fan out in an arc.

I searched for whoever was steering the vessel and my eyes fell on *him*. The inspector.

My breath snagged in my throat. Before I could recover, the yacht tipped at the bow and I nearly tumbled down the steep stairs. Crashing to my knees, I dug my nails into the wooden steps and splinters buried beneath them. I hissed in pain and the man's eyes snapped to mine, the whites of them near-luminescent in the darkness. My body was heavy, not responding fast enough as I tried to crawl away, my blood spiking with adrenaline.

He moved with impossible speed and, in my haste to escape, I slipped backwards. My stomach swooped as I dropped nearly eight feet. With a loud crack, my back impacted hard with the floor, knocking the wind from my lungs. A cough ripped through my chest and my vision momentarily flashed with bright sparks.

Blinking heavily, I gazed up at the man above me, his ragged hair falling forward, his large form framed by the square hole in the deck. The moonlight illuminated his outline as he gazed down at me, predator-like.

He stepped forward, bypassing the stairs and dropping toward me. I winced as his boots slammed into the boards either side of my head, vibrations thundering through my skull.

He tilted his head to one side, amusement dancing in his metallic green eyes. "I knew you were special, Selena."

He dipped down, dragging me to my feet, his hands like ice on my wrists. I flinched away but he held me in place, his grip vice-like.

I gazed up at him, struggling to loosen my tongue. "Where am I?"

"The more pressing question is: what am I going to do with you?" He grinned but there was no kindness in it. Moving suddenly, he whipped me into his arms like I weighed no more than a feather. A scream tore from my throat as I kicked wildly, panic overwhelming me. I wouldn't go out without a fight. I'd survived too much for my life to end at the hands of some stranger.

He laid me over his shoulder like I was no more cumbersome than a bale of hay. Turning, he sprang onto the deck with inhuman agility, holding my legs tight to his chest.

"Put me down!" I screeched, terror juddering through my body.

He ignored me, carrying me to the helm.

Laying me on the deck, he grinned with delight as he knelt

over me.

My instincts kicked in at last and I punched him hard in the chest. My knuckles crunched and I gasped in pain. His eyes flared with that lustful look again. But this time I recognised it for what it was: hunger.

"I've never smelt anything so good," he muttered to himself, leaning down.

With one hand, he took hold of my jaw, turning my head to the side with surprisingly gentle fingers. His cool mouth traced my neck.

I struggled as hard as I could, clawing at his arms, pushing, flailing madly, but he barely seemed to notice.

"No!" I gasped in horror, trying to escape. What was he going to do?

"Varick!" a man shouted from nearby. "Let her go this *instant*."

Varick paused, leaning back a fraction. There was murder in his eyes as he surveyed me like a ravenous wolf.

I trembled beneath him, my frozen hands curling into fists once more.

"Off. *Now*. You know the rules." The voice was authoritative and calm. Perhaps I had someone on my side after all.

Varick made a low, animal-like growl, standing so I was left as a quivering mess on the floor. I wasn't sure if it was the arctic wind that was making me shiver, or the hungry-looking man who had been about to assault me.

My saviour came into sight: a boy around my age with a shock of blonde hair - near white beneath the silvery moon. He stepped warily around Varick, approaching me with his brows drawn low.

"Jesus," he muttered, taking in my form with cool blue eyes.

He bent down, helping me to my feet and I clung to him, eyeing Varick over his shoulder. Perhaps this guy would help me, or at the very least keep that freak away from me.

"You haven't fed me since we left the island," Varick snarled, his broad shoulders squaring. "Do you have any idea how close I am to ripping *your* head off Ignus?" He had at least a foot on the blonde boy, and he wasn't short by any standards.

"And how do you think my father would repay you for that?" Ignus snorted, folding his arms over his narrow chest. "You'll be fed when we return. A girl like this will make us good money."

They were talking like I wasn't there, like I was some sort of chattel. I stepped away from the boy supporting me. He wasn't protecting me for any other reason than me holding some monetary value to him. But that was better than being left to the mercy of the other man.

I glanced toward the dark water a few feet away, my gut prickling. They say you do drastic things to survive life-threatening situations. And I'd been here before. It was life or death again. And I chose life.

Varick grimaced at the boy. "You know as well as I do that there is only so long I can go unfed without losing all rationale."

Ignus huffed a breath. "Well you shall have to wait a little longer!"

I took a step backwards, my thoughts focused on the edge of the yacht and nothing else.

I could do it. I could jump.

The frigid air clung to my skin and I doubted the seawater would be any more welcoming. But I knew with every part of my being, that I didn't want to find out where this boat was heading.

Unbidden thoughts sprang to mind of human traffickers. No one would look for a cold-blooded killer. No one would care. No one but Mum. I was on my own.

My heels hit the barrier at the edge of the boat. I glanced over my shoulder, searching the dusky horizon. Stars speckled the navy sky, doming overhead in an endless expanse of darkness. A huge shape loomed perhaps fifty feet away, catching my eye. Land, I was certain. What else could it be?

I could swim fifty feet, cold water or not. And anything was better than staying there with those two men. My gut twisted at the thought of leaving behind whoever was below deck. But my staying here would do them no good either.

As I made the decision, my eyes locked with Varick's. I'm sure he noticed the determination in my expression so I didn't waste a second, diving into the pitch black depths beneath me.

As I plunged into the sea, it felt more like hitting rocks than water. For the second time that night, the breath was forced from my lungs. It was more painful than I could have anticipated. I lost my senses, unsure which way was up, the ice-cold water making my body feel like lead.

Somehow, I found the strength to kick my legs, to move my arms enough to reach the surface.

As I breached the waterline, I swam for my life. Salt water stung my nose, slipping to the back of my throat and making me splutter.

Impossibly strong arms surrounded me and I cried out, fighting them with everything I had. For a moment, I prayed it was a trick of the cold, the water making me feel trapped. But then I was dragged upwards, water streaming from my body as I sailed through the air, hanging like a rag doll in the arms of my captor.

My feet slipped as they impact with the deck and Varick steadied me, holding my waist firmly against his hip. He eyed me with a keen interest, his tongue pressing into his cheek. Beautiful as his features were, the inhuman quality to them made him seem more beast-like than man.

"Enough of this!" Ignus barked. "Put her back asleep."

I tried to retort, but my teeth were chattering too hard. My bones felt like they'd been dunked in ice. My heart rate was raising to a dangerous level.

"She'll get hypothermia," Varick snapped, his hands still clamped around my waist.

Ignus rolled his eyes and their piercing blue caught the light of the moon. "Sort this out Varick. If she dies on this yacht, I'll make sure you don't get a single drop when we dock."

Varick swore between his teeth as Ignus stalked away, ducking into a cabin out of sight.

His cold eyes found mine and I looked up, feeling as vulnerable as a lamb before a wolf. The grey inmate clothes I was wearing were sodden, hanging heavily from my shivering body.

Varick looked straight into my eyes, his expression relaxing. "Do as I say, Selena." His words were velvet-smooth, full of comfort and holding a warmth to them that nearly took the edge off the ice in my bones. I blinked heavily, shaking the feeling from my body.

"Do as I say," he repeated.

I almost bought into it, my body responding to his strangely magnetic aura. My thoughts became swimmy and a voice in the back of my head coaxed me into the calm lull of the hypnotic feeling.

I blinked again, fighting my way out of it. What was the matter with me? This man was my captor. Why was his voice so disarming in that moment?

"N-no," I managed through chattering teeth.

His eyebrows arched in surprise. "Interesting..." he muttered. He reached into his long, dripping wet coat and produced a syringe.

I stepped back at the sight of it, but he snatched my wrist, dragging me closer with ease. In a swift movement, he grabbed my hair, tugging my head back and placing the tip of the needle to my neck.

"See you on Raskdød." His tortured expression shifted into a grave smile, then he jammed his thumb down on the plunger.

I clasped his wrist in vain, sinking to my knees as warmth trickled through my body, dragging me down into a dreamless sleep.

Selena

All at once, the memories of my kidnap flooded me. I gasped awake, sitting bolt upright, my brain rattling inside my skull. A pounding headache accompanied the sensation and I groaned, shutting my eyes for a few seconds to centre myself.

Where was I? This place was warm, dry...different. I was no longer on the yacht, I was certain.

Opening my eyes, I found myself on a bed of hay, the needles prodding me sharply through my clothes. A soft, amber light filled the air and a haze of dust motes floated lazily over me. It reminded me of a stable, the walls wooden, a single door before me. I lunged toward it, but was immediately yanked backwards by a shackle bolted around my ankle.

Glancing down, I frowned at the clothes I was wearing. A black gown was tethered onto my torso like a corset with swathes of satin hanging over my feet. Beneath them was a thick pair of woollen tights and heavy, army-style boots.

My pulse rose.

What was this?

What was happening?

I ran a hand into my hair – it was like silk. I grabbed a handful, dragging it beneath my nose. It was freshly washed, the scent of lavender clinging to me.

I scrambled to my feet, walking to the end of my tether. If I leant forward far enough, I could reach the door. I counted the steps it took. *One. Two. Three. Four.*

I banged my fist on the wood. "Hello?" I shouted.

No answer.

I gathered my thoughts, taking a slow, calming breath. I walked as far as possible in each direction, finding I could reach the left wall but not the right.

Although this place was infinitely more welcoming than the yacht, I felt no less a prisoner. And something about the pressing silence was the most unnerving thing of all. I'd rather have been back in my prison cell with Cass, dreaming up ways to escape, plotting idol revenge on Kite.

This wasn't happening. It couldn't be.

"Hello?!" I screamed louder, my voice hoarse.

"Selena?"

"Cass?" I gasped in utter relief, falling to my knees, pressing my cheek to the hay to try and see under the door. There was a small crack but only wooden floorboards were visible beyond it.

"Is that you?"

"Yes...where are we?" Her voice was trembling and it was so unlike Cass that it made my blood turn to ice. If *she* was afraid, then I definitely should be. Nothing about this felt right.

"I don't know. We were on a boat. Now we're here. I saw the *inspector.*"

Cass inhaled sharply. She sounded close, perhaps in the room next to mine. I banged my fist on the wall I was able to reach. "Are you in here?"

"Yes." Her fist hammered back.

I laid my palm flat against it, drawing comfort from her presence.

"Thank god you're here," I sighed, my shoulders dropping.

"Can't say I feel the same," she said dryly, sarcastic even now.

I dropped back onto my heels, eyeing the space for anything I could use as a weapon.

Footsteps sounded beyond my stable-like prison and I fell still, listening. My heart beat a frantic rhythm against my ribcage.

"Selena?" Cass whispered, just loud enough for me to catch it.

"What?" I questioned, not bothering to lower my voice. Whoever was out there already knew we were here. There was no point denying it.

"I think we're in trouble."

My door swung open and I found myself gazing up at Varick, his eyes dropping onto me like two dark marbles. I despised feeling small. My stepfather made me feel that way.

My instincts kicked in and I sprang to my feet, raising my fists.

Varick's mouth twisted up at the corners. "How many times are we going to go through this, Selena?"

Why was it that every time he said my name, it felt like something intimate? Like he was running his tongue over my skin, tasting me. I shuddered at the memory of his mouth on my neck. What had he been going to do? *Bite* me? Perhaps he really was as screwed up as he seemed.

I tightened my fists, planting my feet. I might have looked stupid, but I'd rather have taken a swing at this guy and failed, than not fight at all.

He strolled towards me, offering me his cheek. "Free shot."

I raised my brows, shuffling forward so I was closer to him. But not too close.

"Why?" I found my voice and the sound of a body shifted beyond the wall. Cass, no doubt listening to our every word. She was probably confused as hell by what she was hearing.

"Because I clearly still have a point to make with you." His eyes skimmed down to the dress I was wearing, dropping to my feet where the boots were concealed beneath the skirt. As he surveyed me, I tried not to show my fear, but my trembling hands must have given it away. When his gaze grew hungry, a surge of defiance took over me and I took him up on his offer.

I swung my arm, smacking my knuckles against his proffered cheek. My bones crunched against his damn cheekbone like it was cut from glass. Pain rocketed up my arm and I clutched it to my chest, fighting back the scream of pain that was raking at my throat.

"Ffff-" I bit down on my tongue.

Varick threw back his head, barking a laugh. He reached for me and I stumbled back to escape. When his hands encircled my waist, I remembered to fight. Screaming and kicking, he lifted me as easily as if I were embracing him and bent down, yanking at the cuff around my ankle so it broke off. My mind could barely process the strength it must have taken for him to do such a thing.

Keeping me over his shoulder, he walked me calmly from my cell. In comparison to him, I was an emotional wreck; a flightless bird being carried off to the chopping block. But I couldn't give up. Wherever this man was taking me, was nowhere I wanted to go.

Determined not to give up, I twisted around and slashed my nails across Varick's face. With a gasp, I noticed not a single mark had been left on his skin. In fact, my nails were broken, shredded like I'd just used a razor blade as a nail file.

"What..." I fell still in his arms, my body involuntarily beginning to tremble. "What are you?" I managed.

Varick adjusted the slim, black bandanna in his long, unruly hair (the only thing I'd managed to disrupt in his appearance) and continued walking without a word.

Cass's panicked cries carried to my ears and I clambered up Varick's rock-hard shoulders, gazing down the corridor of cobblestones. Rows of wooden doors lined the walls, the place lit by large bulbs hanging from the ceiling.

"I'm okay!" I called in an attempt to comfort her and she fell silent.

"I deserve an explanation," I spat at Varick and was happy when saliva sprayed over his face. Maybe I couldn't hurt him, but I could certainly show him I wasn't yet ready to give up fighting.

He ran a thumb down his cheek to wipe the trickle away, then placed it directly into his mouth. I gasped, leaning away from him in disgust.

"I'm banking on you surviving, Selena. Those mongrels out in the field won't savour you. It'd be such a waste." He eyed me thoughtfully as he headed toward a wide, metal door, then tucked me under one arm like a damn handbag.

My heartbeat thundered in my ears. "Surviving *what*?"

He smirked at me, but offered no further explanation as he shouldered through the door and dropped me to the floor.

My knees crashed into stone, but the woollen tights beneath my dress saved the skin from splitting open. As I glanced up, I inhaled hard at the sight before me. More than twenty girls stood in a row, none much older than me by the looks of them; they were all dressed in floor-length gowns, ranging from crystal blue to shimmering gold. We were in a square tower, rising up toward a dark ceiling. High above, sat in several rows, were people in dark suits, each with a shining white mask over their face.

The girls cowered before them, clutching each other's arms. But one amongst them caught my eye; a girl in a glittering blue gown, navy like the night sky. Her ebony hair was lifted into her usual ponytail and the single tear-drop tattoo sat beneath her eye. Kite looked fierce, ready to take on the whole world if that's what it would take to survive.

Though it was hard to tell, I sensed the eyes behind the eerie, faceless masks watching me and quickly rose to my feet.

A hard push to my spine reminded me of Varick's presence and I struggled to keep my balance as I moved to join the girls. He remained close, his breath cool on the bare skin of my shoulder. "Don't cause trouble."

I glared back at him, but my lower lip trembled, betraying my fear. The girl nearest to me with short blonde hair and a rounded nose shot me a warning look, so perhaps I had faked my confidence better than I'd realised.

"Fetch the last," a deep male voice rang down from the circle of people above. I tried to place the one speaking, but the crowd were statuesque.

"As you wish," Varick said simply, marching from the room in the direction we'd just come.

"That one's from the new shipment," a voice spoke and I recognised him as the boy from the yacht: Ignus. "Varick has his eye on her, father."

I spotted a mask turning to face Ignus and pinned my gaze on the two of them.

"Is that so?" the man replied.

Many of the crowd leaned forward in their chairs, peering down at me through the eyeholes in their masks. I felt naked before them and an icy feeling tracked down my spine.

Varick returned, dragging Cass by the arm. She wore a dress of green velvet with silver buttons up the bust. She seemed paler than ever as Varick pushed her toward me. We moved to meet each other and I wrapped her in my arms, her body shaking in my hold.

Cass pulled away, but kept her arm linked through mine which comforted me much more than she could ever have known. I glanced along the line of girls. Their faces were gaunt; red cuff marks and bruises lined their wrists. They'd certainly been here longer than Cass, Kite and I. Everything in their bodies spoke of prolonged mistreatment.

"Why are we here?" I blurted, focusing my gaze on Ignus, hoping he remembered me. What good it would do, I had no idea. But it was better than focusing on the faceless masses around him.

He stiffened in his seat, his fingers curling over the arms of his chair. "You are about to be part of an age-old tradition, Selena."

My name from his lips took me by surprise. I squinted up at him, instinctively stepping forward. A hand rested on my stomach, pressing me back with ease. Varick's dark eyes blazed at me in my periphery, but I kept my gaze on Ignus. Despite my fear, I knew I needed information, it was the only way I could start working on a plan to escape.

Many of the girls shuffled into one another, muttering quietly, my question evidently sparking their own curiosity.

"Silence!" Varick barked, stepping away from me. Some of the girls whimpered, huddling tighter together.

I flinched, but remained rooted to the spot, not giving him the satisfaction of seeing me recoil. Cass moved closer to me so our shoulders rubbed, clearly trying to move as far away from Varick as she could.

Ignus's father whispered something into his ear and I waited impatiently for my explanation. The onlookers made me uncomfortable and I bit my tongue on pressing them for answers. Luckily, I didn't have to as Kite spoke up.

"We have a right to know! You've kidnapped us and now you expect us to participate in some *tradition*? Well you're wrong." Kite pressed her shoulders back, looking as confident as if she were often kidnapped and laid out before an audience of creeps.

A titter of male laughter sounded throughout the room and my blood ran hot. Kite, on the other hand, looked ready to murder them all.

Varick shifted forward and I side-stepped to avoid him. As I moved, the clink of metal drew my attention to my ankle. Subtly hitching up my skirt, I discovered part of the shackle still remained intact, hanging from a piece of chain. It looked sharp. It could certainly do some damage.

"What do you want from us?" a girl in turquoise called to the crowd, digging her nails into her arms.

Varick's eyes appeared to measure every inch of her. He was surely assessing us, his gaze swinging from one girl to the next. My heart quickened as he focused on me. My fingers twitched as I thought of the weapon at my ankle. Somehow, he seemed to notice, his gaze following mine to the floor. All at once, he came at me, and simultaneously, I ducked down.

Miraculously, I had the jagged piece of metal clamped in my hand within seconds. But Varick was already upon me. I acted on instinct alone. Lunging upwards, I twisted my arm and swung it towards Varick's neck, a scream of defiance ripping from my lungs.

He caught my wrist just as the tip met his skin and a collective gasp sounded around the room, like air sucked through a vent. The sharp end of the metal pressed hard into his jugular, but not even a scratch appeared beneath it. I couldn't quite believe what I'd done and had the terrifying feeling that I'd just made things a whole lot worse for myself.

Varick's grip was iron, squeezing so hard that the metal slipped from my hand, dropping to the floor with a clang that echoed into the silence for an eternity.

"What did I say about trouble?" Varick snarled, so low that I was sure only I could hear.

I was frozen in his deadly gaze, trying not to wince as his fingers crushed my wrist. I lost the battle, my eyes crinkling at the corners.

"Better get used to pain, Grey." There was no amusement in his expression this time.

"Already am," I breathed and his brow lifted a fraction. This man would *not* get the better of me. And neither would any of the other cowards hiding behind those masks.

During our spat, the level of noise had risen around the room; the crowd above were now talking in low, excited voices and the girls were whispering in frantic tones.

It didn't take a rocket scientist to figure out who they were talking about. I shuffled back in to line, trying not to draw any more attention to myself than I already had.

"Enough talk," Ignus's father commanded, standing. Even from here I could tell he was an imposing man, his shoulders wide and his muscular chest nearly busting out of his shirt. "My name is Abraham Van Helsing, and each of you now belong to me."

"Ha," Kite spat and the girls murmured their discontent, spurred on by her defiance. I remained resolutely silent as Cass's fingernails dug into my arm.

"Varick." Abraham jutted his chin at the row of girls. "Prepare them."

Varick nodded, marching down the line. When he spoke, his voice rang out across the room, "You will be spending the night out on the island. Each of you will be armed to face the Vs."

"The what?" hissed the girl in pink next to me, her thick brows drawing together. No one answered her, which only caused more of a panic.

"Leave," Abraham ordered and I glanced up, wondering who he was talking to. My question was soon answered as the masked crowd began filing out of the room through a white door.

The other girls and I were left at the mercy of Varick. But twenty five against one seemed like good odds to me.

He marched past us, pushing everyone into a line. I hurriedly took up position at the end of it, not wanting him to touch me again. Varick stood before us, placing his hands behind his back.

A door opened and a man in white overalls wheeled in a trolley covered with a crimson sheet. He bowed his head to Varick before departing and the tell-tale sound of a lock clicked as he shut the door.

Varick moved to the trolley, whipping off the sheet in a fluid movement. Mutters broke out amongst the girls as we took in the implements laid out on it. White, wooden stakes, twenty five in total, all standing on their ends in rows.

My instincts screamed at me to get out of here. From everything I'd learnt so far, I was certain I didn't want to find out what 'Vs' were. And I definitely didn't want to spend a night out on some island.

"A Vampire can only be killed with white oak. Just a splinter driven into the skin can cause immeasurable pain." Varick took a stake in his palm, shifting it from side to side.

"Vampires?" an auburn-haired girl questioned him in a small voice. She was the slimmest of the group, her yellow dress barely held in place over her non-existent cleavage.

I was equally shocked by the term; some of the girls even broke hesitant smiles like they were hoping this was all some twisted joke. I wasn't so optimistic.

Varick rushed towards the girl who had spoken at an impossible speed, dragging her hair back in his fist to expose her neck. "Who would like proof?" he addressed the rest of us and my heart lurched in my chest. What on earth was he planning to do?

I thought of the yacht and of how Varick had pressed his mouth to my neck. How he'd seemed so...hungry. Lifting a palm, I traced my fingers over my throat, at war with myself over what to believe.

"Leave her alone!" A girl with copper skin and a bob of dark curls tugged at his arm, but he either didn't notice or didn't care.

Varick lowered his mouth to the girl's neck and I was certain not one person in the room could deny the sight of his sharp, perfectly pointed canines, ready to pierce her olive-tan neck.

"Stop! Marie- move!" her friend pleaded in her French accent.

The girl in Varick's arms, evidently Marie, seemed under some trance, gazing up at Varick with unfocused, dreamy eyes.

Varick dropped her and she fell to the ground in swathes of yellow silk as her dress caught around her legs.

"I'm fine, Briony," Marie murmured as the other girl fell to her side, hugging her close so the gold of her dress tangled with the yellow of the other's.

In their distraction, I'd backed up closer to the trolley. Vampire or not, those stakes looked sharp. And leaving them unattended was a foolish move, especially if all twenty five of us stuck together.

I subtly picked one up, clamping the cool, rounded bark between my fist. Varick's eyes flashed to mine and a smile curved his mouth.

"My little rebel," he remarked, rushing toward me in a blur of movement. He paused inches from my face and I found his hand already curled around my wrist. "Like this, Grey." He angled the sharp point between his ribs and to the left. No matter how hard I pushed, it wouldn't budge, but I still clenched my teeth and shoved harder.

"Selena," Cass gasped in warning and I eased my grip, losing my nerve.

"They're weaker than me," he murmured. "You'll manage." He moistened his lips and I shrank away.

Plucking the stake from my grip, Varick turned back to the room, leaving me unattended with the trolley again. "Selena, be a good girl and pass out the weapons."

My eyebrows lifted as I complied, happy to arm everyone in the room. If we all worked together, surely we could take down Varick?

As I met the eyes of each girl, I grew less and less hopeful of my plan. There was fight in their eyes, but fear was staying their hands.

Kite snatched a stake from my fist before I could pass her one. Her upper lip twitched as she recognised me, but she said nothing.

After Varick had shown each of us the weak spot on his body, he marched away, wrenching open the door across from us. The word *Vampire* circled in my head. It couldn't be true. Surely? But the inhuman way Varick moved, his strength, his teeth...I just didn't know if I could deny it any longer.

"We have to get out of here," Cass whispered to me as Varick gestured for everyone to go through.

I nodded stiffly, but had no solid plan to offer at that moment. As we followed the line of girls toward the door, I hesitated.

"Tell us the truth," I pleaded of Varick. "Do any of us have a chance of walking back through that door?"

Varick didn't answer and more of the girls filed past him, keeping close together. He caught my arm as I approached and I shuddered from his touch.

"You have a chance," he confirmed. "And I'm hungry as hell, so I'd appreciate the effort."

My upper lip curled back. "So even if I survive, you'll kill me anyway?"

"No...the Helsings have me under strict orders not to hurt the contestants." He breathed in, pulling me so close his nose was in my hair. "But trust me, you'll soon be *begging* for me to kill you instead of *them*."

Fear flickered through me and I knew Varick sensed it from the way he breathed the air. His grip tightened on me and he sucked his lower lip. "You better find a way to cover that delicious scent of yours, Selena. They're going to smell you from a mile away."

I tried to tug my arm free and he released me, gesturing for me to follow the other girls.

I hugged Cass's side and she took hold of my hand, feeling rattled as she wound her fingers between mine. "Stop challenging him," she begged and I stole a glance at her anxious expression.

My initial retort died on my lips. "I'll try."

"You're not being brave. You're being stupid."

Her grip tightened on my hand protectively, but the insult didn't pass me by. Maybe she was right. Maybe I *was* acting recklessly.

"Do you believe what he said?" I whispered as we passed down a corridor of ancient stone walls. Small, cross-shaped windows were slit into the highest part of them, revealing it was night time beyond them.

Two wooden doors awaited us, forming an arch at the end of the long corridor. Varick moved swiftly to open them, faster than any normal man, making my hair ruffle as he passed. Nothing about this was possible. I prayed I was about to wake up at any moment.

He wrenched the brass handles, revealing a large chapel beyond the doors.

Inside, the room stretched out ahead of us. Arching windows ringed the walls high above; a huge stained-glass window awaited us at the far end. Darkness prevailed beyond them, the night sky oppressively black. The only thing illuminating the space were torches set into brackets around the room. It felt like stepping back in time into some ancient cathedral.

Varick moved behind us, predator-like as he shifted from side to side. He lined us up before the alter, directing us to kneel.

The stone was icy even through the layers of material between it and my skin.

A man in white walked down the line, placing a cloak over

each of our backs, the same colour as our dresses. I wrapped it tightly around me, glancing at Cass. She shrugged, tying the knot around her neck.

"What is this?" a girl in a bright, orange dress addressed Varick as he passed.

"Old tradition. You get five minutes to pray."

My blood chilled and I glanced down the row of girls, some of whom were praying already, Kite included. Others simply sobbed, burying their faces in their skirts.

Before I could even think of what I might ask God for in the first prayer of my life – and possibly my last – the time ran out and Varick ordered us to sit in the rows of pews. It seemed like a twisted joke, him standing at the head of the church.

"I will call your names in alphabetical order. Once you are called, please make your way through the door to my left."

Our heads wheeled towards the metal door that had no place in a church. It looked new, strong as iron, held shut with cogs and wheels.

Cass's hand found mine.

"Angelina Bergström," he called.

The girl beside me stood; she had long blonde hair and the kind of face that belonged in a magazine. Her deep crimson dress brought out her blood-red lips. "Yes, that's me," she said in a soft, Swedish accent. The only thing that made her less beautiful were her blotchy red cheeks from where she'd been crying.

Varick gestured to the door. It took several seconds for her to react, but her resistance only caused Varick to move closer and that made her lurch out toward the door immediately. Angelina looked ghost-like and distant as she passed through it and it swung shut behind her.

Five minutes passed, then ten, the space loud with sobs and girls begging to be released. Varick kept his eyes fixed on a point somewhere over our heads, never responding.

"Marie Chevrier," Varick called at last and a girl whimpered in the row behind me.

I turned, spotting the girl in the yellow dress that Varick had threatened to bite. Her friend was comforting her in muttered French and eventually she made her way to the metal door. I fiddled with the long stake in my hand, my sweat making the bark slick in my hold.

As more of the girls were called, I realised that they ranged from all over Europe. Had they been taken from a prison like me? Were they criminals too?

My heart nearly froze when Varick called, "Selena Grey."

I stood, trying not to show fear as I mumbled a goodbye to Cass and headed to the door.

It opened as I approached and I crept through the heavy door, arriving in a long room awash with blood. My first instinct was that I was about to be executed and I wheeled around, desperately looking for a way out, but the door had already shut behind me.

That was when I spotted the crowd above; the masked men watching, like statues as they waited for something to happen.

One of them stood and I recognised from his thickset form, that he was Abraham. "Selena Grey, you are offered the privilege of competing in the V Games. If you agree, you will have the chance to erase your criminal record and return home with a clean slate."

"What?" I blurted in shock, my pulse skyrocketing. "How can you possibly offer me that?"

"I am a very powerful man, Miss Grey. I have the capabilities and the resources to wipe away your prison sentence. You were given twenty five years for the murder of your stepfather, is that correct?"

I nodded, my mouth agape. The offer was certainly alluring, but how could I possibly trust what this man said?

"What are the rules?" I questioned, my brows tugging together.

"No rules. You must simply survive for a week on the island."

A tingle ran down my spine, a mixture of hope and terror. How could I pass up the chance for freedom?

"And if I refuse?" I asked, trying to ignore the way the crowd were leaning close, talking amongst each other.

"Then you will return to prison where you can fulfil your sentence. And you will never be offered this chance again."

I thought of my mum, of how pleased she would be to have me home. I pictured rebuilding a life with her, a life without my stepfather to haunt us. She must have been so terribly alone now that I was gone. I didn't know if I could trust this man's word, but refusing such an opportunity simply didn't sit right with me.

With a weighing feeling inside me, I knew I'd already made my decision.

"Okay."

A door at the far end opened and a figure ran at me, human-like but animalistic in its movements. It was like something out of a horror film. A thin, emaciated body charged in my direction, its clothes torn to tatters, its body mucky and its hair overly grown.

As I fumbled with my stake, my heart drumming in my ears, it collided with me. I fought with all my might as I crashed into the wall behind me.

I screamed as nails tore at my arms and I shoved the creature back. It came at me again, its mouth open, fangs bared.

I was pinned against the wall, battling with all my strength, terror ripping through to my core. It didn't matter what I'd been told, nothing could have prepared me for this. Teeth gnashed near my ear and I lurched my head away, narrowly avoiding a bite. Now it was up close, it seemed more human, its body all sharp angles from starvation.

I pressed my arm to its neck, forcing it back as its tongue whipped out to taste the air around me. Without another thought, I recalled Varick's instructions and drove the stake up between its ribs.

With a roar of fury, slashing fingernails and snapping teeth, it fell dead at my feet. I was speckled with blackish-blue blood and shaken to my core, trying to process what had just had happened. One word rang in my head over and over: *Vampire, vampire,*

vampire.

A smattering of applause sounded around me, then a bidding process started like I was an item in an auction.

I barely heard any of it, shaking from head to toe, gazing at the dead creature at my feet. The words were a tumble, ringing in my ears, echoing around the space, around my *skull*. The last number I caught was somewhere near a million before a door opened and a woman led me out of the room. She said nothing, clamping a metal cuff onto my trembling wrist and guiding me into a large cell, ringed with bars.

The other girls who had gone before me were there, some flecked with blood, others clean but ashen-faced.

Everyone was silent, carving out their own space on the plain wooden benches laid out for us.

I took a seat at one end, scrubbing the blood smears from my arms as I tried to erase the memory of what I'd just witnessed. Was Varick right? Did Vampires exist? Had I just *killed* one?

Ever-so-slowly, the other girls arrived; all of them, it seemed, had accepted Abraham's offer.

I rushed to my feet when Cass appeared, blood peppering her cheeks. I wiped them clean and she gazed at me, saying nothing, her eyes fearful and her stake bloody.

"What kind of people would do this?" I breathed, but Cass had no answer, sinking down onto the bench beside me, clearly shaken.

Varick reappeared, moving into the cell with a surly

expression. If he was a Vampire, he certainly looked nothing like the one I'd just faced.

He stood by the single wall that the benches were lined up in front of and a screen burst to life behind him. A map of an island was projected across the cream stones, one section of the landmass highlighted in electric blue.

Varick pointed to the screen. "Your objective today, is simple. You must travel from the castle here." He gestured to us on the south-eastern coast of the island. "To here." A red dot was highlighted nearly directly opposite us on the west coast. "You have twelve hours to reach it."

"Or what?" Kite demanded.

"Or...the capsules that were placed in your heads upon your arrival, will release a fast-acting poison that will kill you in less than two seconds."

Silence fell.

I could practically hear my heart galloping in my chest.

"Poison?" some of the girls muttered.

"How can you do this to us?" someone called, then a tumult of noise broke out.

Varick waited calmly, like he'd seen this a hundred times. "You volunteered."

"You tricked us!" a girl in a silver dress cried, wringing her hands together.

I turned to Cass beside me and she set her jaw.

"Quiet!" he roared at last and the room fell deathly silent. "The cuffs on your wrists will provide you with the map and a timer. Simply tap it to gain access to them."

I followed his instructions and a hologram illuminated above my cuff, mirroring the map on the wall. Tapping it again brought up a timer of twelve hours, not yet running down.

"This is twisted," Cass whispered and I nodded, feeling like I was going into shock.

"I've changed my mind, I don't want to play," called a girl with a thick Greek accent.

"Too late," Varick snarled and she fell silent, quivering.

Varick's jaw hardened as he gazed around at us, quickly meeting my eye. "If you make it to the first checkpoint within the time limit, you will be rewarded with food, supplies and rest before the next round."

"How many rounds are there?" asked a girl with almond eyes and purple-streaked hair; I thought her accent might be Finnish but couldn't be sure.

"Five," Varick answered.

A tense silence filled the room, then I asked, "Who are those people in the white masks?"

"Spectators; men who are here solely because of you," Varick responded, his jaw ticking. "The entire game will be fed back here for them to watch. They will be betting on which of you they think will survive."

I felt sick, my stomach turning over and over. I was in the hands of psychopaths, about to play some twisted game for their entertainment.

Varick started handing out backpacks; they were the type a runner would wear, slimline and lightweight. He shoved one roughly into my arms and I grimaced at him, tugging it open. Inside, were several energy bars, a bottle of water, a box of matches and a slim knife.

I scoffed, chucking my bag at Varick's feet. He turned to me, practically snarling. "What is it now, sweetheart?"

"This is a joke," I muttered. "You're sending us to the slaughter. What's the food for, to pretend you're giving us a chance?"

Varick prowled closer as some of the other girls dropped their bags too. "Fine. Go out there without supplies. See what I care? You can take it or leave it." He kicked the bag at my feet and my heart thumped harder in my chest. I glared at the pack, stubbornly considering leaving it simply to spite Varick. But that would only harm my chances of survival – if there were any. With a sigh of defeat, I scooped up the bag and slung it over my shoulder.

"There will only be four Vs hunting you in this round," Varick announced. "The game will get progressively harder. So the quicker you learn how to defend yourselves, the better."

Silence rang out in the room, his words doing nothing to comfort any of us.

"So...if you'll proceed with me to the start of the game," Varick said, guiding us out of the cell.

We passed down a wide hall of pale flagstones and huge, red

and black tapestries, featuring a large letter H bordered by Latin phrases.

I felt the back of my neck, searching for a bump and my fingers brushed over a raised piece of skin. With a sinking feeling, I knew there was no way to escape.

Varick was watching me again and I dropped my hand, not wanting him to see me afraid. But, of course, I was terrified. Of him, of this place, of the creature that had attacked me and, most of all, of what lay beyond the huge wooden door at the end of the corridor. It was held in place by metal chains attached to the ceiling and, as Varick turned a massive wheel on the wall, the door slowly lowered, forming a bridge.

A sheet of snow hid the view beyond it, whipping across the land in a storm. We all huddled together as a horn blared through the castle, deafeningly loud.

Varick pointed toward the bridge and we shuffled out onto it, grouped together in a tight cluster.

I glanced back and Varick's eyes locked with mine, his expression seeming to say, *"Run."*

Selena

Ice. Snow. Night.

There was nothing but those three things beyond the wooden bridge. I squinted to try and see further, but snowflakes skated and danced through the air, forming a curtain before us.

Then something snagged my attention. Something that sent a chill down my already frozen spine.

Bones.

They crunched beneath our boots as we shuffled forward, clinging to each other in a throng of bodies. Bodies, I realised, that were sitting ducks for whatever was out here to hunt us. If anything Varick had said was true, we needed to split up, run, get as far away from this place as possible.

"Cass, move," I hissed, her fingernails tearing into my arm. I treasured the pain, knowing it confirmed her presence, my eyes darting left and right through the veil of snow around us.

The bascule bridge creaked as it moved upwards, stranding us on the island for good.

One of the girls, Maria, in her sunshine yellow dress, darted toward the rising platform, screaming as she tried to reach the edge of it above her head.

"Maria!" Briony screeched, darting toward her as Maria

teetered on the cliff edge. The sea water roared below, crashing against the endlessly sharp rocks. It was barely visible through the fog of snow, but the sheerness of the cliff walls alone was enough to invoke fear.

Maria's boots slipped from beneath her and Briony gripped her waist, dragging her back so they both tumbled to the ground in a heap.

"*Selena*," Cass hissed, but I couldn't drag my eyes from the cliff. She shook my arm until I turned to her, finding her eyes trained on the snow before us.

Dark figures drew closer in the mist. The longer we stood there, the more vulnerable we became.

A sucking, sniffing sounded as they approached.

"Go." I shoved Cass, not wanting to be around when the Vs emerged.

She stumbled over the hem of her long dress, gathering it up in her hands as we darted away from the other girls.

Footsteps pounded after us as the group followed. I glanced over my shoulder and the Vs descended on us.

Kite barged past me, faster than any of us as she took off into the snow and disappeared in an instant.

The wind swept across my path, surrounding us in a fog of white so I lost sight of the girls behind us.

But the screams didn't escape me.

I drew freezing breath after freezing breath into my laboured lungs, trying to focus on nothing but not falling as I ran, keeping my dress knotted up in my hands.

A scream cut short, followed by a vile gargling I knew I would never be able to wipe from my memory. Cass was just ahead, her long legs outpacing mine as I hurried to keep up.

The snowfall never let up, obscuring everything, both before us and behind. I kept my eyes on the swishing, dancing red hair of Cass ahead of me, stumbling over loose rocks and the ice that clung to the ground. The snow began to settle, so much so that we had to slow down, struggling through the thickening inches beneath our boots.

We hurried on for what felt like hours, walking until my legs ached and my lungs were raw. But we never stopped, not once, terrified of what was pursuing us out here.

A rush of air ruffled my hair and I ducked instinctively, clutching the stake tightly in my hand. Wheeling around, I saw only shadows dancing in the mist, but a strangled scream made every part of me shake.

The brief moment of distraction had separated me from the group. Cass was no longer visible and as I turned, left, right, round and round in circles, all I could see was the ever-pressing white mist.

I tried to slow my breathing, but no matter how hard I tried, it continued to drag raggedly from my lungs, seeming as loud as an alarm bell in my ears.

A crunch to my right made me slap a hand to my mouth. My fingers were numb, trembling, turning my lips to ice the longer I held them there.

Whispers filled the air like hushed prayers, working their way into my head. "Be still. Don't run, children. Come to us."

The lulling voice soothed my heartbeat for a moment and I nearly removed the hand from my mouth.

Snow clumped in my hair, melting as it reached my skin beneath and sliding down my neck in a cool trickle. My hand began to move, seemingly of its own accord. I struggled to force the voices from my head, blinking out of my stupor.

I remained stock still, my heart in my throat.

"Here's one," a sharp female voice cut through the mist.

I pinched my noise, my lungs burning for air. Footsteps sounded so close by, I was sure whoever was there was just feet away.

"Come here pretty girl," a rough male voice joined the first.

"Hello?" a girl's voice sounded nearby. I shook my head in horror, wanting to call out to tell them to run, but knowing I couldn't.

"So pretty, all that long yellow hair."

It wasn't me they'd found. And I despised myself for how much relief I felt for that.

"No more games, I'm starving," the male voice said and a scuffle sounded, then a loud thump as something heavy hit the ground.

A blood-curdling scream reached to high heaven, making me want to claw at my ears just so I didn't have to hear it a second longer.

Tears sailed down my cheeks as I used the girl's death to hide my escape, fleeing at a sprint, running faster than I'd ever run before. How could I leave her? What kind of person did that make me?

As I fled, my legs gave way beneath me and I slammed into the ground, the stake flying from my grip. I gasped in horror, desperate to find it, scrabbling through the snow.

"What was that?" a voice hissed close by. Too close.

With a wrenching feeling, I abandoned my plight, standing and sprinting away. I was desperate as I traversed the uneven ground, trying to escape, losing my footing again and again.

A new noise eventually reached to me from the distance: the gushing of fast water. I scrambled my way toward it, practically blind in the snowstorm, clambering down a rocky hill in the pressing darkness.

The tears on my cheeks had frozen to two trails of ice, leaving my face numb from the cold.

As I reached the bottom of the hill, the mist lifted.

Snowflakes melted as they hit the obsidian river before me and the rising, rocky walls made me feel as though I were encased within a bowl. A waterfall flooded the space with a cacophonous roaring that I prayed would cover the sound of my movements.

Picking my way across the rocks, I moved along the shore, growing closer to the falls. The spray clung to my hair so it curled around me, glistening with water droplets and flecks of white snow.

How I was ever going to survive the night without getting hypothermia was challenge enough, let alone without those bloodthirsty creatures hunting me too.

A cave was my salvation; not much more than a dent in the rocks like huge knuckles had once taken a swing at the wall. Inside, it was mostly dry, and that would have to be enough. The cold bit at my skin and I huddled within my cloak, clutching it tightly around my shivering shoulders.

Death lurked in plain sight. Death by teeth, death by ice, death by exhaustion. These were just a few of my options. But in my frigid state, my teeth chattering and my body rocking a rhythmic pattern back and forth, I found a memory to cling to. Admittedly, it could be considered a bitter one. But to me it tasted sweeter than honey.

The moment my mother found me: my stepfather's body slumped on top of mine. I lay panting in a pool of heated blood, blood that had seeped over my skin. I never realised how warm it was, and considering the man my stepfather had been, I'd have guessed he was a cold-blooded creature.

Mum had rolled the body off of mine and I extracted the blade from his belly. He'd died so quickly. I had no idea it would be that way. And in all honesty, I hadn't thought through the process of killing him. But a kitchen knife had been tucked into the folds of my pillow case for months.

As I sat rocking, the persistent rattle of my teeth in my ears and the roar of water beyond the cave, I thought of the way the blood had felt on my skin. I relived the relief, then the resulting tears, hugging my mother until she too was drenched in his blood. We waited too long to call the police. That was my mistake. The one they pinned on me in court. Where was the remorse? What kind of teenager stabbed their stepfather and didn't shed a tear? It didn't matter what I'd said about the abuse. There was no proof. Of course I'd say that. And my stepfather had been an upstanding man in the community. He even donated generously to the local church.

I released a breath, watching as it turned to vapour before my eyes.

Still alive.

Still breathing.

Using the cuff on my wrist for light, I spotted the remains of an old fire, the wood was nearly burnt to a crisp. It had long since been put out and I wondered if these 'games' were held regularly.

Lighting it could be a death wish. The smoke could alert the Vs to my presence. But the snow had soaked me through to the bone and, now that my adrenaline had subsided, I was shivering uncontrollably.

Perhaps another twenty minutes passed before my resolve finally broke.

Taking the matches from my bag, I stripped off small pieces of the box, gathering them into a pile before arranging them beneath the most salvageable log. I crumbled the charred ends of it so more kindling was added to the cardboard before striking the first match. It took three more to set the log alight, but it burned bright, crackling with red sparks as the bark was devoured.

If the spectators were watching, and no doubt they were, many probably just ripped up their betting slips for having chosen me as their winner. I tapped the cuff on my wrist, illuminating the map. Perhaps no more than a hundred acres was highlighted in blue on the hologram. Far to the west of the castle, on a corner of the island that tapered into a sharp point, sat a flashing red beacon: our first checkpoint. I had eleven hours left to make it there. And right then, that didn't seem like much time.

As the fire grew, I shed my cloak, laying it out to dry beside it. My hands soon regained feeling and my lips no longer felt like two lumps of ice clinging to my face.

My instincts told me fire and smoke were bound to draw the attention of my hunters. I just had to hope they had more easy targets to occupy them. However dark that thought was.

Soon, the constant gushing of the waterfall and the flicker of the firelight offered the illusion of safety. I curled up like a child before the flames, thinking over my next move. I couldn't waste much more time. Reaching my fingers toward the fire as close as I could manage without burning myself, I resolved to give myself a little longer in its embrace before I moved. Besides, it seemed like a reasonable idea to wait until some of the girls had journeyed away from this area, drawing the Vs away with them.

Every new sound that reached my ears made my body twitch

and jolt. Soon I'd be plunged into darkness, forced to face the cold once more.

A noise made me sit up; a pebble overturned by a shoe. Standing, I readied myself to face whatever came at me. It was too late to douse the fire. If a Vampire was close, it already knew I was here.

Varick

The Helsings insisted I watched the games. In part, to remind me what awaited me if I disobeyed them. And, I suspected, to keep the spectators in line, too. The Helsings may have had me under control, but the men didn't know that, and I was certain they were left to make their own conclusions about me. To them, I was one of the vicious Vs like those out in the game, tearing the heads off innocent girls. Well, as innocent as their criminal records showed.

Taking girls from prisons was a new idea brought in from the last generation of Helsings. In the modern age, it wasn't as easy to abduct women without the whole world finding out. So the idea was to choose women that few people cared about and Charm anyone who questioned their disappearance. Charming guards into believing a prisoner had died in the night was simpler than convincing the whole world to stop looking for some innocent country girl. The sad truth was, no one cared about anyone who had landed themselves in a maximum security prison. And no one would listen to their families either.

It sat better with the Helsings, too, knowing the girls were a bunch of murderers and felons themselves. They even preached it to their new clients, so they needn't feel guilty for participating in the blood sport. Not that I thought the spectators cared either way.

The numbers had remained remarkably similar for hundreds of years, and I for one, had witnessed the dark nature of these men.

The auditorium was laden with velvet chairs and betting tables where the men could spend more money as they kept one eye on the screens surrounding the room. I sat in the crescent of seats at the edge of the room, remaining in the shadows. My eyes were pinned on the screen showing Selena, curled around a fire.

I'd nearly bitten off my tongue when she'd lost her stake. Now she would have to reach the first checkpoint without a weapon. And though this may have been the easiest round of the game, with just four Vampires released to hunt them, she still had drastically reduced her chances of survival by losing it. My hopes of her survival were, of course, rooted in the fact I got to drink from the winners. And her blood was like nothing I'd ever smelt. The problem was, the Vs in the game would soon figure that out, too. Making her a prime target. And the thought was driving me mad.

My eyes flicked to another girl: the redhead who had arrived with Selena. She'd reached the hot springs on the island and was huddled around a steaming geezer. That area of the island was probably the safest. The scent of the sulphur would cover the girls' own, and the hot water would keep them alive. The only problem was, the Vs knew that. And it wouldn't be long before they ran a sweep through that area to see if any of the girls had stumbled upon it. The advantage was always with them. Unless the Vs were recently turned, they knew the island like the back of their hand. And the games were the only time they were let loose from their holding cells.

If it were me, I'd have been as ravenous as they were. When a Vampire was deprived of blood for months, there was nothing left of us but thirst. So, in a twisted way, I pitied them.

A cry went up across the room as a bald, portly man won a hand at poker. He gathered up the chips which were coloured red, stamped with the H of the Helsings. Money and blood, that's what this place was home to. Not much different from the sea life I'd once lived. But I'd never seen myself like these men. At least back then I had bet my life in a hand for gold, and blood had been spilt from my enemies, not in some organised game.

I'd always managed to keep a healthy distance from this scene, showing my face only as much as I had to during the season. Now, I sat rigidly in my chair and didn't plan on vacating it until I was sent to the first checkpoint to meet with today's survivors. I wondered how quickly they would realise that polar night currently reigned on this island. If any of them were waiting for the sun to rise and save them, they'd be sorely disappointed.

"Varick!" Abraham's voice boomed across the hall.

I tilted my head in acknowledgement as he marched toward me through the crowd. He was dressed in a smart suit and tie, his huge form towering above most of the heads in the room.

As he reached the bottom of the seating area, he jerked his chin, commanding that I come down.

Bored already by whatever conversation he wanted to have

with me, I rose gracefully from my seat and moved toward him.

A hush fell over the room as the men closest to me noticed my movement, all eyes drawn to mine. As I halted on the last step before Abraham, he shot out a hand and took hold of my shirt, tugging roughly forward. I resisted his Hunter strength, but the menace in his eyes warned me to comply.

"Do you want a shot of silver in front of the entire room?" he snarled, threateningly reaching into the inside of his jacket, no doubt to retrieve the remote that could unleash a torrent of pain on me.

I dropped off the last step, brushing the creases from my shirt that his fist had made. "Now, now, Abraham. We both know you'd be hard pressed to do that. I'm your obedient little pet, remember? You wouldn't want your buddies to think otherwise."

He gave me a cold stare through his deep blue eyes. "Even a dog needs a kick every now and then to keep it in line."

I growled at him, baring my teeth. "Go ahead. Kick the dog."

Abraham moved strategically in front of me so his towering height just about blocked me from sight of the room.

"Fetch Mercy for me. She hasn't shown her face since the game started. I need her out here, talking to our clients."

"You mean flirting money out of them," I growled. Mercy had recently turned eighteen, and her father had no shame in flaunting her beauty in front of the spectators. It worked like a charm.

I, however, was less fond of the girl. She'd taken it upon herself to taunt me for her own amusement, trying to tempt me into wanting her like she did every other man that passed through this castle.

"Just fetch her," Abraham snapped before walking away.

With a final glance at Selena on the towering screen, I headed up to the east tower, in no particular hurry to see Mercy.

When I knocked on her door, she called, "Come in!"

I pushed inside, finding the girl sprawled out on the golden sheets of her bed in nothing but a lacy bra and knickers. Her endlessly blonde locks flowed around her like a silky pool.

"Get dressed, your father wants you downstairs," I demanded, turning on my heel to leave.

"Stop," she commanded and my shoulders tensed as I paused in the doorway. My senses were rife with her blood. She was the only one of the Helsings who didn't rub garlic oil onto her skin. Another temptation for my benefit. The little witch.

But the only reason I wanted to sink my teeth into Mercy's neck, was to get my revenge on the family I despised more than anything in the world.

Mercy swung her olive-tan legs over the bed, moving toward me, shrugging on a see-through sliver of chiffon she evidently deemed a robe.

As she approached, her wide, sea blue eyes swept over me. The remote that all of them carried hung around her neck on a silver chain. She was encouraged to keep it there by her father who believed her to be the most appealing to me. And I had no doubt I could kill Mercy if I wanted to. She let her guard down often, all in the name of exerting her power over me. She knew I'd never touch her, I'd be signing my own death warrant if I did.

"I thought they might send you," she said with a smirk, pulling up her coral-pink lips.

"Is that why you were laid out on the bed like an afternoon snack?" I remarked, baring my teeth so she backed up, but only half a step.

The flitter of fear in her eyes turned to excitement. She was perhaps the most twisted of the family, drawn to the danger in me. But she was playing with fire and she knew it.

"Don't worry, Mercy." I sneered. "I'd sooner drink sewage water than your blood." I wanted to my words to dig at her, but we both knew how much I craved her blood.

She twisted a strand of her hair around her finger, her brow furrowing in offense. "Come on, Varick." She stepped closer, splaying a hand across my chest. "There must be some *man* left in there." Her hand sailed lower and I caught her wrist at my waistband, crushing it in my fist.

She let out a squeak of pain, but I didn't let go. "I'll tell Father," she warned.

"You'll tell him what? That you flaunted yourself in front of me?" I released her wrist and she cupped it in her other hand, looking wounded.

"The other men look at me, why don't you?" She pouted, looking very much the teenager that she was.

"Because the only reason I'd ever touch you, Mercy, is to drain every drop of that delicious blood of yours." I stepped forward but she stood her ground.

Sweeping her hair aside, she bared her neck. "Prove it."

I rolled my eyes, but my tongue burned with thirst. "Go downstairs. I won't ask you again."

She played with the tassels on her pathetic excuse for a robe, regarding me. "What will you do if I say no?"

"Throw you over my shoulder and deliver you to your father as you are. Dressed or not." I shrugged. "I don't really give a damn."

She huffed, storming away from me and grabbing a blood-red dress from the ornate wardrobe. Slinking out of her robe, it fluttered to the floor as she pulled the dress over her head. It was hardly much less revealing than if she had remained in her underwear, but I didn't really care. I wanted to get back to the auditorium. For all I knew, Selena could already be dead. When the Vs attacked, they didn't waste much time in killing their victims. Not until they'd fed a little, at least. Then the nastier side of the game came out. It was probably a blessing for some of the girls to have died first. Because if a V caught them after they'd been fed, they were more likely to toy with their food.

They weren't stupid, they knew the Helsings and their vile clients were watching. And some of the Vs revelled in putting on a show for them.

When we returned to the auditorium, Mercy melted into the crowd, immediately descended on by the lustful onlookers in the room.

Abraham stood upon a stage at the far end, clasping his hands together. "Good evening gentlemen. Tonight, the contestants will arrive at the first checkpoint. In order to let both you and they rest, the time they spend there won't be broadcast."

A murmur of ascent went up. "No doubt they'll need a good rest for tomorrow!" called one of the regular game attendants, his shiny, slicked-back hair catching my eye. Brice Edgewater was an Australian beef farmer who had more money than grains of sand on his million acre farm in the outback. It was his third year at the games and he had a streak of picking the winners.

Abraham gestured to me with his chin. "Varick will be heading out to meet the girls and prepare them for tomorrow."

I stood, making my way through the crowd. The men shifted out of my way with haste, tucking the tails of their coats beneath them. I took my time, basking in their fear. Mercy brushed her fingers over my spine, showing me off to the men as her glorified pet.

I shrugged past her, meeting Abraham as he descended from the stage. "The supplies are waiting at the lighthouse. Make sure any girls who survive are well rested for tomorrow."

He gave me a hard stare and I sighed. It was always the same old warnings, as if I would betray him and drink from the competitors. I wasn't fool enough to do so. I knew the value they held to the Helsings and I wasn't going to risk my own neck for the sake of a drink. No matter how desperate I became.

"Of course, sir." I gave him a mocking bow of my head,

moving past him toward the exit. Slipping through the wooden door, I picked up my pace, speeding through the castle toward the bridge.

I knew I was making haste for another reason. I didn't want to waste a second not watching the game. Every moment I was away from the screen, was another moment a V could have stumbled upon Selena. Could have drained her body of life, left her slumped in the snow like a beautiful, broken doll. Ever since I'd first smelled her blood at the British prison, I couldn't force her from my mind. She'd inched her way into my body like a splinter under my skin. No doubt it was due to the desperate hunger I was currently a slave to. The Helsings had been stingier than ever before this game. I should have been fed two weeks ago, but still they denied me blood.

The lighthouse was on the western coast, on a splinter of rock that protruded from the island. It had long since been retired, but the structure still remained; it had originally been built to warn trade ships of the rocky shore. But no ships took this route any longer. The Helsings had made sure of that.

I had over ten hours before time ran out to reach the checkpoint. But in the past, some of the girls would make it there in a few hours. It was a bold tactic, but it often worked. The Vs spent the first couple of rounds weeding off the weaker prey. Much as they were a slave to this game, their enjoyment of the hunt meant they wanted the game to continue for as long as possible. The final rounds were always a blood bath. And though the girls didn't know it, sometimes there was no survivors in this game. The last one to the grave would take the metaphorical crown, for all the good it did them.

I made my way across the frosty landscape, skirting the edge of the island so I wouldn't run into any of the girls. But from time to time, I smelt them on the wind, a mixture of sweat, blood and tears. Someone was injured, and it wouldn't be long before they were hunted down. Even a paper-cut was a death sentence out here. Bodily odours could be covered well enough with mud, or the pungent sulphurous steam of the hot springs on the southern shore. But our senses were finely tuned to the metallic scent of blood, so much so that I could smell a drop of it a mile away.

With the island rife with animals, however, from wild wolves to the caribou in the northern forest, our senses were dulled slightly. I supposed the Helsings had planned it as such, to give the girls a slither of a chance.

I reached the towering white lighthouse and hurried across the rocky outcrop in a burst of speed. Wrenching open the metal door at the bottom, I hurried up the twisting stairway. At the top, another door parted me from the room inside. The place was damp and cold, disused since the previous games last winter. It was my job to make it comfortable for the girls and I was certain to make that a priority, as soon as I'd projected the footage on the far wall.

The game flashed to life and several boxes split across it, the hidden cameras trained on the surviving contestants. It took me three seconds to locate Selena and a small sigh passed my lips as I spotted her alive, still inside the cave. But she wasn't alone.

Selena

"**E**rgh, just my luck for it to be *you* here," Kite snarled as she stepped into the cave.

My hackles rose and I felt instinctively protective of the safe space I'd found. Behind her, was a girl with mousy brown hair and an equally mousy face. Her wide, hazel eyes and small, button nose gave her the appearance of a creature stuck in the headlights of an oncoming car. Her dress was a dark grey, unlike the navy blue of Kite's. It occurred to me that it was an unfair advantage for us to be wearing darker colours, whilst other girls attempted to hide the bright dresses they'd been given to wear.

Kite had her stake clamped in her hand and blue blood, so dark it was almost black, dripped from it in thick globs.

"Did you kill one of them?" I gasped as the girls moved closer, dropping down in front of the dying embers of my fire without a word.

I got to my feet, feeling anxious to leave the cave in case they had led one of the Vs here.

"Yeah. It's not that hard." Kite shrugged and the other girl shifted closer to her.

"What's your name?" I addressed the stranger.

"Tiffany," she replied in a small voice. "Kite saved me."

"I wouldn't call it that," Kite snipped. "That V came at both of us. I was saving myself."

"Still..." Tiffany took her stake from her bag, chucking it onto the fire. "I couldn't do it."

"Idiot," Kite muttered, but spared no time in stoking the fire with the toe of her boot. She turned to me with a smirk that skewed her pretty features. "Why are you still hanging around on this corner of the island anyway?"

"I just thought..." I couldn't finish my sentence, not wanting to admit the truth. I dropped down across from them as the heat of the fire tempted me in.

Kite's smile grew. "You thought the other girls would draw the Vampires away so you could take a safe stroll to the checkpoint." I scowled at her and she tapped her temple with a satisfied smile. "Great minds think alike."

My morals were thoroughly shaken by her words. I didn't want to admit that that was why I was holding up here a little longer than I should have.

The wind picked up outside, drawing the smoke out so it filtered into the sky.

I held my hands above the fire, warming my numb fingers. Tiffany played with the cuff on her wrist, twisting and turning the hologram of the map that was projected above it.

Kite glanced at it. "We should move soon."

"We have hours," Tiffany insisted.

"The quicker we get there, the sooner we're safe," Kite

snapped and I couldn't help but agree.

"As soon as the fire burns down, we'll go," Tiffany said and we nodded our agreement.

Having Kite as an ally didn't appeal to me one bit. But if she'd killed a V already, perhaps she was useful to have around. Her fight wasn't with me any more, but that didn't mean I wouldn't stop watching my back around her.

The wind howled beyond the cave, loud enough to be heard over the streaming river.

My stomach grumbled loudly and Kite rolled her eyes. "Hungry, puppy?"

I ignored her, taking out one of the energy bars from my bag. It was wrapped in black paper with a large H printed on it. The hard oat bar inside didn't look particularly appealing, but I was too hungry to complain, wolfing it down in two bites.

As the fire flickered out, I tried to prepare myself mentally for moving beyond the cave. Already, it had become a sanctuary of sorts and my instincts urged me to stay there. But Kite was right, the sooner we got to the lighthouse, the better. I just hoped Cass had the same idea. I prayed she was still alive, making her way to safety as quickly as she could.

As we readied to leave, I stamped out the remains of the fire and slung my pack over my shoulders, pulling my ebony robe over it.

"A black dress seems like the best deal," Kite muttered, eyeing my clothes. "I reckon someone likes you back at the castle."

I spat a laugh, going to reply when a voice stopped me dead.

"Three little piggies, standing in a cave. Three little piggies, thought they would be safe."

I snapped around to face the smiling Vampire in the cave entrance. He had a mop of grizzly dark hair that hung lankly around his gaunt face. His bright blue eyes were sunken and bloodshot and his lips were drawn back to reveal reddened gums and sharp yellow teeth.

My heart stumbled as I gazed at him, none of us making a move.

He breathed in deeply, his nostrils flaring, his eyes landing on me. "My, my, something smells good in here."

"Go," Kite hissed, but I was frozen to the spot.

She readied herself in a fighting stance, grinning back at the V. "Come and get your cut of bacon, then."

My hands trembled as I prepared to run. Tiffany was twitching with how much she was shaking, clinging to Kite's side like a monkey to its mother.

The V lunged at us in a blur of movement and Kite moved almost as fast, shoving Tiffany into his outstretched arms.

A scream tore from her throat that sliced to my core. I cried out in horror as Kite darted past me, fleeing from the cave.

Tiffany was dragged to the ground in a swirl of grey material and blood splattered across the wall.

There was nothing I could do. Nothing but run.

My legs moved before I even realised I was running and the

cold air engulfed me as I sprinted from the cave. Kite was nowhere in sight, but I didn't care. I wanted as far away from her as I did the V.

I charged in the direction of the waterfall, clambering up a muddy hill beside it.

By the time I reached the top, I was soaked and panting harder than I ever had in my life. I orientated myself on the map then kept running, fleeing into a thick forest, the tree trunks whipping past me, flashing in my periphery.

I didn't stop until I physically couldn't run any longer, dropping down behind a large pine and resting my back against the trunk. I gulped down the freezing air, crushing my knees to my chest as I tried to catch my breath enough to be quiet.

The snow hadn't reached the ground of the forest and it was relatively dry beneath the canopy. The smell of pine needles flooded my senses, a smell I'd once loved. I focused on the peace of the wood and the chattering of small mammals above, assuring me I was in no immediate danger.

I took the bottle of water from my pack, drinking nearly half before I forced myself to save it. I shut my eyes, reminded of the pine air freshener that hung in my mother's car. We'd only ever take her car when we were going somewhere nice. The park was where we took refuge from my stepfather, stealing a few hours of happiness, playing on the swings and soaking in the laughter of the other children.

I clung to the image and opened my eyes, calculating my next move. Tapping my cuff, I orientated myself on the map. The coast was west of the forest and I was thankful I could remain in the dark wood for now. So long as the buzz of life surrounded me in the forest, I convinced myself no Vs could be close. Standing, I started walking at a brisk pace, moving as quietly but as quickly as possible. From time to time I checked my heading, but I never stopped moving.

The trees were dense and the snap of twigs around me was so regular that I soon stopped jumping at the noise. My own boots sounded as loud as thunder as I walked, but there was nothing I could do about it.

As the trees thinned and the moonlight illuminated the snow beyond the forest edge, my heart rate picked up. The second I was out of the trees, I'd have no cover. What if the Vs were waiting out there to pick off the girls as they appeared?

I paused by one of the final trees, tucking myself behind it and peering out. Another twig snapped behind me and I ignored it, staring out at the snowy field before me. Grass peeked through the top of it, so I knew the land was flat.

The hairs raised on the back of my neck and I snapped around, overwhelmed with the feeling of someone watching me. It was irrational, because of course people were watching me. A hundred men betting on me living or dying, I didn't know which.

My eyes flitted from tree to tree, every fluttering leaf causing my heart to jolt. But if a V was waiting there, surely they would have attacked me by now?

I forced my eyes back on the field ahead and stepped out into the snow. In the distance, I could just make out the coast where several black rocks jutted into the sky. Moving to the nearest pine tree, I snapped off a branch with a fan of needles on one end.

Setting my eye on the horizon, I started moving, finding the snow only a few inches deep. As I'd predicted, my boots left deep tracks behind me so I leant an arm back, dragging the branch so it covered them as I moved. It wasn't entirely effective, but unless a V was looking for my tracks here, they wouldn't be easily noticed. And I wasn't leaving anything up to chance.

The plain of land dropped down toward the coast and I spied the lighthouse in the far distance, like a beacon of hope, stark white beneath the moon.

A scream ripped through the air and I froze, searching for the source. It was hard to tell how far away it had come from, but as I waited, the girl was revealed, darting out of a small group of trees in the distance.

Between here and the lighthouse, coloured dots far ahead marked girls running toward it.

I was well behind, but even from here, I could see the blurs of Vampires charging after them across the snow.

I counted four girls and three Vs. Those weren't good odds. Screams rose into the night and all I could do was stand there as the first girl fell and a stream of red flew across the snow.

My legs trembled, urging me to run. Ahead of me was a bloodbath, but going back wasn't an option.

Glancing at the dark rocks at the edge of the cliff, an idea came to me. Praying the other girls were enough of a distraction – and hating myself for doing so – I dropped the branch and charged flat out toward the cliff.

I moved faster than even I thought was possible, leaving great rifts in the snow where I bounded through it.

Screams sliced through the air, over and over, ending as abruptly as they'd started.

My boots hit the rocks, but I kept moving until I'd risen onto higher ground where the sea spray had washed away the snow.

Crouching down low, I caught my breath, gathering up the hood of my robe and keeping my bare hands concealed within it. Then, ever so slowly, I started moving across the sharp black stones, praying I was camouflaged against them. I remained on my hands and knees, despite my dress continually snagging on the rocks.

Every now and then, I glanced up to check the Vs weren't near, but the three out in the field were still feasting on the girls. My stomach churned and I shut my eyes for a moment to force away the nausea. I'd never been particularly squeamish. My mother couldn't even watch trailers for horror movies without feeling queasy. I, on the other hand, could watch blood and gore without batting an eye. Well, I *had* been able to. Seeing it in real life wasn't like the movies. And I was certain this moment would stay with me forever, or for however long I had left on this earth.

As I drew closer, a flash of red hair caught my attention and my heart nearly stopped working.

Cass.

With a guilty breath of relief, I realised it was a female Vampire's hair, flowing over the snow as she fed on a girl's neck.

I closed my eyes, freeing myself from the sight for a second before I continued. I'd moved past two of the Vs already, but the final one wasn't far from the lighthouse, now standing guard, wiping blood from the corner of his mouth and sucking it off his fingertips. A girl was at his feet in a lilac gown, the skirt twisted awkwardly around her legs.

Fear inched deeper into my chest as I approached, keeping my movements to the minimum as I used my own dark dress to my benefit. Perhaps Kite had been right. I didn't deserve this advantage over the other girls.

Foamy sea water sprayed over me as huge waves crashed onto the rocks at the base of the cliff. The lower the cliff dropped, the more water soaked the path I was taking. My hands slipped and slid on the rocks, but somehow I managed to keep going, setting my eye on the lighthouse and nothing else.

I moved as far as I could without risking the final V spotting me. His scraggly locks hung around him; his cheekbones were sharp enough to cut glass.

With him barring my way, I couldn't move any further.

Crawling behind a protrusion of rock, I rested my back against it, keeping hidden whilst I waited for the V to move. A sickening thought ran through my mind as I realised the distraction I was waiting for was another girl to appear.

A howl cut through the air, echoing across the island from the forest.

The two Vs that were feeding on the fallen girls stood upright immediately, snapping around to face the wood.

The red-haired V sniffed the air and called out to the others. "It came from the east."

The V standing guard by the lighthouse stepped forward, nodding to the others. "Go."

They sprinted off into the night, leaving him behind. The wind ruffled my dress and seconds later, brushed through the V's coppery hair. He inhaled deeply then stepped forward, gazing across the field, no doubt having caught my scent.

I counted my breaths to keep calm, ducking my head behind the rocks.

I glanced toward the nearest body; I recognised her golden brown skin and dark eyes, but couldn't remember her name. My gaze fell on the stake that was inches from her outstretched hand.

If I ran, perhaps I could make it to the weapon in time. But that was a big might and I wasn't sure I was willing to bet my life on it.

With a jolt of my heart, the decision was made for me as my hand slipped down the rock and my palm sliced open.

My inhale was echoed by the Vampire standing close by.

In a heartbeat, I was running, sprinting and stumbling toward the dark-haired girl on the ground. The V had a hundred metres to sprint, I had five.

My hand clamped around the stake the same moment taloned nails gripped my hair.

I was yanked backwards and, in the momentum, I swung, kicking and screaming as I angled the stake upwards.

Bone cracked and splintered. Dark blood spewed and the V's grip in my hair released.

I gasped as the full weight of the Vampire slumped on top of me. I struggled to move. To breathe.

The stake was buried so deeply in his chest, I couldn't remove it.

Slithering out from beneath him with a groan of horror, I clambered to my feet, dripping in oozing dark blood as I fled toward the lighthouse.

The outcrop of rock was uneven, the stones skittering under my boots. I was almost at the door when someone cried my name.

"Selena!" Cass's voice made me snap around. My fingers hovered above the handle, but I was frozen in place. I couldn't leave her.

We may not have known each other that long, but she'd been my rock in prison. We were the same now, the two of us fighting for survival on this infernal island.

She was sprinting across the ground, her green dress gathered above her knees, clamped in her fists. A V charged behind her, gaining speed with each passing second.

"Run!" I cried as the lighthouse door swung open.

Before I could move to meet her, a cold hand clamped around my wrist. I turned in alarm, coming face to face with Varick, his expression fierce.

"Inside," he demanded, but I shook my head, trying to free myself of him.

I turned to face Cass, stumbling as she reached the rocks. The V was almost upon her when a flash of black fur and snarling teeth collided with it. Cass smashed into me and I stumbled back against Varick. He dragged us inside, slamming the door and shutting out the freezing air.

Our panting was the only sound to fill the space.

"What ?" I asked, breathless as I turned to Varick for answers.

"Some dumb animal," he muttered, heading up a winding staircase.

We hurried to follow, jogging up the stairs as if one of the Vs might burst through the lighthouse door at any moment.

"Merry as ever," Cass murmured to me and I broke a nervous smile.

"Are there wolves on the island?" I asked Varick.

"Wolves, snakes, bears. You name it, it's probably here."

We entered a vast wooden room with a fire burning on one side. Food was laid out on a long, oak table and mattresses were spread in rows beyond that. One side of the room was taken up by a vast window that overlooked the tempestuous sea.

Ten other girls were already here, helping themselves to food and sitting in rows of chairs that faced a huge screen on the wall.

My gut turned over as I realised the footage was a live broadcast of the game. Kite was amongst the girls already present, as were Briony and Marie, sticking close to one another in two seats at the back of the chairs. I noted only twenty were laid out, despite there being twenty five of us in the game.

"Eat," Varick snapped at us and Cass jumped, hurrying to comply.

I glared at him, unmoving. "Been enjoying the show?"

"It's been riveting," he remarked dryly, glancing me up and down. "Showers are in the back. New clothes, too."

"Another dress?" I raised a brow.

"Of course, and a sleeping suit for the evening."

"Sleeping suit? What are you, from the 19th century?"

"18th actually." He surveyed me closely and a chill ran down my spine. Why did he make me feel so exposed?

"I hope you brought your own dinner," I muttered as I walked away and his dark laughter followed me.

I passed by the table of food, despite my rumbling belly, and headed to the showers. The V blood was soaking through my dress, sticking to my skin. It was cool and thick, unlike any blood I'd ever seen.

The bathroom was lined with creaking floorboards and wooden stalls that barely covered any of my body as I stripped off inside one.

Turning on the water, I nearly sank to my knees with the heavenly feel of the warm shower. I stood beneath the stream until every inch of my blood had reheated and I could finally feel my toes again.

Snug jumpsuits were stacked beside china basins, and I quickly pulled mine from the pile: black with my name embroidered across the back in white. I chucked the vile remains of my dress into a large wicker bin and returned to the main room, helping myself to some food.

"She's not going to make it," Kite was talking to a blonde girl whose name I recalled as Angelina. The two of them were watching one of the girls on the screen who was racing toward the lighthouse with two stakes in her hands. A V took her down before she even reached the rocks and a collective inhale sounded throughout the room. My stomach tied itself in a tight knot.

I chucked my plate down on the table, no longer hungry. Marching toward the door, I found myself desperate to escape this hell. I couldn't sit here watching girls die whilst filling my belly. It was twisted.

Varick flew into my way, blocking the door. "And where do you think you're going?"

I gazed up at him, practically spitting venom. "I can't be in here with *that* playing." I swung an arm back to point at the screen and Cass's eyes wheeled my way. She'd joined Marie and Briony on the seats.

"There's nowhere else to go," he growled.

"This is a lighthouse, isn't it?" I snapped. "Where's the light?"

Kite's voice carried to me. "You could learn a thing or two by watching this, pup."

I ignored her, staring resolutely through Varick's chest as if I could will him to move by sheer determination.

My shoulders sagged as I gave up and I whispered, "Please."

Varick stiffened for a moment then moved aside, taking my arm. "Fine, but I'm going with you. I'm not having you committing suicide off the tower."

"What do you care?" I snipped, following him into the hall and heading further up the spiral staircase.

"Because, if you kill yourself on my watch, I'll get the blame."

"If I wanted to kill myself, don't you think I would have tried hugging a Vampire earlier?"

Varick regarded me with a hint of amusement in his eyes. "Well if you do make the decision to kill yourself, I'd be grateful if you let me do the honours."

I glowered at him as he opened the door at the top of the stairs. A ring of windows surrounded an enormous orb lantern. It was caked in dust, evidently having gone unused for years, but the metal still shone beneath it.

The room was cold but bearable. I moved to the furthest window, dropping down and gazing out at the moonlight shimmering on the dark sea. Yes, this was better. At least it was quiet in here.

The door clicked as it closed and I was painfully aware of being alone with a Vampire. The only thing stopping him from eating me was a bunch of humans running this death game. So I didn't have a whole lot of faith that he would keep his fangs to himself. But I could finally breathe again in here, and I wasn't willing to give that up just yet.

As the silence stretched on, my eyes were drawn to the sky, pin-pricked with a million stars, brighter than I'd ever seen.

"Do you believe in god?" I asked quietly, my mind overwhelmed by the enormity of our surroundings. Perhaps I was here for a reason. Perhaps I was cursed by some higher being.

"What kind of god would let a man like me live forever?" Varick said, appearing beside me. Instead of sitting down, he leant against the railing ringing the windows, looking out at the sea.

"So you were this pleasant as a human too?" I remarked.

He smirked at me and I almost broke a smile. Christ, what was wrong with me? Varick was as sick as the Vs that hunted me out on that island.

I rested my chin on my knees. "Well if there *is* a god, I'm pretty sure he's punishing me."

"And why would he do that?" Varick turned to me, tilting his head to the side.

I dropped my eyes. "I'm a killer."

"Killing a man who tormented you and your mother isn't much of a crime."

I sat up straighter. "You know about that?"

He shrugged casually. "I'm required to read the files of the girls who are brought here. They're condensed into notes for the spectators. To help them decide who to bid on."

I wrinkled my nose in disgust. "I'd like to see *them* survive out here."

Varick's mouth hooked up at the corner. "Oh believe me, Selena, I would too."

The door opened and I glanced around, finding Cass, Briony and Marie creeping through the door.

"Are you alright?" Cass asked, her eyes flitting between Varick and I.

I nodded, standing and moving toward her. She'd changed into a dark green jumpsuit and the girls stood beside her in yellow and gold.

"I can't watch the game," I admitted.

"It's over," Briony said, running a hand through her chestnut hair. "The last girl just got here."

Varick moved past them and Marie shrank against the wall so he didn't touch her. "Be back downstairs in one minute," he barked at us before disappearing down the stairs.

"How can you stand being around him?" Marie folded her slim arms, shuddering.

I shrugged because I didn't really have an answer. Something about Varick was different from the other Vs, not only that he looked like an angel and acted with rationale, but he seemed almost human at times.

We headed downstairs and, thankfully, the screen had been switched off. The showers sounded from the other room where the last arrivals were cleaning up.

One girl, however, was huddled on the floor by the table, rocking back and forth with her head buried in her silver dress.

"Who's that?" Briony whispered as Marie clutched her arm. shrugging.

Varick paced the room, causing girls to jump from their seats every time he walked past. As he reached the sobbing girl, she screamed, crawling backwards across the floorboards to escape him.

"You need to rest," he demanded in a tone that wasn't at all comforting.

I marched over, elbowing him aside. He didn't move an inch so I ducked around him, kneeling before the dark-skinned girl and blocking him out of sight.

"Don't worry about him. We're safe here. Come with me." I took her ice-cold fingers, clutching them between mine and pulling her to her feet. Leading her into the bathroom, I helped her out of her snow-caked dress before guiding her into a shower cubicle.

She shivered beneath the stream, starting to sob again.

"What's your name?" I asked softly, leaning my back against the door of the stall.

"V-Vienna," she stuttered through another choked sob.

"I'm Selena."

"We're never getting off this island, Selena."

"Don't think like that. They said whoever survives will go

home."

"But what do you *really* think they'll do with us?" she demanded, her sobs turning to anger. "Keep us for another game? Throw us to the Vs anyway? They're not going to let us *leave*."

My heart sank at her words, but I had to have hope. Surely we would be able to leave if we made it through the game? It was the only thing keeping any of us going.

The door opened and Varick appeared. "Anyone injured report to me immediately." He stalked away and I sighed as I followed, curling my injured hand into a fist.

Varick was waiting by the table and a small queue of five girls lined up before him. Varick bit down on his thumb and squeezed blood into six small glasses.

"Drink," he ordered as the girls filed toward him, taking a glass with wide eyes and heading away. I frowned as I approached him and his eyes fixed on mine.

"Take it," he demanded, his voice so willful that I nearly gave into it. Glaring at him, I slowly took the glass of my own volition. Varick's blood wasn't like the other Vampires' had been. It was thicker than a human's, but dark red as it should have been. He gestured for us to drink, seeming bored.

"Why would I drink this?" I asked as the other girls gathered nearby. Evidently I was the only one bold enough to ask.

"Vampire blood has healing properties." Varick leant back against the table.

"Ironic," I muttered, but some of the more badly injured girls hesitantly sipped from their glasses.

I watched in disbelief as the cuts on their arms and torsos healed before my eyes. Before I could change my mind, I knocked back the blood in one, figuring 'what the hell?' A vile tang of metal filled my mouth and I nearly spat it out. The resulting tingling in my hand made me pause and within seconds, the cut had stitched itself together, vanishing like magic.

I gazed at my palm in shock, unable to believe what I'd just witnessed.

Kite was amongst the injured group, with long scratch marks down her arm that I hoped hadn't come from another sacrificed girl. She grinned at the sight of her own wounds healing. "So if a V bites me, should I bite them back and start drinking?"

Varick barked a laugh. "I would *love* for you to give that a try, sweetheart."

Kite seemed satisfied by his response, swinging her hips as she walked away.

The room slowly fell silent and all eyes turned to Varick. He gestured toward the beds with his chin. "Bed. Now. No questions."

"Bed?" snapped Angelina. "Surely the sun is going to come up soon?"

"We're in the arctic circle. Polar night reigns here for the next six months."

A murmur of discontent passed through the group.

I huffed a breath, moving to Cass's side and heading over to the mattresses. Vienna crept out of the bathroom in her silver jumpsuit and I gestured for her to join us. Keeping a wary eye on Varick, she did so, dropping onto the mattress beside mine. I was at the edge of the row, the closest to Varick of everyone. He stood by the door, gazing at us unblinkingly as if he were lost in his own thoughts.

The eternal night was playing havoc with my internal clock but as I shut my eyes, exhaustion swept in and I was soon consumed by the waiting nightmares.

◐ ☼ ◐

"Hands flat on the table, Selena," the rasping voice of my drunken stepfather crawled over me.

I whimpered as I obeyed, my six year old hands so tiny on the wide surface of the dining table.

"Are you sorry?" he growled, sipping from a bottle of whiskey. The smell was vile, the putrid stench reminding me of him and him alone.

"Yes, Elijah."

He struck my knuckles with his belt, the buckle looped around his hand.

I cried out as the skin tore and my small body began to shake.

"You will call me dad, do-ya understand? How many more times am I gonna have to say it?!"

"You're not my dad," I squeaked, despite knowing the consequences of my words.

Elijah thrashed my knuckles three more times until blood ran smoothly across the table.

"Please baby, don't," Mum sobbed from the corner, her own arms whipped bloody. "She's just a little girl. She doesn't understand."

"It's been two years, Rachel! She needs-ta understand," he slurred, his blue eyes, peppered with grey, slid over me. "Your waste-a space father abandoned you and ya mother. I'm the one who looks after you both. You get that?"

I shook my head, determined to defy him for my daddy's sake. "You'll never be my daddy."

The belt whipped through the air, the dark brown leather coiled like a snake-

I woke, bolting upright and clutching my head.

"No, no, no," I whispered, raking my nails through my hair. The nightmare prickled my skin like ants scurrying over my body. Sweat trickled down my spine as I clambered out of bed, desperate to find some water. It appeared before me in Varick's hand, his nostril's flaring as he took in my scent. His eyes fixed on mine, dragging me into them like I was falling into the deepest of wells.

"Calm," he commanded and I was almost pulled into the lull of his voice. I teetered on the edge of his ability to control me and pulled back with all my might.

I whipped my head hard to the right, forcing my eyes from his. Wordlessly, he took my hand and placed the glass of water in it.

"How did you manage that?" he breathed, almost to himself.

"I don't know," I hissed. "But I'd be grateful if you stopped trying to worm your way into my head."

"I can't read your mind."

"No? Well I guess that's ten points to Edward Cullen then, isn't it?"

He grimaced at me. "Vampires are a bit grimmer in real life, sweetheart."

"You can say that again."

"Go back to sleep, Selena. I was only trying to help."

I bit back another retort, not wanting to wake the other girls. We all had to face another day on the island tomorrow, and the least everyone deserved was a good night's sleep before it. Not that *I'd* be privy to one of those myself.

I sipped the cool water, tipping it up and finishing it.

I glanced over my shoulder at the mattress I'd vacated, an icy chill running through me. That bed was a gateway back to my nightmares. But if I didn't get any rest before tomorrow, I was going to have to face nightmares of the real kind in an exhausted state.

"If you don't fight it, I can help you sleep," Varick murmured, stepping closer.

"The dreams..." I shook my head. "I'll just wake again."

"Not if you let me help," he urged.

My throat grew dry as he invaded my personal space, gazing down at me with those alluring green eyes. Like the smooth surface of two lakes shining at me.

It took everything I had not to draw away from him. Survival was driving the decision. Rest was vital, and if Varick could offer it to me, I had to take it.

I felt the moment his will butted up against mine. He didn't blink as he gazed at me and I was pretty sure I didn't either. My instincts fought to keep him out, but I battled them back, letting him in.

As soon as I stopped fighting, everything changed. My mind melted into a slushy pool so every thought I had was fleeting, vanishing as quickly as it appeared.

"No one's going to hurt you," he said in a smooth voice. He really was captivating to look at. Ruggedly handsome with dewy skin and an addictive, saccharine scent.

A dreamy smile tugged at my mouth as I bought into his words and their safe promise. "No one," I echoed.

Someone shifted in the bed behind me, but I didn't care to look.

Varick lifted a hand, brushing locks of ebony hair behind my ear. "You'll sleep soundly until I wake you in the morning."

I nodded, a yawn dragging my mouth open.

"Bed," he encouraged and I obeyed, walking back to my mattress and sliding under the covers.

Sleep came swiftly and the sweet nothingness took me away,

void of nightmares, void of all but one thing: a shimmering, green lake.

◐ ☼ ◑

"Up," Varick's voice woke me and I sprang to my feet. The control he'd had on me was gone and the shame of what I'd let him do washed over me. Had I been so weak that I'd let a Vampire into my mind?

I felt Cass's eyes on me as we queued in line for breakfast, helping ourselves to cereals and fruit laid out on the table.

"I saw you last night," she muttered.

"Saw me?" I said in a high voice, piling my muesli with grapes.

"Talking to *him*." She nodded her head in Varick's direction.

My cheeks began to burn. What kind of explanation could I give for what Varick had done?

"I had a nightmare," I admitted, my cheeks flaming further. I sounded like a whinging child.

"So you went to the Vampire for comfort?" she snorted.

I nodded vaguely, reaching for a large jug of yoghurt that I drizzled over my breakfast. Cass snatched my arm, nearly spilling the yoghurt across the table. My heart leapt upwards as she pinned me with a remember-I-went-to-prison-too stare.

"What?" I hissed.

"Don't go making friends with it," she snapped, glancing over her shoulder. "You can't trust one of them."

"I don't trust him."

"You could have woken *me* up if you needed someone to talk to." Her eyes flashed with hurt and my stomach knotted.

"I didn't *talk* to him Cass. I got up to get some water and he was just *there*."

She nodded, giving in. "I'm just looking out for you."

"Course." I smiled. "We'll stick together today, right?"

"You bet." She plucked the jug of yoghurt from my hand and doused her cornflakes in it. Her bowl had a croissant balancing precariously on the side.

"Hungry?" I teased.

"I'm gonna get what I can take. Who knows if they'll even give us food today." She headed past me and I hastily snatched up two bagels in response.

Kite, who had already eaten one breakfast, lined up again beside me. As she reached over me for a bowl of chopped pineapple, she opened her mouth and spat in my muesli.

I clutched the bowl tighter, about to throw it in Kite's face, when a blur of movement occurred in my periphery. Varick appeared, snatching my wrists to halt me.

"No fighting."

"We weren't fighting," Kite said innocently, batting her eyelashes at Varick.

I glared at her, chucking my bowl down and marching off to

join Cass on a group of chairs she, Briony and Marie had arranged into a circle.

"Where's your breakfast?" Cass demanded.

"Not hungry," I grumbled.

Varick appeared a moment later, dumping a bowl of muesli and yoghurt in my lap. "You forgot this."

"I don't want it." I grimaced.

"This one is minus the topping." He strode away and I glanced back at the table where he was already scraping the remains of my last bowl into a bin. He was like the bloody Flash.

Feeling too hungry to complain, I plucked the spoon from the bowl and began eating. I felt the other girls' eyes on me, but refused to meet them as I ate.

When everyone had crammed as much food down their throats as possible, Varick ordered an assembly and we lined up on the rows of wooden chairs.

Varick stood before the screen with a trolley in place behind him. "Today, you'll be heading further north on the island." The screen lit up behind him and a map illuminated, zooming into the new section we would be travelling to today. An area was highlighted in red on the north eastern coast; the other side of the island from where we were now.

A collective groan sounded throughout the group.

"Think of yesterday as a rehearsal, today will be hell," Varick announced, pointing to the screen. "You have twice the distance to cover and twice the Vs to avoid." He swung his finger toward the Helsing castle on the south east coast where we'd started. "The Vs are released from here. So you have about a twenty minute advantage today. Use it wisely." He gave us all an intense look, his eyes landing on me. He turned to the trolley behind him, revealing a row of fresh stakes and bags beneath it. "New weapons, new supplies." He grabbed up a handful and passed them out until everyone was armed. "Get dressed. You leave in fifteen minutes."

Panic broke out and Vienna let out a wail of fear, hunkering down in her chair. "I can't," she moaned and Briony laid a hand on her back.

"Come on, we'll stick together."

"P-promise?" she sobbed.

"Promise," Marie confirmed, leaning across Briony.

The bathroom was mayhem as the girls scrambled to find their dresses. I was the last to reach mine, and when I did, I found only a bright red dress remaining.

My heart stuttered as I gazed around the girls, searching for my dress. My eyes fell on the blonde bombshell Angelina who was being helped into my ebony gown by Kite. I strode towards them, my blood heating with anger.

I thrust her dress at her. "Give it back."

Angelina's pale green eyes swivelled onto me then round to Kite.

Kite gave me an up and down look. "Angelina has light hair. She's already at a disadvantage."

My neck heated up as I felt everyone in the room turning their attention to us. "It's mine," I snarled.

"The Vs like you," Angelina said lightly, adjusting the bust of the dress.

"Yeah, Selena. Why not go complain to your Vampire friend out there?" Kite sneered and some of the girls in the room muttered their agreement.

"He's not my friend," I snarled, my hand tightening around the crimson dress.

Cass appeared in her green velvet gown, glaring at Kite and Angelina. "We can't swap dresses."

"Who says?" Angelina placed a hand on her hip, looking like a dark queen in my dress. "Besides, Selena's already at an advantage with all that snow white skin and black, seaweed hair. She blends right into the landscape."

A few of the girls giggled and my cheeks scorched. Cass stepped forward, squaring her shoulders, but I took her arm, guiding her away.

"Forget it," I muttered, not wanting to turn any of the girls against her. It was dangerous enough as it was out on the island without having enemies amongst ourselves.

"Tell Varick," she hissed as we exited the bathroom.

I shook my head firmly. "That will make them hate me more."

Cass sighed in acknowledgement and I headed toward the beds, grabbing a sheet and asking Cass to hold it up whilst I changed.

Cass laced up the back of the crimson dress and I resigned myself to its colour. Perhaps it was only fair I didn't have an advantage today.

"No!" Varick barked the second Cass dropped the sheet. "Not happening." He moved toward me like a tsunami and grabbed my arm, dragging me toward the bathroom.

"No wait – please," I begged, trying to halt him.

He stopped inches from the doorway, his eyes sliding to mine.

"They already think I'm friends with you. Don't do this. I don't need more enemies out there than I already have."

"This dress is not meant for you," he snarled, revealing his sharpened canines.

I tried to snatch my arm from his grip, but it was like a vice. "Some of the dresses are more advantageous than others, right?"

He nodded slowly, easing his grip on my wrist.

"So maybe it's only fair we swap?" I stared him down and he reluctantly released my arm.

"Fine. But if you lose your stake again today, Selena. I'm going to personally kill you myself."

"You're not allowed to hurt us," I breathed.

"Accidents happen," he growled, shifting closer.

It did nothing to improve my situation as Kite opened the door at that very moment, finding us within inches of each other.

I shrank away from Varick, moving quickly to join Cass, but I didn't miss the mutterings from the other girls as they judged me.

"Right. Out. Good luck. Whatever." Varick pointed to the

door.

We filed through the doorway and Cass clung to my side. "Selena, I'm not ready for another day of this."

"We'll be fine," I said, though I didn't even believe it myself. "We'll figure it out together."

Varick had to force Vienna through the door after us and my gut wrenched at us leaving her behind. Falling back, I kept close to her side as Varick herded us down the stairs. "You can stay with us today, if you like?"

She glanced up and, for the first time, there was hope in her eyes. "Are you sure?"

"Of course."

Briony and Marie were waiting at the foot of the stairs for us and I smiled around in surprise at the group we'd formed.

Varick prowled through the crowd, opening the door of the lighthouse. "Remember. Twenty minutes."

A horn sounded across the island and Varick gestured for us to go.

Everyone started sprinting across the rocks, some pushing and shoving to reach the front. Marie lost her footing and Briony caught her before the other girls crashed into her, pulling her to her feet.

I jogged in time with Cass and Vienna, watching as the girls split off in different directions across the field.

"What's our plan?" Briony shot over her shoulder.

Most of the girls were heading directly east, evidently planning to head up the coast on the other side of the island.

"I say we stay on this coast for as long as we can, then cross to the north, avoid the high ground in the centre of the island in case its difficult to traverse," I said, pointing to the map illuminated above my cuff.

The others assented and we veered left, hugging the cliff as we continued to jog onwards. Vienna was the first to slow, panting and clutching her side. We paused to take a breather and I turned back, squinting toward the horizon where we'd left the lighthouse far behind. I pictured Varick watching us on the screen and wondered what he was thinking. Was he entertained by our deaths? The thought made me ill.

The cliff began to drop down, lower and lower until the rocks met with the water. Trees and moss covered the ground, providing shelter from the prevailing wind.

We moved further into the trees, keeping the sea to our left as we headed north, hiking on for hours.

The land curved inwards, forming a bay where the water gurgled and bubbled amongst the rocks. Our water bottles were already running low, but there was nowhere we could fill them up here.

I tapped the cuff on my wrist and the timer shone above it. We had nearly twenty four hours to reach the next checkpoint. We needed water in that time if we were going to keep this pace up.

"We need to head inland," I urged.

My legs trembled as we paused to take a break, my muscles

tired from overexertion.

"Why?" Cass panted, holding a stitch in her side.

I took out my water bottle, taking a small sip of the final inch at the bottom. "Water," I gasped.

Briony nodded her agreement, shaking her empty bottle as evidence.

"They could give us more than a litre," Marie complained.

Vienna was anxiously gazing toward the forest that clung to the beach edge, jumping at every sound, clearly not listening to our conversation.

I checked our location on the map and found we were still achingly far away from the checkpoint. "If we continue at this pace, it'll take us another eight hours to be level with the checkpoint. Then we still have to cross the island..." I frowned, trying to assess the distance. If my assessment was accurate, it would take at least another six hours to cross the island, and that was without stopping. At some point we would need to rest. That only left six hours spare.

Marie moved over the slippery rocks to the sea's edge, crouching down and using the seawater to wash the sweat from her face. Standing, she gazed out at the horizon, her body stiff.

"What if we built a raft and just...sailed out of here?"

"Then we'd be poisoned, Marie," Briony snapped, pointing to the back of her neck.

"Oh...yeah," Marie sighed, looking crestfallen as she tiptoed her way back up the beach.

Vienna had followed her to the water's edge, her shoulders shivering.

"You've never been the brightest button," Briony teased as Marie joined her side, tugging at her pigtails.

"Let's go," Cass encouraged, her flame-red hair flowing in the wind. I didn't like how much of a target it made her, but I guess my dress was just as eye-catching now.

"Do you think Vampires can swim?" Vienna remarked, turning to us.

"Yes, I do," I said. "And probably really well."

Vienna sighed, picking up the hem of her skirt and heading back to join us on the mossy hill.

With a loud, ear-wrenching snap of metal on bone, a bear trap closed around Vienna's leg. Her scream was unlike anything I'd ever heard: a gut-churning shriek of pain that seemed to echo around the entire island.

Briony charged to her side, clamping a hand over her mouth as the rest of us gazed on in abject shock.

I was the next to act, rushing to her side and dropping to my knees to inspect the contraption. Bile rose in my throat as I took in the damage the serrated teeth had done to her leg.

"Shh, hush now, it's okay," Briony soothed as Vienna writhed in her arms.

"They'll hear us. They'll smell the blood," Marie murmured, her eyes wide as she watched.

"Get something strong – a stick – *something*," I barked at her and she hurried off into the trees lining the shore.

Cass sat opposite me and we dug our fingers into the metal, trying to prise it apart.

Vienna let out another scream and Briony almost smacked her with how hard she pressed her hand to her mouth.

"Hush, please, please," Briony tried. "We'll get you out, don't worry."

But I had no idea how we would do that. My fingernails broke as I clawed at the metal, heaving with all my might to get it open.

I shared a look of horror with Cass, both of us knowing we couldn't open it.

Marie returned with a long branch and hurried down the beach to help. She wedged it between two of the teeth and Vienna spasmed as it knocked her leg.

"Careful!" Briony hissed at her.

"I'm trying," Marie said in a panic, positioning the stick into the trap. When it was wedged in far enough, we all took hold of the branch, pulling in one direction as hard as we could. With a splintering of wood, the branch snapped in two, but the lower piece remained inside, leaving a slight gap.

"We need something stronger," I said, looking to Cass.

After a stretch of painful silence, I huffed as I made a decision, opening my pack and taking out my stake. As I wedged it into the trap, I could almost hear Varick cursing my name, but I couldn't leave Vienna here to die.

I wrapped my hands around the wood and Cass clasped my

wrists, pushing toward me whilst I pulled.

Incredibly, the trap began to open.

I gasped my relief as the gap widened enough for Briony to pull Vienna's leg free. I couldn't hold the stake in place a second longer and tried to yank it out of the trap. It was no good and the stake smashed in its jaws, splitting in half.

I hurried to my feet, pushing the fact that I was now weaponless again far from my mind. Vienna hummed and moaned her pain as Briony tentatively removed her hand from her mouth.

"Don't scream," she pleaded and Vienna nodded, tears sailing silently down her cheeks.

"We have to move," Cass hissed, glancing left and right. "Vs will be coming."

"How is she supposed to walk?" Briony snapped.

"We'll carry her." I shed my cloak. Cass got the idea and removed her own, laying it on top of mine to make a strong sling. Carefully, Briony lowered Vienna onto it and we wound the ends up so she'd be easier to carry.

Marie knelt before her and with a harsh snap of metal on metal, another trap went off, her cloak having trailed over it. She gasped in fright.

I gazed around the rocks and, to my horror, spotted more of them in nearly every crevice.

"Oh..." Cass followed my gaze. We were ten feet from shore. How no more of us had stepped on one was a bloody miracle.

"Oh my god," Marie breathed.

"What?" Vienna groaned and Briony waved a hand.

"Nothing, nothing. Just relax. We'll have to bind up that leg."

Marie inhaled deeply then focused her attention on Vienna's injury.

"Here, give me her stake," I said and Briony fished it out of Vienna's bag. Cass and I stood guard as Marie tended to Vienna's wound, wrapping strips of her cloak around it.

As I watched the trees, shadows seemed to dance between them. Any second now, a V would burst from them, I was certain. I steadied my feet, my eyes flitting from the bear traps to the woods.

"Okay, that should stop the bleeding." Marie stood, taking hold of one end of the cloaks whilst Briony took the other.

Cass glanced at me with a 'we're screwed' expression, but what choice did we have? We couldn't leave her.

"Follow me," I instructed, eyeing the rocks and carefully stepping between them. The girls followed in a tight line and I knew with a frightening certainty, that I was acting as the guinea pig. If any of the traps went off, it'd be me that stepped on it first.

When we'd moved a few feet, a V stepped out of the woods. She had flowing golden hair and her hazel eyes were bright and shining, looking healthier than the Vs I'd seen yesterday.

"Oh dear, what's happened?" She feigned sympathy, bending down and picking up a handful of pebbles.

My heart stalled as I waited for her next move, clutching the stake tightly in my hand. With perfect aim, she threw a pebble at a trap close to the rock I was standing on. It went off with a loud *clap* that nearly caused me to stumble.

"Bitch," Cass hissed. "Why not come and get us?" She raised the stake in her hand, looking fierce.

I tried to imitate her, but was sure I didn't look quite so intimidating.

"But this is so much more fun." The V threw another pebble and Marie squeaked as a loud snap sounded.

Another V appeared up on a rocky outcrop jutting into the sea beside us.

"Smells good." He sniffed the air, his eyes wild with hunger and his black hair patchy where it had fallen out. He was obviously less well fed than the female and I feared he'd be quicker to act.

"What are you waiting for, Genevieve?" the male snarled, licking his pale blue lips. "I'm starved."

"Have a little patience," she replied, but he didn't waste another second, springing forward onto the beach and heading straight for Vienna.

"Lift it!" Briony screeched and, as one, she and Marie yanked the cloaks taught so the V collided with the middle of the stretcher, lost his footing and tumbled back onto the rocks. With a sickening *snap*, a bear trap crunched around his head and black blood spewed into the air, splattering across Vienna.

Genevieve launched at us, screeching her rage as she charged.

Cass and I split apart, prancing from rock to rock. Genevieve was slower in her hunt, evidently not wanting to suffer the same fate as the other V.

"So pretty," she purred at Cass, stalking her, sniffing the air.

Cass positioned her stake and had to move backwards across the rocks, unable to look behind her as she moved. Her foot slipped and Genevieve lunged toward her.

"No!" I cried, but she was several feet away and there was nothing I could do.

Marie and Briony had made it to the shore with Vienna, carrying her up the hill as fast as they could.

"Go!" I shouted at them. "We'll catch up."

With brief nods, they disappeared into the trees, the shadows swallowing them whole.

Cass fell onto her back, her head just inches from a trap as the V straddled her. Cass slashed her stake upwards, but Genevieve swiped it from her hand and it rattled across the rocks. I moved toward them as fast as I could, but I had to watch every step I took.

Genevieve took hold of Cass's neck, pushing her head toward the trap beneath her.

I bit my tongue on a scream, instead hoping to surprise the V as I reached her. I couldn't stab her from the front, so prayed I was strong enough to reach her heart from the back. With all my strength, and a very unfeminine grunt, I buried the stake in her ribs. She screamed out and I was pushed backwards as she threw me off.

Somehow, I caught my balance and shifted my weight forwards. In my momentum, I slammed a foot into the stake. With a horrible, gurgling sound, the Vampire slumped onto Cass and blood spilled over her back, the dark liquid the deepest of reds.

I kicked the V off of Cass and dragged her up by a hand. "Are you okay?"

She clasped my palm tightly, nodding, though her face was pale. I yanked the stake free of the dead Vampire and silently, we hurried as fast as we could off of the beach into the woods.

The darkness was oppressive compared to the silver moonlight out on the beach, but I felt immediately safer amongst the close-knit boughs. The sound of our quickened breaths seemed painfully loud as we moved, but we didn't slow, not even for a second.

I wanted to get as far away from that beach as possible and Cass evidently felt the same way.

"Briony?" I hissed into the night, but there was no response. Their footfalls would have been loud enough to hear if they were close, so we continued on regardless.

When we'd travelled for nearly thirty minutes, we stopped to regroup. I gulped down the last of my water and Cass did the same, but it wasn't anywhere near enough. Sweat trickled down my brow, the collar of my dress already soaked through with it. But the longer we stood there, the more the wind cooled my skin and, without my cloak, I began to shiver.

When we'd stopped panting enough to hear anything else, a musical sound filled my ears. A stream was close by, and that meant fresh water.

We followed the noise, hastening our steps as we drew closer. Muttered voices reached my ears and I gasped in relief, hurrying out into a small clearing where moonlight shone on a narrow stream, winding through the rocks.

Briony and Marie were knelt beside Vienna on the ground, filling their water bottles. Their heads snapped around as we approached and Marie pressed a hand to her heart.

"Thank god it's you."

"Who else?" Cass teased, dropping to her knees and filling her water bottle. I mimicked her, checking the clearness of the water in the moonlight. It looked pure and a small sip revealed it to taste like heaven. I gulped down a whole bottle before refilling it.

Briony held a bottle to Vienna's lips which were turning blue. I frowned, dropping to her side. She was splattered with V blood, covering her silver gown in great globs.

I sucked in a breath in realisation. Dipping my finger into the blood, I brought it to Vienna's mouth. "Drink this!"

"Ew – Selena." Cass wrinkled her nose.

"It can heal her. Varick gave me some of his blood before. It healed the cut on my hand."

Everyone's eyes went wide as they turned to Vienna. She grimaced as she sucked the blood from my finger, then spluttered as it went down.

"That's disgusting!" she spat.

"Better that than die," I insisted, wiping more blood onto my finger so she could swallow it easier.

After three more mouthfuls, she gasped, sitting upright. "No way..." She dragged up her tattered dress, revealing a mess of blood, the remnants of the wound almost entirely healed already.

Marie threw her arms around her. "Oh Vienna!"

Vienna started sobbing and Briony quickly hushed her with a light smack on the arm.

"You need to get this blood off you," I urged, glancing over my shoulder. "The Vs will smell it."

Vienna nodded, standing and testing her leg which was miraculously healed. I sank back on my heels in amazement.

As Vienna started towards the stream, Cass caught hold of her skirt. "Stop. Take your clothes off. You'll freeze in wet clothes."

Vienna whimpered as she undid her dress, baring her skin to the arctic wind. We turned our backs, giving her some privacy as she washed the blood from her body.

She dried herself on the outside of her robe before pulling on the stained dress. Cass took out her knife and cut away the hem where Vienna's blood mixed with the V's. When she was finished, she gathered up our blood-sodden cloaks, took a few large rocks and weighed them down underwater before rinsing off her hands. We'd have to manage without our cloaks, I guessed.

"Okay, we should get moving." Cass stood, checking her map and pointing in the direction we needed to head.

I moved to Vienna's side, holding out the stake I'd taken from her. "Here."

She recoiled from it. "No, please. You keep it. I'm no good with that thing."

I hesitated, not liking the idea of leaving her unarmed. But she was already moving away, her decision made.

We walked on through the quiet wood, travelling for what seemed an eternity. I checked my map from time to time to be certain we were still on course, but we'd lost precious time during our run-in with the Vs.

When we finally parted from the trees, my stomach was beginning to growl, but I was reluctant to take another break. The other girls evidently felt the same as we journeyed on for another two hours across rocky ground, having to make our way carefully because of the ice that clung to it.

"We didn't account for rough terrain. This is going to slow us down even more," Cass muttered as she joined my side.

"The plan was to skirt around this high ground," I said. "We shouldn't have moved east so early."

Cass sighed, clutching my arm and we used each other for support as we tried not to slip on the jagged rocks. The snow had melted in places and I was certain the temperature had risen, if only a fraction.

Hope sparked in my chest as I spotted the sea twinkling beneath the moonlight in the far distance.

"What's the checkpoint?" I asked, bringing up my map again.

The flashing red light that marked the checkpoint seemed to be on an empty patch of land further up the eastern coast.

After another few hours, we finally reached the coast where a sheer cliff dropped a hundred metres onto sharp rocks. We steered clear of the edge, but followed it north, ducking into the cover of trees whenever we could. Most of the land there was rocky and barren, the trees few and far between, leaving us as sitting ducks most of the time. The fact that no Vs had shown up was nothing short of a miracle.

As we passed through another little copse, Marie stumbled to her knees. Briony rushed to help her, pulling her up. "Oh Marie, you're so clumsy."

"I'm exhausted, Briony," she moaned, getting up on shaky legs.

I gazed around the small covering of pines. "Let's take a rest. We have time. We'll take shifts to get some sleep."

Cass chucked her pack to the earthy floor. "I'm game."

Vienna sighed heavily as she dropped down onto the damp earth, propping herself up against a tree trunk.

"I'll take first watch," I said.

"Me too." Briony nodded, placing her stake on a log as she rearranged her pack. I hadn't put Vienna's down since I'd killed the Vampire with it. Coming so close to death had kept me on edge ever since.

Briony and I perched on the fallen pine, sitting side by side to keep each other warm. A fire was tempting but too risky out here on the cliff. So, instead, I wolfed down several granola bars and a pack of dried fruit whilst picturing flames in my mind. It was almost comforting, but didn't do much to banish the cold that was inching into my bones. The other girls managed to sleep despite it.

"So how did you and Marie end up here?" I whispered.

Briony sighed. "The short story is that we were kidnapped from our prison in Paris - like every other girl who's here."

"What's the long version?" I nudged her and she grinned mischievously.

"Marie and I grew up together. She started seeing this boy, Pierre – a complete waste of space in my opinion – but she loved him. Marie's the sweetest girl, but she can be a little naïve at times." Briony glanced over at the girl who was snoozing soundly with her head propped up on her bag. "Pierre started hitting her, and I told her so many times to leave him. But she wouldn't listen." Briony shook her head and her dark curls bounced around her shoulders. "One day, she phoned me saying 'Briony, Briony, you must come help me, Pierre has gone crazy."

I frowned, leaning in closer as she told the story.

"So I rushed to her place, I had to take the bus as I hadn't yet passed my driver's test. I would have taken a cab, but I didn't have a single euro to my name. If only I had..." She gave a weak smile. "When I arrived, I found Marie being beaten by him. By that bastard I'd warned her about all along. I knocked, but no one answered. Then I heard Marie screaming. I climbed through an open window and ran to the kitchen where I found him beating her. I didn't even think, I just grabbed a cooking pot and smacked him over the head with it."

I gasped, my pulse rising. "Is that why you went to prison?"

Briony shook her head solemnly. "I snatched the keys to his car and we ran to it. Marie sat beside me in the passenger seat all bruised up. I was about to drive us far, far away from that place, when Pierre appeared – out of nowhere I tell you – and I don't know what happened...I just *snapped*." She clicked her fingers and the sound seemed to reverberate through the air. "I ran that bastard down and his body went flying. Perhaps we still might have been let off, but that was before Marie took a knife from the glove compartment – apparently he liked to carry them around, that was the kind of freak he was – and she unsheathed this huge blade, got out of the car and just started...stabbing."

I glanced away from Briony, trying to process the story. My eyes fell on the small form of Marie who seemed so innocent and fragile. I couldn't picture her doing such a thing, but if Pierre had been anything like as abusive as my stepfather, I knew what she'd been through.

I took a breath and laid a hand on Briony's wrist, unsure what to say, only that, in a twisted way, I understood. I knew what it was like to snap. I supposed we all had that in common. We had killer's blood and perhaps that's what made us so perfect for this game.

We soon woke the girls so Briony and I could take a turn at

resting. I couldn't sleep a wink, tossing and turning on the mossy ground. Eventually, I gave up and we let Briony sleep for a little while longer before waking her.

"Final push girls," Cass said, stretching her spine. "We can do this. Just think of the hot meal...comfy bed."

The other girls sighed dreamily.

But my attention was elsewhere, trained on the trees beyond them where two, large yellow eyes were staring right at me.

I pointed in horror and everyone flung around. But as I hurried forward with my stake, I found the wood empty. No V, no animal, nothing.

I blinked to clear the fog in my mind. "Sorry," I muttered. "I think I'm overtired."

Everyone seemed concerned by my reaction as we moved on in tense silence, heading north toward our next point of refuge. The frightening thing was, I was sure I hadn't imagined those eyes.

Varick

I returned to the castle as was expected between the rounds.

Nothing had changed. The men were still gambling in the auditorium, the giant screens were still playing live footage of the games. The only thing that was different, was me.

I'd never gotten emotionally involved in the games before. And perhaps 'emotional' was the wrong word for how I was feeling right now, but I certainly felt *something*.

I *hoped* that Selena arrived at the next checkpoint safely. I *hoped* that she wouldn't act recklessly in today's game. I *hoped* she wouldn't lose her stake again.

But apparently, Selena was hell-bent on forgoing her only weapon in other ways today. After witnessing her snap it in a bear trap, I was livid.

Anger was something I knew well, but that kind of fury was rare. How could she be so stupid? Vienna was done for the second she'd stepped on it. Or so I'd thought.

V blood. The trick I had taught Selena. And hell, I even kind of admired the way they'd all pulled together and saved the girl.

But this had to stop. I wanted Selena for her blood, nothing more. When all this was over, if she made it through alive, the Helsing's would let me have my fill of her. And that's what all of this 'hoping' was about. It had to be.

Abraham knew I was getting desperately hungry. He saw it in my eyes the second I walked in the door. The Helsings were Hunters at heart, but nearly three hundred years had passed since they and the other Hunters had gotten the Vampire population under control. The modern-day Helsings were a figment of what they'd once been. But the blood was there, the power they held in their veins. It wouldn't take much for a Hunter to return to his roots.

I ran my tongue across my canines. Perhaps one of these spectators would make a move on Mercy and I could subtly rat him out to her father. Maybe then he'd let me have a feed.

I pushed away the idle thought, moving to the seating area where I could watch the game in peace.

Selena was still with the group she'd chosen as allies. For the most part, they were a strong team, but that Vienna girl was trouble. She was dead weight. I'd watched her in the first round, making it to the lighthouse on blind luck alone. The fact she was still alive today was due solely to the actions of the others.

My eyes swivelled to Angelina, the curvy blonde who'd stolen Selena's dress. She and Kite had teamed up, the two of them already closing in on the checkpoint. Another hour or so and I'd return to the island to meet them.

My burning throat was causing me grief. A few more days and I'd be losing my mind, starting to become like the Vs out in the game. I'd been pushed to my limit healing Selena of her wounds, standing so close to her blood, it was intoxicating, like nothing I'd ever smelt before. Sometimes, my own strength surprised me.

I considered the types of punishment I'd be given and whether it was worth the risk. A shot of silver was certainly bearable for the sake of a precious drink. But something like this would serve a more severe punishment. They might contain me for a while in the holding cells. Let me starve for even longer. Face the sunlamps and the daily shots of silver, and when I was as weak as the Vs in the game, they'd chuck me onto the island with the rest of them.

No, it wasn't worth it. For all the blood in the world, I had to bide my time.

Ignus appeared at the foot of the seating area, grinning at me as he approached, his hands stuffed into the pockets of his tan corduroys.

"Hungry, V?" he taunted and I grunted a response. Ignus would be in charge one day, but until then, I didn't offer him the same respect that Abraham squeezed out of me.

"Mother doesn't like you eyeing the spectators like they're fresh meat. It freaks them the hell out."

My eyes roamed over him. Skinny little runt. How would a kid like that fair against a V? But he was pure Helsing. He probably had skills not even *he* was aware of. Not that I'd be reminding him of that any time soon.

"Unless you've come over here to slit your own wrists in a blood offering to me, I suggest you keep walking."

Ignus laughed. I'd always hated his laugh. It was one of those repetitive cackles that gets right under your skin. "Actually, I might have a snack for you..."

My interest peaked and my expression must have betrayed this to him, because he laughed again in his irritating *'a-ha a-ha a-ha'* style. "But I need a little favour first, hm?"

I would have sighed if I hadn't been expecting it. The only way I ever got extra scraps around here was by doing favours for the Helsing kids. Ignus and Mercy were master manipulators, but I had to give it to them, they knew how to conduct business behind their parents' backs. And I could always cash in on it, seeing as they entrusted their secrets to me.

"What do you want?" I growled and he took an almost imperceptible step back.

He stole a brief glance over his shoulder. "See the twit over there in the breeches?"

My gaze swung toward the man and I took in his youthful appearance, his muddy blonde hair and thickset boots, army style. He certainly stood out amongst the suited men.

Ignus snapped his fingers before my eyes to grab my attention and rage flashed through me.

"Who is he?" I asked, grinding my teeth.

"Name's Ulvic Hund. I'm doing business with him, but he hasn't delivered his end of the deal."

I sat back in my chair, disinterested. "What kind of business?" I knew Ignus well enough to know any business he got involved with was dodgy.

"That's between me and Ulvic." Ignus gave me a slanted grin. "I just need you to give him a little bit of...encouragement, to fulfil his end of the deal."

"And I'm guessing Mummy and Daddy don't know about this little deal of yours?" I smirked at him and Ignus glowered.

"I'm offering you blood, V. So long as you don't kill the guy, you have my approval."

"And what if your father finds out I've been biting spectators? Who do you think is going to the cells for it? You or me?"

Ignus sighed, stamping his foot in a childish manner. "You have my protection, Varick. I give you my word. I'll take full blame if you're caught."

I shrugged, pretending I wasn't that bothered about the blood. But my throat was aching, constricting further and further by the second. "The word of a Helsing isn't much to go on."

Ignus started to turn red, glaring at me as if I were a badly trained dog refusing to sit on command.

"I'll set it up for you."

I stood, rolling my shoulders and Ignus shrank before me. "You'll be there. So if your parents show up, you can't weed out of the blame," I demanded and, after a beat, he nodded.

"Fine." He strode away, heading toward Ulvic and clapping him on the shoulder.

I checked the screens, finding Selena and her group resting in a copse. I didn't have long before I had to head to the next checkpoint, but if there was even the smallest chance of a drink, I was going to hold out for it. Maybe then I could get Selena off my mind once and for all.

After a few minutes, Ignus led Ulvic from the room, winding through the crowd and passing through the heavy wooden doors toward the western tower.

I followed at a leisurely pace, knowing I could catch them in seconds. I followed Ignus's scent of sweat, garlic and lavender soap toward one of the old smoking rooms where the guests enjoyed cigars and whiskey as if they were living in the 1920s.

Hunter blood was notoriously appealing; after thousands of years of war, it was if Vs had a evolved to find their blood extra appetising, craving their deaths more than any other human. Though apparently not Selena's...

Ulvic was already puffing on a cigar as I silently slipped into the smoking room. His scent was inviting, the warmth of his blood calling to me.

Ignus sat opposite him in a red velvet armchair with cherry wood handles, curving beneath his rested elbows.

"I want your entire stock," Ingus was saying. "We can't run a proper test with just the one."

I could only see the back of Ulvic's head as he sat in his chair, sipping from a crystal glass of whiskey. "Can't do it, Ignus. Perhaps in a year or so, when the batch is properly tested."

"It's clear it works," Ignus demanded, his eyes sliding to me. "Money isn't an issue."

"You're not the only Hunter offering me money, Ignus."

Ignus stood, his eyes narrowing to slits. "No, but perhaps I'm the only one willing to threaten you for it."

Ulvic choked a laugh into his drink. "*Threaten* me?"

Ignus gave me a nod and I moved in a flash, dragging Ulvic up by the neck and wrenching backwards so his head hung over the chair. As he cried out, starting to flail in my hold, I didn't waste a second. The animal in me took over and I let it, desperate to sate this craving that was tearing at my insides.

As my fangs pierced the skin of his neck, he screamed. Hot, delicious blood flooded down my throat and I lost all sense of myself. I felt the man's life fading like a dimming bulb, but it was nearly impossible to restrain myself. Ignus roared at me to stop and somehow I managed to recall the memories of the cells, the sun lamps, the way my skin cracked and dried beneath them.

I yanked my canines free, snarling at Ignus whose hand was fisted into my shirt. Ignus backed off, reaching for the metal control in his pocket, holding it out in warning.

I wiped the remaining blood from my mouth as Ulvic slumped down into the chair, unconscious.

"You've killed him!" Ignus roared and I shook my head. The slow thump of Ulvic's heart reached my ears. I tore open my own wrist with my teeth and rested the wound against Ulvic's gaping mouth.

Ignus watched in horror as Ulvic regained consciousness and the bite mark on his neck knitted itself together.

"Go," Ignus hissed at me and I wasted no time in obeying, having gotten what I needed.

My throat relaxed as I headed out of the castle, on my way to the next checkpoint. My blood rushed with heat and I regained my senses. The shame washed in at what I'd done and I saw myself in my mind's eye as a monster feeding on that man. Everything around me sharpened and the pounding in my head finally melted away.

At least tonight, Selena wouldn't tempt me. I was fed at last and that should make this game a whole lot easier.

I quickened my pace toward the north-eastern coast. The first girls could arrive within an hour, but the end of this round was always bloody. The game was about to weed out the weak from the strong. And I tried to ignore the hope I was still feeling that Selena would make it to the checkpoint alive.

Selena

The wind pressed us toward the cliff edge, tugging at our dresses and encouraging us over the sheer drop. We huddled closer together, moving as fast as we could to find more shelter.

My bones rattled with the cold and my breath fogged before me in a repetitive stream. Every now and then, a scream echoed from somewhere across nearby. In my panicked state, I pictured the attacker just up ahead, waiting to pick us off next.

"Can't be far now," Cass whispered near to me.

A glint of blue caught my eye ahead; whatever it was, was positioned near to the checkpoint, according to my map.

"Come on," I urged, increasing my pace despite my burning calf muscles.

I took the lead and footsteps pattered behind me as we moved on as a unit.

I squinted at the blue dot and realised it was one of the girls in a bright turquoise dress. My heart lurched as she started running, directly toward the cliff.

My instincts took control and I started sprinting. A scream tore through the air as she plunged over the edge and a splash sounded a second later.

I hurried to the ledge she'd thrown herself from, nearly

stumbling over it myself from my momentum. I gazed left and right, gazing at the frothing sea below, my heart beating a frantic tune in my ears.

Briony reached my side, taking my wrist and pulling me back a step.

"She jumped," I breathed in astonishment.

The black water below showed no signs of the girl. It was too dark; the moonlight hung low on the western side of the sky so its light barely reached this coast.

"Can't blame her," Vienna muttered, but drew away from the cliff all the same.

"She died the way she wanted to," Cass said, folding her arms. "Now let's keep moving."

"Wait," Marie whispered, her cuff illuminating the map above her wrist. "We're here."

The checkpoint blinked on the map, a small red dot exactly where we were standing.

I automatically glanced down at the floor as if expecting to see something, but only the rocky ground stared back at me.

The longer we stood there, the more the icy wind crept under my skin. My gaze swept to the sea and with a jolt, I put two and two together. I huffed at my own stupidity. "That girl didn't commit suicide!" I pointed at the sea. "The checkpoint must be down there."

Vienna practically lurched away from the cliff, her dark hair flying around her in the wind.

"Down *there*?" Marie echoed in a small voice.

"We have to jump?" Briony asked, wide eyed.

I nodded as Cass moved toward the edge, assessing the fall. "Must be safe." She shrugged, turning back to us. Her eyes flitted over our heads, becoming wide with alarm.

I swung around to face whatever she'd spotted and fear slid through me. Vs were charging out of the trees, a hundred or so metres away. Ahead of them were several girls, fleeing in our direction.

"We have to jump – now!" Cass demanded and I joined her at the edge, gathering up the tattered hem of my dress. It was jump or die.

Blood-curdling screams tore at my ears as the first of the girls fell.

Briony and Marie held hands as they approached the edge, keeping close together. Just as I braced to jump and throw my life into the hands of fate, praying I wouldn't smash my head on a rock, Vienna whimpered.

"I can't," she moaned and I snapped around.

She was moving tentatively toward the edge, one tiny footstep at a time.

"Come on," Cass urged, looking ready to take on the world.

My gaze slid from her to the oncoming Vs and I made a decision. "You guys jump, I'll help Vienna."

Without a word of complaint, Briony and Marie clamped their eyes shut and launched themselves forward, hand in hand. Cass didn't move, rooted to the spot as she gazed at me.

"Selena, I won't leave you."

I took Vienna's arm, guiding her closer to the edge as she started to sob.

Footsteps pounded close by, warning us of the deadly stampede heading our way.

"Go, Cass!" I roared, staring her down.

With a dark look of acceptance, she turned and threw herself over the edge in a flutter of green fabric.

I managed to get Vienna to stand at the edge on wobbly legs.

"Look at me," I demanded and her bloodshot eyes found mine. She was starting to hyperventilate, her entire body quaking in my hold.

One of the running girls reached us, screaming as she threw herself over the edge. Vienna lurched away from me, clawing her hands into her hair. "I can't, I can't!"

She was working herself up into a complete panic and I knew we didn't have any more time to waste.

I stepped toward her, determined simply to throw her over the edge myself.

She held up her hands to halt me, evidently reading my decision in my expression. "No, don't. No, no, no, n-" A blur of movement and a rush of air, then something collided with Vienna.

A V launched her off of the cliff, wrapped around her as they plummeted toward the sea. Vienna screamed bloody murder and I called out her name in horror as a foam of white exploded as they hit the surface.

I'd hesitated too long, and suddenly girls and Vs descended on the cliff. Screams ripped through the air as the Vs caught girls mid-air like hawks on rabbits. Some of the Vampires simply dove into the sea, preying on the stragglers swimming there.

Somehow, I was still standing rooted to the spot, watching the bloodbath unfold.

It took two more seconds for a V to take me out. The wind was knocked out of me. I flew backwards and sharp claws raked my neck and back as the V clutched me to him. The stench of blood on his breath ran over me in a wave, then everything went black as we plunged into the sea.

I couldn't breathe, I couldn't see. I didn't know where the cold ended and the clutching talons of the V began. I was turned upside down, rolling and rolling until I had no idea which way was up.

A pain like fire ripped through my shoulder and I battled with all my might against it. My hand was no longer clamped around the stake, it was lost to the sea.

With a violent jerk, we hit a rock, but luckily for me, the V took the blow. He lost his grip and I sprang into action, kicking my legs in a frantic movement, rising and rising until I finally breached the surface. I gasped down a lungful of air, coughing and spluttering as the seawater filled my nostrils, burned my eyes, and choked my senses.

The surface was chaos. Splashes of water, red and white foam as Vampires feasted on their victims. The screams were unbearable. It took everything I had to block out the noise and focus on my destination: a dark ocean cave overhung by the jagged cliff rocks.

As hard as I could, I swam into it. The cold numbed my body and it felt like using leaden poles to move myself, but inch by inch, I made progress. I stole the odd glance over my shoulder, trying to catch sight of my friends, but nothing but splashes and the frenzied Vs caught my attention and I couldn't bear to watch a second longer.

My teeth chattered as I reached the cave, and my eyes locked with another girl who made it at the same time I did. Kite was as pale as a ghost, the tear drop beneath her eye standing out starkly against her skin. We swam into the darkness together. My joints ached, my shoulders protested with every turn of my arms, but somehow I kept moving.

The darkness soon engulfed us and all that seemed to exist was the freezing water, the endless black tunnel and the continual screams that reverberated off of the cave roof.

"Selena?" Kite's voice reached to me, a rare note of vulnerability in it.

"I'm h-here," I managed through chattering teeth.

Her fingers found mine in the water and it took a second to register her touch through the numbing cold.

"Keep m-moving," I encouraged, releasing her hand so we could swim again.

"I can't see," she whispered. "What are we even swimming toward?"

Her question gave me an idea and I quickly tapped my cuff so the map illuminated beneath the water. It gave us enough light to swim by and Kite seemed to relax a little as we made progress.

Moonlight glimmered up ahead, confusing my senses, assuming we were swimming deep underground. As we approached, the cause became apparent as we swam into a small pool that led up to a rocky beach. Looking up, I found we were enclosed in a hidden cove, the cliffs towering up around us on all sides. As the water became shallower, we dragged our way up the shore, collapsing down on the pebbles as the quiet tide lapped our feet.

It occurred to me that if we had continued further up the cliff, perhaps we would have come across this cove from above. Perhaps the water was deep enough to jump directly into this place of safety.

My thoughts were confirmed as a huge splash signalled someone had thrown themselves from above. Moments later, Angelina joined us on the beach, shivering and pale, but otherwise unharmed.

Kite scrambled to her feet, launching herself at the girl. "Jump *together*? Isn't that what you said!?"

Kite grabbed a fistful of white locks and pulled until Angelina screamed.

"I saw the Vs, Kite! I ran for it!"

Kite shoved her to the ground and she crawled backwards on her hands and feet. A knife appeared in Kite's hand; the one we were all given in our packs.

"Enough!" a booming voice roared.

I lifted my head to see Varick appear from a shadowy corner amongst the foliage, but my body was too stiff with the cold to move further.

"Inside. Now," he commanded and the two girls hurried through an enormous, wooden door set into the cliff face.

I, however, was pretty sure my body was becoming an eternal part of the scenery. I could barely lift a finger.

"Up, Selena," Varick ordered, but not as harshly as he had before.

I shut my eyes, focusing on moving my arms. My joints creaked, but I managed to lift myself half way up before collapsing again.

Varick took hold of my waist, lifting me with impossible ease. My body craved the warmth of another human being, but he didn't provide that comfort, his chest like a firm wall as I buckled against him.

"You're bleeding," Varick said in a tight voice, like his throat was constricting around the words.

I glanced down, finding blood flowing freely over my shoulder, my arms. My skin was torn to bits from the Vampire who had knocked me off the cliff, only I couldn't feel it at all.

Splashing sounded, joined by the frantic whimpers and cries of girls who had managed to make it through the cave. My vision blurred as I turned to them. I wanted to locate my friends but darkness curtained my eyes. My legs gave out beneath me, but the harsh crunch of stone against my knees never came, I simply sailed away into nothingness.

◐ ☼ ◐

The first thing I was aware of was fire. Flames flickered and danced through my eyelids and heat washed over me so powerfully that I was practically burning.

I woke in a sweat and scrambled away from the fire that was at the heart of a huge cave.

I reached for the cuts on my shoulders, but found nothing there, no blood, no wounds, as if I'd imagined them.

I pushed the heavy blanket off of my legs, drenched in sweat as I hurried to my feet, gazing around the black walls that glistened with water.

The girls were split apart around the space and I was overcome with desperation as I searched for Cass and the others. It was clear we'd taken a hit in numbers, only fifteen girls now remained. As I span on my heel, I came face to face (or face to chest) with Varick.

"Better now?" he asked and I lifted my chin, glowering at him.

"You mean *you* were the one trying to roast me on that fire?"

His eyes slid over the sweat pouring down my throat. "I don't feel the heat."

"But you know that fire cooks things, right?" I huffed, marching past him toward the girls, spotting Briony and Marie huddled together in blankets on one mattress. I didn't know why I was angry with Varick. Perhaps because he was one of *them*. That he could just as easily have been the V that knocked me off that cliff and tried to tear me limb from limb.

"What happened?" I jogged the last few paces to the girls. "Where's Cass? Vienna?"

Briony pointed across the room and I spotted Cass filling a plate of food from a stone table. My shoulders dropped dramatically and I had the urge to run over and hug her. But with Kite and Angelina watching, I didn't want any more of their snickering.

"Vienna didn't make it," Marie said in a tiny voice.

My heart tumbled in my chest as I took in the news. She'd been so frightened up on that cliff.

Cass joined us and I gripped her wrist. "I thought you might be..."

She nodded, giving me a grim smile. "I thought the whole lot of us might be." She lifted her plate, offering me food and my stomach growled in response.

I must have resembled a hungry wolf because Cass quickly extracted her plate from my reach and said, "On second thoughts, you can get your own."

I broke a small smile, but the news of Vienna's death weighed heavily on me. It wasn't logical to get attached to the other girls. We weren't all going to make it, and many of them had already died without me really registering their deaths. But any day now, that faceless, nameless death could be mine. And only Cass would care. Perhaps Briony and Marie, too, but their interest was clearly in getting each other through this hell. And I didn't blame them.

Half-jogging across the room, I approached the table. A buffet of battered fish, mashed potatoes, steamed vegetables, pies and gravy was all laid out before me. It was like some twisted joke after everything the Helsings had put us through today. Like a pat on the head for being good. It made me want to start a hunger strike, but I knew not eating would only harm myself. And what was the point in that?

So I ladled heaps of food onto my plate, taking a bit of everything, considering this could be my last decent meal before I died. I felt eyes on me and glanced up to find Varick standing guard by a huge wooden door that had been built into the natural entrance of the cave.

I was sure he looked different to the last time I'd seen him. Like he was better rested, or...

I realised with a sick feeling in my stomach that he must have recently drank blood. Just like the Vs out in the game who appeared more human the more blood they got their hands on.

Varick raised an eyebrow at my expression and I realised I was grimacing at him. "Problem, Grey?"

I stuck up my chin, determined not to back down. "Have a nice drink today? Perhaps you thought you'd have a little fun of your own and run around with your V pals on the island?"

I turned away and, in a flash, he was at my side, his hand around my wrist. "How hungry are you right now?" His upper lip was curled into a snarl and the beauty of his face twisted enough that I glimpsed the true monster beneath the facade.

I pulled away from him but he held tight.

Pinching my lips together, I refused to answer.

"I'd bet you're pretty ravenous," he growled and I wet my lips, giving away my salivating mouth from the smell of the cooked food beneath my nose.

"Imagine feeling so hungry that you *wished* you could feel the way you do now." His eyes darkened and a shiver ran through me. "Imagine claws raking at your insides, your mouth burning, *scorching* with hunger."

I shivered, knowing he meant this was how he felt without blood.

"I'd die before I hurt someone," I breathed.

He spat a laugh. "Tell that to your step-father."

Before I could punch him, slap him or defend myself at all, he was gone, half way across the room scaring some of the other survivors.

He bothered me so much more than he should have. I didn't know what it was about him, but he worked his way under my skin, making my blood boil before he even spoke a word.

I remained quiet for the rest of the evening, a drab mood descending on me. Tomorrow would be worse than today. And more of us would be killed. I was as likely to die as the next girl. Black dress or not, I didn't think any of us would have much of an advantage going forward. The more Vs that hunted us, the less chance we had of escaping.

As everyone settled down for the night, I found myself pacing the cave. Varick watched me silently, back and forth, back and forth, like I was the ball in a tennis match. The longer I paced, the more worked up I got. How could we be kept here like animals in a cell? What kind of people were sick enough to force us onto this island, day after day? Did the Helsings really have enough sway to eradicate our prison sentences? What if it was all a lie, just to make us play along?

I turned mid-stride, marching toward Varick, hell-bent on seeking some revenge. It was futile, I knew, but I had no one else to take out my fury on.

"Who are these Helsings? What are they getting out of this?" I hissed, keeping my voice low so as not to disturb the exhausted girls snoozing in the far corner.

"Hunters," Varick replied with a sour expression.

I waited for a further explanation and he sighed, taking my arm and leading me toward the door. Unbolting it, he guided me out into the moonlit cove, which was sheltered from the icy wind.

He perched on a large boulder and I hesitated to do the same, simply standing before him with folded arms. It irritated me further the way his skin shone in the moonlight. He was too perfect, why didn't the other Vs look this way? Or would they too be beautiful if they drank enough human blood?

"Hunters are human, for the most part. Except their blood is ancient and strong. They can live for hundreds of years, their strength is unequalled by normal men and women. And their one, defining purpose is to destroy creatures like me."

I frowned, moving a step closer. "So why don't they just round you all up and be done with it?"

Varick grimaced. "Wish they would sometimes. But if there's no hell-born beings left to play with, what fun is that for them?"

"So there aren't any Vampires left in the world? Apart from here?"

Varick tilted his head as he considered it. "Some. The other Hunter clans keep Vs for their own purposes."

"Like...?"

"More games, entertainment. We've become their playthings." He glanced away from me, evidently ashamed.

It was the first time I actually felt any pity for him, but I battled it away. "Why not fight back then?"

He tapped the back of his head. "Can't do it, sweetheart. They've got the same kill trigger in my head as they do in yours."

I mimicked him, running a hand down my own neck and feeling the bump beneath it where the Helsings had inserted a capsule full of poison. One second late over the finish line and it got released. I shuddered, dropping my hand. "I guess fighting back is suicide," I mumbled and he nodded.

I glanced out at the dark cave that had led us here, my neck prickling at the memory. "Why do the Vs keep out of the checkpoints?"

"The Helsings will detonate the capsules in their heads. Some have tried in the past. They've learnt it's not worth it."

"How long have the Vampires been here?"

"Some as long as me, some longer." Varick shrugged. "They bring fresh ones in from time to time, to replenish the numbers lost in the games."

"Where from?" I shivered in the wind.

Varick's brows drew together, then he stood, gesturing for us to return inside and evading my question. "Come, let's go in. You need to rest before tomorrow."

"Is tomorrow worse?"

"Much worse," he growled and my heart sank like an anchor.

Varick

Ever since I'd died, time had become a wheel; no matter how much passed, I always ended up in the same place. I recalled the gift of life, the fragility of it. The plans, the ambition, the possibilities. Now, I had an eternity to achieve anything I ever desired, yet somehow the allure was gone. Why did a human spend their life rising to the top in their career? Or fall in love, create a family, build a home with their own two hands?

Achievement. To say they'd actually done something with the time they'd been given. But if you're given forever, what did it matter? No one would remember me, because I had no expiration date to be remembered beyond. That was, so long as a Helsing didn't decide to end me. Or I didn't rip my own head off out of the sheer exhaustion of merely existing.

As I stood watching the girls sleep, or, should I say, watching *her* sleep, I thought on these things. And I thought about my reason for still being here. Why did I remain? What was holding me back from ending it all? I'd lived longer than any man ever should.

Initially, I'd spent many years enjoying the freedom immortality had given me. I'd achieved everything one *could* achieve under such circumstances. And then the Helsings brought me here and still I remained. Still clung to life like a leech on skin. *Something* had kept me here.

I couldn't simply go on living as I had been, owned by the Helsings, doing their bidding. I was starting to feel something watching the games. Rage. Revulsion. Even regret. And I wasn't sure I could see this one through.

As the time arrived that I had to wake the girls, I decided I wanted things to change. Because, dammit, there had to be more to immortality than this shit.

As the girls roused and made their way to breakfast, some of them began discussing tactics for the day ahead. Selena was weaving amongst them with a bowl of porridge clamped between two hands. I tried to split my attention between the other contestants, but somehow my eye was always drawn back to her. The dark, waterfall curls that flowed over her shoulders, the cool determination in her inky eyes, the curve of her lower lip. I jolted as I realised I was appreciating her beauty, not just her enticing scent. That was a first for me since I was turned. And perhaps due to my recent drink. Sometimes, after a decent fill, human emotions were dragged up to the surface for a while, putting me back in touch with humanity for a few fleeting hours. Maybe that was why she was still of interest to me.

I let myself bask in the feeling, picturing that small, crooked smile she gave her friends, replacing the glowers she saved for me. Her contempt for me wasn't surprising. None of the girls ever enjoyed my company, but most ignored me once they accepted I wasn't a threat. Selena, however, turned her attention to me occasionally. Like she wanted to provoke me, to take out her frustration.

If she knew a better fed V like me was actually ten times stronger than those she faced daily, perhaps she'd show me more respect. But, in a way, I liked our back and forth conversations. She jabbed at me, and not in the way the Helsings did. Selena was trying to suss me out. For what purpose, I had no idea. But it felt good to be seen by her. Even if all she saw was a monster.

When the girls had finished eating, I gathered them together in a semi-circle. Several pairs of bright, round eyes gazed at me. The contestants were always attentive after the second round. Hoping anything I said could offer them a lifeline.

Fifteen left.

How many would reach the next checkpoint? Would Selena make it through this one?

An uncomfortable, prickling feeling ran through my gut as I projected today's map onto the wall.

"Today, you will be heading here." I pointed to a red dot on the map further north and inland.

"But that's only a few miles," Angelina said, her pale eyebrows lifting in hope. I noted with a flare of anger, that she was once again wearing Selena's dress. Why Selena let her get away with it, I had no idea.

"Yes," I confirmed. "But you won't be done once you reach that spot." I remained vague, as was ordered of me, but the fear that flashed across the girls' faces was disturbing.

"What's there?" Selena demanded, catching my eye.

More than anything I wanted to tell her, so she could be prepared. But if the Helsings found out I gave any of the girls an advantage, I'd be executed without hesitation.

I grabbed a handful of the small backpacks on the floor, passing them out.

Kite yanked hers open then her head snapped up. "This is it?" She held out the single energy bar they'd been gifted today. "How long does this round last?"

"You have six hours." At my words, a commotion broke out. I raised my voice louder as I continued and they quickly fell silent once more. "Having less time is a disadvantage, as you may have already figured out. In this round, it can be a death sentence."

"What does that mean?" Cassandra asked, glancing at Selena beside her.

Determinedly, I kept my gaze on her as I answered. "You will find out soon enough."

I grabbed fresh stakes from a rack on the wall. I passed them out one at a time and when I reached Selena, I held onto hers for half a second more. "Use everything in your packs today," I said directly to her, but loud enough that everyone could hear.

She gave a small nod, eyeing me curiously as I moved away.

When the girls were armed, I led them out of the cave into the cove. The Helsings had constructed a wooden lift there hundreds of years ago, scaling the sheer cliff wall. Endless fun for me, as I got the job of hoisting the cable that caused the lift to rise. Ushering them all onto the rectangular platform, I dragged across the wooden gate and moved to the pulley system.

I yanked down on the steel cable and the lift rose up the side of the cliff with a jerk. I continued to pull, hand after hand, dragging the cable down as they raised toward the cliff edge high above.

As it reached the top, I waited whilst the girls filed out, a niggling feeling in my stomach distracting me. I didn't have any time to dwell on it as the castle horn blared across the island, and round three of the game began.

Selena

I was crammed at the back of the lift when it juddered to a halt at the top of the cliff, swinging precariously on a metal crane.

Cass was at my side, her shoulder rubbing mine as we shuffled toward the exit. A horn blared in my ears, echoing across the island, sounding the start of the third round.

Six hours and counting.

As one, all fifteen of us started running across the rough terrain. I tapped the cuff on my wrist, eyeing the red dot we were moving toward. Just three miles to the next checkpoint, but I knew it wasn't going to be that simple.

Kite tore away from the group, splitting off to the right. I glanced at Cass as more of the girls broke off into groups, darting away left and right until just ten of us remained together. We were taking the most direct route to the checkpoint. But perhaps also the most deadly.

Briony raised a hand to Cass and I in farewell, before turning away and running into a nearby group of trees with Marie. The rest of the group swiftly followed, dividing into small units and vanishing into the woods around us.

"Guess it's just us then," Cass panted, her cheeks flushed red from the cold.

I slowed our pace, taking her arm. "Do you think this route is safe?"

"I don't think any route is safe, but the quicker we get to the checkpoint, the better."

"It's too easy," I breathed as we moved on, the crunch of leaves and twigs under my boots making me nervous.

After another cautious mile, Cass checked her map, finding the red dot just up ahead. The trees thinned and we arrived in a clearing where a large trap door lay open on the ground. I approached it with my stake raised, glancing into the trees for signs of the other girls.

Tiptoeing to the edge, I found a ladder disappearing into the dark abyss. My stomach turned over and I took a step back.

"Christ," Cass cursed as she joined my side. "The checkpoint's down there?"

"Looks like it." The red dot on my map hovered above this very spot.

Cass moved toward the ladder with purpose and I hissed, "*Wait*," dropping my bag from my shoulder.

She watched as I opened it, rummaging through the gear we'd been provided. Just three items lay inside. The single energy bar, a torch and a knife.

I sighed, taking out the torch and switching it on. It was bright, but small enough to hold between my teeth.

"Good idea," Cass mumbled, mimicking me.

Whilst she prepared herself, I took the lead, dropping onto the first rung. I tucked my stake into the top of my dress and held onto the iron ladder tightly, the metal bitterly cold beneath my palms. I glanced up at Cass as I descended, the moon casting a halo around her head.

"How far down does it go, do you reckon?" Cass asked as she turned, stepping onto the first rung and placing the torch between her teeth.

I grunted a response around the metal torch in my mouth and she broke a small laugh. Her torch fell from her teeth, swinging and wheeling as it whizzed past my ear.

I turned to watch it fall and several seconds later, it clunked loudly down below. I could make out the light far beneath us, but nothing was visible beyond it.

Cass swore as we continued on, trying to make as little noise as possible on the rungs. A scream echoed up to us from deep underground and both Cass and I stalled. My heartbeat thundered against my eardrums and my hands trembled so much I was worried I'd lose my grip on the ladder.

Whatever awaited us below, wasn't going to be a table of food and soft mattresses.

When we eventually descended the ladder, my boots hit hard ground. Two passages led away either side of me, both of them thick with darkness.

Cass dropped down beside me, ducking down and picking up her torch. I plucked mine from my mouth, holding it out to illuminate one of the tunnels. Pressing walls and a winding path lay ahead. The other tunnel didn't prove much more enticing, but the path was straighter, allowing us to see further ahead.

"This one," I encouraged, leading the way. Cass jogged at my side, tapping the cuff on her wrist. No map was provided for us, only an arrow that pointed to our left, no matter which way we turned.

"Guess we're following that then," Cass said, pointing to an opening.

Tentatively, we moved into the dark corridor, swinging our torches across it to be sure it was empty. As we moved, I tried not think about the pressing walls and tight spaces that we could become so easily trapped in.

The next turning led us to a square room, lit by a dim bulb hanging from the centre of the ceiling. Doors surrounded us and as we assessed which route to take, footsteps filled the air. Cass pressed me back as three girls ran into the room, sprinting flat out.

Their expressions were panicky, but before I could ask any of them what was going on, four Vs spilled through the doors.

Chaos ensued.

Everyone split apart. I lost sight of Cass, but heard her screaming, "Run!"

I charged toward one of the doors, picking it a random. I fled into the darkness, my torch flashing against the wall as I ran.

Pursuing footsteps made me run even faster, until my lungs burned and my legs ached. I couldn't outpace a V, that was all I could think. But still I ran on, as if I could defy everything I'd witnessed about the Vampires so far. Their speed, their ferocious nature, their unending desire for my blood.

I smashed into a dead end, nearly knocking myself out on the stone wall as I failed to stop in time. Wheeling around, I wrenched the stake from my dress-

The V collided with me.

The force with which she hit me knocked the wind from my lungs. I gasped as I awaited the feel of teeth ripping into my skin, claws sinking into my flesh.

But none came.

The V sank forward, her ebony hair -the same colour as mine- wet with dark blood. I trembled from head to toe as I tried to work out what had happened. And as the fog of fear lifted from my mind, I realised the stake in my hand had pierced her heart.

Gasping in relief, I could hardly believe my luck. The V's own momentum had impaled her on it. I pushed her body from mine, dragging the stake free with a grimace. Vampire blood was spilled down my dress, staining it in patches of black gloop.

When I managed to stop shaking, I tapped my cuff to check the timer. Four hours remaining. How had so much time passed already?

The torch was somehow still in my hand, so I swung it around, finding two more passages left and right. The arrow provided by my cuff illuminated the way in a blue shimmer. I took the left passage, curving in what I hoped was the direction of the checkpoint.

The dark was pressing and the close walls made every sound seem achingly loud. The echo of my own footsteps caused me to jump more than once, as if someone was just behind me, about to pounce.

After meeting several dead ends and walking in circles, I checked the clock on my cuff again, conscious of how much time was wasting. I had just three hours left to find the checkpoint.

That was long enough. *It had to be.*

Moving down another corridor of endless grey stone, I came across a trap door that led deeper into the maze. I dropped my torch into it – purposefully this time to illuminate the passage below - and it clattered as it hit the floor about ten feet down. I descended to the next level, the temperature plummeting dramatically.

Ice glimmered on the walls as I continued, using my torchlight to guide the way. After another hour of twisting and turning through the endless corridors, I took a break, eating my energy bar. These winding halls were like a labyrinth, drawing me round and round in circles.

I slumped against a wall at an intersection, keeping a wary eye on all of the exits as I chewed. It was overly sweet, filled with dried fruit and too much sugar. The taste lingered on my tongue long after I'd eaten it.

Footsteps approached, slow and steady. Whoever was around the next corner seemed in no particular hurry. If it was one of the other girls, they surely would be rushing around. So it had to be a

V.

Clicking off my light, I waited. And waited.

My heart rate notched up and it became harder and harder to keep calm. Holding my breath, I held out for the footsteps to pass. But it soon became apparent whoever it was, was pacing.

I steeled myself, gripping the stake tighter in my hand. I had to move, staying put was a death wish. But rounding the next corner seemed like one too.

Creeping forward, I pressed my back to the wall and stole a glance around the corner. The snarling and grunting of the haggard V caught my ear. Luckily, his back was to me as he paced, blocking my way to an open metal door at the other end of the corridor.

Perhaps that was the checkpoint. Perhaps all I had to do was take down this single Vampire and I'd be safe.

My hands shook as I tried to calm my nerves enough to spring an attack. I recalled Varick's words. These Vs were weaker than him. And this one didn't look well fed. Maybe I had the upper hand.

Before I knew what I was doing, I ran. My muscles flooded with adrenaline, my arm was raised with the stake in my fist.

In a blur of movement, the Vampire turned and in a heartbeat, he was upon me.

The force with which he hit me sent me tumbling into a wall. His fingers dug into my shoulders, holding me in place. Drool dripped from his fangs, the stench of his breath a vile mixture of rot and blood.

Before I could even attempt to fight him off, his teeth sunk into my neck. I screamed out, shoving him back, but it was no use. My legs began to buckle with his pressing weight, his movements frenzied as he sucked on my throat. The pain was nothing compared to the disgust I felt at him drinking from me. But the longer it went on, the more woozy I grew, my vision blurring.

My mind became foggy; my only thought was that I had to survive. Somehow, I had to get out of this. I had to get back home. *For Mum.*

With as much energy as I could muster, I slashed upwards with the stake. The V screeched so loud that it hurt my ears, but the single moment of weakness gave me back a chance.

I'd buried the stake too low. I yanked it out as the V launched at me again. And this time, I didn't miss. The V gasped, inches from my ear, his fingernails raking down my arms as he died.

I shuddered as he crumpled to the floor at my feet. I didn't waist another second, knowing the commotion could draw more of them.

I fled toward the door, darting through it and speeding into the darkness. With a wrenching feeling, I realised I'd dropped my torch.

Wheeling around on the spot, I turned back to the fallen V, now far at the end of the corridor. The torchlight glowed by his fallen body, illuminating both him, and the two Vs standing above him. It took a moment for me to register what I was seeing.

I was drowsy from blood loss and the world seemed to be tilting around me.

Their bloodshot eyes locked with mine and my instincts tore me in half: I could either try to reach the open metal door and shut it in time. Or, I could run.

The Vs sped toward me and I abandoned my hopes of shutting the door, fleeing into the darkness, cursing myself for not acting sooner.

The only guide I had was my fingers brushing the walls. Every time a gap appeared, I darted into it. Turning, left, right, left until I was lost in the abyss. The only thing I could hope for was that I was lost to the Vs too.

Everything seemed louder without my sight. Screams reached to me from far away, the aggressive shouts of Vs, their voices too distorted by echoes to catch what they were saying.

I continued running, trying to focus my muddled thoughts. I wasn't even sure if my eyes were open; the dark was so pressing and I could only punctuate it from time to time with my cuff, unable to keep the light on it for longer than a few seconds.

The cold was biting and pain shot down my neck from where the V had fed on me. I held a hand to it, finding my shoulder slick with blood. I winced, moving on, keeping one hand clamped down on the wound and the other on the wall beside me.

I moved on and on, eventually stopping to check the time. The corridor was cast in an eerie blue glow, the icy walls twinkling either side of me.

My heart plummeted.

One hour.

Getting lost in these tunnels had drained the precious time I'd had left. And I still had no idea if I was even close to the checkpoint.

For a moment, I simply stood, sucking down icy breaths, trying to keep myself from panicking. A knot was tightening in my chest, pulling and pulling.

It would be so easy to give up now, to break down. My body was pushed to its limits and I was on the verge of giving in to fear.

I shut my eyes, thinking of home. Of the past few years and how I'd already survived so much. My stepfather's voice rung in my ears, as crystal clear as if he were standing next to me.

"You'll never amount to anything, Selena. Like your mother. Worthless, wastes of space, the two of you. You should be grateful I'm here to look after you."

I gritted my teeth, that same anger fuelling me now as the day I'd killed him. "I don't need you," I hissed into the air, the words giving me enough strength to move my feet. What the spectators would make of that, I had no idea. They'd probably think I was losing my mind. But in fact, I was starting to feel sane again. Strong enough to go on.

Using the arrow on my cuff to guide me, I found an opening leading in the right direction. Praying I was close, I picked up my pace, jogging then flat-out sprinting. With every corner I turned, I expected to see the checkpoint, tapping my cuff to illuminate the space for a few seconds before the hologram evaporated and plunged me back into darkness.

Around and around I went, every corridor looking the same until I was certain I was going in circles. Nothing but blank walls and hollow rooms awaited me. But there was a fire in my belly now, forcing me to keep moving. If I was going to die, it would have to be by the capsule in my head. I couldn't give up until the choice was taken out of my hands.

I urged my legs on, speeding around a corner.

With a collision that felt like I'd hit another wall, I slammed into someone. My arm came up with the stake in hand, but they'd gotten there first. The pain rushed to meet me; the sharp tip of white oak had slid deep into my side.

I choked down a rattling breath, lifting my chin to face my attacker, illuminated by a torch strapped to their wrist: Angelina.

Her fair hair was lank with sweat, her eyes wide as she registered what had happened.

As if in slow motion, I sunk to my knees, clawing at her arms to try and stay upright. My chances of escape faded in a flash.

Angelina shook her head, gazing at me with parted lips. "I'm sorry," she breathed. "I'm so sorry." In a blur, she ran on, darting through a doorway and leaving me in the dark.

I clutched the wound and agony ripped through me, nearly making me cry out. I forced myself to keep silent. If I was going to die, I didn't want it to be at the hungry mouth of a V.

My hands trembled as I ripped swathes of material from the hem of dress, managing to bind it around my waist. It stemmed the blood flow, but the damage was done.

Still, I wanted to move. I wanted to fight until my last breath was snatched from my lungs.

Tapping my cuff and leaving a bloody print on it, the arrow shone brightly, pointing directly behind me.

I crawled toward the door Angelina had disappeared through, moving in the direction of the arrow.

A dark trail of blood followed me and I feared the worst. The Vs would smell this. It was only a matter of time before one of them found me. That was, if the timer didn't run out first and a shot of poison was injected into my brain.

I groaned my agony, unable to stop myself as my stomach muscles contracted with every move I made.

Numbness slid through my body. My hands, my legs, everything was starting to let me down.

"No," I said through gritted teeth, dragging myself on. "Not now. Not here."

I'd been through too much for this to be the end. Life owed me so many things. So many happy days had been stolen from me. And I was going to buy them back. I was going to make it home to Mum and make up for every peaceful day Elijah had taken from us.

With a jolt, I remembered the V blood on my dress. Reaching down, I tried to wipe enough onto my hand for me to drink. But it was already dried into my clothes. Life was evading me at every turn.

My energy ran out. I was forced to stop when my belly dragged across the floor, my strength failing. I propped myself up against a wall, sucking in my final breaths. Each one became slower and my vision started to fade.

I checked the timer and found I had just five minutes to reach the checkpoint. The clock reflected on the wall, enlarging tenfold. I sighed, watching my life tick away by the second.

"Selena," a voice whispered, so quiet I wasn't sure if I was imagining it. I wanted to answer back, certain I recognised the voice. Male. Deep. Someone I knew.

I slowly wheeled my head around, trying to spot the source, but no one was visible.

"Selena!" Cass's voice rang through the air.

And as I blinked, focusing, I saw a door, just ten feet away where Cass was being guided forward by Varick. He practically shoved her toward me but she didn't even stumble, already racing in my direction. She dropped to her knees and smeared something over my mouth, shielding me with a curtain of her hair.

I tasted the sharp metallic tang of V blood and, in an instant, life flooded back into my veins.

"Up," she whispered, ever so quietly. "Not too fast."

I wrapped an arm around her shoulders, struggling alongside her, despite feeling stronger with every step. The timer ticked down on my cuff. Just thirty seconds.

Twenty seconds.

Ten.

We quickened our pace, rolling over the doorstep with just five seconds to spare and I fell at Varick's feet, sighing my relief.

I gazed up at him and his eyes blazed into mine.

My attention was dragged from him as a high-pitched wail sounded in the corridor. I snapped around, clambering to my feet as I spotted a girl in a pale pink gown collapsing to the ground just metres from us.

"Come on!" I cried, but blood was already pouring from her unseeing eyes, running down her cheeks in two streaks.

"The poison," Cass breathed as we gazed on in horror.

Two metal doors slid closed between us, locking us away from the maze.

I blinked, trying to register what I'd just witnessed. My palms were sticky with sweat and all I could think was *that could have been me'*. I was rooted to the spot, disgusted with myself for thinking that way. Despising myself for being grateful that I was standing here and not her.

Varick touched my elbow to encourage me further into the room. And for the first time, I didn't recoil from him. Because I was sure, without a doubt, that it had been his blood that had saved me.

Selena

Cass clutched my hand. I was drenched in sweat and still shaking, probably resembling the undead.

"I'll take her from here," Varick commanded as we entered a large room where the survivors were gathered.

I found Angelina amongst them and my upper lip curled back. I had half a mind to launch myself at her but Varick took hold of my arm, guiding me firmly away. At a glance, I would have guessed there were perhaps twelve of us remaining. Thankfully, Briony and Marie were amongst them, their eyes wide with fright at the sight of me.

Cass let me go with less objection than I expected. I must have looked pretty rough if she was willing to let me wander off alone with Varick.

He led me to another room, shutting the metal door behind him with a loud clunk. Bunk beds sat on either side of the small room and jumpsuits were laid out on each.

Hastily, I sank down onto a bottom bunk, shivering in the freezing air.

"I know what you did," I said as Varick placed a metal chair before me and perched on it.

"And what was that exactly?" He raised a brow.

"The blood." I touched my lips. "You let Cass heal me."

His eyes fixed on mine, dark green and deep as always. "And why would I help a contestant, Selena?" He was clearly trying to play dumb, but I knew the truth.

"Your blood is stronger than the others. I know it was yours."

He leant in close, his jaw ticking. "Well let's keep that between the three of us, shall we?"

I nodded, wide-eyed. "Of course." The idea that I would rat him out after what he'd done for me was ludicrous. But I simply didn't understand why he had done it at all. "But Varick-"

He halted me by raising a hand. "You need more blood." He brushed the matted hair away from my neck where the V bite had been. "Your injuries were serious."

I nodded and he slit open his wrist with his teeth, holding it out for me. I leant back with a frown, my nose wrinkling at what he was suggesting.

"Drink," he demanded.

Tentatively, I took his raised arm, but couldn't force myself to do anything more. Varick lifted his wrist, encouraging me. "Trust me."

Even after what he'd done for me, it was a difficult thing to do, but I had to get better if I was going to face another day.

Sickened with myself, I pressed my mouth over the wound.

Surprisingly, the blood was warm, not as hot as a human's, but so much more than the cold sludge that resided in the Vs' veins out in the game.

I felt Varick's eyes on me as I drank and I tried to block him out, feeling strangely self-conscious.

"That'll do," he said at last and I released him, frowning at what I'd done.

"My turn." He took my wrist and I lurched away as he started laughing. "Too soon for jokes?"

I shook my head at him. "You're twisted, you know that?"

His mouth hooked up at the corner, but he said no more. He gestured to my jumpsuit. "There's no showers here." He stood. "Get changed. Come eat. You've got twelve hours before round four."

I sighed, hanging my head as he walked toward the door.

"Varick?" I called and he paused. "Thank you."

He nodded, his gaze lingering on me a moment longer before he exited the room. An electric charge seemed to dispel from the air and I was able to relax again. There was something about him I couldn't figure out. Everything he appeared to be on the outside, was hiding something softer. I had no doubt he could be vicious, dangerous even, and yet I sensed some vulnerability in him, too.

Cleaning myself up as I best I could with the single, leaky sink in the room, I changed into the warm jumpsuit and braided my blood-coated hair into a long plait. It was the best I could do with the basic facilities provided for us, but I felt miles better than I had in that dress. If I ever got out of here, I didn't know if I could wear a dress again without thinking of this awful game.

A sudden longing for home overwhelmed me. I'd expected to

be locked up in prison when this kind of homesickness kicked in, not on some godforsaken island fending off Vampires on a daily basis. I shuddered, curling up on the bottom bunk and pulling the thin, woollen blanket over me. If this cold persisted, I'd never get a good night's sleep.

What would Mum think if she knew I was here now? I'm sure she would tell me to *'hold out for brighter days'*. That was her motto when things got really bad. Mum was strong, even though she hadn't been strong enough to leave home. Perhaps killing Elijah had been selfish. I'd saved myself. I'd landed myself in prison and, in a roundabout way, put myself on this island too. In doing so, I'd abandoned my mum. The one person who wanted to keep me safe, even if she hadn't always been able to do so.

I curled tighter into a ball, passing from dreams to reality as the cold continually woke me.

Eventually, Cass brought me some food and I was glad at least to find it was a hot broth, even though it tasted of very little. I wolfed down two bowls before I felt better, the taste of leeks remaining on my tongue long after.

"Thought you were a goner," she said quietly, slipping under my blanket and bringing her own one down from the bed above so we'd have an extra layer.

"Me too..." I lowered my voice and said, "Angelina stabbed me."

Cass gasped, looking like she was about to storm from the room to confront her. I grabbed her arm.

"It was an accident, we ran into each other around a corner. It could just as easily have been the other way around."

"But she left you there," Cass said in disbelief.

I bit my lip, giving a slight nod. "It's not her fault. We're all just trying to survive here."

"Some more than others," Cass muttered, but seemed to drop the issue.

"Thank you for coming back for me."

"Of course." She nudged me. "When all of this is over, we're going home together."

I nodded, breaking a hopeful smile, trying to ignore the niggling doubt that it wouldn't be so simple.

With Cass sharing my bed, we were both warm enough to sleep. Dim bulbs lit the room, flickering from time to time, their amber glow filtering into my dreams.

After a few more hours of fairly decent sleep, I was forced to get up, feeling agitated. I knew I should try to rest longer, but my brain was on overdrive. What did tomorrow hold? How many of us would survive it? The thought of losing Cass seemed more unbearable every day. Now that she'd risked her life to save me, I felt a bond between us that wouldn't easily be broken.

The other girls had joined our room, snoozing soundly on the other bunk beds - apart from their persistent shivering. I slipped out of the room, part of me hoping Varick would be waiting there.

He was sat on one of the chairs, facing the wall where the game had presumably been projected.

"What's it like? Watching us?" I asked and he didn't jump, evidently knowing I'd been there all along.

His gaze remained fixed on the wall. "Routine mainly. I've watched hundreds of these games. Watched too many girls die."

"So it bothers you?" I approached him slowly, taking in the icy room and the dark walls.

He considered his answer then said, "Now it does."

"Why?" I blurted and he finally turned to me.

There was something about him, something that drew me in and wouldn't let go. Perhaps all the Vs were capable of it. Maybe it was just another way they lured their victims to them.

"Guess I'm just seeing things in a different light this time round."

"But why?" I pressed, approaching him, placing my hand on the nearest chair.

He gave me a hard stare, taking in my shivering shoulders. "I don't usually drink during the games. Perhaps I'm feeling a little more human this time."

My neck tingled.

"Who did you feed from?" I asked quietly, not sure if I wanted to know.

"One of the spectators," he said with a satisfied smile.

I mirrored him; whoever he had drank from had probably deserved it. "Did he die?" It was twisted, but I hoped he had.

"No," he replied with a grimace. I wasn't sure if he was disgusted with himself or the fact the man still lived.

A cold wind rattled through the space and I wrapped my arms around myself to keep warm. "What is this place?"

"An old storage bunker for the castle. A long time ago, this island was a fortress for the Norwegian king. A fleet of ships once surrounded it to protect Norway from invading countries...and pirates."

Something in his tone made me question the last part. "Pirates?"

"Mhm. People like me." He smiled at some memory, but there was sadness in it too. And loss.

"You were a pirate?" I asked in surprise, his appearance suddenly making much more sense.

"I was a captain." He scoffed at himself, raising his hands. "King of the bloody north sea. Now look at me."

I frowned, dropping into a seat a few down from his. "At least you did something with your life." I threaded my fingers together. "I screwed mine up. Probably deserve to be here."

"No one deserves to be here," he snarled and I fought the urge to recoil from his bared fangs.

"At least the Helsings pick a bunch of murderers to take part in this game."

"They didn't always. And don't make the mistake of thinking that's some kind of decency. The only reason they take girls from prisons is because they're easier to bury. I have to Charm a lot less people into thinking you're dead."

My heart twitched. "*Dead*? Does my mother think I'm dead?"

Varick shifted in his seat. "I'm sorry, Selena. It's protocol. I only Charm the guards. They would have informed your mother afterwards."

Tears burned my eyes. My mother had no one left but me. She'd be distraught thinking I'd died in that prison.

The walls suddenly seemed pressing and my lungs couldn't drag in enough air. I stood, clutching at my chest. "I can't do this any more. I want to go home. My mother deserves to know the truth." I sounded weak, but I couldn't help myself.

"You can go home if you survive the game," Varick said in a serious tone.

"You swear?" I asked through my teeth. "Do you *promise* they'll let me go?"

After a moment, he nodded. "They will."

I sighed, rubbing my eyes, certain he was telling the truth.

"I'll make sure everyone forgets you were ever in prison. No one will know you killed your step-father but you. The Helsings will make sure of it, too."

I released a shuddering breath, clinging to the glimmer of hope.

"Come." He stood. "I'll take you for some air."

I raised my brows but he gave no further explanation, moving across the room and heading through a bolted door. I followed him into a metal shaft where a ladder led upwards, a sheer climb giving us access to the island.

I gasped and moved toward the ladder, but he halted me,

moving onto it himself. "I'll go first. Some of the Vs may still be out there."

I nodded, fear trickling into my gut. But my desire for fresh air overrode it. This place was oppressive and I needed to escape it, if only for a few minutes.

Varick scaled the ladder in a flash and I moved after him, climbing as quickly as I could. My arms ached by the time I reached the top, scrambling over the edge. Varick helped me to my feet and I took in our surroundings. We were at the base of a mountain, its tip peaked in snow, and streams of water running down its sides. One of them passed close by, causing small waterfalls as it ran over the black rocks. A few pine trees gave us cover from the wind, but we'd be fairly exposed if any Vs came our way. I wondered how Varick felt about killing his kind.

"Am I allowed to be out here?" I asked, breathing in the fresh air.

"No." He gave me a crooked smile. "Another one of our secrets."

I rolled my eyes. "Are we starting a collection?"

His grin widened and he took my arm, leading me further into the woods. "When you're not being hunted like an animal, this place has its charm." He guided me to a waterfall where a deer was lapping at the moonlit pool beneath it. Her head whipped up at the sound of us approaching. Well, *me* approaching, considering Varick didn't seem to make a single noise as he moved across the ground.

"Go." I waved my hands, not wanting the creature to be around if a hungry V showed up. The deer rushed off into the trees and my heart rate settled.

"Will she be safe?" I whispered.

"The Vs don't bother with animals whilst human blood is on offer." Varick turned to me, taking my braid between his fingers, his jaw ticking. "Speaking of which. You should wash the blood from your hair in the stream. A V will smell this a mile off tomorrow."

I undid my sticky braid and Varick turned his back, his shoulders hunching. The blood was clearly bothering him, but I trusted he wouldn't bite me, considering his recent efforts to keep me alive.

The water was icy cold, but I dunked most of my hair in it, washing it clean to make sure the blood was gone. I'd rather face the cold than a hungry V tomorrow.

When I was done, Varick shed his leather coat, wrapping it around my shoulders. I gave him a smile of thanks and he started walking back toward the ladder.

"Wait," I begged. "I can't go back. Not yet."

"You'll freeze out here."

"Just a few minutes longer." I dropped onto a rock by the stream.

He moved to my side, hovering by the rock and I patted the space beside me. Raising his brows, he dropped onto the boulder. His arm brushed mine and my heart dipped.

"Do you feel the cold?" I asked, my breath coming out in a puff of vapour.

"No." If any breath left him, there was no trace of it in the air. "Not the cold. Not heat. Nothing." There was a bitterness in his tone.

My brows lowered. "That's kind of sad."

He huffed a laugh. "I feel more when I've fed."

"What do you miss the most?"

He remained silent for a while, thinking over his answer. Everything he did seemed to be deliberated. Like he was in no hurry at all. I guessed that was due to the fact he had an endless amount of time to spend. "The sun. Sunset, sunrises. Nothing beats that out at sea. The colours..." He painted his hand through the air. "Makes you believe there really is something worth living for."

"And now?" I asked quietly.

He released a low growl. "Now, there's nothing left. Me and an eternity of darkness, craving blood. Watching these damn games."

Something twisted in my chest. I shouldn't have pitied him. He had a hand in these games, even if he was a prisoner to the Helsings. But there was such a loneliness about him, that it hurt me to imagine. All that time alone, a slave to the Helsings with no end in sight. It didn't bear thinking about.

I rubbed my hands together, the cold setting in. But for some reason, I didn't want to end this moment yet.

"You need to survive, Selena." Varick turned to me, lifting a hand then dropping it awkwardly.

"Why do you care?" I had to know. What interest did this Vampire have in my survival? How did it affect him?

"There's something special about you..." His brows drew together. "I don't know what, but I can sense it."

I shook my head determinedly. "I'm no different than the other girls. Most of them are stronger, better at surviving."

"I'm not talking about the game. You're more desirable than the others. Your blood...it's like a drug."

I almost shrank from him, knowing he must be able to smell my blood now. He must have wanted to drink it. Perhaps coming to a secluded place in the woods with him wasn't the best idea. But somehow I still trusted he wouldn't hurt me.

"I won't touch you," he said, echoing my thoughts.

"I know." I hung my head. "You wouldn't have helped me today if you wanted me dead."

"*Or* I was just waiting for a quieter moment in the woods."

I glared at him. "You're not good at making jokes."

He laughed and the sound was deep and human. I hid my own smile, turning away.

Bloody Vampires. The sooner I got off this island, the sooner I'd never have to deal with one again.

The crescent moon sat low in the sky, coloured amber tonight as it peered through the passing clouds.

A howl cut through the air and my bones shook from the

sound. Perhaps it was misguided, knowing there were much worse things than wolves to worry about on this island. But Varick was suddenly alert, springing to his feet in an aggressive stance.

"What is it?" I hissed, but my question was answered as a V stepped through the trees. He was a huge man, thick with muscle and his straggly blonde hair hung around him like a mane. He was clearly well fed, but his eyes were still bloodshot and ringed with dark circles.

"Varick," he snarled, his gaze flitting between the two of us. "How kind of you to bring me a midnight snack."

"We were just leaving, Ravenos," Varick said, reaching back and gesturing for me to move.

I hurried to comply, pressing into his shoulder and peering toward the V across the stream. His movements were slow and controlled, his pale face turning to me, making me shiver.

"Pity, pity." Ravenos took a step forward and Varick nudged me back.

"You know you can't take me on, brother," Varick said in a smooth tone.

"Hunger will make you do crazy things, *brother*." He spat the word. "But I suppose you wouldn't know about that, seeing as the Helsings keep their pet well fed."

"You don't know anything about my treatment. I'm as much a slave as you are."

"Nice to be up in that castle though, isn't it? Must be quite comfortable. And here you are, taking a bite out of one of the girls meant solely for us." He tutted, baring his fangs. "Greedy, very greedy."

"You'll have your chance out in the game tomorrow. You know the rules." Varick shifted me further behind him and I stumbled from the force he used. My heart pounded in my ears, so loud that I was certain both of the Vampires could hear it.

"Liar," Ravenos hissed and spittle flew from his mouth. He lifted a hand, pointing directly at me. "That one has ancient blood and you know it. Does he drink from you, sweetie?" His pale grey eyes shifted over me as he sniffed the air.

"No, it's against the rules," I choked out, leaning around Varick, my mind racing. What did he mean 'ancient blood'?

Ravenos turned back to Varick. "Come on, friend. We'll share her. The Helsings won't notice if one goes missing."

Varick's body tensed, coiled like a loaded spring. "You're wrong. She's the favourite to win. The Helsings would have both our heads for it."

My heart flipped over at his words. Was that true? Why on earth would the spectators bid on me more than anyone else?

Ravenos took a step into the stream. "Maybe *your* head. But not mine. You were the one who brought her out here unprotected."

"She's not unprotected!" Varick barked.

Ravenos retreated like a cowering dog. "Alright, have it your way." He slunk back toward the trees, his eyes never leaving mine. "See you tomorrow."

"Maybe she'll introduce you to her stake," Varick growled.

Ravenos cackled a laugh. "Not if she meets my fangs first."

The second he melted into the shadows, Varick half-dragged, half-carried me back to the ladder. "Down!" he ordered and I didn't hesitate, dropping onto the first rung and hurrying into the safety of the bunker.

Varick met with me a moment later, seeming furious as he led me back to the main room, bolting the heavy metal door behind us.

He started pacing, raking a hand through his hair and cursing profusely.

"It's fine," I said in an attempt to placate him.

"It's not fine," he hissed, probably trying not to wake the girls. "He could have killed you."

I moved toward him, tentatively resting a hand on his arm and he froze. "You said yourself, you're stronger than him."

"Yes, but I shouldn't have put you at risk. Do you have any idea what the Helsings would do to me if they found out?" He shut his eyes for a moment and I extracted my hand, resting it over my erratic heartbeat instead. "And if you died, I'd-" he cut off, clutching his throat as he looked at me.

"You'd what?" I pressed, shrinking before his penetrative gaze.

"Nothing," he growled, recomposing himself. "He'll hunt you tomorrow for sure."

"You said they're after me anyway, what difference does it

make?"

"Ravenos is getting stronger every day. He may disregard the other girls for the sake of seizing you."

An icy chill crept up my spine. I removed Varick's coat from my shoulders, placing it on a chair.

Varick looked tense, his brow heavily furrowed.

"I'll be okay, Varick. I know how to kill them."

He sighed. "Ravenos is cunning. He'll grab you from behind so you can't use your stake."

"Oh," I breathed.

"Try not to turn your back on him. But if he does get a hold of you, don't fight. Let him bite you."

"What?" I said in alarm and he glared at me to keep my voice down.

I bit my lip then repeated in a quieter voice, "What do you mean? *Let* him bite me? Are you insane?"

He shook his head. "Vs are weaker when they're feeding. He'll be too distracted, plus you'll have access to the back of his neck." He turned around, pushing up his hair and pointing to a soft patch of skin at the base of his skull. "Strike here with the stake. With any luck, you'll have a chance at breaking the capsule of silver inside his head."

He turned back to me and evidently I looked completely baffled because he turned me swiftly around and tugged me into a tight hold. For a second I actually thought he was hugging me, then realised he was showing me how Ravenos would attack. My cheeks flamed from my foolishness and I was glad my back was to him so he couldn't see.

Shifting my damp hair aside, he lowered his mouth to my neck, almost touching. My throat went dry from his proximity. He could so easily hurt me. He probably wanted to. The rigidity of his body told me he was struggling to restrain himself.

"Lift your right arm."

I did so, reaching behind his neck which I now had access to in this position. "Okay." I felt a little better, knowing I at least had an idea of what to do if I got caught.

I tried to shift from his hold, but Varick didn't let me go, making a low noise of frustration in his throat.

"*Varick*," I said in a whisper.

His grip tightened further and I shut my eyes, trying to let myself trust him. It was nearly impossible, from all I'd ever known about men in my life, none of them seemed trustworthy. Least of all one with jagged teeth who liked the taste of people.

"You have no idea how hard this is..." He dragged in a breath that ruffled my hair and, for some reason, I relaxed.

"It's okay," I said, my voice quavering only a fraction. "You wouldn't hurt me." I was only ninety nine percent sure of my words, and that one percent was playing havoc with my heart.

After a second longer, he released me, pushing me rather more forcefully away from him than was necessary.

"Bed," he commanded, not looking at me.

As I trailed toward the bedroom, a question rose to my mind, and despite his dismissal, I asked it anyway. "What did Ravenos mean when he said I had ancient blood?"

Varick's expression changed; for a moment he actually looked worried. "It just means your blood is more desirable to the Vs, that's all."

I wasn't sure if he was being entirely honest, but the look in his eyes told me I wasn't going to get any more information from him.

"And none of the other girls have this...problem?" I asked in a small voice.

He shook his head stiffly. "I've never craved anyone so much. I barely notice the others." His Adam's apple rose and fell. A tense moment hung between us where I could almost hear the tension thrumming in the air.

"Now go to bed," he snapped.

I scowled as I walked away, feeling chastised. It wasn't *my* fault he was a blood addict. But I headed to bed all the same, not saying another word.

Selena

In my dreams I watched Ravenos kill the small deer in the woods. It was worse than if he'd been hunting me. There was something so innocent about the creature, her elegant beauty and quiet nature.

As I munched on a dry bagel in the morning - my writhing stomach not feeling up to much else - I found myself watching the other girls. None of us were innocent. We had all done something terrible, perhaps many things. Most of us were killers, so perhaps being here was some poetic justice.

My gaze eventually settled on Cass. Cass the arsonist. Though she'd said her ex hadn't been killed in the fire she'd set. Surely that wouldn't have landed her in a maximum security prison?

A hand dropped onto my shoulder and I jumped out of my seat, electricity crackling in my veins. Twisting around, I found Varick there, silent as ever.

"You should wear bells or something!" I gestured to his body in general. Damn V, sneaking up on me.

There was no amusement in his expression, only darkness. "Get dressed. Be ready to run today." He gave me a small nod, cementing the strange alliance we were forming and I was left feeling too sick to finish my bagel.

Christ, what had I gotten myself into taking *him* on as an ally? If that's what I could call him. Perhaps his sole interest in my survival was so he could get his own teeth into my veins. If I was as much of a delicacy as he said I was, perhaps that was his intention all along.

For now, I had to cling to the small advantages he was giving me and deal with the consequences later. I tried to reach my black dress before Angelina got there today, but found her already twirling around in it in the bathroom - the room no more than a twelve foot metal locker.

Suddenly, I'd had enough. Storming toward her, I started unknotting the laced-up back. She shrieked, turning and slashing out at me with her palm.

I snatched her slim wrist, squeezing tightly and glaring at her. "I think the least you owe me is my dress."

Some of the other girls halted putting on their own gowns, watching us with interest.

Angelina squealed from the tight hold I had on her. Something had changed in me. Or perhaps it had been there all along and only now my killer instincts were rising to the surface.

"Don't you think?" I pressed and Angelina screwed up her eyes.

"Fine," she huffed.

"And remember, I don't die that easily. So the next time you consider leaving me in a pool of my own blood, I'd have serious second thoughts. Because I won't be so forgiving in future."

Angelina nodded, biting her lip from the pain.

I released her, folded my arms and waited for her to strip. Cass caught my eye over her shoulder, grinning from ear to ear. I fought a smile in return, satisfaction spreading through me. If I was going to die today, I was going to do it on my own terms. Starting with *this* bitch.

Angelina threw the dress at me and I span on my heel, marching into a toilet cubicle where I changed into it. Her body had already warmed the material which was an added benefit for me. Behind the toilet door, I let myself really smile.

As usual, Varick was waiting for us in front of a projected map of the island. The mountain I'd seen last night was highlighted on the new section with a seemingly endless forest on the other side of it.

I sat in the back row between Marie and Cass, watching his presentation with a fierce determination. That was, until his next words.

"You will spend three days out on the island. The checkpoint will not be open until the third day."

Chaos broke out in the form of angry shouts and muttering.

"Quiet!" Varick roared, his eyes flaring. "You are about to face your first real test. As well as the Vs, you will need to consider how you are going to find food, water, shelter-"

"You aren't giving us any food?" a girl I think was called Sakura, cried out. Her hair was streaked with pink and purple, the dye having faded drastically since we'd arrived.

"No," Varick said simply and my pulse rose. No food, no water? It was bad enough evading the Vs without having to worry about such things.

"There are sources on the island, you only need look for them," Varick encouraged, but no one seemed particularly comforted. He picked up packs from the table behind him, passing them out. When I received mine, I tugged it open, like everyone else around me was doing. There was a large bottle inside – empty –, a knife, a flare, a single match and some kindling bound together with twine.

A tense silence fell on the room and as Varick passed out the stakes, no one said a word. I was certain we were all thinking the same thing: a lot of us were going to die in this round.

Varick led us to the ladder we'd ascended last night, but I felt nothing of the brief moment of freedom I'd felt then. More than ever, I felt like a prisoner, being marched into a firing line.

"I don't want to die," I heard Marie whisper.

"Suffering is worse than death," Varick muttered to himself.

A murmur of disquiet ran through the group. Varick certainly wasn't adept at comforting people.

"One at a time," he commanded. "Wait at the top of the ladder. If you move before the horn sounds, the capsule in your head will detonate."

Yes, comforting people definitely wasn't his forte.

I moved into line behind Cass, gazing up the shaft so icy raindrops peppered my cheeks. Sakura was the first up the ladder and we followed, one by one, after her. As I climbed, amongst the last to go, I shot a glance over my shoulder at Varick. His Adam's apple bobbed as he fixed his attention on me. A silent goodbye passed between us, because the chances were, I wouldn't survive this round.

Rain battered me as I reached the top, sweeping across the island in great sheets of grey.

I stood, shoulder to shoulder with the remaining twelve girls, waiting for the horn to announce the beginning of round four. I tapped my cuff, finding the checkpoint on the other side of the mountain. Zooming in, a cave system became clear within it. It was the most direct route to the checkpoint, but perhaps the most treacherous, too.

The horn sounded through the howling wind and rain, seeming more distant than it had before. It was the first time a round hadn't started in an outright sprint.

The girls divided into groups, some splitting off singularly and picking their way across the stream in the direction of the mountain.

Briony, Marie and Cass kept close and I nodded toward the direction Sakura was taking, following the path Varick had shown me last night.

Tugging up our hoods, we followed her, keeping our stakes drawn and our communication short.

"Over or under?" I muttered, tapping my cuff.

They knew what I meant. The route over the mountain would

be exposed, perhaps more dangerous in terms of the elements. No one was keen to return underground, but my gut told me it was the quickest way.

"There'll be water, shelter..." I reasoned.

"And probably a hundred Vs cornering us in the dark again." Marie shook her head. "Yesterday was bad enough."

"Cass?" I turned to her, spying raindrops sailing over her cheeks.

"I'm not a fan of the rain. If this storm gets worse, we'll wish we took the underground pass."

Briony took Marie's hand. "We'll take the long road."

I didn't like to split up again, but it made sense. There was no point sticking together if we didn't agree on the same strategy.

"Alright." I nodded, hugging each of them in turn. "We'll see you on the other side."

They gave stiff smiles that said neither of them were sure we'd ever see each other again, but none of us said it. It was easier to say goodbye if we pretended it wasn't forever.

"Good luck!" I called as Briony and Marie took a path that led up the mountain.

Sakura had increased her pace ahead, and though we hadn't spoken during the whole game, I increased my own pace, keeping her colourful hair in sight.

"How are we going to find food underground?" Cass voiced my own concerns. One of which we didn't mention; the fact we hadn't been gifted with torches in our packs. Would the route below ground be entirely dark? If so, we might have to rethink things. I wasn't sure I could face the pitch black again.

Without warning, a V burst from the trees, knocking Sakura to the ground, the skirt of her dark mauve dress snagged around her ankles.

I shouted out, already running toward her with my stake raised. I kicked the grey-haired V who had her on the ground. Thinking of Varick's advice, I aimed the tip of my stake at the base of his skull and brought it down with force.

The second the stake pierced skin, the V reared away, screaming, flailing on the ground. Liquid silver poured from his eyes, his nose, the corners of his mouth. With a sudden jerk, he died and Sakura gasped her relief, scrambling to her feet.

"What the hell?" Cass reached my side, gazing at the V.

"Guess they have a kill switch in the back of their heads, too," I panted, covering for the fact that Varick had tipped me off. If the Helsings were watching, I didn't want them to think I'd been cheating.

Miraculously, Sakura was unharmed. Her eyes fell on me and the bloody stake in my hand. "Thanks." She brushed down her dress. "Reckon I could have managed myself though."

"I bet you could," Cass drawled, marching past her.

I moved to follow, but Sakura caught my arm. "You're the one Varick likes." Her eyes flitted between mine and I noticed she had one blue eye and one green. With her wild, colourful locks, it somehow suited her.

"He doesn't like me," I snapped, overly defensive, but unsure why.

Sakura tongued her cheek. "Whatever. I'm sticking with you. Maybe he has some insider tip about who's most likely to survive."

I shrugged, heading onwards. "Suit yourself. But I'm no different than anyone else."

"Tell that to that Vampire who keeps staring at you. It's like he's high or something."

"He doesn't stare at me," I insisted, my cheeks flushing hot as I became aware of the hidden cameras feeding all of this back to the spectators and the Helsings. I didn't want Varick to get in trouble.

"Er- *yeah* he does. Like constantly." Sakura suddenly ducked low, picking berries off a bush. "Blackberries."

I raised my brows, dropping down to help her gather them, glad of the distraction from our topic of conversation. Like a fool, I would have walked right past them. Maybe our new ally was a useful one to have.

Cass found another bush and started making her own pile. Ripping off some of the material on our dresses, we packed them up and carefully placed them in our bags. The more food we could acquire now, the better.

The persistent rain made for a miserable journey as we walked on through damp bushes and low-hanging leaves on the surrounding trees. My cloak was soon soaked through and I decided, dark or not, cutting through the caves had to be the better option.

According to the map, there were several entrances to the underground passages. We headed for the furthest one, figuring the other girls would seek shelter as soon as possible. And that could draw the Vs away from the other cave entrances.

The rain washed away the last of the snow. The world was sapped of all colour until we were left in a monotone landscape, drudging on for what felt like an eternity.

I thought of the sun, picturing a summer's day, lazing on the small garden lawn outside my home, sipping lemonade with Mum, enjoying the few safe hours we'd had whilst Elijah was at work.

I craved daylight, and it made me think of Varick and the hundreds of years he'd spent in darkness. Perhaps immortality wasn't all it was cracked up to be.

Cass found the cave entrance first, hidden behind a mass of vines. We'd managed to gather a fairly decent amount of food, hopefully enough to see us through the pass. Our horde mostly consisted of berries, but Sakura had dug up a couple of roots she said were edible.

Pushing past the vines, we tentatively made our way inside. As I'd hoped, fresh water trickled down the cave walls and we spent some time filling our bottles from the small rivulets.

Sakura took the knife from her bag, cut the metal boning from the upper part of her dress and tugged it free. She bent a small piece of the metal, tucked one end under her cuff and pressed the other atop it. The map sprang to life and remained in place when she removed her finger from the cuff.

"Light," she announced brightly, heading into the cave.

"How'd you do that?" I asked, wishing I'd known of such a technique back in the bunker yesterday.

"The metal makes a circuit between your skin and the receptor. Simple really." Sakura twisted the remaining metal in her hand until it broke into pieces and she passed bits to Cass and I.

Copying her, I arranged the metal in place and was proud when it worked. Sakura definitely seemed handy to have around.

As we headed into the cave, the ceiling became lost high above into the darkness. Every step seemed to echo on for miles, making me cringe over and over. A Vampire would hear us a mile off, but taking our boots off on the wet ground didn't seem like an appealing idea.

Thankfully, the cave soon grew narrower and we made less noise as we progressed, winding into the depths of the mountain. None of us spoke. The only sound was the persistent dripping from the cave roof, the sound tenfold as it echoed through the caverns.

Sakura cursed from up ahead and as I caught her up, I found out why. The trail we'd followed dropped away into a dark abyss, the sheer edge before us stopping us from progressing. On the other side of the cavernous space, I could just make out a passage through the light thrown from our cuffs.

"How the hell do we get over there?" I asked.

A horrible, screeching noise sounded behind us and fear flashed through me.

I looked left and right for a way across, certain this couldn't be it. Cass reached into her bag, took out her flare and snapped it, chucking it into the empty space before us.

We watched in silence as it span away, the glowing red flames lighting up the pit as it hit the rocks below. It illuminated one other thing: a natural bridge of rock just a few feet below us, perhaps half a foot wide.

"Great," Cass muttered.

Sakura shrugged. "No point whining. I'd rather walk across that than wait for a V to catch us." With swift skill, Sakura dropped down onto the ledge below. She was graceful in her movements, raising her arms either side of her like a gymnast on a balance beam, making her way across.

I steeled myself before following, dropping with much less grace onto the bridge of rock and planting my feet.

Cass watched from above, her pale face illuminated in the hazy blue glow of her cuff.

"You can do it," I encouraged and she nodded, taking my hand as I helped her down. We wobbled precariously and I immediately let go of her, crouching down and finding my balance. Carefully turning, I spotted Sakura almost at the other side already.

"Damn show off," Cass muttered and I broke a shaky laugh.

As I stood on trembling legs, I thought of my stake, and how it would be near impossible to take on a V here without falling.

As I moved, one step at a time, I focused on the ledge that Sakura was scrambling up to. My breaths came in small pants, my heart faltering with every movement I made.

A rush of air was the only warning I had of the V that landed before me, having jumped from the ledge above. With a shout of alarm, I acted instinctively, shoving hard against the V's chest. She was slimmer than me and smaller in height, but as she tumbled from the ledge, she grabbed my arm, dragging me after her.

"No!" Cass cried out.

My arms flailed as I plummeted off of the bridge, my heart in my throat, my vision a blur of blue and red.

The V clawed into the rock with its free hand to halt her fall and I grabbed her other arm, saving myself. Suddenly, the Vampire was my only chance of survival and I desperately gripped her wrist with both hands.

I kicked at the rocks, trying to find purchase on the side of the bridge, but they were slick with water and made me swing precariously from the V's arm.

"Selena!" Cass called.

"I'm here!" I choked.

The V snarled and snapped at me, but I couldn't escape. She seemed barely human, her face skull-like and her eyes sunken. She dragged me up with her free arm, bringing my neck to her mouth. I dug the stake into a crevice for support as she clutched me to her skeletal body, ripping at my cloak with her teeth. Fear juddered through me as I desperately tried not to fall and equally to keep away from the ravenous Vampire.

"Cass, pull me up!" I begged, shaking off the V's hold on my arm and reaching upwards.

My fingers grazed the top of the bridge and a cold hand clamped down on them.

The V scrambled upwards, biting deep into my neck and I fought back a scream, a pained groan passing my lips instead.

"Up, *up*," I begged as Cass's grip tightened on me.

I tried to jerk out of the V's grip, but it was no good. Despite her emaciated condition, she was still stronger than me.

As Cass took my weight, I managed to pull the stake free of the rock. Before Cass could pull me up, I twisted my arm between the V and I, and pushed the tip as hard as I could against her.

With a roar of anger, she shoved me back against the rock, knocking my head against it. My vision blurred and my grip loosened on the stake.

Another hand joined Cass's and suddenly I was yanked upwards.

A foot flew threw the air, smashing into the V's shoulder. She lost her grip on me and tumbled backwards with a screech of rage, a distant *smack* sounding her impact.

I gasped my relief as Sakura and Cass dragged me up onto the bridge. Blood dripped from my neck, streaming over the rocks.

"Oh hell, Selena." Cass pressed her hands to my neck, stemming the blood flow.

"I'm alright. Just go." I managed to crawl toward the ledge and Sakura helped me up onto it.

As Cass joined us, she ripped a large swathe of material from her dress and held it to my neck, absorbing the blood.

I panted my thanks, dropping my head back onto the rocks as I caught my breath.

"Here." Sakura brought my stake to my lips and I grimaced as I licked the blood off it. After a few moments, the pain in my neck and head eased and I felt ready to move again.

Cass helped me to my feet and we journeyed on, huddling together through the narrow passage leading away from the canyon. The metal wire had come loose from my cuff, but as we rounded a corner, I discovered I no longer needed the light.

Glow worms illuminated the cave roof, like stars in the night sky.

Cass and Sakura extinguished the holograms on their cuffs and we followed the silver trail above us deeper into the cave system. Soon, we reached a dark pool of water where the twinkling lights reflected in its inky surface.

"We have to go through," I said, pointing to the passage on the other side.

"Take your cloaks off, put them in your bags," Sakura suggested, shedding her own and tucking it away.

We moved into the pool, holding our packs above our heads.

The water was numbingly cold and I was soon up to my waist in it. I tried not to think of the monsters I imagined living in the depths of this pool, but every splash made me jump. By the time we made it to the other side, we were shivering and our teeth were chattering violently.

"H-here, we'll start a f-fire," Cass said, moving to higher ground where the floor was dry. Taking her kindling from her bag, she arranged it in a neat pile before striking the single match she had. The flames took and we worked quickly to encourage the fire, ripping small slithers of material off of our dry cloaks to burn. The fire burned low, but it was enough to warm us up and, within a couple of hours, we were dry enough to stop our persistent shivering. Eating a handful of berries each, we resolved to continue on, following the map into the belly of the mountain.

As the hours ticked by, I grew worried about the lack of Vs we'd come across. "Where are they all?"

"Maybe they're chasing the other girls," Cass replied.

"Hope so," Sakura remarked without remorse.

I shot her a glare and she rolled her eyes.

"What? You'd rather it was *you* they were hunting?"

I remained silent, taking the lead as guilt tugged at my gut. I wanted to be good enough that I didn't think that way. But I knew Sakura was right. I'd rather the Vs were off hunting someone other than us.

We reached a sheer wall, blocking our way. Milky white stalactites hung from the roof, so sharp they looked as though they'd be lethal if they fell on us.

"Where now?" I asked, turning back to the others.

A pool of water lay at the base of the rock and Cass splashed through it, following it along the wall. "This water has to go somewhere."

The rushing sound of an underground river confirmed her theory. Sakura perched on a rock, taking a drink whilst we hunted for a way out.

The further Cass moved into the pool, the deeper it got and she was soon submerged up to her chest. She gasped then dropped under the water.

"Cass!" I cried, splashing through the pool after her.

Her cuff illuminated beneath the water and disappeared into the darkness. I gazed left and right, the cold water making me panic.

The blue glow of her cuff reappeared and Cass resurfaced, dragging down a lungful of air. "There's a way through."

Relief spilled through me.

"I am *not* going down there," Sakura said from her rock, shaking her head.

"Suit yourself," Cass said, turning to me. "Come on. It's not that far."

I nodded, taking her hand and readying myself mentally for what I was about to do. Before we disappeared under the rocks, Sakura sprang to her feet.

"Wait! I'm coming."

"Hurry up about it, then," Cass urged, huffing her frustration.

Sakura waded into the pool, reaching for my hand. I clasped my fingers with hers, finding them trembling.

"It'll be fine," I said and she nodded, not looking convinced.

"Follow me," Cass said, gulping down some air and diving under again.

I took out the flare in my bag, snapping it and letting it sink to the bottom of the pool, illuminating the way in a red flow. I dragged Sakura after me as I dove under, squinting through the dark pool and following the light. Sakura's hold on me was vice-like, making it difficult for me to swim. But I couldn't deny, I was reassured by her presence, too.

I kicked as hard as I could, pressing my hand to the rock above my head as I moved through a large hole beneath it. The light of Cass's cuff disappeared and I swam harder, panicking as I lost sight of her.

There was nothing I could do but swim on. My lungs burned for air, my chest compressing with the cold.

Dark thoughts crept into my mind. I wasn't going to make it. The water was weighing me down like a tonne of bricks. I kicked out violently, desperate to find air.

I needed to get out.

I had to reach the surface.

Despite my flailing, Sakura never let go of my hand and, somehow, my head breached the water. I threw my head back, gasping down as much oxygen as I could.

In a heartbeat, I knew something was wrong.

Cass's light shimmered on the roof as she flailed on the rocks at the edge of the pool, battling against an emaciated V. I couldn't tell if it was male or female, its body so thin it was practically bones.

The snapping of its jaw sounded through the cave as Cass fought it off with all her might.

I shook off Sakura's hand, scrambling toward the edge of the pool. The rocks were slippery as I tried to drag myself out, digging my fingers into the cracks, desperate to reach Cass.

The V's head snapped around and all I saw was a tangle of matted hair and sharp teeth as it lunged toward me.

I reared backwards, but the V never made contact. Cass appeared above it, slamming her stake between its ribs. The V died with a jerk and a grunt and bluish blood poured into the water around me.

Sakura cursed loudly, swimming to my side.

Together, we crawled out of the pool. Cass stood there, breathing heavily, clutching her neck.

"It bit me," she whispered and I tugged at her arm to the see wound.

"It's alright," I encouraged. It wasn't deep. The V had barely gotten its fangs into her.

"Why did it stop feeding on me?" Cass breathed.

"You." Sakura gazed at me with a look of dismay. "It went after *you*."

A chill ran through me and I tried to shrug off the comment. "Don't be ridiculous." But my conversation with Varick filled my mind. If I really *did* have more desirable blood than the others, it was a miracle I'd gotten this far.

The chances of me getting through this round seemed to dim before my eyes.

"I'm not going to turn into one of them, am I?" Cass thankfully changed the subject, giving me a wide-eyed look of horror.

I quickly shook my head. "No. I don't think it works like that." Of course, I didn't really know what I was talking about. I'd never thought to ask Varick how someone became a Vampire. But I'd been bitten before and hadn't felt any strange effects from it, even if I had been healed shortly after.

"Think you have to die first, then you'll change," Sakura said, wringing the water from her skirt.

"After you've been bitten?" Cass asked in horror.

Sakura shrugged. "I heard one of the girls talking to Varick about it." She stood up straight, flicking her hair back which looked as dark a purple as her dress now that it was wet. "He's kind of hot, isn't he? In a psycho sort of way."

I wasn't sure what to say to that. And the knowledge that Varick was almost certainly watching us right now made me blush. What the hell kind of a reaction was that? I just prayed the dark and the blue lights on our cuffs had hidden my response.

"He's a V, Sakura," Cass spat. "How can you even look at him that way?"

I busied myself by starting to search for an exit to the cave, pretending to be entirely uninterested in their conversation.

"I'm just saying. Guy like that was probably model hot *before* he died. Now he's like, a super Vampire."

"I don't care what he looks like," Cass snarled. "If any Vampire comes near me, they all get the same treatment. A stake through the heart."

"Can we drop this?" I said as lightly as I could. "I'd like to get out of this cave, *today*."

"Well this was your great plan, Red, now where do we go?" Sakura folded her arms, lifting a brow at Cass. Cass looked ready to punch her.

"How about *you* make a suggestion for once?" Cass barked. "This was *our* plan, why not go make your own?"

Their voices were raising and it was making me nervous. "Guys, please. Can you shut up and help me here?"

I moved along the cave wall, shining my light around the space, searching desperately for a way forward. Their arguing continued, both of them completely ignoring me.

I sighed, shuffling along a narrow edge beside the water. I didn't want to get back into it any time soon. My core temperature had plummeted and the sooner we got somewhere dry, the better.

My heart juddered as I found a way out: a tiny crawl space at my feet, just big enough for us to squeeze through. Maybe.

When I turned back to the others, who were shouting at the top of their lungs, I lost it.

"Shut the hell up!" I barked and they fell silent. I lowered my voice to a whisper. "You wanna bring every V in these caves down on our heads?"

They shifted guiltily in front of me.

I sighed, pointing to the gap in the rock. "This is our way out."

Cass marched away from Sakura, joining my side. A blood-curdling shriek sounded from across the room and we all swung our lights in that direction. On the other side of the pool, high up on the wall was a dark hole that led out of the cave we were in. And something was shuffling its way through it.

"*Go*," Sakura hissed, waving her hands at us to head through the hole at my feet. Before we could duck into the space, Sakura dived ahead of us, wriggling through head first on her belly.

Cass looked like she was about to stake her, when I pressed a hand to her arm.

"Calm down. We're all going to get out of here."

Cass went next, slipping into the tiny space with more grace than I knew I would manage.

I dropped to the floor, flattening myself and wriggling forward as fast as I could. After a bone-squeezing minute, the tunnel widened just enough that I could crawl, but the walls still pressed down heavily on my shoulders. I tried not to think about the fact the weight of an entire mountain was resting above me and continued moving, following Cass's feet ahead.

The blue light of my cuff kept blinding me as I moved my wrists and I soon had to turn it off, focusing solely on Cass's light which was filtering around her.

A snuffling, grunting sounded behind me and my heart raced into top gear.

"Go," I begged and Cass sped up. I shuffled after her as fast as I could, panic setting in. My knees tore against the rocks and my palms were rubbed raw. I tried not to think about the fact I was leaving patches of blood behind me, probably alerting more Vs to our whereabouts.

Cass suddenly stopped and I was crawling so fast I nearly ran into her.

"What are you doing? Move!" I begged, the hairs on the back of my neck standing up.

"I'm stuck!" Sakura cried and Cass grunted with effort as she tried to move her.

"Oh god," I breathed, the rasping sound of a Vampire's breath rattling its way behind me. I tried to turn my head to look, but the space was too narrow. I tucked in my knees, squashing up as close to Cass as I could.

"Push her!" I practically shrieked.

"I am – she won't budge!" Cass cried.

Claws sank into my ankle.

I screamed as I was dragged backwards, rolling onto my spine as I did so. The position gave me enough room to kick out and I felt my heel connect with bone.

The V made a horrible, screeching noise and I wriggled backwards as fast I could, my head knocking against Cass's boots.

"If we die because of you, Sakura, I'm going to kill you," Cass said in a strained voice, evidently still shoving her.

The V launched at me again and I scrambled for the stake tucked into my dress. I drew it out, but there was no way I could get near the V to defend myself.

I kicked my legs wildly, trying to evade its hold, but its fingernails dug into me again, dragging me toward it.

I screamed as its jagged teeth sunk into my leg, and with a forceful stomp, my boot connected with its face.

"Selena – move!" Cass's voice reached to me.

In the brief second I had whilst the V recovered from the blow, I moved. Using my elbows, I scrambled backwards as fast as I could, dripping blood in a trail. There was hardly any light for me to see by now, but the dark shadow of the V was moving toward me. Closer and Closer.

Being smaller than the other two gave me some advantage, and I managed to squeeze through the tiny gap that Sakura had evidently been stuck in without stopping.

Hands grabbed my shoulders and I was wrenched out into a wide cave, the V snapping at my heels.

As it darted out of the hole on all fours, Sakura took action, kicking it onto its back and slamming her stake into its heart.

I lay, panting and quivering, my hand clamped so tightly around my stake, it hurt.

I had only a moment to recover as another snarl sounded from the tiny passage.

Cass dragged me to my feet and I hobbled on after them. The cave we'd emerged in was wide and light was filtering into it from up ahead.

"There! It's a way out!" Sakura announced, rushing toward the moonlight.

We sprinted across the loose stones, rising and rising, the promising smell of pine trees washing over me. I could almost taste the fresh air as we clambered upwards, forced to climb on our hands and knees toward the waning moon.

As we emerged from the cave, we crashed down a steep ridge, bursting into the foliage as damp, prickly under-brush tore at my dress. I skidded to a halt in the mud with Cass and Sakura in a heap on either side of me. A laugh of relief escaped me, but it was swiftly silenced by our surroundings. A thick forest surrounded us and a blanket of fog filtered through the boughs.

But it wasn't that that frightened me. It was the dark shapes approaching through the grey mist, emerging, one by one. There had to a thirty of them, or perhaps it only seemed that way because of the tree trunks that swayed and moved too, tricking my mind.

The first of the Vs loomed from the mist, my blood soaked knees and ankles giving us away to them.

It occurred to me that the Vs were here on purpose; they probably knew every cave exit across the entire mountain. And why waste energy hunting us beneath ground? When we'd all eventually end up here, walking straight into their waiting jaws.

Heading the mass was a face that had haunted my dreams last night. I should have known I'd meet with him eventually. And Ravenos looked delighted by our reunion.

Varick

The next three days would be hell. I returned to the castle, striding to the auditorium to watch the game. My presence wasn't ignored as I'd hoped and Abraham soon cornered me, asking me about last night.

"How's morale in the group?" he asked as some of the spectators drew closer, wanting a tip-off as to who was a weak link.

"Low, as can be expected," I drawled, trying to move past him.

Abraham swung out an arm, halting me. "Are you making sure they're well rested before each round?"

I tried not to grimace at his words. He didn't care about the girls, this was about his reputation. He wanted to put on a good show, and if the girls dropped in numbers too quickly, the last round may not be so entertaining.

"Of course," I insisted. My gaze trailed to the men hovering around him who backed off as I eyed them.

"Good. This round should harden up the surviving group for the finale." Abraham seemed satisfied, running a hand over his slicked-back, white hair. "My bets are on the redhead. I like her spark."

Some of the men muttered their delight and my stomach

churned as they grabbed Abraham's attention, offering him more money to place on Cassandra.

The betting didn't end until the final day, due to the fact the highest bidder on the winning contestant would be awarded a prize. One that made me physically ill. Perhaps it wouldn't have done in the past, but knowing Selena was in the running changed things.

"The Grey girl is clearly the most desirable to the Vs," a lean man was saying to Abraham, sipping on a crystal glass of brandy.

"Yes, it's rather brought her ranking down. The Vs choose her over the others," Abraham remarked and my blood began to boil.

Selena wasn't the first girl to have desirable blood in the games. But she was the first that made even *me* lose my focus. She wasn't just desirable, she was a god damn rarity. And the more blood the Vs drank, the more aware they became, able to focus their attention on her.

I moved away from the men, their attention having passed on from me. I continually glanced at the screens as I made my way to the seating area. Plenty of spectators were sat there today, the game now drawing all of the attention in the room. I moved to the back rows as men shifted out of my way, taking a seat alone, away from their sneering faces.

The only others sat in the back row were Mercy and a man whose lap she was perched in.

His head snapped up as he spotted me sitting a few seats down from them.

"Oh don't mind him," Mercy purred, turning the man's face so his eyes returned to hers. "He's just moping because he can't run around on that island himself."

I ignored her, watching the screen, quickly locating Selena who was squeezing her way through a tight space in the mountain caves. My breathing grew shallow as I spotted the V crawling through the passage after her.

"If you want a drink, baby, be my guest." Mercy thrust her arm at me and the man she was straddling looked on in horror.

"You don't let it drink from you, do you?" he asked her, hugging her tighter to him.

"Na. He's under orders. You can't touch me, can you Varick?"

I continued to ignore her, sitting forward in my seat as Selena battled with the emaciated V beneath ground. It'd be weak for sure. He didn't look as though he'd fed for almost a year. The Helsings were clever like that. Feeding different groups varying amounts of blood to make sure there was a mix on the island. From the strongest to the weakest. It gave the girls more of a chance, and I supposed made for a more riveting show.

Mercy snapped her fingers beneath my nose and it was like a thunder crack in my ear.

"*Don't*, you'll anger it," the man breathed.

I turned to them as Selena escaped the V and the purple-haired girl Sakura dispatched it. "Mercy doesn't bother me. But being referred to as 'it' is about to get on my last nerve." I stared down the man and he hid behind Mercy's golden locks.

She threw her head back, giggling wildly. "Oh Varick you're such a tease. Leave him be."

"Tell him to keep his opinions to himself, or I'll gladly rip out his tongue so he never shares another thought with me again."

The man stood, hastily dropping Mercy into her seat – not so gracefully – and scurried away like the vermin he was.

"Oh *now* look what you've done." She pouted, rising to her feet, brushing down the non-existent, wisp of a dress she was wearing and moving into the seat beside mine. "You're so angry today." She ran a finger up my arm and I determinedly ignored her. She wore no garlic on her skin and instead of the lavender soap that so often made me ill, she was splashed with a light, sweet perfume. My throat constricted as the scent of her Hunter blood reached to me. Painfully tempting.

"Go be a harlot somewhere else, will you?" I demanded.

She huffed. "I'm not a *harlot*."

"In my day, whores wore more clothes than you are now. Unless you genuinely forgot to put on trousers today?"

She glanced down at her legs, dropping a hand onto her thigh. "You like it really."

"I'm a V, Mercy. Or have you forgotten? All I give a damn about is blood. So if you really want me to take notice of you, I suggest you slit your wrists."

Her mouth fell open and I hid my satisfied smile. Winding Mercy up wasn't the worst thing in the world, I supposed.

Mercy followed my line of sight to the screen where Selena

was clambering her way out of the cave mouth. My heart nearly stopped – and that was saying something considering it barely beat more than once a minute anyway – and I sprang to my feet.

Fifteen, no *twenty* Vs, moving through the forest, heading toward Selena and her friends. "No, dammit. Don't you dare." I spotted Ravenos leading the line, marching through the fog with a smug expression slapped across his face. My eyes darted from screen to screen, my mind racing. If only there was some way to communicate to Selena. But there was nothing I could do but watch as she tumbled down a hill directly into their hands.

"Uh oh," Mercy sang. "Looks like Grey's out of the running."

The fact that she didn't mention the other two drew my attention to her. Mercy was smiling, but there was no kindness in it.

"Think I haven't noticed you gawping at her?" She laughed cruelly. "It's pathetic really. And here I am flaunting Hunter blood at you when you've got a taste for that pale bitch in the game." She leant in close, her heated breath on my ear. "And I know your little secret, Varick."

My spine straightened as I turned to her.

"What secret?" I feigned ignorance.

"Grey shouldn't have made it in the last round. Funny how she got up and walked the ten steps to the checkpoint, when she couldn't even crawl that far before the redhead came to help her."

"So?" I snapped. "What's your point?"

"My point is...only V blood could have cured an injury like

that. Strong blood, too. And Redtop didn't have a splash on her when she reached the checkpoint."

I ground my jaw, trying to keep my flaming anger under control.

She leant in close again. "Don't worry, Varick. Your secret is safe with me. So long as you do as I say from now on."

"Not much of a threat, considering I have to do anything you say anyway."

She smiled a twisted smile. "Not everything."

I shifted away from her, trying not to think of all the screwed up things she'd asked me to do in the past. She was right, I often refused her. But I never thought her little games were anything more than that. Surely she didn't actually want me to bite her? If Abraham found out, he'd have my head on a spike, or mounted on the wall in his trophy room.

But if Mercy told him I was helping a girl in the game, he'd do the same thing. He'd believe his daughter over me any day of the week.

"What do you want me to do?" I growled, knowing I had no choice.

She leant in close again and the urge to bite her nearly overwhelmed me. I could practically taste the blood on my tongue.

"If Grey survives this round, I want you to kill her."

I lurched away, gazing at Mercy in horror. "That's impossible. Abraham will have my head for it."

"Not if you make it look like one of the girls did it. Drive a knife into her heart, be subtle. I know you can do it."

My stomach lurched at the very idea. "No," I said firmly.

"You'll do it, or I'll tell Daddy what you did and he'll have both of your heads for it."

I shrank from the girl, feeling trapped. She stood, glancing down at me with a satisfied smile. "Oh, and come to my room tonight. Midnight should be late enough for no one to notice."

She left me sitting there, trembling with rage. But in moments, my thoughts were forgotten as an ear-splitting scream rang out from the game.

Selena

Sakura made a dash for it. A V had her pinned to the ground before she'd made it ten feet. The V's reddy-brown locks fell around Sakura's face as she grinned viciously down at her screaming prey.

"Hold it, Melinda," Ravenos ordered and she stilled, turning to him.

"You said you only wanted the raven haired girl."

"I know what I said!" he roared and the wood fell deathly silent.

Cass crawled to my side as we lay in the damp grass, awaiting our fate. My stake was clutched in my hand as I ran over and over in my mind what Varick had taught me about Ravenos, but what use did it do me now? If *he* didn't kill me, there was nearly twenty other Vs that would.

"I'm glad we met, Selena," Cass whispered. "Made it pretty far, didn't we?"

"Don't talk like we're dead," I hissed back, though I couldn't see any possible way out of this. I simply couldn't give up. Not yet.

The Vs stood as still as statues, some veiled in the mist, others as pale as ghosts, gazing at us with hungry expressions.

"We take them to the Blood Caves. Remind the Helsings what we're capable of." Ravenos smiled, marching toward me and snatching a hold of my hair. He dragged me to my feet, tugging me close as he breathed in my scent. I used the moment to my advantage, angling my stake upwards and ramming it toward his chest. He caught my wrist with ease, laughing in a low chuckle before plucking the weapon from my grip.

"Take the other one, Iskender," he ordered a nearby V with wet black hair that hung in a mop over his shoulders. He was broad and thickset, approaching Cass at a terrifying speed. Taking her weapon, he chucked her over one shoulder and she screamed bloody murder.

"Quiet, woman," he ordered in a thick, Turkish accent.

Ravenos snatched my waist and threw me over his shoulder, mimicking Iskender. I kicked out, but if my impacting boots affected him at all, he didn't show it. We moved through the forest at speed until the world was a blur of green and grey. My gut writhed with nausea and I shut my eyes to try and save myself from vomiting up the berries I'd eaten earlier.

We stopped abruptly and I was strung upside down, my ankles aching as rope was tethered around them. My pack and cloak were ripped from my shoulders and someone stuffed my skirt between my legs so it didn't fall over my face. I groaned as my vision swum before me and the dim red glow of a cave became visible. The light was emitting from fiery torches, planted upright in the muddy ground. From the growth of moss across the walls, I guessed we were still somewhere in the forest. The earthy scent of it remained in the air.

The cave stretched away into the darkness and Vs gathered hungrily from the shadows. I could tell from their expressions that they'd been here before. And probably done this very thing to previous contestants. Ravenos stood before me, my neck swaying at mouth height, painfully vulnerable to him. I swung up a hand, slashing at him with a shriek of defiance. He caught it, raising my wrist to his mouth and breathing in. "Two more entire days, until those capsules in your heads detonate. We're going to have quite some time together, you and I." He opened his mouth and sank his fangs into my wrist.

I whimpered, but didn't scream, not giving him the satisfaction of my pain. The more he drank, the more woozy I became, and the more the other Vs grew restless.

Ravenos released me, wiping his mouth before gesturing to the other Vs to approach Cass and Sakura who were strung up either side of me.

"One at a time," Ravenos ordered and the Vs took turns drinking from them. No one touched me, but the Vampires sniffed the air near my swinging body, evidently tempted to take a bite. When a female with a bald head got too close, I spat at her, making her strike out at me with her nails. They slit my cheek open and, in an instant, Ravenos was upon her, wrenching her head off with two hands.

I watched on in horror, twisting my ankles in a desperate

attempt to escape.

The other Vs backed up, eyeing Ravenos with caution.

"I said, she's mine!" he bellowed at them and a murmur of ascent ran through the cave.

I caught Sakura's eye as Melinda fed on her arm. She was quivering, but a steely determination flared in her expression. She hadn't given up yet, and that gave me hope.

Blood was rushing to my head, making an ache grow behind my eyes. My arms swung uselessly below me as my hands grew heavy.

Ravenos fed from my wrist again and I closed my eyes, shutting out the feel of his cool mouth on my skin. With a jerk, he pulled away from me, clawing at his head. His eyes met mine, filled with horror, disgust. He remained silent as Vs filed past him, taking their turns feeding on Sakura and Cass.

Ravenos gazed at them like he was seeing them for the first time. He touched his mouth, his hands shaking.

"What have you done to me?" he snarled and I gazed on numbly, my body weak from blood loss.

"GET OUT!" he roared at the other Vs and begrudgingly, they obeyed, melting away into the darkness, heading deeper into the caves.

Ravenos launched at me, snatching hold of my neck. "What have you done, witch?" he spat at me.

I shook my head, trying to breathe through the press of his fingers. "Noth-ing," I choked out.

He released me, covering his face and wailing in horror. He didn't seem in any physical pain. I had no idea what was happening to him.

I stole a glance at Cass, but she was passed out, blood dripping from her wrists to the floor. My heart raced, labouring to pump the remainder of my blood around my body.

Sakura was still with me, swinging back and forth, trying to reach her feet. It was no use, she could barely touch her knees.

Ravenos started crying. I wasn't sure at first, but there he was, sobbing on the muddy floor whilst we swung above him like animals rigged up for the slaughter.

"What's wrong with him?" Sakura hissed and I shook my head, having no answer.

A snarling and snapping of teeth made my insides constrict. I tried to understand what I was seeing in my upside down world as a flash of ebony fur moved through the cave. The beast launched at Ravenos and I realised what it was with a jolt of disbelief. A black wolf, tearing at Ravenos's neck. The V didn't have a chance to scream as the wolf snapped its jaws violently and he fell still, red blood seeping across the ground.

I almost screamed, but clamped my lips together, not wanting to draw the Vs back to us. The wolf rounded on us and I tried to lift my head out of its reach.

It was no good. The animal was huge and no doubt it could jump as high as the rope holding me in place.

The wolf paused before me, gazing into my eyes with a tilt of its head, then padded toward Cass, opening its deadly jaws.

I thrust an arm in her direction, trying to stop the animal from hurting her.

The wolf easily dodged my feeble attempt, snapping at me. It darted back toward Cass and I flapped my arms, desperate to keep it away from her.

Before I could make any more pathetic attempts at saving my friend, the wolf licked the side of her face, cleaning the blood that was dribbling down her cheek from her neck.

"What the-" Sakura started, pausing mid-sentence as Cass woke up; she came nose to nose with the animal and screamed to high heaven.

"No!" I hissed, trying to quiet her.

The wolf sprang into the air before her, making her writhe in her bonds, trying to keep clear of its sharp claws. With a loud clap, its teeth locked around the rope and broke it in two. Cass slammed into the wet earth, swinging her legs around as she tried to right herself. She scrambled to her feet, backing away from the wolf, but it bowed its head, stepping away from her to show it wasn't a threat.

"Cass," I hissed to get her attention.

She stumbled dizzily towards me, bent down and took a knife from her boot.

She reached up, and slashed the rope holding me in place. I smacked into the ground, my hands sinking an inch into the mud.

"Ow," I mouthed, finding my way to my feet whilst Cass cut

Sakura free.

When I found my balance – still shaky from blood loss - I spotted the wolf hovering in the cave entrance. It padded back and forth as if it were waiting for us and I tentatively took a step closer. Moving to Ravenos's body, I bent down, extracting my stake from the back of his waistband.

The wolf made a whining noise and my hackles rose. "What does it want?" I whispered to the other girls, adjusting the stake in my hand.

"Looks like it wants to help," Sakura said, moving toward the animal.

I threw out an arm, halting her. "Are you crazy? It just ripped off that Vampire's *head*."

The wolf moved toward us and I backed into Sakura, my heart flipping over in my chest. Slowly, the animal pressed its head into Sakura's hand and she smiled.

"See," she said, following it from the cave.

The sound of footsteps pounded from deep inside the cave system. Without a word, Cass and I broke into a sprint, grabbing our discarded packs, cloaks and stakes on the way out.

As we darted out of the cave, Cass grabbed my arm, dragging me sideways toward a boulder where we ducked down behind it. Sakura was already there, pressing her back to the rock. The wolf howled and we all flinched from the noise as it darted off into the forest, disappearing into the thick mist. A group of Vampires followed it into the trees and we held our breaths whilst they passed.

"Everyone saw that, right?" Cass whispered and we nodded, wide-eyed.

"What kind of wolf was that?" I asked in astonishment.

"The kind I like having on our side." Sakura stood, looking out toward the trees. "This whole place is screwed up. Maybe the animals have been messed with too."

I scrubbed my eyes, trying to process what had just happened, but my mind was still in a daze from the blood I'd lost.

Sakura's legs wobbled beneath her. "We should find somewhere to rest. I'm not going into that forest until this fog lifts."

"Agreed." Cass stood, rubbing the bite marks on her neck. She gazed back in the direction we'd come.

"What?" I breathed.

"We should go back for Ravenos's blood. To heal."

Sakura placed her hands on her hips. "I'm not going back there. Only half the Vs followed that wolf. Which means there's a pack of Vampires still sniffing around that cave."

Cass sighed and I gave her a comforting look, regretting not having taken advantage of the V's blood back in the cave.

"I don't know if I'm glad I stuck with you guys or not," Sakura muttered, wrapping strips of her dress around the bites on her wrists.

"Well, you're still alive, aren't you?" I said.

She broke a smile, the first I'd ever seen her break, showing she had dimples. "I think that's because there's something special about you, Selena."

"What's that supposed to mean?" I huffed.

"That V had some kind of breakdown after drinking from you. If that's not special, I don't know what is."

I pursed my lips, having no retort to give her. She was right after all. Ravenos *had* acted strangely, but I couldn't figure out what exactly my blood had done to him. "Other Vs have bitten me. None have reacted like that before."

Cass looked awkward as if she didn't want to side with Sakura over me, but clearly felt the same way.

"None of them had that much blood though, right?" Sakura folded her arms, gazing at me like I was a puzzle to be solved.

"No," I murmured, checking my map to try and get firmly off of this subject. "Let's look for somewhere to regroup, get some rest." I glanced toward the dark forest, still thick with mist. With the way I was feeling, I could have slumped down in a bush and fallen asleep right there and then.

"We could move up the mountain a bit," Sakura suggested, gazing up the steep hill that led away from the cave, back in the direction we'd come. "I reckon most of the Vs will stick around the forest, waiting for girls to pass through. It's the only way to the checkpoint."

It was as decent a plan as any, so we followed Sakura up the hill, forcing our way through the brambles and low bushes that lined the mountainside.

After a few hours, we found a fairly level patch of ground, sheltered from the wind by an overhang of rock. We made camp beneath it, making the damp ground as comfortable as possible using our cloaks as blankets. Our meal consisted of berries and nothing more. We started a small fire to keep warm, praying it didn't draw any unwanted attention, but desperate to dry out our damp clothes. It was worth the risk; the freezing air combined with our wet attire was a dangerous combination.

Huddling close under the rock, we took turns taking watch. Cass went first, and Sakura and I snuggled together for warmth as we tried to get some rest. It wasn't easy, considering what we'd just been through. And I knew Vampires awaited me in my dreams. But better those than the real ones who were waiting for us out in the woods.

Varick

Midnight arrived.

I'd watched on in horror as Ravenos had fed on Selena, trying to force myself not to run out onto the island to save her. My palms itched with it. My body physically hurt. But if I interfered with the games on camera, I was screwed.

I had to hope Selena could survive this on her own. And thanks to some rogue wolf, she had. I was certain the Helsings had a hand in that beast. Probably a new creation to keep things interesting. I guessed Ignus was involved. He was always enthusiastic about bringing new elements to the games. But one that actually helped the girls was surprising. That wasn't his style. Perhaps it was an experiment gone wrong.

Knowing she was safe for now, tucked up high on the mountain where the Vs weren't bothering to venture, I made good on my deal and went to Mercy's room. The polar night made tracking time difficult, but the grandfather clock in the entrance hall told me it was time.

I dreaded to know what she wanted from me. But the sooner I got it over with, the better.

I knocked on her door, and when she didn't answer, pushed inside.

Mercy was tangled under the sheets with someone who she quickly kicked out of the bed. I waited with folded arms as the guy Mercy had been straddling down in the auditorium appeared. He scrambled for his clothes, holding them up to cover his modesty and charging from the room like he was on fire. *Perks of being a Vampire.*

I regarded Mercy with contempt, but she smiled at me innocently like she was enjoying the fact I'd walked in on her. I knew her well enough to know this was planned.

I grimaced as she pulled on her flimsy robe, flaunting her naked body in front of me. A moment later, she approached me, swaying her hips. "You came."

"You told me to," I answered.

"Oh come on, Varick. Lighten up. What's the matter? Grey get her head eaten by a V?"

I kept my expression impassive.

"No? Oh well, I'm sure you're looking forward to having the task yourself."

"It's not right to interfere with the games," I snarled.

"Then why did you?" She placed a hand on my chest and I raised my eyes to the ceiling, suppressing a sigh. Her usual attempt at seduction was tiring. She knew I couldn't feel that way about her, even if I'd wanted to. Which I certainly didn't. But she seemed to like the challenge anyway. Pretty pointless in my opinion, but still she persisted.

"Why did you ask me here?" I demanded, my body tensing

under her touch. The scent of her blood reached to me, the heat of it practically rolling over my tongue.

"Perhaps I just wanted the delight of your company." She laughed at her own joke, turning away from me.

I suppressed the urge to march straight from her room. But I had to play along if I was going to survive.

"I have a little secret."

"Another one?" I drawled.

"Yes, I like keeping secrets. Life's no fun without them." She dropped down onto the bed, dramatically raising an arm over her head to rest on the pillow. "Want to know what it is?"

I shrugged.

"Oh *do* act like you care, Varick. It'd be so much more interesting."

"Fine," I snarled. "What's your secret?"

"I know why Ravenos reacted to Grey's blood."

My ears pricked up. That *was* something worth knowing. I was deeply curious myself. I took a step forward. "You do?"

"Uhuh." She waved a hand in the air. "Well, it's just a theory. But I'm quite sure."

"What is it?" I growled and she patted the bed beside her.

"Come join me, won't you? It's awfully lonely over here."

I sighed, moving to the bed and perching on the edge like a bird about to take flight.

Mercy's arms snaked around my waist and I fought the urge to push her off.

Play along, I reminded myself.

She leant up to my ear, whispering into it. The words she spoke made my blood run cold – if I had any warmth in my veins to cool.

"You're wrong," I snarled, but her theory had a ring of truth to it I couldn't deny.

"You'll still kill her."

I snapped around. "Why?"

"You broke the rules, Varick. There has to be consequences." She slumped back onto the bed, writhing in the sheets so her naked body was nearly on show.

I grimaced, turning away.

"Drink from me." She dropped her wrist into my lap. "Just a little. I want to know what it feels like."

"No," I said instantly. Drinking from a Helsing was about the most dangerous thing I could do besides walking directly into the morning sunrise. Abraham would have me killed. Probably tortured first. "Your father-"

"My father won't know a thing." Her tone was harsh, like her mother's. She had all the authority of her family with a little insanity thrown in. "I told you, I like keeping secrets."

She lifted her arm, holding her wrist to my mouth. It was about the most tempting situation I'd ever been in, bar the time I'd spent with Selena. Mercy was calm as could be, her body in the perfect state to be fed from. And the scent was simply intoxicating.

"Do it," she urged and I did. I sunk my fangs into her wrist and she moaned like she was enjoying it. The blood was the best I'd ever tasted. I grabbed hold of her arm, keeping her in place, though she didn't fight me at all.

I hated the spell she had over me. The near blinding frenzy I was falling into. It would be impossible to stop. I couldn't. I bit deeper, taking more, more than I should have. More than she wanted me to. She started fighting, her skinny limbs kicking out at me. I was aware of her cursing my name, begging me to stop, but I couldn't. I was lost to the taste, the way my senses sprang to life and my heart beat harder than it had in years.

"Varick!" she shouted, pummelling her fists against me. She was a Hunter through and through. I felt the blows, but the blood was making me strong. I pinned her down, driven nearly to madness with need. The need for every, last drop.

I thought of Selena. Of how Mercy's death would equal my own. How I wouldn't be there in two days time to greet Selena at the checkpoint.

And somehow, miraculously, I stopped.

"Bastard," she breathed. Then she started laughing, delirious as she hugged her arm to her chest. "Now give me some of yours."

I slit my thumb open, offering my arm back to her. She sucked my thumb – much more provocatively than was necessary – but I was a slave to my thoughts, new emotions rising in my chest that had been previously lost to hundreds of years of Vampirism.

Mercy released my hand, gasping her relief. "You could have killed me." She sounded delighted, like she'd just returned from a trip to Disneyland.

I stood, facing her. The sight of her naked body suddenly seemed more inappropriate and I turned away, heading toward the door.

"Tomorrow! Come back tomorrow," she instructed, giggling.

I grunted in confirmation, hurrying through the door and heading back to my room. My pace increased until I was flat out sprinting, panic rising in my chest.

I wrenched open the door, flicking a switch that projected the game onto one entire wall.

I found her in seconds. Selena had managed to fall asleep, which I was grateful for. She'd need to build up her strength for tomorrow. Especially considering how much blood Ravenos had taken from her. She might not be herself again for days.

I tugged at my hair, anxiety darting through me. I lay down on the large bed at the heart of my room. I never slept. I rarely used the room at all, only if I wanted an escape from the Helsings. When the games weren't running, my refuge was out on the island. I felt more myself out there. The rugged landscape reminded me of my life at sea, sailing between the northern lands. Those memories came to me now, tugging me down into them. I couldn't dream any longer, but I knew that if I could, I'd dream of those days. I'd dream of the sun and the azure sky, the flutter of white sails and the rush of the wind across my cheeks, peppered with the salty taste of the sea.

I was dragged back to the room by the sight of Selena. She

seemed to be sleeping peacefully for once and that was a relief to me. *Stress*, that's what I was feeling. Mercy's blood had brought back some of my more human qualities. But apparently only the agonising ones. Knowing Selena was out there alone, when I could so easily defend her, was driving me to insanity. The longer the night stretched on, the more I felt the presence of time. The way it dragged because, for once, I wanted it to pass.

Two more days on that island. Would she survive? Would she be there at that checkpoint on day three, shivering, grateful for the food? Perhaps even willing to spend a moment or two with me again? I shouldn't have wanted that, for her sake. I was the same as the Vs who hunted her daily. It could just as easily have been me out there, starving, desperate for a kill. And now I was bound by a promise to end her myself.

I pressed my fingers into my eyes, wishing to take away the guilt that was stabbing like knives into my heart. If I refused Mercy's order, I'd be sentenced to death. So either Selena died in the remainder of this round, or she died at my hand. And neither of those options seemed acceptable to me.

Selena

Waking up the next day was probably one of my worst experiences in the game so far.

The bites on my legs from the V I'd encountered down in the caves had become infected, turning a deep red around the jagged cuts. Coupled with those Ravenos had given me, and the overall blood loss, I was in a bad way.

"We need to move," Cass said softly as I shivered uncontrollably at her feet.

Sakura was pacing anxiously in front of me.

"I c-can't," I said through chattering teeth. Cass looked tired. She'd barely slept, leaving me to rest longer than I should have. She'd laid her cloak over me too which helped, despite it still being a little damp.

"Where's that damn wolf when we need him?" Sakura muttered, checking the clock on her watch for the hundredth time. We had just over a full day left to reach the checkpoint. There was no way I was going to make it.

"We'll have to build up the fire, to get Selena warm," Cass decided, taking out her knife and moving to the dry roots that were crawling up the overhanging rock above my head.

"Are you kidding me?" Sakura snapped. "We don't have time.

We need to go."

Cass ignored her, continuing to work.

I fixed my gaze on Sakura, knowing there was no point trying to talk Cass out of this. But there was no need for Sakura to stay as well. "G-go," I managed.

Sakura frowned, her dark brows drawing together. With a final glance at Cass, she marched off, heading down the hill.

"Good riddance," Cass muttered, placing the dry roots onto the small flames at the heart of the fire. Taking out the damp kindling from my bag, she laid it around the fire to dry. As she fed the flames, the space began to grow warmer. Cass continually moved about, laying out our clothes to fully dry, helping me out of my dress, keeping me covered in the cloaks.

Slowly, but surely, as the hours ticked by, I stopped shivering. Cass mashed some of the berries up on a flat piece of rock and heated them over the fire.

They were sickly sweet, but immediately gave me energy and the heat of them helped warm me through to my bones.

"How do you feel?" Cass pressed a hand to my forehead with a concerned frown.

"Better," I sighed, not mentioning the agonising pain still flaring up from my ankles. Or the fact I knew exactly the effects an infected bite could have. When I was six, I'd been bitten by our neighbour's dog. I'd been playing with him and one of his tug toys and, seeing as I was half the size of a Siberian husky, his teeth had done me some serious damage. I still had the scar on my forearm.

It had hurt like hell, but I'd been so worried about the dog being put down for what had happened, that I wrapped a scarf around the bite and didn't tell anyone. For a six year old, that lasted about half an hour before I went running to Mummy.

Veins were already spreading up my arms by the time I got to the hospital. Infections can move really fast, I learnt that day. I'd made Mum promise not to hurt the dog and I remember her words even now. *"You protect everyone but yourself, Selena. Promise me you'll learn to look after yourself, too."*

Her words had more meaning now than they had then. Was I looking after myself now? Would she be proud that I was trying to survive?

"I need to take a closer look at your wounds," Cass said quietly and I nodded, screwing up my eyes as she gently removed my boots, tugging down my tattered socks. She sucked in air through her teeth and I knew it was bad. Gently, she used the water from her bottle to wash the bite marks and I groaned as the icy stream rushed over them.

"I need antibiotics," I whispered.

"No." Cass stood. "You need V blood. All we've gotta do is get you some."

I shook my head in defeat. "Cass..."

"Don't say it," she demanded and my brows lowered.

"How do you know what I was going to say?"

"You were going to tell me to leave you here, right?" She

planted her hands on her hips and I gave a small nod in confirmation. The longer Cass remained here, the less time she had to reach the checkpoint. I couldn't be responsible for her death.

"Cass, look at me." She met my eye and sank to her knees. "I'm not getting out of this one."

She touched my cheek which was burning from a fever.

Elijah had turned up at the hospital after I'd been bitten all those years ago – probably furious that we weren't at home – and said, *"Why did you bring her here? It's just a bite."*

My mother had bowed down to him on more than one occasion. But perhaps she'd felt stronger that day, surrounded by nurses and the bustle of patients in the corridors.

"Because she's my daughter and I love her more than anything!"

The implied fact she loved me more than Elijah had drained all the colour from his face. The doctor kept me in that night and when my mother returned the next day, I expected her to be beaten bloody. Apparently, Elijah wasn't stupid enough to hit her where the bruises would be on display to nurses all day. But *I* saw them. The ghosts of brownish-grey skin peeping from beneath her sleeves, her collar.

I'd asked her that day – still not having learned to button my lip at that point – why she wouldn't leave Elijah. Why didn't we run away into the woods like they did in fairytales and start a new life?

"Because, my darling, he'll find us. And he'll hurt you."

Of course, that didn't make any sense to me at the time. Elijah *did* hurt me. Not regularly, not at that age anyway. But I'd received the slash of his belt more than once. It wasn't until I was bordering on fourteen that I realised what she'd meant. Elijah was fully capable of - and willing- to kill us. One rainy, Saturday afternoon, he'd waved a knife at my mother. The second my mother stepped out of line, he'd said, he'd drive the knife into my heart. That's when I knew it was time to act. That's when I started keeping my own knife under my pillow.

It's easy for an outsider to judge. That's what court had taught me. *Why didn't you go to the police? Why didn't you show someone the bruises?* They might as well have asked, *why were you so weak?*

As if it wasn't possible that two people could live under the roof of a man that tormented them for so long without them doing something about it. But there was one thing those people were forgetting: fear.

Fear was the most powerful emotion in the world. I believed it was even greater than love. Fear stopped my mother from telling the police, from reporting Elijah, from taking me somewhere safer. She loved me and yet her fear kept us trapped in that house. And Christ, I didn't blame her. I knew what he could be like. I knew the creak of his shoes on the stairs, the jangle of his keys in the front door. Those sounds became warning signals. And somehow, Mum and I adapted to that life.

Cass strapped the wounds up on my ankles with pieces of her dress, helped me back into my socks and shoes then dragged me to my feet.

"We're making it out of here," she said through gritted teeth, slinging my arm over her shoulder.

Every step hurt; the ache of my ankles was nearly unbearable. But I clung to Cass, desperate to survive, buying into the small sliver of hope that I still could.

As we moved, guilt burrowed into my chest. Cass was sacrificing her chance to help me. I should have forced her to leave. Told her to go. But I knew she wouldn't listen. And secretly, I was glad that she'd stayed.

We made it down the hill and the fresh air awakened my senses. The mist hadn't lifted, not even a fraction between the deathly dark trees that awaited us.

"All we have to do is reach the other side of the forest," Cass murmured and I broke a delirious, probably infection-infused laugh.

"Oh, well if that's all we need to do..."

We steeled ourselves, moving into the thick fog, engulfed by it immediately. The world was a sweeping plane of grey and, as we moved, the looming tree trunks seemed to shift and shuffle before us. I had to squeeze my eyes shut more than once, forcing away the visions. The mist tasted of something acrid, leaving a vile flavour on my tongue. Perhaps I was imagining it, but the more I breathed it in, the more the world seemed to spin.

The trees aren't moving.

There are no Vs near us.

The clink and tinkle of keys caught my ear and I swung around. *That* sound. I knew it well.

I forced Cass to stop, clawing at her arm, my breathing coming in ragged pants.

"What is it?" she whispered, turning to me.

Through the darkness I saw her squint at me, then pull away in horror. I nearly fell over without her support.

"What's wrong?" I gasped as she shrank from me.

"You're one of them!"

I touched my face as if I could feel what she was seeing, but nothing was different. I reached for her and she smacked my arm away, raising her stake at me.

"Cass!" I gasped, stumbling backwards.

Her hand trembled as she pointed the sharp tip of the stake at me. "I'm sorry," she whispered, shaking her head, then darted off into the trees.

My spine hit a tree and I nearly jumped out of my skin. My breathing grew shallow and panic swiftly moved in to fill the hollow space in my chest.

I ran my thumb across my teeth, searching for fangs, for any sign that I'd somehow become one of the Vs. But I hadn't. I was me. Nothing had changed. So why did Cass think that I had?

The tinkle of keys made me lurch forward again and my boot caught on a root. I stumbled, finding my balance at the last second. Swinging around, I pointed my stake toward the mist.

A blanket of white surrounded me. I was disorientated, turning left and right.

The crunch of boots made my body quiver.

"Selena, it's time you grew up." My step-father's voice. The same words he'd spoken to me that night.

I groaned in fear, shrinking to my knees and hugging them to my chest.

"Where's Mum?" I'd asked. It was morning. Early. I hadn't gotten out of bed yet.

"She's gone to the supermarket. We have an hour or so." He locked my bedroom door.

I pulled the covers higher up my legs, thinking of the knife I'd stashed under my pillow all those months ago.

Elijah was muscular, thickset, tall. As a local policeman, he'd become something of an icon in our community; he'd saved a child from a car that had driven off a bridge, plummeting into the river that ran through town. All a disguise. All an act. Covering his back. Mum and I were the only ones that saw the real him.

He ripped back the quilt from my bare legs. He'd been looking at me strangely for weeks. Since I'd turned eighteen.

There were two ways I could have acted that day: the same way I always had, ducking my head and waiting for his punishments to be over. Or, the way I dreamed that one day I *would* act. And that day, I'd had enough. Enough of the pain, of the fear, of the terror induced by simple sounds like keys in locks and the clink of a whiskey bottle against his watch. I was done. And I wasn't going to let him take a single thing more from me.

I recalled the weight of him, the familiar acridity of his breath. The way his belt got stuck as he tried to unbuckle it. I wasn't in any way stronger. But I was sober. Faster. Quicker with that knife than he ever could have seen coming.

Belly deep. It took a moment for the blood to appear, for the shock to register on his face. He was already hemorrhaging by the time he tried to fight back.

After the autopsy, I discovered that I'd stuck him in the liver. Apparently you can die pretty fast that way. Funny really, Mum always prayed his liver would take him out.

The mist revealed a figure, the wind thinning it briefly so I spotted him moving toward me. Everything about the way he walked: those lumbering, heavy steps he took after he'd had a drink. I knew it was *him*.

I crumpled to the ground, burying my face in my hands.

It wasn't real. He couldn't be here.

Screams sliced into my head, far away and near at once. I blinked as a heaviness weighed over my mind. The fog wasn't just out here in the trees, it was in my head, clouding my thoughts.

A shadow loomed over me. The stench of whiskey flooded my senses.

I moaned in agony, trying to shuffle away. Elijah stepped out of the mist, grimacing, his eyes fixed on me.

I crawled backwards, cowering against a tree. "No, no," I

begged.

My vision was blurry at the edges. Everything seemed out of focus; everything but Elijah. I gritted my teeth as he approached, bending down, his hands reaching for my throat. I thrust the stake upwards with a screech of defiance.

Blood poured down my arm, hot and fast. So real. The blood *had* to be real.

I blinked as the vision evaporated and I found my stake up to the hilt with how deep it was buried in the yellow swathes of a satin dress.

Marie sunk to her knees, blood spilling from her mouth as she came eye to eye with me. I shook my head in horror, wrenching the stake free. She slumped backwards, her body twisted on the earth.

"No," I breathed, falling forward, reaching for her pulse.

Nothing. She was gone. Her lifeless, glassy eyes gazed up at the canopy of the tree. She hadn't even been able to see the sky through all this fog.

Pain tore at my core and I screamed, part of me wanting to bring the whole forest down on my head. I cupped her cheek, falling forward and sobbing into her dress. I lifted my head a fraction, knowing Vs would be upon me at any moment. Marie had a swathe of material tied around her throat, cut into a diamond like she'd been using it to cover her mouth and nose.

I gently took it from her, wrapping it around my own neck. The mist had done this, not me. I told myself over and over again, but no matter how much I spoke it in my mind, I didn't feel any better. Marie was dead because of me. Not the Vs, not the mist, not the Helsings. *Me.*

My hands stopped trembling as I tied the yellow piece of cloth over my nose and mouth. After a few moments, my vision improved and the world seemed more steady.

I closed Marie's eyes, saying a silent apology and vowing to hurt the people who had put us here. Who had led us to this moment.

Next, I used the thick mud on the forest floor to cover every inch of myself to hide my scent. It was easily done; the mud was wet and sticky. The scent of the earth rushed through my senses as I covered my face, carefully covering the bandanna that was assisting my breathing. Then I took Marie's stake, pressed myself back into the shadows of the trees and waited.

I'd made enough noise. The Vs were coming. It was only a matter of time. I had no choice but to wait, because, for once, I needed their blood as much as they needed mine.

Varick

The mist was a spectator favourite. Ignus had developed it a few years back, driving the girls mad with visions in that forest. The men whooped and cheered around me as Selena drove her stake into Marie's heart because of some entity the fog had conjured.

I felt sick. Ill, even. Mercy's blood was giving me too much of my old self back. I couldn't watch this any more. With every passing moment, I had to battle the urge to run out into those woods and take Selena into my arms. Carry her somewhere far away from harm.

Plans ticked over in my mind. Could I reach the yacht before the Helsings stopped me? Could I get Selena out of here?

Despite the torrent of ideas swimming in my mind, I knew, deep down, that it was pointless. The Helsings would catch my attempt at saving her on camera and send a pack of Vs after us. And when they caught us, we'd be ripped limb from limb as punishment.

My torment didn't go unnoticed by Mercy whose eyes continually found mine across the auditorium. The game was inescapable, projected tenfold on the wall until all I could see was blood and mist. The Vs were hunting in packs, taking down girls one at a time. There were only seven left, now. And Selena wasn't looking like she was going to make it.

With her wounds, she couldn't move fast enough to get through that forest unseen.

As she caked herself in mud, lying in the shadows close to Marie's body, I tried to figure out what she was thinking.

A stake was clamped in each of her hands. So I knew she hadn't given up yet. But the group of Vs heading her way weren't going to be beaten by a single girl. It wasn't possible. Even if she killed one of them, there were four others, including Melinda who was growing stronger every day.

Some of the men were clapping Ignus on the back, congratulating him on his ingenuity. While I, on the other hand, was tempted to snap his neck for it.

Mercy weaved her way toward me through the crowded seats, falling into the single empty one beside me.

"Got to give it to her. She's a determined little minx."

"Fairing better than you would, I expect." I shrugged off her arm as she tried to lay it on me.

"You'd do well to have a little more faith in me."

"I'm pretty sure I had the upper hand last night."

She thumped my arm. "Hush, will you? People are looking."

I leant in close so a curl of her hair brushed against my cheek. "What's the matter? Afraid of everyone finding out you have a thing for being fed on?"

Her top lip curled back. "Shut up."

My attention was drawn to Ignus across the room, chatting in low tones with Ulvic. I tried to drown out the din of the room to hear them, but there was too much clamour even for my senses to penetrate it. Ulvic had a worn look about him since the night I'd drank from him, avoiding me at all costs. Whatever Ignus had wanted from him, it looked like he'd gotten it.

"What's your brother up to?" I asked Mercy.

Her eyes whipped toward him. "Nothing that concerns you."

"So you know?" I raised a brow.

She nodded slowly, giving me a hard stare. "And you're not going to find out."

I'm not sure if I even wanted to know. Ignus had a twisted of idea of what fun looked like. Especially when it came to the games. Whatever he was planning, no doubt had something to do with the island, and my instincts told me it was nothing pleasant.

"What would it take for you to tell me?" I growled, staring her down.

A challenging smile grew on her features. "Even *you* couldn't do enough to make me tell."

I frowned at that. Even *me*?

Mercy shifted closer, her hand snaking under the arm of the chair to lay on my knee. With a rush of understanding, I realised what all of this torment was about. Maybe it was the newfound humanity she'd instilled in me that allowed me to see it at last. I wasn't just some plaything she liked to torture. Mercy, as improbable as it was, *liked* me. Perhaps more than liked. The way her eyes glowed at me. The way she flaunted herself in front of me on a daily basis. Why she'd given me her blood. She actually *wanted* me to fancy her back.

It took several seconds for me to process this new information. And though I had streams of doubt running through me, I couldn't shake the feeling that I had hit the nail on the head. I'd finally sussed out her weakness. And incredibly, it was me.

I wasn't capable of love any more, but even if I had been, no part of me would ever be drawn to Mercy Helsing. She was as despicable as the rest of her family. Demanding the girls be starved before the games. Even once trying to have her father beat them into submission. Always the pretty ones.

I did something then that made my skin prickle with revulsion. I took her hand, winding my fingers between hers.

I have you now, I thought.

She stiffened, but didn't extract her hand. My suspicions were confirmed. Whatever way her mind worked, she was now convincing herself that there was a possibility I liked her too. But Mercy was by no means a fool. So I knew I had to tread lightly.

"Your blood...it's changed things," I said quietly and her baby blue eyes widened to saucers.

"It has?" she breathed.

In all honesty, I wasn't lying. It *had* changed things. But only in so much as me feeling the weight of how monstrous this whole island was. And I was done playing a part in it.

"I can't stop thinking about last night." Again, I wasn't really lying. Her blood played on my mind a lot. Why it was giving me such a powerful sense of who I was before I became a V. Why, of all the people I'd drank from, she had somehow provided me with more humanity than I'd ever received before. Not enough, though. Not enough to stop me from wanting to murder her. Brutally. Painfully.

I inclined my head and her grip tightened on my hand. The feeling in my chest was akin to a violent implosion. Her touch sickened me to my core. But I could see an advantage here, if I just let this play out far enough. I could get the upper hand.

"I'll see you tonight?" she confirmed and I nodded, flashing her the briefest of smiles – pretty much all I could muster even with my newfound acting abilities.

She released my hand, heading away and my mouth fell into a grimace as I returned my attention to the screen. There was a new, tantalising feeling growing in my chest. One that had evaded me for so long, it took me some time to figure out what it was.

Hope.

Selena

Humans are capable of terrible things when they're forced to survive. That's what I thought about now as I lay in the mud, waiting for the Vs to arrive. I didn't know if they could smell me through the thick layer of earth that surrounded me, but all I needed was a brief advantage.

I was certain this was all futile. But I wasn't the type to die easily. I wasn't about to give up. Maybe I would have once, before the day I snapped and killed my stepfather. But there's only so far a girl can be pushed before she becomes her own hero.

I wasn't ready to die, and yet I knew it was imminent. Two white stakes and a lot of gall, that's what I had. I shut my eyes, counting the soft footsteps. These Vs didn't move like Varick, with silent grace. And I reminded myself they weren't as strong either. At least four of them, I was certain.

The first arrived, falling over Marie's body immediately and ravishing her neck for blood. It was a female who looked malnourished, her bones protruding from the tatter of clothing she wore.

I counted them, my body starting to shake. With cold, with fear, with desperation. I was alive with terror.

One.

The second arrived. Iskender, the Turkish V; large and brutish. But not looking as strong as Ravenos had been. He fell next to the first V, feasting on Marie. I shut my eyes briefly, trying to block out the horrible sight. *That could be me next.*

Two.

Remorse did Marie no good now, so I forced it away.

The third and fourth burst into the clearing. Thankfully, they were like the first, perhaps even more haggard and weak, like the cave Vs had been. But their grotesque appearance only made me more afraid. The well-fed Vs looked deceptively human, but these creatures were monstrous.

Four.

Then the final one: Melinda, the female who had carried Sakura to the Blood Caves. Tall and lean, she moved through the trees with absolute poise, not even cracking a single twig under her boots. She had clearly grown strong. Probably having fed on countless girls.

Five.

Pushing away the weaker Vs, Melinda took her fill of Marie. And somehow that made me angrier than the others. She was more human than them, less animal. There was no doubt she'd done terrible things to the girls that joined me in this game. And if she was about to tear me apart, I was going to get my revenge for them first. For Vienna. For Marie.

One of the weaker Vs was flung into my path, scrambling and writhing in the mud as it tried to return to the feeding frenzy.

Adrenaline fuelled my actions as I shifted forward on the ground, my pulse pounding in my ears.

Slamming the first stake into its heart, the V didn't even have time to scream before it was dead. I trembled like mad, wincing as I waited for an assault to come from the other Vs.

Incredibly, the advantage was still mine: none of the others had noticed their murdered comrade.

Grimacing, I licked the blood from my stake, desperate for strength. I needed to heal, and the more I drank, the quicker I recovered. The pain in my ankles reduced to nothing and I fought back a sigh of relief.

Perhaps I should have ran away, but watching the Vs feeding on Marie, who only lay there because of my actions, I felt determined to fight back. With my strength returned, courage slid into my chest and I made a decision that I was sure I'd soon regret.

Slinking forward like some serpentine swamp creature, slithering across the ground, I knew my second attack would not go unnoticed. With two stakes in hand, I planned my next move down to a T.

I raised my hand – it wasn't shaking any longer – angling the stake directly above the back of Iskender's neck. A rattling breath left my lungs as I drove it down, tip first into his skin with all the strength I could muster. Iskender screamed and wailed from the liquid silver that was pouring through his head.

The weakest V noticed me, its head whipping up, blood

pouring from its peeled-back gums. With a gasp of fear, I twisted sideways, trying to prepare for his attack. He fell atop me with force and I was crushed beneath his weight.

This was it.

This was how I died.

The V scrabbled for my neck, biting, snapping and snarling. Somehow, I slammed my second stake into its back, screaming my defiance in its face as the tip met its heart.

Melinda tore the dead V from my body, chucking it aside. The final weakling ran at me on all fours, launching through the air. Melinda caught it in a headlock, snapping its head right off.

Death hung in the air like a poisonous gas. And I knew I was its next victim.

I swung my legs around, smashing into the side of hers, trying to bring her to her knees.

It was no good and she snarled as she bent down, taking hold of my neck and plucking me from the mud.

I hung in the air, choking as her nails dug into my throat. I kicked out and my foot connected with her stomach. She roared in pain. With all my might, I kicked again and she dropped me.

I felt for my stake on the ground, lost in the mud. Melinda gripped my hair, pulling me to my feet just as I got a hold of it.

I turned, kicking out at her shin and a sharp snap sounded. Melinda screamed in agony. I didn't waste another second, throwing my arm through the air and sinking the stake under her ribs, right on target.

She gasped, unable to believe what I'd done. I staggered back in shock, staring at her as blood began to run down her chest.

She sank to the ground and I wrenched the stake free, panting as I drew down lungfuls of the freezing air. Her eyes misted over and she fell in a heap at my feet, her red hair swirling around her in the mud.

Iskender was still gargling through the silver that was pouring over his cheeks. I moved to finish the job when more footsteps sounded through the trees. Cutting my losses, I turned on my heel and ran.

The mud had seeped through my clothes, turning my skin to ice. But the more I ran, the more my blood pumped around my body, heating my veins. I checked the map, hurrying on through the trees. Nothing would stop me now. Miraculously, I was still alive and that gave me hope that I stood a chance of making it to the checkpoint.

My calves burned as I forced my legs to move as fast as humanly possible.

The mist eventually began to thin and when I was sure it was no longer a threat, I tugged the mask from my mouth so I could breathe more easily.

The forest was endless and the dark pressing. I soon had to slow to a jog, clutching my side as a stitch ripped through it.

I journeyed on and on, encountering no more Vs along the way. It was as if the trees themselves were hiding me, bending closer and giving me cover. I moved as quietly as I could, but as quickly too. I knew I'd tire soon, but every tree I passed was one closer to the checkpoint.

It couldn't be nearby yet. There was a third day remaining for this hellish round. And what lay up ahead surely wouldn't be an easy path toward safety.

The ground dipped away into a valley and an ache grew in my toes as they pressed against the inside of my boots. Eventually, the ground evened out into a rocky terrain, still surrounded by arching trees. Pine needles lay in a bed on the ground, softening my footfalls. I was thankful for it because I knew, with absolute certainty, that the Vs were still out here, hunting us. Hunting *me*.

I was weary with how far I'd travelled and the timer on my cuff revealed I'd been walking for hours.

The flow of water soon filled my ears and I discovered a river that met with a wide lake. The trees thinned toward its edge so I remained within the cover of the forest. If I was going to survive another night, I needed to find somewhere I could light a fire. Whenever I came across firewood, kept dry beneath overhanging rocks or fallen trees, I stuffed it into my bag.

As I followed the river to higher ground, I spotted a cave, sat back into the rocks, kept hidden by a sheet of Ivy.

I numbly marched toward it, creeping inside to check it was empty.

Apart from a few bones which I prayed didn't belong to a girl from a previous game, the place was perfect. It stretched back almost ten metres and there was even a small opening at the far end I could potentially scramble out of if a V entered from the other.

I set my pack down, preparing the wood I'd found in a pile at the heart of it. Then I returned to the river, picking a shallower pool that met with an uproot of rock, the water being slowed by the obstacle.

I washed away the muck on my body, scrubbing my hair, my face, my arms. As I returned to the cave, I came across some flints that I scooped up and took with me.

Inside, I began bashing the flints together. Over and over until finally a spark sailed into the smaller pieces of wood and took light.

I sighed as the fire grew, quickly warming the space. The smoke filtered out through the hole in the roof of the cave and I prayed that no Vs were near enough to smell it. Or at least, that they were distracted enough to ignore it.

The time ticked by slowly as I waited for my things to dry. I pulled my cloak around me, tugging it tight to halt my persistent shivering.

Sleep dragged me down to the cave floor. I fought it for a while, afraid that a V would find me here unawares. But without it, I would be useless tomorrow. So I sank into darkness, hoping that what awaited me in my dreams wasn't Elijah, or Marie's horrified expression as she realised what I'd done.

Perhaps, in a way, I was like the Vampires. I'd met with death once, and survived. Something had changed inside me. Years of fearing what my stepfather would do to me. The creak of a door in the dead of night, my mother sobbing into a pillow in the next room, the stench of drink on his breath.

There was only so much I could go through before I didn't feel it any more. The first thing I'd truly felt in years was the twist of that blade in his stomach. It felt like breathing again. It felt like resurfacing from a mile-deep lake. That day I was wide awake. There was no guilt, no pain, nothing. It all went away. I didn't know if he took it from me, or if I gave it up willingly. But the part of me that feared him, was finally gone.

But no normal girl can kill someone and not feel it, right? So what made me different from those bloodthirsty Vs? From Varick who wanted nothing more than to taste the hot stream of blood down his throat? They wanted to feel again and so did I. We were all chasing life and it was evading every one of us.

I'd seen survival shows from time to time. And I thought what everyone probably did whilst they watched them: could I do that? Would I survive a life or death situation? Now I knew.

But I wasn't prepared for the reality as I woke up who-knows-how-many-hours after I'd fallen asleep in that cave. The cold, the thirst, the hunger. You can't imagine those things until they're tearing at your insides, demanding to be dealt with. And whilst I sheltered in that cave, watching snow begin to fall in thick clumps, bashing flints together over and over to bring the fire back to life until my hands bled, I realised, Varick was right. Suffering was worse than death. And we were all the same on this island, humans and Vs alike. We were all in pain, driven nearly mad by our needs.

As I struck the flints together once more, a spark shot from them into the mass of dry twigs I'd saved from the night before. But most of my stash had been burnt the previous day. A tiny, glimmer of a flame caught hold and I moved quickly to encourage it. Bending low, I gently blew on the mass of dry foliage until the pile went up in smoke. Tears leaked down my cheeks as I sagged onto the ground beside it, religiously feeding it every few seconds. My hands were numb and bloody and, as I gazed at them, I panicked.

Blood covered the flints, speckled my fingers, my dress. I had nothing to conceal it with. This game was designed to kill me. If the Vs didn't find me, the cold would drive its way into my bones. And at that moment, both were imminent.

The crunch and muffled stomp of approaching boots sounded beyond the sheet of white snowfall that whirled behind the ivy. Shuffling backwards, I reached for the white oak stake, clasping my fist around it so it was stained with a red print of my hand.

Perhaps a V had been close and caught the scent of my blood on the wind.

I shifted the stake in my right hand, angling it down, doing as Varick instructed. It was ironic that he was a lifeline to me now. His few words of advice were offering me advantages I wouldn't have had.

A blur of red passed through the mist.

Panic consumed me. Yesterday I'd been fuelled by pain, by a need to avenge Marie. Now, I was a sitting duck in this wretched cave. I could try to sneak out the back, but the thought of a V tearing at my legs whilst I climbed kept me rooted in place.

Done for, done for, done for.

My breath misted before me, perhaps one of the last to ever pass my lips.

I positioned my feet, crouching low, making myself a smaller target. I had one thing on my side, and that was desperation. I'd fight tooth and nail to survive. I'd cling to life even when it tried to shake me free. I was ready to bleed, I was ready to hurt, but I still wasn't ready to die.

I rushed to meet the shadow that came at me through the curtain of ivy.

Fight or die.

I was in that murderous place again, blood rushing through my veins, heating me to the core. Adrenaline was my friend, fuelling my muscles, readying me to face my predator.

"Selena!" Cass exclaimed, her crimson hair a mess of tangled leaves and mud, her pale skin so white it was nearly translucent. The olive-green dress she wore hung limply from her shoulders, the hem torn and tattered around her booted feet.

I ran to embrace her, unable to believe she was really here. But as I reached her, she shuddered and collapsed in my arms, sinking to the stone floor unconscious.

Her head lolled in my lap and I groaned my anguish as I dragged her to the fire, laying her beside it. Surely the world wouldn't be so cruel as to bring her here just to die before my eyes?

I fed the flames with all I had left, ripping strips of material from my dress to offer it more fuel.

It grew large enough to heat the space and, despite the sweeping snowstorm just feet away, the cave began to grow warm once more. Perhaps it was an illusion, perhaps if I'd sat in this cave on any other day, I'd have frozen to death. But today was different. Today we were going to live.

"Cass," I rocked her gently, resting her on my folded legs to offer her any warmth I had.

Her lips were nearly blue. The only thing that comforted me was that she continued to shiver, assuring me she was alive.

I checked the timer on my watch. We had fifteen hours to make it to the checkpoint. But all I could do at that moment was rock back and forth, hugging Cass to my body.

My eyelids soon began to droop. Sleep was dangerous. Sleep could get us both killed. But I hadn't had enough rest. The night had been long and I'd met with all kinds of horrors in my dreams, waking me in pools of sweat.

To keep my thoughts sharp, I began to sing. The song that sprang to mind surprised me. I hadn't heard it in years, not since I was a child. My mother used to sing it to me to help me sleep. She'd curl around me in bed and I felt so safe that I truly believed nothing could touch me. Not even Elijah. Mum was my shield, she was my saviour on so many nights. And I never had a chance to tell her.

Varick

There was a time in my human life that I went six days without food. Our supplies ran short on a voyage from Norway to Sweden. Hunger like that was agony, it near drove you mad. When you're pushed to your very limits, all those instincts born through thousands of years of evolution come rising to the surface.

I was reduced to an animal, my mouth salivating at the thought of fresh meat, the crunch of bread between my teeth.

Now, I'd take that kind of hunger any day to abate the pain that tore at my throat. I was a slave to the thirst. Before I'd drank from Mercy, I'd been plagued with violent visions, tearing at the necks of those girls out in the game. Especially *her*. Selena. The pain had eased to a dull ache, barely noticeable and giving me some of my old self back.

I'd watched Selena on the twelve foot screen in the auditorium, shredding the arms of my velvet seat with my nails whilst she took on five Vs. *Five.*

Never in the history of the games had any girl taken on so many and survived. The money poured into Selena's bids, skyrocketing. She was the favourite again. And I was, for now, on the side of every man in this room.

Selena's camera briefly took up the central screen, the volume emitting from it. She was cradling the red-haired girl in her arms, singing a soft, lulling song that reminded me of my time at sea. I shut my eyes and let the past in. It was always waiting, haunting me, the life I'd once loved. The memories remained crystal clear. I could practically hear Jameson's voice, shouting over the roar of the churning sea.

Autumn, 1803

"Batten down the hatches, men! She'll be on us before dawn!" Jameson leaned hard to the right as he swung the helm, countering the tilting hull.

The night had been unbearable. Not even I could sleep when the north sea tossed and turned us like a cork in a bottle.

My open shirt blew around me in the freezing wind. There was no time to finish dressing, I'd barely managed to fasten my sword to my hip as I'd run to the tiller to help.

"Captain, the storm'll be upon us in less than an hour," Jameson informed me, sweeping back the dark blonde locks that had come loose from his braid.

One of my crew, a newbie by the name of Pud Jessops, retched full-bodily over the stern side, coughing his guts up into the sea.

"Why'd you recruit the weed?" I sneered. A man needed two things to survive aboard a ship: a strong stomach and sturdy sea legs. This boy didn't seem to have either as he stumbled

backwards, nearly falling on his arse.

"Forgive me, Varick. The boy's a cousin of mine. And he may be a weak hand on deck, but he knows more tales of the sea than you or I. He's a born storyteller, and in them days without woman or rum to entertain the men, I figured it'd do us no harm to have some other form of entertainment."

I rolled my eyes at the comment, but let Jameson have his way. He much too easily bought into the idea of mermaids and beasts of the deep for my liking. I believed whatever my eyes proved to me, no more and no less. But if he needed his stories to find excitement in the seven seas, then so be it. I, on the other hand, found passion in gold, women and blood.

Jameson could have his fish-tailed fantasies, but I would lay with real women and search for true satisfaction. Of course, love wasn't my goal. I wouldn't be so cruel as to let a woman fall for a pirate who spent less time on land than a seabird. I was a free spirit. And no one would tie me down.

Jameson, however, had a woman waiting for him at every port. Lovelorn and doe-eyed at the sight of him, as if they really believed he only had eyes for them. If they knew what a womaniser he was, they probably wouldn't have given him the time of day.

But if there was one thing I'd learnt from my time at shore, it was that women were trouble. They gossiped, they plotted, they schemed to win the most eligible men. It was our gender that were the fools, writing them off as simple-minded creatures. But in a partnership, they often held all the cards, they just didn't let their husbands realise it.

I had a strict no-women rule amongst my crew. I'd heard of ships that kept women aboard, no doubt for the type of entertainment that Jameson so clearly craved. So I'd let him have his story boy. Better that than bringing a temptress onboard.

Selena's scent still reeked havoc on my senses, her saliva, her skin. It was a narcotic, tempting me to take more. Driving me to insanity. Yes, women still had the upper hand. I was their slave. Especially to a girl like her. Only, they didn't win if I took an interest in them. When I'd had my fill, I'm not sure I won either.

I was caught in a never-ending cycle of craving, sating and despising myself.

Some of us were different. Some of the Vs could suppress their emotional responses. But I'd never taken council from a V. No one had taught me the ways of coping with my new self, it had come to me through practice alone. But look where that had landed me. At the hands of the Helsings. Watching this twisted game they played to fund their cause. Why didn't they just kill us all and be done with it?

I half concentrated on the screens encompassing the far wall. Six girls now remained from the twelve that had started this round. More than I'd expected by this point. I wasn't sure whether that was to do with the Vs' weakness or the girls' strength.

Either way, one had to win out. I just hoped Selena came back to me. Because if I had to sit here, witnessing another V drain her body, I'd be at breaking point. I didn't understand the new emotions I was feeling toward her. I'd convinced myself it was to do with her blood, but a niggling voice in the back of my mind told me it was something more than that. Though what that was, I couldn't quite comprehend.

Ignus caught my eye from the front row, glancing over his shoulder with a dark grin. That kid was as screwed up as they came. And no wonder, considering he'd rarely left this island. His parents were practically brainwashing him, forcing him to be the good little heir they needed to ensure this island had a future.

Rotten luck for me, seeing as I was cursed with an eternity of serving whichever Helsing happened to reign here. Unless I could escape. But two hundred years had passed since my last attempt, and the mere memory of what they did to me still haunted me.

Midnight had rolled past and I hesitated to go to Mercy's room, not wanting to take my eyes off of Selena. Many of the men forwent sleep at this stage in the game. No one wanted to miss the next death, even though the Helsings had an alarm system hooked up to their rooms that warned the men if Vs were getting close to any of the girls.

As the hours ticked by, I knew I couldn't wait any longer. Rising from my seat, I headed toward the east tower. My pace was slow; I was in no hurry to meet with Mercy again. But how I behaved with her tonight was key to my survival. And perhaps Selena's too.

I knocked on the door and she wrenched it open barely a second later.

"Where have you been?" she demanded, taking my wrist and encouraging me inside.

"The men were asking my advice," I lied and she huffed, dropping onto her bed in her slinky nightgown.

"Well you'll have to make up for lost time." She grinned, beckoning me with her finger.

My throat tightened with revulsion. I moved to the bed, taking her wrist and drawing it to my mouth.

She tugged it free, shaking her head. "My neck today."

I suppressed a shudder as she took my arm, guiding me forward and shifting the golden locks from her throat. I bent low, tempted to take a deep bite, but resisted, putting my plan into action. "I can't hurt you," I said softly, drawing away with a feigned expression of pain. The only pain I was feeling was the sickness in my stomach. I hated this girl right down to the pit of my soul.

"Oh," she breathed and I heard her heartbeat rise, felt the heat radiating from her blood.

I backed away, rubbing my eyes. "It's too much Mercy. The way I feel about you. It's all too sudden."

"Oh Varick, it's my blood. It's let you love me at last." She raised her arms, wriggling across the sheets with her joy.

"I think you're right," I said with a taut frown.

"Come, drink more," she offered, tilting her neck toward me, but I shook my head.

"No, I wont. I can't."

She stood, hurrying across the room just as I laid my hand on the doorknob. Damn.

My escape had been so close.

She offered her neck to me again and I knew I had no choice. Not that drinking her blood was in any way a misery for me. I had no qualms about sinking my teeth into this wretch. But the fact that she enjoyed it made me uneasy, not to mention the fact Abraham would have me hung, drawn and quartered if her found out.

I sank my fangs in all the same, taking what I wanted and what she gave willingly. She cupped my neck, pulling me to her, and despite the delicious drink running down my throat, all I could focus on was her hands on me. My skin itched with how much I wanted to push her away, but I remained in place.

Today, being well fed already, it was easier to stop. Combine that with my general ill-feeling about this whole thing, and I was probably only at her neck for half a minute.

"It's too much for me, Mercy. I need time to process these feelings." I wrenched open the door and Mercy gazed on triumphantly as I slipped away.

A grin crept onto my mouth as I wiped the blood from it, heading back toward my room.

Hook, line and sinker.

Selena

Cass finally came to and I fed her the last of the berries from both of our packs. She had no signs of injury, but fatigue had set in. She must have been running around this forest longer than I had.

"How'd you make it here?" she asked when she woke.

I wanted to hide the fact that I'd killed Marie. But Cass had been through enough that I didn't want to keep secrets from her. When I told her what had happened, she didn't glare at me or walk away, she hugged me, wrapping me in her limber arms.

"It wasn't your fault," she said. "The mist must have been poisoned. I kept seeing things..."

Tears slid down my cheeks, reality finally settling in. I'd murdered another person. She may not have been entirely innocent, considering her past, but she'd had a good heart. And killing her boyfriend hadn't been any more noble than me killing my stepfather.

"I'm so sorry I left you," Cass said, a single tear escaping her eye.

"I understand," I breathed.

"I want to get out of this forest," Cass whispered, glancing toward the cave exit. "We could make it to the checkpoint within hours. It's close."

I nodded, clutching onto her a moment longer, knowing the pain at what I'd done would never leave me.

As we gathered up our things, I became aware of how little I really knew about Cass. She never spoke about her past and I was sure there was more to her than met the eye. A survivor like her wasn't born this way, she was made. But how, I wasn't sure.

As we gathered up our things and headed into the eternal night, I plucked up the courage to ask her. "Who were you before all of this?"

Cass glanced at me, before her gaze fell to the ground. "I told you. I was in for arson."

"Why did they send you to a maximum security prison? No one died, did they? You said you only tried to burn down your ex's place."

She nodded, digging her teeth into her lower lip. As we crossed over the river, tiptoeing across protruding rocks in the stream, she turned to me.

"I hurt a lot of people, Selena." She shook her head.

My foot slipped on the rock and she steadied me, holding me in place. "You're a good person. You hurt someone that hurt you. You shouldn't be here with the rest of us."

I untangled her fingers from my cloak. "I'm not, Cass. No more so than you or anyone else. You've saved me more than once. I wouldn't be standing here without you."

Cass choked out a dry laugh. "You don't understand."

"Then help me to," I demanded. "What does it matter now? We'll most likely be dead before tomorrow."

She sighed, making her way across the rocks and I followed her onto the dry ground.

"My ex's home was in a block of flats. The one I set light to." She stopped walking, keeping her gaze fixed on a tree ahead of us. "Families died, Selena. Couples. Teenagers. *Kids*." She covered her face, a rattling sob rolling up from her throat. "I was so angry. I never thought about the consequences. And that bastard wasn't even in the flat."

I touched her arm, anguish flaring through me. "You didn't know."

"I *did* know!" She cupped her hand to her mouth, horrified by herself. "I knew other people lived close by, that should have been enough. But I wasn't myself. I was a wreck after I found out he cheated on me. I acted stupidly. I wasn't thinking."

I gripped her arm. She'd forgiven me of everything I'd done. I needed to offer her the same courtesy.

"Are you sorry?" I asked quietly.

"*So* sorry...I'd do anything to take it back." She wrenched her arm from my hold. "I tried to kill myself. But the police found me swallowing the pills. Had my stomach pumped before they arrested me."

I sucked in a breath, eyeing the bunched muscles in her shoulders. I could see how much pain she was in. I'd admired her strength so much through this game, but clearly she was broken inside. She'd made mistakes that had cost people their lives. But now I had too. So how could I be angry with her?

I reached for her again and she shrank from my touch, spinning around. "I want you to survive this, Selena. You're the only one that deserves to."

"Don't say that," I bit back. "I'm as guilty as you are."

"No..." She stepped forward, squeezing my arm. "You're not like us. You're a survivor, not a killer. That's why you're still here. Whereas the rest of us..." She sighed.

"There's no difference. People have died at my hand, it equates to the same thing."

She shook her head, pressing her lips together.

"Stop it," I demanded. "We're here, still standing. And that's all that matters now. We can go home, start fresh-"

"There's nothing for me back in England." Cass moved away from me, heading on.

"Then why are you still walking toward the checkpoint?" My question hung in the air and she didn't answer, continuing to weave through the trees.

I huffed, heading after her. We moved on in tense silence, not even the birds daring to make a noise between us as we walked.

It was so quiet that it didn't seem natural. Fear crept up my spine as some sense warned me that we weren't alone. I twisted around, suddenly sure that we were being watched. My heart started thumping faster and my palms grew slick as I tightened my grip on my stake.

Movement caught my eye ahead of us as a V suddenly charged out of the undergrowth, a feral shriek escaping it. I froze but Cass started running, sprinting straight toward the V with a cry of her own.

She collided with the Vampire, shouting out with effort as she brought it down, sticking her stake deep into its chest. The starved V fell to the ground, but Cass didn't stop there. She started stabbing and stabbing and I stood, watching in horror as she took out her rage on the fallen V.

Cass finally stood, dripping in blood, a grimace on her face. She wiped a splash from her cheek and set her jaw. "I may not deserve to be here, and I sure as hell don't know what surviving this game means for me. But I *do* know I don't wanna die any more."

I nodded, wide-eyed. "You're not going to die."

She thrust up her chin. "Correction: *we're* not going to die."

She stomped off into the woods and I hurried to follow her. Christ, Cass was formidable. Together, maybe we really did stand a chance.

We finally passed the tree line and a steep downhill descent led us toward a beach. At the edge of it was a large cabin. Smoke pumped out of a chimney, the scent of burning coal reaching to us on the wind.

"That's it," Cass sighed, checking the map on her cuff.

It was quiet. Too quiet. The waves lapped against the shore. All we had to do was walk a hundred metres to the cabin and we'd be safe.

I moved forward but Cass caught my arm. "Wait," she hissed, pointing past me.

My neck prickled as I followed her finger, finding a row of Vs lined up along the tree line. They were gazing at us, hungrily licking their lips, but none of them made a move.

"What are they doing?" I breathed, clutching Cass's arm as I stumbled backwards.

Before she could answer, a flash of purple shot past us as Sakura sprinted down the beach. Other girls, evidently hiding amongst the boughs, followed her lead, making a dash for it.

The Vs' ever-watching eyes made me nervous, but as they started in our direction, Cass and I followed the other girls.

I spotted Kite and Angelina stumbling over the rocks, splitting apart to make their own way to the cabin. Briony was just ahead of us and a girl I didn't know with short, strawberry blonde hair sprinted after her.

I shot a glance over my shoulder, expecting the pursuit of the Vs, but they remained sentinel, standing in rows, just watching us. As if they were waiting for-

A scream tore through the air and I flung around, trying to place it. The girl with short hair had disappeared, but I couldn't figure out where to until Briony dropped out of sight, too.

My heart plummeted and I dug my heels in, forcing myself to a halt.

Cass wheeled around. "What are you doing?" But I was

already heading toward where I'd last seen Briony. The Vs were moving at last, circling around an area where the blonde girl had been running. I spurred my legs on, desperate to find her. After what I'd done to Marie, I couldn't leave her.

I reached the place where the blonde girl had disappeared and gasped, finding her in a deep pit, laid across a bed of spikes, her body torn and broken.

"No." I backed away in horror. My head snapped up as something moved in my periphery; Briony was clambering out of a ditch several feet away. I sprang into action, running to help her.

Something clicked beneath my feet and suddenly the ground disappeared.

I acted on instinct, thinking of the spikes. Of the blonde girl's unseeing eyes, her body speared on the wooden spikes. I threw out my arms, reaching for the stony wall as it rushed past me. I managed to dig my fingers in, stopping my fall with a jerk.

Glancing down, I saw the first of the spikes just inches from my feet. I dug in my toes, desperately clawing my way upwards. The top of the pit was a few feet above me, too high to reach on my own.

Vs came into sight, leering down at me with hungry grins on their faces.

I grunted my frustration. I was too damn close to the checkpoint to go out of the game like this. I grabbed my stake and used it to heave myself up the wall.

A V flew through the air with a scream as it landed on the

spikes. It hadn't been killed, but was evidently stuck on the sharp poles, unable to get free. More fell and I ducked my head as reaching fingers swept past me.

"Selena! Grab my hand!"

I reached upwards toward my unexpected saviour and Kite took hold of my fingers. More hands found me and I was heaved out of the hole, planted on my feet and forced to run again.

Kite, Cass and Sakura were my rescuers. Sakura, who had already reached the checkpoint had actually come back for me. And Kite who had despised me since day one. I had no time to think about it as we ran as a tight group toward the cabin where Briony was already darting inside.

We stumbled onto the beach, rushing through the door which was open and waiting for us.

Heat flooded over us from a nearby fire; it was like being dragged out of a horror movie and dropped into a romance. Champagne awaited us on the table beside a bowl of strawberries and cosy blankets were laid over the plush chairs. We collapsed around the room, exhausted, drained and filthy, but alive.

Varick sat in an armchair, plucking stalks from strawberries. My mouth fell open. "Comfortable?"

Varick's mouth hooked up at the corner as he took me in. "Very." He gestured to the hall beyond the lounge. "Wash. Sleep. Drink. Kill yourselves. Whatever you feel like."

Cass took a purposeful step toward him, her stake raised. "How about I off you? 'Cause that's what I feel like doing right now."

He opened his arms invitingly. "Have at it, sweetheart. I could use a laugh."

I pressed Cass's arm down. "Come on, let's get changed."

She glowered at Varick as we walked past him, finding seven bedrooms. Enough for each of us and more, like they knew no more than seven of us would make it here. I cursed the Helsings under my breath, picking a room at random and shedding my filthy clothes. An en-suite led to a small bathroom where I stood under the shower for an age.

When I was dressed in the warm jumpsuit that was folded at the end of my single bed, I pulled on a pair of woollen socks and headed back to the lounge, my stomach growling with hunger.

The other girls were already present, sitting around the room, some sipping on champagne.

Varick turned the projector off; it had been running highlights from today's round.

"Do you have to watch the game or do you just enjoy it?" Sakura addressed Varick with a scowl.

He was sat on the only spare sofa and no one seemed keen to join him. "Well how else would I know how many glasses of champagne to pour?"

A grumble of contempt passed round the room. Figuring there was nowhere else to sit, I joined him on the two-seater, snatching a handful of strawberries from the bowl.

"Do we get a real dinner, or is this it?" Angelina demanded, turning her nose up at the strawberries.

"Cook's not brought it yet." Varick shrugged, eyeing me as I ate strawberry after strawberry. Cass avoided the bowl, evidently having had enough berries to last her a lifetime. I, on the other hand, was famished and wasn't about to turn down free food.

"So you don't make the meals?" I questioned, raising a brow.

A small smile pulled at his mouth. "I haven't cooked in three centuries, sweetheart. I think you'd rather eat mud."

"How long until the next round?" Kite asked, perching on the edge of an armchair that Angelina was sat in.

"You have twenty four hours," he replied.

"That long?" I murmured and he nodded.

"Get as much rest as you can. You're not at the finishing line yet."

"Noted," Cass muttered, marching from the room.

The girls slowly trickled after her, none of them seeming too keen on Varick's company. As Kite filed out, I caught her eye and mumbled, "Thank you."

"For what?" she spat, quickening her pace as she exited the room. I frowned, having no idea why she was pretending she hadn't helped me today.

I lifted my knees to my chest, hiding my face in them, thinking of Marie. What would Briony do if she found out what I'd done?

"You did well," Varick said quietly.

"I killed someone. I don't classify that as doing *well*."

"The Helsings are responsible for this, not you. You're only trying to survive."

"I'm sick of people saying that to me. *I* make the choices out there." I pointed to the door. "Choices that are turning me into someone I never wanted to be."

"You're still you. You're just being pushed to your limits."

"Well I don't like my limits!" I snapped, my pulse rising. What did he care? He was a blood sucking V. This kind of stuff was a daily occurrence for him.

The room fell quiet and guilt stabbed at me for lashing out at Varick. It wasn't his fault. He was only doing what the Helsings ordered him to do.

I sighed, voicing what was at the root of my agony. "They didn't deserve to die that way," I muttered, an ache in my heart at witnessing so many deaths.

"It's not so bad," he said softly. "Death is silent. Death is peace."

"Oh what do you know?" I hissed. "Your death is eternal. And you don't look much at peace to me, Varick."

His jaw hardened as his eyes locked with mine. "Well maybe you should be grateful they aren't cursed with an eternity in hell, Selena."

"Grateful?" I snarled. "You want me to be *grateful*?" I stood, my rage rising too high.

He shook his head with a weary sigh. "That's not what I meant."

The door opened and my head whipped up. A team of people

in white uniforms walked in, carrying tray after tray of food. They said nothing to me or Varick, heading straight through the cabin.

"Food." Varick stood, leading the way to the feast they were laying out in a small dining room. Five places were set with silverware and crystal glasses. A decanter of red wine sat at the heart of it all. When the table was laid, the Helsings' staff exited without a word.

Varick fetched the other girls and left us alone to eat together.

Cass stood, taking the wine and pouring us all a glass. "Screw sobriety, girls. We all deserve a reward."

We clinked our glasses together, but no one said anything. Everyone seemed deep in their own thoughts as they sipped moodily on her drink and dished out helpings of stew and freshly baked rolls.

Sakura sat at my side, having polished off one glass already.

The wine was dry on my tongue but warmth spread through my body as it sank into my stomach, providing me with some sorely needed peace of mind.

"How many of us do you think are going to make it over the finish line?" Kite asked casually, sipping on her wine.

"Do we have to talk about that?" Sakura muttered. "We get a few hours away from the games in here."

"Pah," Kite spat a laugh. "We aren't away from the games, Sakura. Giving us food, soft beds. It's just another way to screw with us."

"Why don't we make a break for it?" Angelina hissed, leaning in closer.

"And go where?" I asked, shaking my head. "We have chips in the back of our heads."

Angelina huffed. "I'm just making a suggestion. Why don't we cut them out?"

Briony stood. "That's not a bad idea." She picked up a sharp knife.

Cass nodded keenly, standing too.

I folded my arms, watching this madness play out. "Come on, that won't work. You're more likely to bleed out."

"Do it." Kite moved the food aside and bent over the table. Briony hurried to her side and Cass held Kite's hair back. Briony felt for the bump on the back of Kite's neck, just above her spiderweb tattoo.

"This is crazy." I stood, panic fleeing through me.

Angelina shook her head. "It's genius."

Briony poised the blade above Kite's neck – a bread knife no less. Just as the tip pressed against skin, the door flew open.

"Out. Now," Varick demanded, snatching the knife from Briony's hand in a blindingly fast movement.

Kite straightened, glaring at him. "Why don't you help us, Vampire? What fun is this for you?"

Varick pointed toward the door, a deadly look on his face. "Get out!"

Before I left, he caught my arm, giving me a look that said he wanted to talk to me. The other girls were already disappearing around the corner.

"Meet me outside," he said.

"I'll wait till everyone's asleep," I breathed, slipping away.

I didn't know why, but I wanted to spend some alone time with Varick. The other girls hated him, but I couldn't shake the feeling he was just like us. Stuck here on this island, playing games.

I lay on my bed, my heart hammering in my ears as I waited for the minutes to pass. Maybe I was crazy, but the brief moments I'd spent with Varick outside of the game gave me something to focus on other than all the death I had to face daily. Which was ironic, considering he was death reincarnated.

I managed to doze off for a while, feeling physically exhausted from the last few days. When I woke, I was certain everyone must be asleep and pulled on the spare boots that sat by the door. Creeping out of my room, I listened for any sound of the other girls, but all was quiet. I hated feeling like I was betraying Cass as I walked down the hall. She despised Varick and would judge me heavily if she knew what I was doing. But I couldn't stop myself.

I crept out into the night, heading across the pebbly shore. The moon hung low over the sea, casting silver across the calm waves. The snow had passed on, leaving the sky clear of clouds and a bitterly cold wind.

Varick was sitting on a boulder in a small cove. I glanced back at the light streaming from the cabin windows and moved on. Perhaps it was Varick's superior strength to the other Vs that made me feel safe out here. Whatever the reason, I wasn't worried about an ambush. Even though I could easily imagine Vs waiting in the trees that clung to the hill leading up from the beach.

"I wasn't sure you'd come," he said, moving to meet me.

"I fell asleep."

"Thought as much. You had a hard few days."

I nodded, wrapping my arms around myself against the cold.

"Come. Let's walk," he instructed and I followed him down the beach, moving to a more secluded area where plants protruded from the pebbles.

"Is everything alright?" I asked, sensing something off in his demeanour.

"Yes...and no."

I waited for further explanation, but he didn't give me one.

When we reached a small inlet, he led me into a seclusion of trees. It was dark and my skin prickled all over from the cold.

"I'm in trouble, Selena," he growled, moving toward me.

I instinctively backed up, my spine pressing against a tree trunk. "Trouble?" I questioned, my tone too high.

"One of the Helsing's knows I helped you through the third round."

"Oh," I breathed. "What are they going to do about it?"

Varick sighed, shifting from foot to foot, moving closer. My mouth went dry, but still I wasn't scared.

"They've asked me to undo what I did."

Had I been so foolish to trust him? Coming out here alone in the dark, it wasn't exactly sensible of me. But what was the point in being sensible, when tomorrow a V could be feasting on my neck?

He moved closer and I knew there was no point in running. He'd outpace me in seconds. And after everything I'd been through, I wasn't going to die like a coward.

He bared his teeth, his milky fangs glistening at me in the lambent moonlight.

I fell still, my heartbeat slowing. It had only been a matter of time before I ended up here. And a small part of me was relieved. There were worse deaths than this, much worse.

I tilted my chin up, baring my throat, my rampant pulse no doubt visible to him.

"Make it quick," I panted, the adrenaline subsiding from my veins.

I'd put up a good fight in the games. I'd never go out without one. I'd beaten a superior opponent before. But not this time.

As Varick closed in on me, I recalled the last man who had me cowering in this way, at his mercy.

My stepfather.

After everything, here I was again. Perhaps it was my fate to die this way after all.

He pulled a knife from his jacket and I shuddered. "No teeth?" I questioned.

"I'm supposed to make it look like one of the girls did it."

I nodded, a tear leaking from my eye. I hated myself for it, but death wasn't something I embraced easily.

Varick chucked the knife and it flew out into the sea, disappearing with a splash.

"I won't do it," he said firmly and my heartbeat slowed a fraction.

"Why not?" I gasped.

He moved closer and I wasn't sure whether to be frightened or not any more.

"I can't. Selena I-" He shook his head, moving closer still. "You've given something back to me. Something I thought I'd lost."

"What?" I breathed as he closed the distance between us. My feelings were split down the middle. Strangely wanting him closer and equalling wanting to push him away.

"I feel hopeful again. I can't explain it...it's not just you. It's everything lately. I feel more like my old self. Who I was before I was turned. Who I want to be again."

I nodded, trying to understand. He looked pained, his expression dark.

"We might not meet again after today," he said in a low tone.

A weight pulled at my chest. Did he not believe I was capable of making it through the final round? "Why not?"

"I've disobeyed the Helsings..." He lifted a hand, cupping my chin and tilting it upwards. "Do you hate me like the other girls do?"

I shook my head. "Perhaps I should."

"The fact that you don't is enough to change the whole world,

Selena."

I frowned, not understanding. But before I could question him further, he kissed me.

I was frozen in place and yet warmed to the bone. His kiss was slow and hesitant; he knew I wasn't prepared for this. But suddenly we were just two people, trying to find something to live for on this godforsaken island. I wrapped my arms around his neck and he pressed flush against me, knotting his hands in my hair.

My veins were charged with energy, my thoughts scattered, leaving me abandoned to this crazy, beautiful moment. I didn't want it to end; I didn't want to deal with the realities of what this meant. His kiss became more fervent, his hands sliding down to my waist. I was certain he knew as well as I did that this kiss would be both our first and our last. Nothing could come of this. It was a brief moment of light in an eternity of darkness.

When he finally released me, I was breathless. He of course, wasn't, which simply made my cheeks scorch with embarrassment.

"Why did you do that?" I breathed, his body so close all I could do was stare into his eyes.

"I wanted to feel human again. Why did you let me?"

I considered my answer for a moment then admitted, "Same reason."

"Hm." His mouth pulled up at the corner as he drew away from me.

There were tiny threads forming between us, like a spider spinning our fates, entwining us with one another. I couldn't understand the pull I felt toward someone whose intentions were far from noble. And yet, if I ignored all logic and reason, all that remained was the calmness of his presence and the quiet, unwavering certainty that we were supposed to have met.

"The real world is waiting for us," he growled.

I sighed, letting him draw me away from the tree and back toward the cabin. There was something hanging in the air, something neither of us were saying. And I was pretty sure it was goodbye.

◐ ☼ ◐

I woke early, teeming with all the things I should have said to Varick last night. Funny how I could never think of the right words in the moment. But when the time had passed, suddenly I had a hundred things to say.

I should have asked him more questions. I should have offered solutions.

I slipped out of my room, hunting for a glass of water in the small kitchen. As I searched the cupboards, I noticed all of the sharp knives had been removed. Evidently Varick didn't trust us not to start cutting the devices out of our heads. I could hardly blame the girls. It had been a reasonable enough idea if I wasn't fairly sure the Helsings would have taken that into account. I bet those things would explode the second I could touch one with a knife tip, like the ones in the Vs' heads.

I poured myself a glass of water, tipping the cool liquid down my throat and gazing out of the small window across the beach.

"Morning."

Varick's voice made me jump and I nearly dropped the glass. I turned to him and his dark expression brightened a fraction as he met my eye.

"What's going to happen to you?" I blurted. Perhaps I could have chosen my timing better, maybe eased into this conversation a little. But I felt we were on borrowed time as it was.

Varick sighed, moving toward me. "I've lived for a very long time, Selena."

I started shaking my head, a knot of terror tightening in my chest. I knew what he was saying and some part of me couldn't bear it. It was more than his death that angered me. It was the Helsings' absolute power on this island. Who were they to decide his fate? Or mine, or any of the other girls forced to play their game?

I moved toward him, resting a hand on his chest. He gazed down at me with uncertainty. I knew I had to explain. So I had to find the words, and fast.

"Why don't we stop playing along?" I whispered and Varick's brow lowered. "What if we refused?"

"They'd start killing you off until the rest of you continued the game." Varick took my hand in his, squeezing softly. The action did strange things to my heart.

"You can't surrender to them," I demanded, my pulse rising. I knew from my entire upbringing, that if you let cruel people have their way, they would continue to push boundaries. To find new ways to break you. The only way to stop them was to refuse to give in, no matter what the consequences.

Varick tilted his head to the side, looking at me like I was a riddle he needed to solve.

"Selena, I've been a part of the terrible things here. I've stood at the sidelines and done the Helsings' bidding for too many years, feeling nothing inside me but a hollow void." He reached out, cupping my cheek and gently grazing his thumb across it. "You've reminded me of who I am, but that doesn't change what I've done."

"We've all done terrible things," I said, breathless as tears pooled in my eyes. Varick had become something of a guiding star to me. Maybe I was experiencing Stockholm syndrome. Maybe I'd formed this attachment to give myself some kind of relief from the game. Whatever it was, I couldn't shake it. "You can make things right again."

Varick shook his head. "I let this happen."

He turned away from me and I caught his arm. "Then *stop* letting it."

He glanced back at me and pain lanced through his eyes. He was trapped by his captors and I knew what that felt like. I knew how lonely it was, how empty.

Cass walked through the door and I made the conscious decision not to release Varick. I wasn't going to hide my alliance with him. If I was going to ask him to stand up to the Helsings, then I had to start by standing up for my own beliefs.

Cass's eyes slid from Varick's arm to my hand. "Morning," she said tersely.

I nodded and Varick walked away, heading out of the kitchen. I hung my head, knowing the fight Varick needed could only come from him.

"What's with you and the V?" Cass asked, making herself a cup of tea.

"Oh, lay off me, will you?" I snapped, my anger spilling over.

Cass looked affronted, pausing as she poured hot water onto a tea bag. "I just don't think you should be hanging around with it."

"*Him*," I corrected. "And if you actually took the time to talk to Varick, maybe you'd realise he's not all bad. And maybe you'd start to realise that those Vs out on the island are forced to be here as much as we are."

"Are you actually defending them?" she asked in disbelief.

"I'm just saying. Sometimes, it doesn't do any harm to see things from both sides."

"So what? You want us to make friends with the Vs now?"

I huffed, walking away from her, but as I stepped out of the kitchen, I realised her suggestion wasn't all that crazy. Okay, so I couldn't exactly have a rational conversation with a V whilst it was hunting me down on the island. But maybe Varick could. We all had a common enemy, after all.

I went to find him, but found the living room filling with people. Men and women in white overalls were moving through the front door, carrying large metal boxes.

"What's going on?"

None of them answered, but continued to set up whatever equipment they'd brought with them.

Varick appeared, leading the girls into the room.

"Today you'll be prepared for the final round," he announced.

"Prepared how?" Sakura demanded, eyeing the newcomers with suspicion.

"You'll be pampered," Varick said, not managing to hide the note of disgust in his tone.

The men and women laid out massage tables across the room, pushing the furniture aside to make room for them. One of them placed a speaker down which started playing ethereal, classical music.

I folded my arms, surveying them.

"Why?" I snapped and Varick shot me a glare.

"Just play along," he demanded, striding from the room and locking the door.

Angelina was the first to strip out of her clothes, laying down on a table as one of the women gestured for her to do so. Slowly, one by one, all of the girls followed. Everyone but me.

Cass gave me a look that said she agreed with Varick for once.

Play along.

The girls started to receive massages from the surrounding beauty crew. I resisted a moment longer before stripping off and laying face down on the final table. I was in desperate need of a massage, so I wasn't going to pass one up. And I supposed if we were going to spend the entire day here at the cabin, I might as well take the opportunity to try and relax.

When every inch of us were massaged and my body felt like jelly, the beauty therapists started waxing our legs, filing our nails, washing our hair in sweet-smelling soap. It soon became apparent that the crew were not permitted to speak to us. So the other girls and I proceeded to ignore them.

"Why do I feel like I'm being made pretty just to get torn apart by Vampires?" Sakura asked as one of the women dyed her hair, restoring it to its bright colour.

"Who cares?" Kite drawled; she was half way through a foot massage and didn't seem to have any qualms about bossing the therapists about.

"We're the final six," Briony said in a quiet voice. "What if we've already won? What if they're getting us ready to attend some victory ball?"

I shook my head, causing the woman brushing my hair to drop her comb. "Varick said there's another round."

"So?" Briony chipped in hopefully. "Maybe the final round is eating cake and celebrating."

"Yeah right," I muttered.

"Well what do you think this is all about then?" Angelina demanded. She already looked twice as radiant as she had before. Her skin was glowing with a tinted moisturiser and her eyes had been painted in golden shadows.

I considered it and could only come to one conclusion. "I think the Helsings are putting on a show for their spectators. The prettier we look, the more money they'll bet on us."

"Why? What does being pretty have to do with it?" Angelina demanded.

I sighed, sinking back into the head massage my therapist was giving me. "They're men, Angelina. It has everything to do with it." At least, those were certainly the type of men who'd attend a sick show like this.

"Not all men are pigs," Sakura said quietly.

The other girls, me included, scoffed.

"Never met a good one myself," Kite said. "Killed a lot of bad ones though." A smug grin settled on her features and a pang of curiosity went through me. Is that what Kite had gone to prison for?

"Well *I* have," Sakura said proudly. "In fact, he's waiting for me back in Finland."

Cass rolled her eyes, but I couldn't fight my intrigue.

"You have a boyfriend?" I asked and she nodded.

"His name's Rico. We met in school." A dreamy look filled her eyes.

"And he's never hit you?" Briony narrowed her eyes and

Sakura shook her head.

"Or cheated on you?" Cass asked and Sakura declined again, a smile growing on her face.

"Well he probably will," Kite sang. "He's probably off screwing your best friend while you're here-"

"Shut up," Sakura growled. "He loves me. He would never hurt me."

Silence fell over the room. I guessed I had more in common with some of the girls than I'd realised. We'd all been hurt in some way or other by men. But maybe Sakura was right, maybe there *were* good men left in the world.

By the time the beauty team were finished with us, everyone was practically sparkling. The effect was lost on us a little as we were helped into our ball gowns, ready for another round.

Varick returned, his gaze immediately turning to me. He stilled for a moment, then cleared his throat. "You first." He nodded to me and I frowned with curiosity, following him out of the room.

"What's going on?" I whispered as he guided me down the hall. I caught sight of myself in a long mirror hanging on the wall and barely recognised myself. My lips were painted red, my eyes powdered with greys and blacks. My skin seemed to glow and my cheekbones were much higher than I recalled them being before.

"The Helsings like to create profiles on the last girls. To help the spectators choose who to place their final bids on."

I nodded, my belly swimming with nerves as he led me into the kitchen. He opened the small back door that led onto the beach, and I was immediately out of my depth.

A huge green screen was erected before me and a camera crew stood before it, being bossed about by a woman in high heels – not appropriate for the pebbled beach – and blonde hair that flowed effortlessly around her in the wind.

She rushed forward when she spotted me, her bright blue eyes piercing through me. Her features were small and her mouth sticky with pink lip gloss.

"This is Dawn," Varick introduced her. "She's a cousin of the Helsings."

"Oh my, what wonderful work they've done on you, Selena." She patted my cheek and I felt the sting of her patronising tone. She was perhaps in her forties but it was hard to tell through all the make-up she was wearing.

"Stand over there for your photo shoot." She pressed me toward the green screen and I gritted my teeth, stomping toward it, with half a mind to refuse.

I stepped into place, feeling like a lemon as several cameras glared at me.

Varick leant back against the cabin wall, watching me, making me unbelievably self-conscious.

"Smile, cherry pie," Dawn encouraged, painting a smile either side of her cheeks to try and encourage me.

I glowered at her, at the cameras, having no intention of pretending I was at all happy about being paraded like an idiot. "I haven't got much to smile about."

"Nonsense!" She waved a hand. "You could be a winner of the V Games soon. That's no easy task."

"Still not smiling," I said through my teeth as camera bulbs flashed at me.

Varick caught my eye, grinning at my stubbornness and I tried to fight back the urge to return it. A tiny smile pulled at one corner of my mouth and a hundred flashes blinded me.

"Perfect," Dawn announced with a satisfied grin. She gestured to someone beyond the green screen and a moment later a girl appeared, pushing a V forward on a restraining pole.

I backed up, glancing to Varick for reassurance. He gave me a small nod, but his eyes were dark.

Someone placed a stake in my hand and directed the V in my direction. He was skin and bones, barely human beneath his long hair and anorexic body.

"Kill it," Dawn instructed, wafting me toward the Vampire.

I shuddered in horror, taking a step back. "No," I demanded.

"Oh why must you be so difficult?" Dawn muttered. "It's all for show. This one's weak. It'll only take a quick stab."

My upper lip curled back in disgust. "I'm not going to kill some chained up V. It's not a fair fight."

Cameras were rolling now, capturing every second of my defiance.

"*Do* cooperate, Selena," Dawn pleaded. "I have five more girls to get through today."

I folded my arms as the V snapped and snarled at me from a

few a feet away. "I'm not doing it."

Dawn's light-hearted expression became cold. "If you don't kill it willingly, I will make you do so."

I stood my ground, glaring at this vile woman who so boldly tried to control me.

I chucked the stake at my feet. "Then make me," I snarled, my hands beginning to tremble with rage. I was done being told what to do. Forced into killing when I never had a choice in being here.

Dawn gave a brief nod to the girl holding the V at the end of the pole and, with a wide-eyed look, she released it.

The V ran at me.

I gasped, dropping to the floor, scrambling for the stake on the ground. I had no choice. It was kill or be killed again.

Before it reached me, Varick bolted into its path, snapping its neck in seconds. Bending low, he helped me to my feet, his eyes flitting between mine.

My cheeks grew hot from the intensity of his gaze and even hotter as I realised the cameras were still rolling.

"Perfect," Dawn announced smugly.

I sensed something deadly in her tone. I felt some secret had been revealed between Varick and I. And dread slid through me as I realised the whole of the Helsing family were going to watch that footage.

Varick evidently felt as nervous as I did about it, his expression cold as he moved swiftly away from me, trying to cover his tracks. "Shoot that scene again. I'm sure Selena will comply this time."

"No need," Dawn said lightly.

"There *is* need," Varick growled.

"Not the way I see it." Dawn took out her lip gloss, painting the thick gloop onto her mouth. "On to the interview."

"Interview?" I breathed, looking to Varick, but he was striding purposefully away from me, not looking back.

I pictured what they might superimpose behind me on the green screen.

My heartbeat stuttered and my legs became shaky as Dawn gestured for me to return inside.

"Not to worry, there are no cameras for this part. I'm just going to ask you a few questions."

We sat opposite each other at the small kitchen table and Dawn took out a notepad.

"So Selena." Dawn was suddenly all business, her pen poised above a list of questions already printed out on a sheet in front of her. "Do you have anyone waiting for you back home? A boyfriend perhaps?"

I shook my head. "Just my mother." I shifted in my seat then added, "She's probably missing me terribly." Perhaps I could win some sympathy points with the spectators. Though I'm not sure what good it would do me. And I'm pretty sure Dawn didn't write that part down.

She tilted her head. "And would you define yourself as heterosexual? That is, you desire men, not women?"

"What kind of question is that?" I blurted.

She wound her pen through the air, trying to encourage me to answer. "I just need a yes or no answer."

I gaped at her, but she simply waited for my answer.

I sighed, giving in. "Yes...I'm into men."

"And are you a virgin, Selena?"

I stood up, glaring at the woman in fury. "That's none of your business." Why on earth was she asking me that?

She pressed her sticky lips together, eyeing me. "Just a yes or no answer will suffice."

"You have no right to ask me that." What kind of interview was this?

"You are being very difficult," she sighed. "Some of the men think virgins are more desired by Vampires. Old wives tales, that's all. But it effects their betting strategies all the same."

I gritted my teeth and spat, "Fine. Yes, I'm a virgin."

She clucked her tongue, writing down my answer. Her interview descended into a probing questionnaire about my life, much of which I refused to answer and gave short, yes or no responses to. I didn't see what difference this would make to my survival. So what was the point? This was all about the spectators, trying to pick their winner. And I didn't want them betting on me, even though I wanted to survive. I didn't want them making money off of my misery.

When Dawn dismissed me, I gladly slipped away, returning to my room before Varick fetched one of the other girls. I felt torn apart. Like this was all some plan to rip into the last ounces of who I was and lay me bare for the Helsings. It made me hope they'd all bet on me, then I could kill myself just to spite them. But that went against my nature. Really what I wanted, was to survive the game then cut down every last one of the Helsings before sailing home to England and never looking back.

My options were limited. Like I was being squeezed through a tube of toothpaste, with only one possible way out. If I tried to leave, I'd die. If I refused to play, I'd die. The only way that equalled my survival was reaching the final checkpoint unharmed.

I screamed into my pillow – something I used to do to relieve my frustration when I heard my stepfather beating my mother. The memories fuelled me now. I'd been too young to do anything about her pain then. Now I was old enough and big enough to fight back, but my nemesis had grown too.

A knock came at my door and I looked up as Cass walked in. Blood was splattered across her arms and a dark look swam in her eyes. She didn't have to say anything, I simply lifted an arm and she joined me on the bed, hugging me close.

"I want them dead," she breathed and I knew she meant the Helsings.

I squeezed her tighter, knowing what she had just been through. "We cross the finish line, then we find a way to kill them."

"Promise?" she whispered.

"Promise."

◐ ☼ ◐

I gazed at myself in the full length mirror hanging on the wall. What would my school friends think of me now? So many of them judged me when I was arrested. I supposed I couldn't blame them. The press had torn me apart, painted me as some kind of manipulative witch. It didn't matter what I said after that. Mum had told me, *"People will believe what they want to believe."*

But why, after eighteen years of school and a handful of friends I'd known most of my life, did they *want* to believe that about me?

I laced up my boots, determination filling me. It didn't matter any more. The only way to prove who I really was, was to prove it to the whole god-damn world.

A knock came at the door and I found all five of the other girls standing there, dressed for the final round. Before I could say a word, they filed into my room, surrounding me.

"We've decided to team up," Cass announced and my brows lifted.

"We can all win if we stick together," Sakura said with a small smile.

Briony looked on at me hopefully.

"Are you in?" Kite demanded, folding her arms.

Angelina gazed out of the window, not seeming onboard with this idea in the slightest.

A grin broke across my features. "Of course."

Everyone visibly relaxed at my agreement and that seemed odd to me. Why wouldn't I want to team up? Surely that would give us all a better chance at surviving?

I had no time to question it, however, as Kite led the way out of the room toward the lounge.

As usual, Varick was waiting for us before the screen. It was strange to be sat around with so few of us for his presentation.

Before he said a word, he sighed, sinking down onto the edge of an armchair. "Look, I know you all hate me." I noted he included me in that scenario, though after last night I was fairly certain he knew that wasn't the case. "But I think this whole game is as screwed up as you do."

"Oh no, you're not growing a conscience are you?" Kite teased, smirking.

Varick threw her a smile that made my stomach tighten. "Apparently."

"And what are you going to do about it?" Cass demanded, narrowing her eyes at him.

"What would you like me to do? If I try to help you, we'll all die. If I try to take on the Helsings, they'll kill me, then kill all of you. So the only chance you have of walking off of this island, is surviving the game."

A tense silence filled the room as the truth settled over us. We had to finish this round. We had no choice.

"So how can we survive today?" I asked.

Varick seemed to be avoiding my eye as he stood, gesturing to the screen. A map illuminated across it in blue tones, pinpointing us at the cabin and, just under a mile away, the checkpoint.

Varick pointed to it. "Today's round will last four hours."

"That's it?" Brony gasped and he nodded firmly.

"You have one task." He tapped the red dot that marked the checkpoint. "Get to this tower and reach the top of it before the timer runs out."

"Let me guess, it won't be that easy?" Cass snipped.

Varick nodded, looking grim. "Not even a little."

"Great," Angelina sighed, her gaze focused on the window. I followed her line of sight toward the lapping sea. Perhaps she was trying to soak up one, final calm view before all hell broke loose.

"But if we get to the top, we can leave the island?" Sakura asked hopefully and everyone drew their attention to Varick, eager for his answer.

"Yes," he said, lifting his chin.

"Today?" Kite asked hopefully.

Varick's expression grew sour. "Not today. But soon."

"You swear it?" Cass snarled, thrusting out a hand to him. Hesitantly, he took it. "I swear."

"The word of a V's not much to go on," Angelina muttered.

"Why would he lie?" I snapped, my neck heating up irrationally.

Angelina turned to me, raising her brows with a I-know-you-have-a-thing-for-him expression. "Give over, Selena. Has he really got into your head that much?"

"He's telling the truth," I insisted.

"We're not leaving this island," she muttered and I stood up.

"Then stay here and wait for the capsule to blow in your head if you really believe that."

She pursed her lips, saying nothing.

"Are we quite done?" Varick stared me down until I dropped back into my seat, but there was a flash of admiration in his eyes too.

"So if we reach the top in time, we *all* get to go home?" Briony's small voice filled the room.

"Yes," Varick said in a softer tone. "Any number of you can reach the finish line. But only the first there will be crowned the winner."

"What difference does it make?" I asked and Varick's eyes swam with some emotion I couldn't place.

"It's just for the sake of the spectators," he muttered.

He turned to the trolley behind him, taking our stakes and passing them out, ending the conversation. No bags. I guessed we didn't need any supplies for the sake of four hours. But it would be strange travelling without one.

When we'd pulled on our cloaks, Varick led us onto the beach where the icy air caused goosebumps to rise on my skin. As we lined up in a row, I glanced back at him. Before I could think of anything to say - a goodbye or a thank you, perhaps - he mouthed something to me that made my blood run cold.

"Don't win."

Selena

The horn cried out across the island and I had no more time to think about Varick's warning as I started running. We remained as a pack, rushing along the pebbled beach and circling toward the next checkpoint. When we'd passed the booby-trapped beach we'd encountered yesterday, we turned inland, climbing up the pebbly ground and skirting the edge of the forest.

Heading north, we jogged on until we could avoid the woodland entirely. A silent agreement passed through us that no one wanted to return to the shadow of the trees.

The hill began to climb, higher and higher over rocky terrain. We were forced to slow down as the hem of our dresses continually snagged on the sharp stones.

Bending low, I took hold of my hem and ripped it half way up my calves. Nothing could slow me down today.

The other girls paused, mimicking me.

We stood in a circle, stakes in hand until everyone was ready to continue.

The soft braids that had been plaited into Angelina's hair were being tugged free by the wind. By the end of this round, I didn't expect any of us would look particularly beautiful.

"I look like a Disney Princess." Briony scowled, her thoughts following mine.

"You better show them how well Beauty can kick the Beast's ass then." Kite smirked, leading the way ahead.

We followed her up to a high ridge that overlooked the sweeping valley below.

I sucked in a breath.

At the centre of it was an enormous tower of black stone, reaching high into the sky. But that wasn't the most concerning thing. It was the hordes upon hordes of Vampires circling it, standing guard. There had to be fifty of them, if not more.

As one, we dropped to the ground, crawling closer to the edge to get a better look.

"Christ," Cass hissed. "How the hell are we going to get past them?"

"I guess we'll just have to run through," Briony breathed, her eyes rounding into saucers.

"Are you crazy?" Angelina spat. "We'll be killed in seconds."

"We need a distraction," I said, deep in thought. How were we going to shift fifty Vampires away from that tower?

A low growl made me spin around and I came eye to eye with the enormous black wolf that had saved us. Angelina let out half a scream before Kite slammed a hand over her mouth. The two of them scrambled backwards together, staring at the animal in fear.

Briony shifted forward with her stake in hand, but Cass, Sakura and I all grabbed her, yanking her back.

"He helped us before," Sakura explained in a whisper whilst

Briony trembled in her arms.

The wolf bowed its head before me and I tentatively reached out a hand. "Good...wolf," I said uncertainly, resting my hand on its head.

"Do you think he wants to help again?" Cass breathed.

"I don't know." I shrugged, unable to take my eyes off of the immense animal.

The wolf turned its head, licking my hand, then with a quick nip, drew blood on my palm. I gasped and Briony tried to lunge at it again.

"*Wait*," I demanded, gazing at the small cut on my hand. The wolf pushed its head into my palm, smearing the blood across its brow.

My mouth parted as I realised what he was doing. "He's going to draw them away."

Cass swiftly slit open her palm, brushing it across the wolf's ears. "Sure you can outrun them, boy?"

The wolf bared its teeth in answer and I prayed that meant yes.

Sakura helped, running her cut hand down the wolf's neck. "Why is it helping us?"

"Who cares?" Angelina hissed, rushing forward with a blood stained palm. The wolf snapped at her and she reared backwards, her skirt nearly flying over her head.

Cass snorted a laugh and I couldn't help but grin.

"He doesn't like you," Sakura whispered, rubbing the wolf's muzzle.

He dipped his head, and moved away, padding down the hill and circling toward the Vs. My heartbeat became rapid as I watched him approach the horde.

"He'll be okay, won't he?" I breathed.

Cass clamped her hand around mine, saying nothing.

My stomach churned as the wolf padded around the edge of the valley. The Vs began to shift, catching the scent of blood on the wind.

Sakura passed out strips of her purple dress to bind our hands until all three of us had matching bandages.

"Do you *trust* that wolf?" Briony asked in disbelief.

"He saved our lives," Cass said, her brows knitting together.

Angelina was muttering something to Kite that I couldn't hear. It made me uneasy. Neither of them were easily trusted. But Kite, at least, had helped me yesterday. So I had to believe she would keep her word on our truce.

A streak of lightning tore across the sky, followed swiftly by a crack of thunder. A storm was blowing in from the sea, meaning the moonlight we had to see by would soon be gone.

A howl sliced through the air, making my bones quiver. Everyone fell silent, waiting, watching as the Vs began to move. Not all of them, but many. Perhaps half, were rushing toward the trees in the direction the wolf had taken.

"It's now or never, girls." Kite stood, her mouth pulling up at the corner before she launched herself down the hill.

"See you at the tower," Briony called, charging after her, stake raised.

Angelina was holding back, but I didn't hesitate a second longer, running after the other girls, hearing Sakura and Cass following me closely.

My lungs ached from the freezing air, my hair dragged back behind me, and my jaw was set in a snarl as I tore toward the first line of Vs.

Cass was screaming her fury like she was charging into battle and Sakura was already swinging her stake, taking out the first Vs she collided with.

I got further than I expected as I met the throng. The Vampires were ravenous, wheeling around, desperate for blood. But in their frenzied, starving state, they were making mistakes. Claws slashed over my head and I reared upwards, bringing my stake up with force. The second the tip hit its target, I wrenched it back, wheeling around and piercing the heart of another oncoming bloodsucker. Another one crumpled to the floor, practically nothing but bones.

Through the crush of bodies, I spotted a huge figure with silver streaks burnt into his cheeks: Iskender.

My heart lurched into my throat as he spotted me. Somehow, he'd survived a stake to the back of his head. And there was vengeance in his silver-flecked eyes as he locked his gaze on me.

I started moving, ducking and darting past the weaker Vs, dispatching any I could. I fixed my gaze on the tower, now only twenty metres ahead. Nails tore at my dress, my arms, my neck, but I kept moving. Screaming my desperation, I threw myself at the final two Vs blocking my way, breaching the line.

In my momentum, I stumbled to the ground, the material of my dress bunching up around me. I rolled onto my back, desperate to get up as a hungry V launched at me. Before he could reach me, Iskender caught him by the neck and threw him aside with a cracking of bone.

I gasped, crawling backwards, trying to get up but losing my balance in the mud.

Iskender fell on top of me and the weight of him had to equal a horse. The breath in my lungs squeezed out of me in a splutter. His hands curled around my throat, twisting my neck to the side until I was sure it was going to snap. Then he lowered his mouth to my ear and whispered. "For Melinda..."

His fangs ripped into my neck and I screamed, battling him with all my might. It was no good, my arms flailed uselessly beside me; I couldn't even bend them from the way he held me. I was pinned, completely at his mercy as he flexed me like a doll to gain further access to my neck.

Snapping teeth and a sudden blur of fur announced the wolf's arrival. His jaws clamped around Iskender's entire head as he dragged him backwards.

Sakura was there, her purple and pink locks streaming about her in the wind. Her stake was clutched in her hand, her features set into a snarl worthy of the wolf's. As the animal dragged Iskender backwards, Sakura stabbed his chest with a roar of defiance.

Iskender reached for her with taloned nails, slashing her across the belly as he died. She gasped out, hugging the bleeding gashes on her stomach, dropping to her knees.

Two Vs darted toward her, drawn by the blood. Struggling to my feet, I half-crawled, half ran toward her. She'd saved me and there was no way I could leave her behind.

A V descended on her, but before he could even touch her, I lashed out, killing it with a twist of my stake under its ribs.

The second V was more cautious, circling us, her bloodshot, yellowish eyes trained on Sakura. She launched toward her and I put myself between them, taking the full weight of her and dropping on top of Sakura so the three of us were trapped in a tangle of limbs. Teeth snapped close to my ear and I jerked in fright, trying to escape the scrabbling arms and sharp nails that were trying to tear us apart.

Lifting my knee, I kicked upwards as hard as I could. She flew backwards and I launched after her, ramming the stake into her heart. Thick, blackish blood slid down my arm as she fell atop me, dead.

Sakura was still beneath me, crushed, probably unable to move. I rolled away, crawling toward her in the mud and lifting my bloodied stake to her mouth. With a jolt of horror, I found her two-toned eyes gazing glassily back at me.

"*No*," I murmured, pressing the blood to her mouth. She just needed to drink. That was all. Then she'd wake up.

When she didn't move, I hoisted her arms over mine, dragging her towards the tower. The wolf was in a vicious fight with the nearby Vs, keeping their attention diverted from me as I moved.

Angelina appeared, wrenching open a metal door in the wall. Her dress was in tatters, her back riddled with claw marks. As she darted inside, I collided with the door. She was tugging it closed, making my heart stumble.

"Open it!" I screamed and the door released.

I crashed inside with Sakura's limp body weighing down my legs, shutting it behind us with a deafening clang. We were in a stairwell; the walls and floor were white-wash and clean; a stark contrast to our previous surroundings.

Angelina leant back on a metal stair railing, panting heavily.

"You tried to shut us out!" I accused and Angelina shook her head.

"I thought you were a V."

"Liar," I snarled, turning back to Sakura. I checked her pulse and firmly shook her shoulders.

"Wake up, you have a boyfriend to get home to," I whispered, dripping more of the blood into her mouth. Her stomach was torn badly, her dress ripped to shreds around her belly button. She wasn't healing. And the longer I waited, the quicker my hope faded.

"What happened to the others?" I turned to face Angelina with a heavy heart.

"There are other doors," Angelina said through ragged breaths.

"I saw Cassandra go through one."

I sagged with relief, glad at least that Cass was safe.

"Is she dead?" Angelina gestured to Sakura with her chin.

I glowered at her, not wanting to confirm it. Her tone was so cold, so uncaring. She was the last person on earth I wanted to be stuck with now.

"We should move," she said, checking her cuff for the time and preparing to head upstairs. Surprisingly, she waited for me to join her.

With my heart weighing in my chest, I left Sakura propped up next to the door, having done my best to cover the bloody wounds across her stomach. It hadn't done much good. She looked like a broken doll, her head lolling against her chest and her skin deathly pale. An ache grew in me as I left her behind. Would I soon be like her? Adding to the Helsings' death toll?

If I ever got out of this place, I made a mental note to find out how many lives had been taken here. It seemed important now. Like every corner we turned held some ancient death. Someone's daughter, whose parents had never found out the truth about them. Perhaps even been Charmed into forgetting them altogether. It wasn't right that these women were never mourned. The Helsings had already stolen so much from us.

If I died now, would my mother continue to believe I'd been killed in some prison brawl? Would she blame herself? That's what my mum did, always shouldering everyone else's misgivings. As if she were somehow responsible for the cruel actions of other people.

It had been impossible to bear during the trial. She'd blamed herself for all of it. Went over and over all the 'what ifs' and the 'if only I'd done that's'. But I couldn't change the past. And there was no point talking myself in circles. It would drive anyone mad. I'd made my decisions and she'd made hers; all we could do was find a way to live with them.

As I climbed the staircase, the lights on the ceiling were so glaring that I felt I was under scrutiny. Which of course, I was. I was the centre of an entertainment show for a group of men who had nothing better to do with their money than to fund some illegal bloodsport. I'd envied the rich growing up, of their nice things, their easy lives. But now I despised them for it. Money bred power and power bred evil. Nothing was ever enough. And even if they'd burned the entire world down for their own entertainment, no happiness awaited them. Only a pit that could never be filled.

On the next level, we found a single, metal door that slid to the left, offering us access. Angelina headed through it, taking a defensive stance as she tiptoed into the room.

The second I followed, the door slid shut behind me, trapping us. Light flooded the space, the walls themselves seeming aglow; it took a moment for my eyes to adjust.

A door on the other side of the room opened and Cass, Briony and Kite appeared, rushing inside. They were splattered with blood and Kite's dress looked like it had been nearly torn from her shoulders.

I rushed to meet them, embracing Cass.

"Where's Sakura?" Cass asked, glancing over my shoulder.

I shook my head in answer and the light in her eyes extinguished.

"Oh," she sighed and I squeezed her arm.

On either side of us, four white doors slid open in the walls. Eight Vampires launched at us; weak, bedraggled, but moving at speed from all sides. Metal plates had been welded to their bodies, covering their chests and necks. My heart span in my chest. It would be impossible to land a killing blow.

Everyone prepared to defend themselves, but the Vs were suddenly yanked backwards by silver chains around their necks, stalling them a few feet from us.

"Congratulations girls," a deep male voice sounded through the room. I recognised Abraham Helsing's voice with a sick feeling in my stomach. "The five of you have made it to level one of the tower."

We shuffled closer together, keeping our distance from the snarling Vs that surrounded us.

The white walls morphed into screens, and suddenly we were surrounded by all five of our video profiles, evidently put together by Dawn. Vs were rushing toward us in the recordings, and there was Varick, moving to save me. My cheeks prickled with heat as eyes swivelled toward me.

The other girls cut down their Vs mercilessly. There was no

remorse for the starved Vampires, only hate. And something about that didn't sit right with me.

The screens faded and the walls returned to their stark white colour.

"Answer this simple question and I shall let you pass to the next room," Abraham said and we waited for him to continue.

My gaze was continually drawn to the Vs, snapping and snarling, their hands reaching toward us with desperation. I tried not to panic, keeping my fear under control. But it was impossible.

"Which of you murdered the most people before you were sent to prison?"

Silence.

My heart rushed into top gear as I gazed around at everyone.

Kite lifted her chin. "It's got to be me."

"Are you sure?" I asked, not wanting to find out what would happen if we got the answer wrong.

"I'm not even sure how many it is," Kite said like she was proud.

"Okay, go ahead," Cass encouraged, gripping the stake firmer in her hand.

"Me," Kite said to the ceiling.

After a moment, Abraham's voice filled the room in a sharp tone, "Incorrect."

With a rattling of metal, the Vs surrounding us were given an extra foot of chain.

Briony squeaked in alarm, pressing against me as the Vs shot toward us, yanked back just in time.

I took a few, slow breaths to calm down.

Kite snapped around, glaring at us. "Who is it then?" She scowled at Angelina. "You said you only killed five."

"I did!" Angelina insisted.

"What about you?" Kite marched toward Briony.

"Just one!" she said and Kite's eyes slid to me.

"One," I announced and with a pang of dread, I realised who it was. All eyes slid to Cass and her face drained of colour. Perhaps she had never seen what she'd done as murder. But now she was. All those people who had died in the fire. How many could it have been?

I rested a hand on her arm, nodding my encouragement.

"Me," she sighed.

Abraham's voice filled the room. "Correct."

A hatch in the roof fell open, but there was no way we could reach it without helping each other up to it.

Abraham continued, "The number of people Cassandra killed will equal the amount of seconds you have before the Vs are released."

A red number 43 flared up on all the walls, immediately starting to run down. I had no time to process it as we smashed into each other, everyone desperate to be the first into the hatch.

We'd already wasted ten seconds when I shouted, "Stop!"

The clinking of metal drew my attention for half a second and

I realised the Vs' chains were growing longer.

I held out my hands, locking my fingers together. "Angelina, help me," I demanded. Of all the girls I didn't want up there before me, it was her. I didn't trust her one bit not to run off the second she was out.

"Cass first," I demanded as Angelina begrudgingly locked her fingers with mine. The one person I could count on pulling me up, was Cass.

"This isn't fair," Angelina muttered.

"We don't have time for fair!" Kite barked, helping Cass up onto our hands. The press of her boots weighed down our arms but after a beat, she dragged herself into the hatch. Turning, she immediately reached down to help the next person. Kite followed her, scrambling up with ease, before the two of them helped Briony into the hole.

"Me next,"Angelina demanded, unlocking her hands from mine.

I noted the timer on the wall. Ten seconds.

"Just go then!" I snapped and she reached up, taking hold of the girls' hands above. I readied my stake, pressing closer to Angelina as she kicked her legs, trying to get up. The Vs were just a foot away, their gnashing teeth making me feel ill.

Five seconds.

"Go!" I screamed at Angelina, allowing her to use my shoulder for purchase. With a harsh kick, she launched up into the room above.

Cass practically hung out of the hatch to reach me. I tucked my stake away and leapt into the air, taking hold of her arms.

The timer ran out and the white walls turned red.

I screamed, kicking my legs as the Vs smashed together around me. Claws snagged at my dress as Cass heaved and heaved. Miraculously, I lifted from the room, kicking sharply at the Vs below and connecting with some of their heads.

Several pairs of hands dragged me into the pitch black space above and I lay panting, my entire body trembling.

Lights flared to life around us, illuminating the enormous glass tank we were inside. Below us, the Vs were visible, their arms raised as they spotted us above.

I clambered to my feet, the glass floor making me queasy.

Abraham's voice greeted us again. "To ascend to level three you must answer this simple question."

We waited, clustering closer together.

"How many Vs have the five of you collectively killed during the game?"

A hush fell over us as we turned to each other, trying to mentally count our kills. I reached eight, but my mind was fuzzy. *It had to be more than eight.*

The game was a blur, all the Vs' deaths merging into one.

"I think I killed twelve," Briony said, which I was surprised by. She didn't seem as confident in killing as some of the others. But I saw the truth in her eyes.

"Eighteen," Kite said proudly.

Cass looked torn, frowning at me as she tried to work it out. "Eleven maybe."

"Nine," I said uncertainly.

Angelina nervously rung her hands together. "Three," she breathed.

"Fifty three," Cass announced to the room with a shrug.

Abraham's voice cut through the muffled air. "Incorrect."

Two enormous pipes were attached high up on the glass walls and, at his word, water poured into the tank in torrents. With a loud clank, one of the glass panels beneath our feet fell away, opening a small gap in it, falling into the crowd of hungry Vs below. Briony was closest to the fallen pane and lurched toward us. We gathered together, my heart beginning to beat an erratic tune.

"Count again," Kite snapped as water sloshed over our feet, rushing so fast that the tank began to fill up, despite the hole in the floor.

I shut my eyes, thinking, trying to keep my breathing steady. But all I could concentrate on was the rising water, already halfway up my calves. It was icily cold, seeping into my boots and freezing my toes.

"Ten?" I guessed, shaking my head.

Kite and Angelina stuck with their answers but Briony and Cass tried again.

"Thirteen," Briony said with a look of fear in her eyes.

"Twelve," Cass said with a shrug.

"Fifty six!" Angelina called to the ceiling, looking panicked as the water rose to our knees.

"Incorrect."

Another panel dropped away in the floor and I lurched aside. My foot had been right on the edge of it. The water poured in quicker and I gasped as it splashed over my midriff. The Vs in the room below us were getting soaked as water streamed through the holes in the glass floor.

"Come on!" Angelina screamed at us. "Get it right!"

I shook my head in dismay. I simply didn't know. I couldn't think straight under this pressure.

"Fifty seven!" Angelina cried in desperation.

"Incorrect."

Another panel fell away and the water rushed in harder through the pipes.

"Fifty nine!" Angelina shouted again and Kite lunged at her, smacking her across the face.

"Incorrect."

"Shut up!" Kite snarled at her.

The water started dragging us down, pulling us toward the empty holes in the floor.

"Think again," Cass begged us all. "Try and remember."

All I could see was a hundred different Vs, running at me, biting me. Blood, pain, teeth.

I shook my head, starting to panic.

"We have to guess!" Angelina screamed and Briony suddenly

sided with her.

"She's right." Her cheeks were pale as the water rose to our shoulders.

We had to tread water, trying to keep afloat as the holes beneath us sucked at our legs.

"Fifty two!" Briony shouted and Kite splashed toward her, trying to fight her.

"You're going to get us killed!" Kite barked.

"Incorrect."

The water rose so high that we had to swim. Angelina started screaming.

"I can't swim!" she flailed in the water and I moved toward her, scooping an arm under her shoulders.

"Just kick with your legs," I demanded and her soft blue eyes met mine. I flitter of vulnerability passed through them as she nodded, doing as I said.

The water rose dramatically until the tank was nearly full. I kicked up with all my might, keeping Angelina at my side, our heads dunking under again and again.

A metre of air was all we had left.

"Fifty one!" Cass shouted, seeing as no one seemed to have the right answer.

Kite didn't fight her this time, looking panicked as the water rose and she pressed a hand to the glass roof.

We had only a few seconds of air remaining, then we wouldn't be able to give an answer.

A clamour of noise rose as everyone started shouting answers and Abraham's repetitive tone followed again and again.

"Incorrect, incorrect, incorrect."

I felt the drag of the holes below us, like a giant plug, tugging us into the vacuum. Just an inch of air was left, our mouths gasping, nearly pressing to the glass ceiling.

"Sixty," I breathed as the water filled the space.

Silence prevailed as I sank under, having been so panicked that I'd forgotten to drag down one final breath.

Below me was turmoil, the water rushing through the open panels in the floor, so many of them, causing whirlpools, sucking us down.

I lost my grip on Angelina and her arms waved madly as she tried to hold on. A whirlpool took hold of her and she span like a rag doll in it, dragged down, down, down.

I wanted to scream, to cry out. I kicked my legs, reaching for her, but it was too late. Her body slipped through the hole.

Through the remaining glass floor, I watched her fall.

All eight of the Vs were loose, waiting for her. Her body writhed as she hit them, dropping to the ground, gazing up at us as we hung suspended above her in the tank.

The Vs fell on top of her and with a twist of my gut, I knew she was lost.

Suddenly, hands were on my back, pulling me up, heaving me out of the water. Cass lay me down atop the glass ceiling. A panel had opened in the roof, incredibly, freeing us.

Cass hugged me tight, her body shuddering. Briony and Kite sat nearby, their faces ashen and their eyes haunted. We were dripping from head to toe and the weight of my dress was tenfold as I rose to my feet. Evidently, my final guess had been correct.

"She got what she deserved," Kite muttered, leading the way ahead toward a frosted glass door.

"And what do *you* deserve Kite?" Briony snapped.

Kite shrugged as the door slid aside and we hurried after her. My hands wouldn't stop shaking, my heart was on overdrive, pumping blood through my veins as hard as it could. I hadn't liked Angelina much, but she'd been scared, just like the rest of us.

I had no time to process her death as we entered a brightly lit, square room. Footage burst onto the walls, encompassing everything we could see. Clips from the game played all around us, showing us running, hiding in caves, taking down Vs, looking fiercer than I ever could have imagined.

Abraham spoke, calm and collected, as if he hadn't just watched one of us die. "You have all done things to survive. But who has kept their humanity? Who deserves to survive the game?"

His question hung in the air as the footage changed. I watched as Kite threw Tiffany to the V that had attacked us on the very first day. A shot of Cass played, staying hidden whilst two girls were taken down by a group of bloodthirsty Vs. Briony fleeing with Marie, away from a girl who'd been badly bitten, lying in a writhing heap on the forest floor. Then there was me, stabbing

Marie in the belly, her eyes going wide in recognition.

The screens faded to white and a tense silence crept into the room. I felt Briony's eyes on me, but refused to meet her gaze, guilt washing through me.

Abraham spoke, saving us from doing so. "Only three will leave this room. You will decide who stays."

I sucked in a breath, gazing around at the group. We were being pitted against each other like dogs.

Briony launched at me, shoving me hard. "You killed her!"

"I didn't know!" I begged. "It was the mist. I didn't know it was her."

"Liar," she sobbed, tears streaming down her cheeks.

Cass tore her away from me, putting herself between us. "Stop fighting. That's what they want."

Kite was on the other side of the room, flipping the stake in her hand. "Selena killed one of us."

"So did you!" Cass barked and Kite shrugged.

"We've all done bad things," I tried, searching Briony's eyes for forgiveness but there was none there.

"Selena stays," Briony snarled and my heart flipped over.

"Wait – no," I tried but Kite rounded on her.

"Or why don't *you* stay Briony? Go be with your little friend."

Briony's eyebrows lifted dramatically. "You can't be serious, I never hurt anybody!"

"But you didn't *help* anybody either," Kite said with a shrug. "Why should you get to leave this room?"

Before she could answer, Cass spoke up. "We should draw straws. None of us are innocent."

Slowly, we agreed and Cass tore strips off her sodden dress, ripping them into different lengths. When she was done, she turned her back, clamping them in her fist before facing us once more.

She offered her fist to me first and I pulled one from her grip. It wasn't too long, but perhaps long enough to survive. I tried not to pay attention to the death stare Briony was giving me, guilt already tearing at my insides.

Briony went next, taking a longer strip than me and she finally relaxed.

Kite pulled out a short one and her mouth fell into a thin line.

Cass opened her palm and the longest one remained inside it.

"That's it then, decision made," Cass muttered and Kite glared at her, the small strip in her hand clamped so tightly in her fist that her knuckles were turning white.

My stomach flipped over as I gazed at Kite. It wasn't right to do this. How could we simply leave her here to die? After everything she'd been through?

Cass pushed me toward the door on the opposite side of the room, not giving me a moment to hesitate. As we reached it, an ear-splitting scream cut through the air.

I span around, my heart in my throat as I spotted Briony on the floor, a pool of blood forming around her. Kite's stake was buried in her chest, a sneer turning up her lips.

"Bitch!" Briony spat, trying to fight back, but it was clear she was already weakening.

"How could you?" I roared, launching myself at Kite. She shoved me back, but I smacked her hands away, tearing at her dress.

"Did you really expect me to roll over?" Kite snarled. "To give in after everything I've been through to get here?"

Briony slumped backwards and I clambered over Kite, cupping Briony's cheek in my hand.

"I'm so sorry," I breathed as the light in her eyes dimmed to nothing.

I didn't know if she forgave me, but my heart told me she didn't and that was a bitter pill to swallow.

Tears dripped down my cheeks, pooling in the crevice of her neck.

A hand clamped around my arm, pulling me backwards.

I moved into Cass's embrace as she led me from the room. Kite was already standing beyond the door. We were in a small, four by four space and, as the door slid quietly shut behind us and Briony's body was forever concealed, I realised we were in a lift.

It sailed smoothly upwards and the tug of gravity made my stomach lurch uncomfortably.

"I'm not dying in this place," Kite said quietly, wiping the blood off her stake onto her dress.

In a way, I understood. None of us owed any allegiance to one another. And I wanted to survive as much as she did. But would I have done something so terrible if I'd pulled the short straw?

I prayed not.

Selena

The lift slowed to a halt and the door opened, revealing a wide corridor running away from us.

"Perhaps this is it," Cass murmured, evidently trying to move on from the horrors we'd just witnessed. "Maybe this is the end."

Behind us, another door at the back of the lift slid open. Ten haggard Vs stood there, their eyes flashing with murder as they spotted us.

"Run!" I roared, fleeing down the corridor ahead. Kite and Cass were close on my heels, but so were the Vs.

The passage veered to the right; a staircase was the only way forward. We started sprinting upwards, higher and higher until my calves ached and my lungs burned.

Cass outpaced me, flying up the stairs two at a time with her longer legs.

A scream from behind caused me to turn back. A snarling V had hold of Kite's hair, dragging her into his arms. I kicked out at it, yanking her forward as my boot smashed into his face.

We ran on, her hand still clinging to mine as we rose, higher and higher up the seemingly endless flights of stairs. I knew I couldn't keep this pace up much longer. But if I stopped for even a second, I was dead.

To my left, a door flew open and a well-fed V charged at me. Kite shoved me aside at the last second, taking the blow herself. She twisted her stake up, slicing it through him, but his teeth had already sunk deep into her neck.

I dragged her free of him, encouraging her on, the V's body causing an obstacle for the others as they tried to pursue us.

"Now we're even," she panted, but I couldn't manage an answer.

Blood dripped in a thick stream to the floor and Kite groaned as we soldiered on, licking her stake as she climbed at my side.

We caught up with Cass who looked exhausted, her feet dragging as she slowed to match our pace.

The screeches and high-pitched cries of the Vs closed in. I was breathless and aching all over.

Finally, the stairs led to another corridor and we flew down it at high speed, the level ground a reprieve from the hellish climb. The Vs had caught up, running just behind us, their fingers clutching at the ends of my hair.

I barged through the door at the other end and nearly lost my footing on the vertical drop immediately before me; we were outside edge of the tower, the island stretching out ahead of us. Kite pushed me aside in seconds, the two of us tumbling onto a platform beside the exit, just wide enough to stand on. Cass hadn't been so lucky, falling forward and catching herself on the edge, dropping her stake as she hung from it with white-knuckled fingers.

I reached for her in desperation as Vs poured out of the door, falling with twisting, writhing bodies as they plummeted toward their deaths.

Kite clung to my side, blocking my path to Cass.

"Help me!" I begged, trying to reach her scrabbling fingers.

A buzz of a helicopter hummed in my ears and the huge machine swooped past us; the rush of wind that followed it nearly dragged us off the ledge. Kite screamed profanities at it that would have shocked me under any other circumstances.

It circled around, hovering several feet from us, the side door open and waiting for us.

As the last of the Vs fell the hundred feet to the ground, Kite slipped back into the doorway, ducking down and grabbing hold of Cass.

I crashed to my knees, crawling back inside, my cloak whipping around me in the wind. Together, Kite and I managed to drag Cass inside. Her back was clawed with marks from the Vs that had fallen, trying to save themselves. Her cheeks were pink from the wind and her lips were trembling.

"We have to jump," Kite said, gesturing to the helicopter before us.

Terror ripped through me. "Are you kidding?"

"Go, you can do it," Cass panted, catching her breath as she huddled in the wind-swept corridor.

Kite stood, pulling me after her. I glanced at the helicopter with a sick feeling in the pit of my stomach.

Kite turned to me, tonguing her cheek. "Always kind of admired you, Grey." She grabbed my head and pressed her lips to my mouth. I was so stunned, I simply froze in her hold.

Pulling away, she shot me a grin, then dove toward the helicopter.

Time seemed to slow as I watched, my heart nearly failing as she sailed through the air. Her arms were outstretched, her fingers reaching, her dark hair sailing about her in the wind. She looked like a hero, diving through the sky. And though I knew she wasn't a good person, in a way I admired her too.

Her fingers grazed the metal railing beneath the door. And with a horrible, gut-wrenching certainty, I knew she'd misjudged the jump.

Her fingers brushed the metal, then she was falling, rushing toward the ground. A scream tore from her lungs and I called out her name, clinging to the edge of the doorway.

She hit the ground, looking like a fallen angel amongst the broken Vampires around her.

I gasped, unable to drag down enough air. I couldn't breathe. I was frozen by fear, gazing at the way ahead and knowing I wasn't strong enough to go on. I stumbled backwards, my legs hitting Cass. She gazed somberly up at me and I dropped to my knees, taking her hand.

"We can do it together."

"Can't do it, Selena." She knocked her head back against the wall and that's when I noticed how damaged her legs were. A V had surely hung from them, tearing her skin to shreds.

I started shaking my head and tears pooled in my eyes. "You can do it. You just have to jump." I lifted my stake in the hopes of finding V blood, but it had been washed clean in the water tank and I hadn't used it since.

Cass tapped her cuff and two minutes illuminated on the timer. "No. *You* have to jump."

I started sobbing, hugging her to me, refusing to go on without her.

"Selena, you have to go." She pushed me back, acceptance in her eyes. "I don't deserve to win this thing," she breathed. "All those people..." She grimaced, the guilt in her expression tearing at my insides.

"You didn't mean to do it!" I cried, clutching her icy fingers and trying to pull her up.

"I lit the match," she whispered.

"Please," I begged. "All you have to do is jump."

She shook her head, a tear sailing down her cheek. "You've got to make it home." She lifted the cuff higher.

Thirty seconds.

Our cuffs started flashing red, warning us that the capsules in our heads would go off if we ran out of time.

"Selena," she said firmly, clasping my neck, her emerald eyes blazing at me. "Make sure they pay."

I nodded, sucking in a breath as I found something to hold onto: revenge. For her, for Kite, all of them.

I nodded and she pushed me up, squeezing my hands one last time.

I turned, a breath rattling around my lungs as I faced the helicopter.

"Go!" she commanded and I forced my legs to move, running flat out toward the edge. I screamed my defiance as my boots hit the edge and I launched myself into the air.

The wind pulled tears from my eyes as I flew toward the helicopter. My muscles flexed as I reached with desperation, the image of Kite falling running through my mind over and over and over.

The timer hit two seconds just as I collided with the metal floor of the helicopter. I skidded forward, crashing into a row of seats.

The helicopter pulled up and I turned back to Cass, her body slumped in the dark, rectangular hole in the side of the tower.

As the timer hit zero, her head dropped forward and my heart split in two.

"Cass!" I screamed, my voice breaking. I huddled on the floor, shivering in my damp dress, wishing this helicopter would fly me all the way home. So I'd never have to face the monsters that did this to me. Part of me had hoped Varick would be here to greet me like all the other times. But I was alone. Entirely alone. A flame was snuffed out inside me as I considered the possibility that Varick had been executed by the Helsings for helping me.

As the helicopter sailed over the island, a sound caught my ear:

a wolf howling, the haunting note somehow comforting me in my moment of anguish.

The castle came into view on the horizon, just a hulking shadow on the cliff edge. My hands curled into fists as the helicopter circled the enormous building, flying past its four immense towers, one on each corner. At the heart of it, a flat roof awaited us and the helicopter lowered, swaying left and right as it came in to land.

With a soft jolt, we touched down. But I didn't move. I remained huddled on the floor, not wanting to face anyone. Unable to drag myself out of the dark place my mind was retreating to.

"Selena?" a deep voice called to me, but I didn't move. Incredibly, Varick was here. Alive. But even he wasn't enough to take away this pain.

"She's going into shock," a woman said, then a needle was digging into my leg.

I barely fought it, the sting hardly registering with me. Whatever I'd been injected with provided peace. And I slipped away into numbness, where nothing but darkness awaited me.

Varick

The moment Selena jumped, everything changed.

The auditorium was a raucous of cheering and all the while I stood, silently watching, praying she'd make it. I'd hoped that Kite would make it too, that she would reach the finish line before Selena. Because what awaited her now as the winner of the game, didn't bear thinking about.

Mercy had tried to corner me more than once, but if she was planning on giving me up to her father, she didn't yet show it. Which meant I had a little more time. And I was going to use it wisely.

When Selena was brought inside, forced into a coma and taken for medical attention, I knew I had to face Mercy at last.

Returning from the helipad, I found her in the auditorium, plucked her from a group of men and led her into the corridor.

She delivered me a dark scowl.

"You promised me you'd kill her," she hissed.

"Yeah, about that-" I slammed my hand against her throat, thrusting her back against the wall.

She gasped, clawing at my arm to try and escape.

"You tell your father that I helped her, and I'll tell him you have a thing for Vampires." I released my grip on her throat so she could answer and she spluttered, "He'll never believe you."

I smashed her back against the wall. "Want a bet?" I snarled, willing to gamble my life on this. "I'll Charm every man I can, force them into thinking they saw us together. I'll plant my memories in their heads. Show them you had your hands all over me. Which isn't untrue, is it Mercy?"

She gasped, shaking her head. "You wouldn't."

I released her throat and she sagged forward, coughing.

I waited for her to recompose herself and she stood up straighter, her brow furrowing. "Fine, I won't tell," she sighed.

I nodded, turning from her but she caught my wrist. I glanced back and her expression became vulnerable. "So you never liked me?"

I shook her off, grimacing. "You repulse me." I marched away, hoping she'd keep her word. I didn't much care at that moment, forcing Mercy to the back of my mind as I headed in the direction of Selena.

I descended to the dungeons which the Helsings had converted into a high-tech prison, capable of holding Vampires. A low blue light illuminated the long corridors, each filled with rows of cells. Silver bars kept the Vs in individual pens, above which were sunlamps, capable of roasting a V alive if they stepped a toe out of line. A memory crawled over me as I recalled being held here myself.

Personnel were rushing around as Vs were rounded up from the island, ushered into their cages. I grimaced as I paced past them, keeping my attention on Selena.

As I approached the final cells, I spotted Ignus there with Ulvic, prodding something in a cage. The black wolf from the island became visible behind the iron bars. Ulvic pressed a needle into its neck before two men heaved it into one of the V chambers. Exiting the cell, they released the hatch on its cage with a long pole.

The wolf launched at the bars, the silver doing nothing to it as it snapped its jaws around it, saliva flying everywhere.

"Why isn't it working?" Ignus demanded, rounding on Ulvic.

"Give it a minute," he insisted, folding his arms.

I moved past them, going unnoticed as I slipped toward the science labs. Ignus conducted all manner of horrors in these laboratories. It wasn't a place I liked to spend time, but Selena had been taken here for medical attention. And nothing would stop me from seeing her now.

I knocked on the door of the room she was being held in, hearing the comforting sound of her heartbeat in my ears. A nurse was with her and I backed up as the woman marched from the room.

"She's not awake yet," she told me, adjusting the collar on her white overcoat.

"How much longer?" I demanded.

"I'm just about to remove the capsule from her neck, then I'll wake her up." She rounded on me, her eyes flicking up and down. No one in the dungeons feared me. They dealt with Vs on a daily basis; this woman had probably done unspeakable things to them.

"As you're here, you might as well donate some blood for the healing process."

I ripped back my sleeve as she produced a vial. She moved toward me with a needle – silver tipped so it could penetrate my skin – but instead of letting the repellent woman touch me, I ripped open my wrist with my teeth. The blood dripped into the vial and she left me to it, returning to the room.

My skin healed over before the vial was filled and I had to slit it open twice more to finish the job.

The nurse – if you could call her that – returned for the blood and I tried to follow her into the room, but she slammed the door in my face.

I snarled, my patience wearing thin. I started pacing outside the room, grinding my jaw, growing desperate to see her.

I was filled with purpose for the first time in hundreds of years. My life had meaning again. And Selena was at the root of it all. Why the girl affected me so much, I had no clue. But I was fixated, in awe of her and all that she'd done. Did she have any idea how implausible it was that she was still here? Having passed more trials than any person should in their life.

The fact that I'd kissed her continued to play on my mind. I hadn't felt desire for a girl since I'd been changed. I didn't know it was possible. But even if I were blind, I couldn't miss the light of her. She shone with the power of a thousand suns, brightening the shadowy corners of my black heart, perhaps even enough to return to me the ability to love.

The door opened and my heart stopped.

"You can go in now," the nurse said, stepping aside.

Suddenly I was rooted to the spot. Would Selena even want to see me? After everything that had happened to her, what if she blamed me now? And why wouldn't she? I'd had a hand in all of the pain she'd been through. I'd been there every step of the way, giving her directions, weapons, maps.

My heart seemed to freeze over.

"Varick?" the nurse prompted and I crept toward the doorway.

I decided then, even if she despised me, I had to see her.

One last time.

Selena

My eyes flickered open and all I saw were white walls and glaring lights. I jerked upwards, thinking of the tower, terrified that I was still there.

In a wave, I realised I must be at the castle. My body was warm and every part of me felt healed. I gazed down at myself, finding I'd been dressed in a long gown of golden silk, the bodice made of cream lace that wound down my arms.

I swung my legs around, dropping off of the hospital bed, my bare feet colliding with cold tiles.

The door opened and I lunged for a syringe beside my bed, spinning around to face whoever entered. If it was a Helsing, I wouldn't hold back.

I came face to face with Varick, looking out of place in a deep, ebony suit. A choked noise escaped my throat, overwhelmed by him being here. That he was still alive. That there was still someone I cared about on this island.

His eyes caught mine and I dropped the syringe, grief flooding me.

I flung myself at him, knowing he was the only person left who could possibly offer me any comfort. Who knew what I'd been through, what I'd seen.

He crushed me into his chest and I let myself come undone, sobbing into his soft shirt.

"I'm sorry," he muttered into my hair.

I gripped him tighter, never wanting to leave his firm embrace. Not wanting to face anyone but him.

"Can I go home now?" I asked in a broken voice. I'd come apart, desperate for reassurance like a small child. The game had unravelled me.

"Not yet, but soon. I promise." His deep voice rumbled through his chest, the vibrations thrumming in my ears.

I released him at last, dipping my head self-consciously. "Sorry I-"

He cut me off. "You've been through hell and back, Selena. If you weren't upset, I'd be concerned."

I nodded, lifting my eyes to meet his. They blazed with admiration. I hated to be looked at that way. As if I'd achieved something great, when all I'd done was cling to life while others had lost theirs.

"Cass..." I breathed and Varick cupped my cheek. His palm was cool, cooler than it had been last night when he'd kissed me. It seemed like a strange dream, a small pocket of calm in an endless storm.

"She wanted you to live," he said quietly and I felt my legs become weak. I wanted to curl up on the bed and hide beneath the sheets. But I had to get out of this place. This nightmare wasn't over yet.

"Selena," Varick sighed, stepping toward the door. "The Helsings are waiting for you. They'd like you to attend a ceremony tonight, held in your honour." His upper lip curled into a sneer, and I knew he had no part in this.

My insides seemed to shrink and I started shaking my head.

Before I could object, Varick muttered, "It isn't optional."

I managed a dry laugh, nodding. "What happens now? After this *ceremony?*" I spat the word.

"It will all be explained tonight." He seemed conflicted, his brow growing taut as if he wanted to tell me more.

"You'll stay with me?" I asked, hopeful.

His expression softened. "Of course."

High heels were laid out for me by the door, six inches, encrusted with jewels. I turned my nose up at them, figuring I'd rather not lose the capability of running in this place and headed through the door.

Varick followed me, taking my arm. His cool fingers halted me and I turned, raising a brow.

"I won't let anything else happen to you," he swore, his grip on me tightening. "I should have got you out sooner."

My heart ached at his words and I placed my hand on his. "Then we would already be dead."

"Selena-" he started, then sighed, unable to find the words he was searching for.

We headed on, entering a wide corridor of cells. The Vampires inside them recognised me and many spat and cursed my name.

Varick was practically snarling by the time we found our way out, heading upstairs into the grand hallways of the castle. He was acting like my bodyguard, shadowing my every move.

Music reached to me from two large oak doors up ahead, some strange electronica that tapped and clunked in my ears.

The flagstones were icy against my bare feet, but I wasn't sure I could ever feel the cold again in the same way. The biting, icy winds on the island would forever remind me what true cold felt like.

Varick held the door handle – a black iron ring, one of a pair – and fixed me with a dark stare.

"Whatever happens in there, remember I'm on your side."

I gave a small nod, my cheeks aflame for a moment. I suspected guilt was at the root of his kindness. A duty to set things right with me. Whatever it was, I was grateful.

Varick opened the door, the massive panel creaking on its hinges, announcing our arrival to everyone in the grand hall.

A sound like rain grew in my ears and it took half a second for me to realise it was applause. The room was heaving with suited men, bashing their hands together, leaning past one another to try and get a better look at me.

If I had been nervous before, my feet had now taken root in the ground. My mouth parted in dismay at the waiting crowd. A soft touch to the base of my spine ignited life back into my bones and I moved at Varick's side. It was soon clear where he was escorting me as we circled the masses at the heart of the lavish space.

A stage, raised above the crowd, upon which the four Helsing family members were stood. Though I hadn't set eyes on most of them before, I knew them from their resemblance to Ignus. Power that seemed to emanate from all of them.

The back of my neck prickled and I instinctively reached to the top of my dress, where I'd been keeping my stake for days.

Varick swiftly took my hand, evidently aware of exactly what had just run through my mind. His fingers squeezed mine and for less than a heartbeat, his mouth was at my ear.

"Timing, sweetheart."

He released me and I ascended the stage on shaky legs, the applause still surrounding me like thunder. I gathered up my dress, afraid of stumbling. Despite that being the least of my worries, it suddenly seemed important that I put on a strong front. Any weakness and I suspected these people might swoop down on me like vultures over a dying animal.

Katherine Helsing moved to greet me on skyscraper heels. All four of them wore gold to match me and I despised that I'd been lumped in with them. As if I somehow belonged here.

She bent low, placing a kiss on my cheek that lingered there long after she'd stepped aside. I resisted the urge to scrub my cheek clean.

Mercy curtsied and Ignus bowed his head. And then I was left to the fate of Abraham, whose entire, massive hands encompassed mine as he placed a kiss on my forehead.

Cheers reached to me from the crowd and as I was turned to

face them, spotlights blinded me, making me blink like a deer in the headlights.

"The winner of the first game in this year's season of the V Games: Selena Grey!" Abraham spoke into a microphone, his voice magnified tenfold across the room.

Mercy appeared before me with a medal in hand, her dress a mere sliver of what mine was. I leant back as she placed it over my head, her eyes trailing over my face with too much interest.

"Congratulations," she said, adjusting my hair so it was pulled from beneath the ribbon.

"What an honour," I said through my teeth. "You should really play yourself sometime."

Mercy's perfectly composed expression faltered at my remark, her eyes swiveling over my head in the direction of her mother. Then she moved on. A breath I hadn't realised I'd been holding passed my lips. I dropped my head, gazing down at the heavy golden disc attached to the ribbon, weighing down my neck.

A large H was engraved in the middle of it, striked through with a silver stake; words circled the emblem, marking me as a winner of the V Games.

When the applause died down at last, Abraham addressed the room once more. "Now, the moment you are all anxiously awaiting: the winning bid. As you know, whoever placed the highest bet on Selena Grey winning the game, will not only receive the 25 to 1 payout, but a full night with the girl herself-"

I didn't hear any more. Men were catcalling to me, whistling and making gestures I wanted to rip their throats out for.

My ears rang, like a warning bell going off in my head. I took a wary step back from the edge of the stage, stealing a glance at the Helsings. Mercy was smirking, but her brother seemed bored, paying more attention to his nails than me. Katherine had her hand on her husband's shoulder, smiling and nodding as he spoke.

I hunted for Varick in the crowd, finding him at the side of the stage, his expression entirely blank. I searched for comfort, but found none. Had he betrayed me after all?

Abraham's voice cut into my head again.

"The winner, bid just over 2.5 million in total, and bet on Selena Grey from the start." Abraham paused for dramatic effect whist my eyes trailed over the sea of spectators. "Congratulations to Brice Edgewater!"

A raucous of shouts and cheers went up from one side of the room and I spotted a group of men, patting their friend on the back. I couldn't get a good look at him, but with the feeling of a block of ice melting in my stomach, I vowed to kill the man before he laid a finger on me.

Abraham was speaking again, drawing me out of my blinding rage.

"But first, Selena will be spending a night with our esteemed Vampire friend, without whom this game could not be possible, please welcome to the stage, Varick Cartwright."

Two things became apparent to me: the first, that I couldn't trust Varick. And the second was that, even if I did get out of this place, the Helsings were going to make sure I was broken. Apparently surviving the game wasn't enough to warrant sending me home. I now had to be subjected to a worse kind of hell.

Varick was guided to my side and he thanked each of the Helsings in turn. I was sick, trembling, ready to lunge into the crowd and start ripping limbs off (and other body parts these men deserved to have removed). But I had no time to act as I was led off of the stage.

Varick's hand clamped around my wrist. He must have sensed how much I was shaking, and I prayed he mistook it for fear and not the absolute rage that was coursing through me.

I just needed a weapon.

One of the men placed a drink in my hand and I immediately chucked it in his face, snarling my rage. Instead of getting angry, he started laughing, seeming delighted by my mood.

Varick's arm slid around my waist and I twisted free, glaring at him.

"We're leaving," he demanded and I shook my head, backing up so I nudged into a few of the men.

"I'm not going anywhere with you," I hissed.

Hands slid up my back and I lurched away from the crowd, finding their eyes trailing over me with a hunger that scared me more than a V's.

Varick snatched a hold of my waist, tugging me against him and practically spitting venom at the men who had touched me. They backed up, the smiles falling immediately from their faces.

I tried to wriggle free again, but Varick held on tight, guiding me purposefully toward the exit. The music grew louder and the lights dimmed as we reached it, the party getting fully underway.

I gave into Varick as he guided me out of the room, not wanting to spend a second longer in the company of those people. Many of the men were already drunk and the last thing I needed was to be trapped in a hall with all of them.

At least Varick was just one man. Or Vampire. And I had defeated plenty of them already.

The second we were out the door, Varick pressed me back against a wall. "Calm down, I'm on your side."

"Ha," I spat. "You seemed pretty cosy up there with the Helsings."

His upper lip curled into a snarl that sent a tremor through me. "Do you have any idea what they'll do if they even *suspect* I'm going to help you?"

My mouth opened then closed. "But you get a night with me, like that other man – the bidder."

Varick shut his eyes, seeming physically in pain. "For blood, Selena. They give you to me to drink from."

"Oh," I breathed, my body slowly halting its trembling.

A group of men burst from the door, laughing and joking.

"Scream," Varick demanded, pressing his mouth to my neck.

My eyes flew open in surprise and I started screaming, thrashing against him. It certainly felt good to get some of my rage out. And miraculously, Varick didn't take a bite.

The men fell silent, eyeing us with awe and excitement.

I wanted to chase after them, to make them pay for watching me go through the games, gambling my life for their entertainment.

They passed round a corner and Varick released me, taking my hand and hurriedly leading me away from the hall.

I wasn't sure what to think, continually stealing glances at him as we walked. I had to trust him. Why would he lie now? What would he gain? He could have bitten me then if he wanted to, but he stayed his hand. That *had* to mean something.

"Where are we going?" I breathed as we headed up into the west tower. The spiral staircase circled ever upwards, making me dizzy.

"My room," he muttered, seeming deep in thought.

Eventually, he led me through a wooden door, the room placed at the far end of a pale stone corridor.

He didn't touch me, keeping his distance as he gestured for me to enter. I moved into the room, finding a large space with a king size bed and velvet furniture dotted around the flagstones. A crimson rug lay across the heart of the room, but apart from that, it was cold and void of life. A door led off from it toward what I presumed was a bathroom. I span on my heel, turning to Varick who was bolting the door locked.

Suddenly, I had to make a decision. I desperately needed someone to trust in this place and it had to be him.

He seemed to guess what I was thinking as he raised his hands and promised, "I won't hurt you."

I dropped onto the edge of his bed, nodding, thinking of tomorrow. Varick may not hurt me, but I wasn't leaving this island until I'd spent a night with Brice Edgewater. And there was no way I was going to make it through even an hour without murdering the man. Then the Helsings really *would* never let me go.

I sunk my head into my hands, trying to think of a way out. But I felt more imprisoned than ever, still playing games. The only difference was, the enemy wasn't Vs any more, it was men.

Selena

Varick was a dangerous ally to keep. I was very aware that he desired my blood. But he had stayed his hand so far. And I had to hold onto the hope that that meant something. Even so, I wasn't going to risk him changing his mind and I'd been deliberating all evening what that meant for me.

"Varick," I snagged his attention, pulling my knees to my chest.

He kept his distance from me as I sat on the bed, always ten feet away, pacing or sitting in the red velvet armchair. He seemed at war with himself, fighting some secret battle in his head.

"Selena?" He raised a brow; his eyes were growing bloodshot and I suddenly realised why he seemed so agitated.

"You're hungry," I sighed.

"Is that a joke?" he drawled, his sharp fangs glinting at me.

I rubbed at my wrists, the skin tingling there. "If you don't drink from me, what will happen?"

He sighed, knocking his head back against the wall. "I imagine the Helsings won't let me keep you much longer."

"And then what?" I pressed, making a decision in my mind. The hairs on my neck crept up with what I was about to offer and I dug my fingernails into my skin. If I drew my own blood, would that mean I was in control of what came next?

"Then they will have to feed me something else," he snarled, raking his nails down the walls so great gauges of plaster ripped off.

I shuddered, dropping my eyes, wondering if there were other girls already waiting in the holding cells lined up to play their sick game. Would Varick drink from one of them? Why was I any different?

As the skin finally slit open on my wrist, Varick's head snapped up. Our eyes locked and I raised my arm.

"Drink," I commanded, my voice trembling only a fraction. Plenty of Vs had gotten their teeth into me during the game, but this was different. This was an exchange, a show of trust.

He groaned his desperation, shutting his eyes and bashing his head back against the wall again. It was hard enough to knock a normal man out, but Varick seemed unharmed.

"Do it," I insisted, my voice quaking only a fraction.

"No," he snarled. "I promised I wouldn't hurt you."

"But if you don't feed, you'll be distracted. And I need you to help me, Varick. Please." I lifted my wrist and he looked like he was going to rush at me. He didn't, instead shutting his eyes and shaking his head.

"Stop, Selena," he begged. "I won't do it."

I stood, tentatively moving toward him. "Varick, it's alright," I insisted, taking his hand. His palm was rough against my fingers and I grew curious about his human life. Had those callouses been made then?

"You don't know what you're saying," he growled, opening his eyes, the whites of them shaded in red. He shook his head as he gazed at me. "You've given enough already. I won't take anything more from you."

"I'm asking you to," I urged, a tear slipping from my eye, surprising me.

In a flash, he caught it then wiped the mark from my cheek. "Please don't ask that of me. I won't be able to forgive myself for it."

"If you don't drink from *me*, then you will from someone else. Won't you?" I whispered and Varick slowly nodded.

"Someone who deserves it," he snarled.

"But if you drink from one of the men, they'll know you aren't feeding on me."

His eyes darkened and he sighed, trying to walk past me without touching me. I shot out a hand to halt him, lifting my torn wrist to his mouth.

"Drink, Varick. For both our sakes."

He quivered as he resisted a moment longer, then his hand curled around my arm, pulling my wrist to his mouth. His fangs sunk into my veins, so gently that it only stung for a second.

His grip was iron and his bite was deep. The longer it went on, the more I grew to bear it. I'd expected the pain the Vs had inflicted on me in the game. But this was a different experience entirely. I found myself watching him, hardly daring to blink.

He seemed desperate as he drank from me, his eyes squeezed shut like he was in agony. But he continued to be impossibly gentle. Finally, he dragged himself away with a breath of relief, turning from me before I could catch sight of his expression.

I eyed the pin-prick marks on my wrist, running my fingers over the slightly raised bumps. He certainly looked better for the blood; the translucent quality of his skin was gone. He actually looked more human, his cheeks slightly tinted with colour, his deep green eyes brighter and his lips fuller.

I didn't know where to look and he evidently felt the same as we stood across from each other.

"You should know, I rarely restrain myself," he admitted in a dark tone.

My heart flipped over as I nodded. "Good to know."

His jaw tightened as he surveyed me. "Are you alright?" He was eyeing my wrist where I was still trailing my thumb over the bite marks.

I dropped my hand. "It didn't hurt, not like in the game."

"That's a first for me, I think." His brow lowered and he slit his wrist open, offering the blood to me to heal.

I shook my head. "Better to keep the marks as proof to the Helsings that you're feeding from me."

He gritted his jaw, nodding and I noticed that the skin on his wrist had already healed over.

A tense silence fell between us. It was as if a moment had passed between us that was even more intimate than the kiss we'd shared the other night.

"Why are you helping me?" I asked eventually, puncturing the quiet.

He started pacing. "Call it instinct, a gut feeling, whatever you like. But the only reason I'm standing here today is because I've paid attention to that feeling in the past. So that's what I'm doing now."

I fell quiet at that, moving back to the bed and dropping down. I knew that feeling too. It had saved me more than once from my stepfather's anger. Sometimes just the sound of the front door opening set it off in me. I simply knew he was in a bad mood. I could slip out the window and head to the park, or pretend I was asleep before he came for me. Sometimes it worked, sometimes it didn't. But at least I'd had a chance to do something about it.

His mouth twitched as he watched me.

"What?" I asked, glancing away to escape his unblinking gaze.

"Nothing," he grunted, returning to his pacing.

I sighed. "If we're going to be allies, Varick, I'd rather you were honest with me."

"Allies?" he questioned. "Is that what you think we are?"

"What would you call it?" I challenged.

He shrugged. "Friends maybe."

I gave him a small smile. "Let's not over-do it."

He laughed and the sound took me by surprise. He sounded so human, so at ease.

"Alright, *allies*." He air-quoted the word, making my smile grow.

I explored his features, the way they had softened and the dark circles around his eyes had faded. "You look...different."

He dropped onto the far end of the bed, surveying me. "Blood makes me more human. And not just on the outside." He tapped his head. "There's a lot going on up here right now."

"Like?" I lifted a brow.

He tongued his cheek. "Give me a minute. I'm trying to work it out myself."

I gazed down at my hands, knotting them together. My thoughts drifted to Cass and pain lanced through me again. "Varick?" I breathed and he tilted his head, waiting for me to go on. "Why am I still alive? And...not the others?"

A tense line appeared on his brow. "I don't know why, Selena. Maybe you just tried harder than the rest of them. But I doubt it, don't you?"

My gut stirred uncomfortably. I didn't like that idea one bit.

He reached out, taking my hand. I inhaled sharply, finding his palm warm to the touch. "You're-"

He nodded, a slanted smile pulling at his mouth. "Feels good. But it won't last." His fingers ran over mine briefly before he released me. "Forgive me," he said quietly. "It's like waking from a nightmare. Everything's new again for a while."

My heart tugged at his words; it was strangely painful to see him experiencing life for the first time in god knows how long.

"Does your heart beat?" I asked softly.

"Only once every minute normally...but now..." He took my hand and lifted it to his chest. I stretched my palm flat, feeling the soft drum of his very human-seeming heart.

I glanced up, my own heartbeat rising to match the rush of his. "Did you know your heart beats in time with the music you listen to?" I blurted, the words spilling from my mouth. I'm not sure why I'd said it, but it was one of those beautiful things I loved about life. My mother had told me so when I was younger so I could listen to soft tunes when my heart rate elevated. It helped me keep calm. It saved me from the fear of *him* for a while.

"Is that so?" Varick raised a brow, dropping my wrist so I parted contact with him. The beat of his heart seemed to linger on in my palm.

Varick stood, moving to the top-of-the-range laptop on his bedside table. Flipping it open, he traversed his way through reams of music before pausing on a particular song.

I settled myself on the bed as *Ain't No Grave* by Johnny Cash played into the room. I choked on a laugh.

"Fitting," I remarked.

"I always was a fan of irony." He grinned and I felt as though I was seeing him for the first time. Or at least glimpsing the man he'd once been.

He dropped onto the bed, laying down beside me, resting a hand on his heart and shutting his eyes.

My own heartbeat seemed to spike rather than be calmed by the slow music. I dragged my gaze away from his still form, but he patted the space beside him, encouraging me to join him.

I shuffled down the bed, gazing up at the ceiling. My white-walled prison. Though the bars kept changing, I hadn't been free since I'd walked into the women's penitentiary back in the east of England.

"So what else do you feel?" I asked in a quiet voice. It felt odd to be lying there on a bed beside the same man who had earmarked me for his lunch the first day I'd encountered him. But I was drawn to this human part of him, curious as to who he once was.

He cleared his throat, his hand remaining on his chest. "It's hard to explain to someone who's never been dead."

A confused smile tugged at my lips. "Well, try."

He sighed, closing his eyes again. "Nothing leaves you the day you become a Vampire. Memories...the things you like...don't like. They're all still there...just, faded. The thirst takes priority over any other need. And the longer you go without it, the more it consumes you. The less the memories mean. My emotions became detached from my past until all that was left was hunger...rage."

I shuddered. "That sounds awful."

"Yes..." His tone was bleak. "But blood restores some of my humanity. Until my next feed anyway. Everything fits together again for a while. I remember exactly why I loved the sea, not just that I once did."

"You were a captain, right?"

He snorted. "If you can believe that."

I stole a glance at his expression, trying to work him out. This wasn't the hungry beast I'd been in the room with just minutes ago. "How long will it last?" I needed to know. He'd had a taste of my blood, so what was to say he wouldn't want more? And I wanted to be prepared to offer it again.

"If I'd had a full feed...maybe a week." He shrugged and I wrinkled my nose.

"A full feed...as in, if you'd killed me?"

Gingerly, he nodded and I had my answer.

"How many people have you killed?" I breathed and he sighed heavily.

"Too many."

"Do you feel bad about it?" I whispered, my skin prickling.

His brow became taut. "Do you?"

The question hung in the air, slicing through to my soul. I'd never once felt guilt for what I did to my stepfather. Perhaps that was messed up, but when you'd spent years under the roof with someone who drove terror into your heart on a daily basis, their loss was nothing but a relief. Marie's death, on the other hand, was a heavy weight I would have to carry around with me forever.

"You don't kill bad people," I commented, deflecting the question.

He blew out a breath. "I take what I can get. Either that or become one of *them*."

"The Vs?" I questioned, shuddering at the memory of their emaciated bodies, their bloodshot eyes and decaying skin.

"Mm."

"Have you ever been like that?" I whispered.

"Once," he replied in a low voice.

I didn't press him further; his body had become rigid. I supposed whatever it felt like for him to be hungry, the Vs out in the game had it worse. Much worse.

"How old are you?" I asked as the Johnny Cash song ended.

"Three hundred and something. Stopped counting about fifty years back. It does things to your head...seeing life pass by like that. I try not to remember how long I've been this way."

A harsh knock came out the door, silencing the next question that sat on my lips. I wasn't sure I should have asked it anyway. Varick no doubt wouldn't share with me whether or not he truly wanted to be a Vampire. But I couldn't help but wonder, did he choose to become this or was the choice made for him?

"Get on the floor," he commanded in a rough tone.

I gave him a questioning frown as me made his way to the door. He shot a snarling look in my direction and I hurried to comply. Whether he felt more human or not, he sure didn't look it at that moment.

I dropped to my knees as the door opened.

Ignus stood there with his arms folded and a slim metal device in his hand. "Have you fed yet? Our winner is anxious to get his hands on her."

Varick placed a palm on the door frame, refusing him access. "None of your business, Ignus. She's mine to do with as I please. And the deal is, she's mine for the night."

A sick feeling filled my gut. What would happen to me if they took me away from Varick? Vampire or not, the Helsings were in control here.

"Get it done, Varick. Or hand her over. She's yours to eat, not torture."

"And what do you care?" Varick snarled.

Ignus tilted his head to the side and his bright blue eyes landed on me. His gaze roamed over my body as if searching for wounds. I had no doubt it was to confirm Varick was feeding from me, not to check that I was okay. "I have need of you. Ulvic-"

"I get my twelve hours!" Varick roared, making me wince. He smacked his hand against the door frame and a chunk of wood snapped off, careening in Ignus's direction. My chest bubbled with hope. The boy seemed frightened, perhaps Varick *did* hold power over him.

Ignus took a wary step back, holding out the silver device in his palm. "Remember who's in charge here, V. You've got a sweet deal on Raskdød. Or would you rather we sent you into the games?" He jutted up his triangular chin, but the fact he was nearly a foot shorter than Varick did nothing to help his attempt at intimidation.

Ignus looked to me again, his mouth twisting grimly. He seemed as though he wanted to say more, but thought better of it at the last moment, turning on his heel and heading away.

Varick slammed the door, his shoulders heaving with deep breaths.

I stood, moving toward him and placing a hand on his spine. He whipped around in a flash. "We'll be left alone until tomorrow." Varick sat me down on the bed with surprisingly gentle hands.

I nodded, unable to unravel the snake that had coiled around my throat and strangled me into silence.

"You should get some rest." Varick began pacing the room, running a hand through his long hair. He pushed the bandanna free, shaking it loose so a tangle of dark hair fell around his face.

I sighed, dropping back onto the soft pillows. My mind was a whirlwind, but the last week had taken a lot out of me. And for the first time in a very long time, I felt safe.

I yawned broadly, rolling onto my side and finding Varick watching me from across the room. "Stop staring," I murmured, my eyelids growing heavy. The angular planes of his face were tempting in my drowsy state; half asleep, my fingers flexed at the thought of reaching out to feel them.

A grin tugged at his mouth - a perfectly human smile. Well, if you discounted the fact Varick looked like an Armani model with the temperament of an angry polar bear. "Goodnight, sweetheart."

Varick

It was the first time in god knows how many years that I actually *missed* sleeping. Standing guard while Selena slept, curled up on the bed like a cat. It made me want to tear my tongue out just so I could stop thinking about her blood. But my thirst for her was battling with some other emotion now. I craved *her*, not just her blood. And perhaps those lines were starting to blur...

The only thing that made her scent more bearable was the fact she'd been bathed, using the same lavender soap of the Helsings. A smell which made my skin crawl with abhorrent memories.

I recalled the cell I'd been kept in; the iron bars, the sunlamps suspended above me, flashing sporadically whenever one of them visited me. The way my skin peeled as it seared beneath the unforgiving light...

Pressing my fingers into my eyes, I forced the images back, but my damn mind was sharper than ever, flooding me with them. The way my skin had decayed on my bones, my jaw had ached with the thirst. It had been torture of the highest form and all it took was removing blood from my diet for a few weeks. I was a slave to it, as I was to *them*.

That was, until I met her. Selena had a streak of fierceness in her that could serve us both well. I just had to figure out a way to stop Brice Edgewater getting his hands on her, without the Helsings killing her for it.

I gazed at her still form, wondering what it would be like to experience such peace again. To be able to switch off my mind and escape for a while.

My memory of sleep was strange. When a need no longer became necessary, it was easy to forget exactly how it felt.

I moved towards Selena, creeping onto the edge of the bed and laying across from her. I was a pro at keeping silent, and if she woke, I could move before she even spotted me.

I watched her in fascination, desperate to know what it felt like to dream again.

I shut my eyes, trying to turn off my thoughts, to encourage the tug of tiredness, drawing me into oblivion. Strange, to be free of such a thing. Was it a curse for a human to spend nearly half their lives unconscious, or was it a sweet blessing that a creature like me could no longer indulge in?

Immortality may have been worth the absence of sleep, of hunger. But not the absence of time. The days meant nothing. Each merged into one, an endless strip of forever that had my name etched into its path. I was here until whatever doom befell the earth. So long as the Helsings didn't end me first. And sometimes, I considered angering them enough that they would. Perhaps I'd rip off Katherine's head and let her husband rain down hell on me.

It was a dreary thought, but one with which I'd flirted more than once. Without time, life had lost meaning. The things I'd once wanted had lost their allure. My friends were gone. My family. All that had remained was me and an eternity of serving a family I despised.

But then *she* showed up. The little survivor. And I now had a purpose again: to get her the hell off this island. No matter what the consequences.

I'd had more than one noose around my neck in my human lifetime. Literal and figurative. And she escaped harm in the way I used to: by the skin of her teeth. That seemed like a handy trait to have in my new 'ally'.

o ☼ o

Winter, 1803

"We sail for Melwick's gold," Jameson muttered to me in my quarters, spinning a dagger in his hand.

I sighed, rubbing my eyes. "It's too soon. We aren't ready."

"The crew need a reason to believe in you again, Varick."

I bashed my fist down on the table between us and Jameson automatically pushed my tankard closer, encouraging me to take a drink. I knocked back the dark rum, wiping the residue from my beard.

We'd been days at sea. A storm had taken four of my men and snapped the mizzenmast. We were travelling on bitter determination alone, and I was sick and tired of Jameson suggesting we head for the gold.

"They have a reason," I snarled. "I'm the son of their last captain. A great man. He owned half the islands in the north sea."

"He owned them once, Varick. Now they're in the hands of our bloody English King."

"The aristocracy think they own everything," I spat. "But do you see the king himself sailing north to lay his claim?" I topped up my rum from the bottle. "I'm more of a king there than some fat blueblood."

Jameson barked a laugh. "Perhaps if he spent more time sailing than eating, he'd have put an end to piracy by now."

"Lucky for us." I grinned and he tapped his tankard to mine.

We drank until my head swam, then Jameson made his way from my cabin, singing old sea songs as he staggered across the deck.

After a while, the sound of Pud's voice caught my attention and I headed onto the deck, finding the majority of my crew gathered around the boy. He was propped up on a barrel, drinking ale as he told his story.

Jameson shot me a grin, joining the crowd. I leant back on the stair to the tiller, listening to Pud's tale.

"-had white teeth, so sharp they could cut through skin and bone. And their beauty was unequalled to anyone I'd seen before. The women were pale-skinned and their bodies bewitchingly desirable."

The men cheered and I rolled my eyes. Pud's drivel was keeping the men merry, had been for months now. So I let him stay. Despite the fact he was about as useful onboard as a rat in the kitchen.

"Even the men lured you in with their eyes. As soon as they spoke, a calm washed over me. My body was no longer mine. They drew me into their arms and I went willingly, letting them take what they wanted from me."

"No one would want your skinny arse, Pud!" Jameson hollered from the crowd to a mass of roaring laughter.

"They wanted my blood!" Pud shouted over the noise and the clamour fell to quiet mutterings.

"They bit my neck, I have the marks to prove it!" He twisted his head to the side, pushing back the locks of curly blonde that had grown so long in the short time he'd been with us.

Even squinting, I could see nothing on his neck, but some of the men disagreed, pointing and gasping.

I'd had enough, walking out into the crew, slowly clapping my hands. "A good tale, Pud. But I think blood-sucking humans are beyond any stretch of the imagination."

"It's the truth, Cap'n," Pud said, straightening his spine. "I'd swear it on my mother's grave, I would."

"No doubt you would," I remarked. "Selling your mother out for the sake of your stories seems a little low, however."

The men eyed me with sour expressions. I stared them down until they diverted their gaze, shuffling around like mistreated dogs.

"Get back to work," I commanded, turning and heading back to my quarters.

"They spoke of you, Captain Varick!" Pud called after me and I paused, glancing over my shoulder with a snarling expression. This boy was asking for trouble.

"They said the son of the Sea King will soon be theirs."

I snapped around, marching toward Pud, my crew hastily getting out of my way. I grabbed him by the scruff, dragging him from the barrel with brute force. He screamed in alarm, huddling protectively at my feet. "No please! I only speak the truth."

"Enough, boy! Tell your stories if you must, but leave me out of them. The next time I have to tell you, you'll be skewered on the end of my sword." I snatched his collar, pulling him up to face me and a whimper passed his lips. He was barely a man, not more than fourteen. At his age, I'd been the mate to my father. I'd learnt how to run a tight ship, how to command a crew's respect. This boy clearly hadn't had such guidance.

Dragging him to his feet, I landed him upright, brushing off his shoulders. "If you wish to stay onboard, you'll learn to do more than weave a good tale, Pud. Tomorrow you'll rise at dawn and come to my quarters. I'll teach you what it takes to be a part of my crew."

I released him forcefully and he gazed up at me with fear and respect in his eyes. The men around him observed me with similar expressions and I knew I'd done my job.

Tomorrow, I would treat the boy as my father had once treated me. And in doing so, I'd remind my men why they followed my orders.

My eyes flickered open and I jerked backwards on the bed, fully conscious. But surely I had been conscious moments ago, too? Sleep wasn't possible. But my memories, they had been so vivid...

Selena still slept beside me, but my movements had stirred her.

My tongue suddenly burned for more of her blood. She had returned to me the ability to sleep. How was that possible? I'd drained entire bodies before and never managed to become so human.

I stood, lifting a hand to my heart which was only slightly slower than it had been immediately after drinking from her. How long would her blood keep me this way? The amount I'd drunk should already have worn off a little.

I moved to the bathroom, eyeing the shower with longing. Would I feel it on my skin? Would the water heat my blood and soften my muscles like it used to?

I rushed into the stream, forgetting to remove my clothes. It had been so long since I'd attempted such a thing. My body didn't sweat. I wasn't a slave to the secretions of a human any longer. The closest I had come to feeling – truly feeling – water on my skin had been out on the island. When it didn't snow on Raskdød, it rained. Bloody poured. And I'd stood in quiet determination out on the eastern cliff, letting it wash over me, trying to feel it again. My body was continually cold, but I didn't feel it the way I had as a human. I hadn't been uncomfortable, but at that moment, I'd wanted to be.

I'd wanted to feel what the sea spray felt like on my cheeks, the way the wind bit my skin and brought the blood to the surface. I recalled standing on that cliff in a violent storm, beneath the black clouds and above the frothing, angry sea.

The rain had soaked my clothes, my hair, plastering it to my body. The drops had run down my neck, my spine, and still I'd felt nothing. Not a shiver or the rush of adrenaline brought on by a thunder crack. I might as well have been one of the rocks, ravished by the elements, its state unchanging in a thousand years.

What life was that? Even if I'd thrown myself from the edge, I'd have lived.

As I stepped into the heated stream of the shower, a breath of hot vapour rushed over me. The lavender soap stung my nose and I quickly removed it from the shower, tossing it into the toilet so I could bear its vile scent.

The hot water distracted me quickly. As it flooded over my body, it soaked into my shirt, my jeans. I sucked in a breath, the steam rising in plumes around me and with a jerk backwards, I realised it was scolding.

Selena was suddenly there, shooting out an arm, turning down the heat and hissing as her own skin grew red beneath the stream. She swore between her teeth, yanking her arm back. "What are you doing?" she demanded.

"I can feel again."

I shut my eyes, recalling the sun in southern France, sailing through the azure waters of Greece, chasing the sunset in Portugal. I'd been free once, more than I'd ever realised.

A noise of grief passed my lips as I finally felt the loss of it. So many years had gone by and never once had I grieved the life I'd left behind. Selena had given me the chance to regret again. The chance to miss it with all my heart. No blood had ever given me that.

Selena laid a palm on my shoulder and it was only then I realised I was shaking.

"Go," I demanded, but her hand didn't leave my skin.

"You're more alive after you drink," she whispered and I span around, burying the grief in my chest.

"Not alive," I snarled. "I'll never be *alive*."

Her eyes flashed with indignation. "Living is overrated," she muttered.

"Get out!" I snapped and she shrank from me, clutching her hands to her chest like I was about to rip out her heart. Perhaps if I did, I could save us both a lot of trouble.

Her face became stony, then she walked from the room without another word. I ached as I watched her go, hating what I'd done.

A while passed before I turned the shower off, marching out into the bedroom, leaving a trail of water behind me. Selena was perched on the edge of the bed, clawing her hands into the sheets.

"Don't ever complain about your life, Selena," I bit at her. "If you didn't want it, you'd stop trying to survive this place."

She sprang to her feet, glaring at me through dark eyes. "When I die, it will be *my* choice. Not someone else's." Her expression spoke of pain and some shadow in her past that haunted her. I knew it wasn't the games that had planted that darkness in her heart. I'd seen it that day at the prison. The girl seemed to be living just to spite the rest of the world.

"Your strength will run out," I said. "Then what will you have left?"

She glared at me with venom in those obsidian eyes. "What *you* have, I guess," she snapped. "Nothing."

My insides shrank. She saw right through me. I was a husk of the person I'd once been. I resembled him, but everything he'd once possessed had been taken from me the day I was turned.

She dropped her eyes, sucking the insides of her cheeks. "I didn't mean that," she breathed. "I'm sorry."

I couldn't remember the last time I'd been apologised to; I felt completely out of my depth. "No, you're right about me."

She shook her head, guilt etched in her features. I moved toward her, bending low and taking her hands. The warmth of them made my heartbeat quicken and something seemed to expand inside my chest. "But helping you has given something back to me. Something to hold on to."

She gripped my palm, her nails digging in and I almost felt the pain of it. "Please, don't let them send me to that man."

I ground my jaw, the mere thought of it reeking havoc on me. I wasn't used to all these feelings; my head was a rush of confusing signals. But above them all, one thing prevailed. Saving her.

"I promise."

She kissed me, her mouth burning hot against mine. And I felt all of it, unlike last time when I'd only been half awake. Now I was fully, unbelievably present. My heart fought against my chest, my blood rushed harder through my veins. My desire for her met boiling point and I detached myself, fearful of hurting her.

For a moment, I considered telling Selena Mercy's theory of why her blood was special, why Ravenos had reacted to it when he drank it. But even *I* wasn't sure I believed it.

Her fingers entwined with mine and a sigh passed my lips. Whatever any of this meant, could not be discussed now. I tugged her toward the door.

"Where are we going?" she asked.

"I'm getting you out of here."

Selena wanted an explanation but I hushed her, moving past two guards stationed along the corridor. They eyed her suspiciously, but said nothing, which was predictable. The Helsings may have had the upper hand over me, but their guards were as human as they came. And they knew better than to challenge me on anything.

I led her downstairs, keeping her hand firmly clamped in mine.

There was only one way we were going to walk off this island alive, so I headed to Brice Edgewater's room, hunting him down by scent.

Selena was leaving this island. Today.

Selena

"**N**o matter what happens, I need you to trust me," Varick said as we walked. I noted his clothes were still sodden from the shower he'd taken. It didn't seem worth mentioning; he either didn't notice or didn't care.

As we walked, I felt that I was balancing on the edge of a knife, one slip would end me. But I'd never felt more alive, or more reckless. I knew what was driving my actions now. Kissing Varick had made my heart beat faster. And reminded me I was still here, still fighting.

Thoughts of Cass flitted in and out of my mind. Of Briony's closing eyes. Of Kite falling, her fingers grazing freedom. I was standing here because of all of them. And I wouldn't forget that.

Varick bashed his fist against Brice's door; it was located in the northern tower, each level housing the men in corridors full of rooms. A group of men passed us and I felt their eyes eating into me. My chin was held high, and I stared right back at them, mentally killing them over and over in my head.

The door opened and Varick immediately thrust me into Brice's arms. I prayed he had a plan, because I was being thrown to the wolves here.

Brice was younger than I'd expected, perhaps in his early

twenties. Attractive too, not the kind of guy who needed to bid for a night with a girl. Certainly none as plain as me.

His fingers curled around my wrist and the warmth of them was more disconcerting than Varick's cold hands had ever been.

"She's all yours," Varick said without emotion and Brice pulled me backwards into the room.

Varick swiftly followed, shutting the door with a kick.

"Some privacy would be appreciated," Brice said, pushing me toward the bed and heading for a bottle across the room. Whiskey. Typical.

My mouth curled into a sneer, but I quickly reconstructed my expression into fear as Brice turned to face me.

Varick moved toward him at speed, knocking the crystal glass from his hand. He gripped his neck, forcing his eyes to meet his.

"Relax," he commanded and Brice went slack in his hold, but Varick didn't release him. "You will tell the Helsings I brought Selena to you. You spent the night together and she left in the morning."

"In the morning," Brice murmured vaguely.

My heart lifted with hope as I watched.

Varick glanced at me. "I'd appreciate you covering your ears for the next part. A guy like this would share the details with his friends."

I screwed up my face in disgust. "Can you at least make him think I put up a good fight?"

Varick's mouth pulled up at the corner. "I doubt he'd expect anything else." He fixed his gaze on Brice's dreamy eyes once more and said, "*Ears*."

I sighed, covering my ears, feeling idiotic.

Varick started speaking and I was too curious not to listen. I lifted my palms and immediately clamped them back down, my cheeks flaming. Damn Vampire. Where did he get ideas like *that*?

I found myself sinking onto the bed, my back to them so I didn't even have to watch Varick talking about me like that. A glint of silver caught my eye beneath the pillow and I lifted it, immediately springing to my feet. My heart thumped loudly as I took in the chains ringed around the bedposts. At the heart of them, lay a silver dagger.

I was suddenly there again, beneath my stepfather. What if I hadn't had that knife to save myself?

My breaths grew ragged as I considered what this man had been planning to do to me. And I grew angry. Angrier than I'd ever been in my life. After everything I'd been through, everything I'd survived and this monster had been planning to rip the last piece of humanity from me.

I grabbed the dagger, murder flooding my veins. Varick's words halted and he snapped around, sensing my approach.

I screamed out, slashing the dagger at Brice, but Varick caught my wrist, his eyes blazing at me.

"Selena!" he warned, then his eyes slid over my head, taking in the chains on the bed. I saw the same thing break in him that had broken in me and without a second thought, he snapped Brice's neck.

I lurched backwards at the sound of the sickening crack, the dagger dropping from my hand. *"Varick,"* I gasped in shock.

His shoulders were hunched, his breathing heavy as he tried to regain control. A barrier dissolved around my heart; one I hadn't realised had been in place. Varick had protected me, without thought, without even a brief hesitation.

I laid a hand on his back, tears filling my eyes. "Thank you."

He stiffened, turning to me and dragging me into his arms. His heart thumped against me, hard and fast and so very human.

A knock came at the door and we split apart, gazing at it in horror.

"Hey mate, you in there? We want a look at her."

I shuddered internally and ducked down, taking the dagger into my hand.

"Let them in," Varick growled in a deadly tone, but I shook my head, knowing we had to leave.

"We have to get out of here." I glanced toward the window with a sinking feeling. We were half way up the tower. How could we possibly escape?

Varick followed my gaze, looking to me then back to the door. He shut his eyes, his hands visibly trembling.

"Calm down." I rested a palm on his chest.

In a flash of movement, he grabbed me, chucking me over his shoulder so a scream of surprise escaped me. He climbed onto the bed, pushed open the window and clambered through it.

I gasped, clinging to him as I hung like a doll over his shoulder. I bit down on my lip, forcing myself not to scream again as he started shimmying down the wall, using the gaps in the ancient bricks as hand and foot holds.

Snow was falling, obscuring my view. Flakes caught in my hair as it swung below me and the arctic wind froze me to the bone in seconds.

When we hit the ground, Varick started running, so fast that I felt sick. It was like the time Ravenos had carried me, but even faster, the world just a stream of white passing me by.

We halted so abruptly that my head smacked against his spine.

"Put me down!" I demanded and Varick complied, planting me on my bare feet before him. I was so dizzy, I immediately dropped to the floor.

"Sorry, sweetheart." He scooped me up like a baby and I clung to his neck, having no choice but to hold onto him as my mind spun in circles.

A noise reached to me that made every hair on my body stand to attention. The rise and fall of a screaming alarm, like a bomb siren, whirring in my ears.

The creak of wood and lap of water caught my attention and I managed to focus enough to find us walking along a pier.

My vision restored as Varick carried me onto a yacht: the same one I'd been brought to this island on.

Varick set to work, hurrying around me, readying the boat to sail. I was useless, watching him, having no idea what he was doing. He headed into a cabin and, after a minute, a motor hummed in my ears.

The cry of nearing Vs sounded across the island and I sucked in an icy breath, realising they were coming after us.

"Go!" I urged Varick, hurrying to his side in the cabin.

The snow sat in the calm bay, the flakes falling, sheeting us in a curtain. I prayed it gave us enough cover to escape.

Varick turned to me, his eyes hardening to steel. "Press this lever forward. When you're ten miles south of here, you'll be able to use the radio to call the Norwegian coastguard."

I was already shaking my head. "Aren't you coming?"

His brows drew together, forming a sharp V between his eyes – strangely marking him as what he was. "They'll kill me the second they realise I'm gone." He pointed to the back of his head and a sobbed escaped me.

"I can't leave you," I blurted, knotting my hands into his shirt. It was still damp, colder than his chest beneath it.

Through the silent snowfall, I heard Vs hit the water, splashing over the pier into the icy bay, hunting us.

His lips met mine for the briefest of moments, just long enough that I shut my eyes to savour the feel of them. Then he was gone.

"Varick!" I shouted, running to the edge of the yacht, spotting him down on the pier, casting out the yacht. The Vs brought him to his knees and I screamed out again.

It was only then I realised, he'd already pressed the lever

forward, causing the yacht to sail into the bay. The sweeping storm engulfed the sight of him, surrounded by the Vampires.

I dissolved into tears, my hands trembling as I brought them to my mouth.

Impossibly, the moment I'd been imagining for so long was finally here. I was going home, leaving this nightmarish island far behind. But now there was no part of me that could bear to leave. Not without Varick. Not when the Helsings still lived, still playing their sick games.

And then there was the promise I'd made Cass. One I knew, deep down in my heart, that I could never break.

A promise for revenge.

Epilogue: Varick

A river of my own blood surrounded me, my skin healing over from the damage that had been inflicted by the sunlamps, the silver chains, and many more of Ingus's contraptions. As I lay in the Helsings' dungeon, Mercy's whispers ran through my mind: the words she'd spoken about Selena. Of what she suspected she was.

From the moment I'd been turned, I had made it my mission to seek out a cure. Something to reverse the Vampire curse that had been laid upon me and tarnished my soul. But I'd given up hope after too many years of searching, at last surrendering to the half-life I'd been left with.

Ravenos had been powerfully affected by Selena's blood, and so had I. I hadn't felt this human since I'd actually been alive. But if Selena's blood could return a V to its human form entirely, then she was in danger. From both Hunters and Vampires alike. And now helping her to escape on the yacht was starting to seem like a terrible mistake. Because I could no longer protect her. And the agony of that knowledge was worse than the literal torture I was being subjected to in this cell.

For some reason, my mind drifted to the day I had been turned. Somehow, it comforted me to relive the last few hours before my human life had been stolen from me. Back when my crew had walked at my side...

Spring, 1804

We'd travelled south for days on end. My King wasn't so keen on me or my men, it seemed; the English were sentencing twelve pirates to death every day. Or so I'd heard. And my information was weak seeing as it came through the flapping mouths of whores into the ears of my drunken crew. Exaggeration was in their nature, especially if Pud caught word of a story. By the time he'd retold it to my men, the details were exaggerated and unrealistic.

So we sailed for Clew Bay on the west coast of Ireland where a safe haven awaited us. My father had struck a deal with the pirate clan who resided there, which was of great fortune to us seeing as anyone not in allegiance with the clan were blasted out of the waters upon sight.

As we sailed into the bay, the colours of my father's ship were raised high on the main mast, surrounded by the rising land and calm Atlantic waters, we dropped anchor and made our way to shore. The pebbled beach rose to meet a single tower known as Rockfleet Castle, though it was barely more than a glorified tower. Sheer grey walls rose upwards to meet a ring of turrets at the top. It may have been small, but I was aware of the power this clan held. Not least by the many ships they had floating in the bay. If the cannons atop Rockfleet couldn't take us down to meet with Davy Jones, those on the Pirate Queen's fleet certainly could.

Kaitlin walked down the shore to greet me, a courtesy that didn't pass me by. Her mother and my father had been close and, as such, our bond remained in loyalty to them.

Her flame-red curls danced in the wind behind her as she moved into the water in sturdy boots. Unlike most of the women I came across, Kaitlin was no stranger to men's clothing. Her breeches were a dark green and she even had a velvet doublet on to match. The only feminine piece of her clothing was the knitted shawl she had gathered around her shoulders. And I could hardly blame her; the wind was biting.

"Varick." She beamed a crooked smile and rushed to embrace me. The teasing from my men didn't surpass me and the moment Kaitlin released me, I rounded on them. "Kaitlin's more man than half of you lot. I assure you, many have had a slit throat instead of a hello from her."

Kaitlin eyed my men with raised brows. "So this is what passes for men these days?" she asked in her celtic tones, clicking her tongue.

"Apparently," I muttered and she shot me a grin.

"Perhaps they'll learn a thing or two from the women of

Rockfleet." She turned on her heel to a chorus of whistles and I slid my sword from its holster in warning.

My men fell silent and my gaze landed on Pud who was stumbling up the rocky shore, his nose buried in a notebook as he furiously scribbled something down. He had come to annoy me less since I'd taken an interest in his training, but his stories were ceaseless. I had to enforce silence on him during his training, lest I lose my mind.

Jameson joined my side, adjusting his belt. "Why did you never bring us here before?" He gazed after Katilin with such intent that it made a laugh burst from my throat.

I clapped a hand to his shoulder. "Good luck laying her, mate. I'd reckon you're at risk of losing more than your dignity in trying."

Jameson ran a hand over his braided blonde hair, smoothing it back. "If anyone has a chance, it's me. Always did have a thing for redheads." His eyes slid to mine. "Or perhaps you have a previous arrangement with the girl?" He started pumping his fists by his hips and I jabbed him with the butt of my sword. He wheezed out a breath, clutching his side, still smirking.

"I'll take that as a yes."

"You can take it however you like, James. Kaitlin's family-" I gave him a stern stare. "-are not for bedding." Not that I really thought he had any chance of doing so. But his attempts may not have reflected well on me.

Pud halted before the tower that jutted into the sky above us and began furiously sketching on his pad.

*I jerked my chin at him. "Round that one up, Jameson," I
ordered, marching ahead to join Kaitlin's side.*

*She linked an arm through mine as we waited for the door to
be unbolted from the inside. It was a simple wooden arch, no
good for keeping out an army.*

*"Perhaps you need a little more reinforcement here," I
remarked. "A ram could knock down this door in two seconds."*

*Kaitlin shrugged. "An army would have to reach my door first.
And if they did, I would be ready." As the door swung open, I
came face to face with a canon of gold and inlaid emeralds
shaped into shamrocks.*

"Jesus," I muttered, running a hand into my hair.

*"Come, you must be tired. How far have you travelled?"
Kaitlin asked as we headed through a dark room of wooden
furniture with a roaring fire before the hearth. The only daylight
in the room came through the arrow-slits high up on the next
level. It was accessible by a wooden staircase, circling the room.
It creaked underfoot as we climbed, and as we reached the third
level, Kaitlin directed us between several rooms.*

*"As captain, you have your own." She passed me a brass key
and I took it in hand, thanking her.*

*"I'll have baths drawn up for your men, and a feast will be
made in your honour."*

*"You're too kind, Kaitlin. I wish I had a home to welcome you
into to return the favour." A dull sigh parted from my lips as I*

thought of my childhood. My mother had been an English maiden, a servant girl to a grand estate on the Kentish coast. She'd met in with my father after he visited Redwood Manor to meet with the Lord of the house. My mother was a victim of abuse, not even my father had divulged the details to me. But he recounted driving a sword into the man's neck after he found him beating my mother. He told her he could drop her at a pirate port of her choosing to start a new life. And whilst he sailed her to the West Indies, they fell in love. And my mother never parted from him thereafter.

As Kaitlin left me to rest in my room, I tried to conjure an image of my mother. But all I had was the descriptions from my father. An angel of hazel hair and lake-green eyes. Eyes, which I had supposedly inherited.

"Every time you look in the mirror, you see her," *my father would tell me, but it had never provided much peace of mind.*

I moved past the four-poster bed, hung with crimson curtains, walking to the vanity stand where an oval mirror was perched. A woman's brush and powder pot sat beside a Flintlock pistol. Typical Kaitlin. Perhaps she'd forgone her own quarters for me tonight.

A beard took over my jaw. Days at sea, with a rough course to sail, gave me no time to shave. But when I docked, I always took care to trim it back. The men said I resembled my father with a sheet of stubble and that was something I used to my advantage. After all, they had been his crew previous to his death, so I would use all the tactics I could to maintain command over them.

My eyes were deepest green, so dark that at times they appeared black. I had my father's thick ebony hair and the cut of his jaw, but she lived on there in my eyes.

A year after I was born, she'd been killed in a battle with a pirate known as Mad Melwick. Though she'd been in the Captain's quarters, soothing me as a battle raged on between the two ships, a cannon ball had taken out the hull where she remained concealed. The resulting shrapnel had ended her life.

My father had found her, with me still held tightly in her arms, just an infant. Even I hadn't avoided damage, a slither of a scar across my forearm was a reminder of what had happened that day. My father had hunted Melwick until his revenge was taken from him in gold and, most importantly, blood.

Gold which was now hidden on an island in the north sea and only I had the knowledge of its whereabouts.

It took a while for me to relax enough to sleep. I'd grown accustomed to the rocking of a ship to lull me into resting. Here, the world was still, calm. Not at all what I was used to. But eventually, sleep came for me.

Cannon fire woke me- a single shot. My hearing rang with the proximity of it. It took a moment for me to realise I wasn't aboard my ship.

Screams tore through the tower and I was suddenly on my feet, my sword in hand.

The door burst open and a woman walked in, her eyes a deep grey that seemed to go on forever. Beautiful didn't come close to *describing her. She shone like starlight, her features were sharp and flawless, the only mark on her was a smear of red around her lips.*

"Drop it," she commanded in a silky soft voice and my fingers opened on the hilt of my sword. It clamoured to the ground, but I wasn't afraid, my mind awash with her calming presence.

"I've been looking for you for a very long time, Varick." She moved toward me with easy grace, her hips swaying in a dress that was far too flimsy for the brutal weather on the Irish coast.

"Looking for me?" I questioned, trying to focus my thoughts. But each one I had slipped away before I could grasp it.

She slipped a finger under my chin, coming eye to eye with me. "You have the smell of fate about you, Varick Cartwright."

"Fate?" I echoed.

She laughed softly, the sound like a sweet song in my ears. "There is so much we have to talk about."

I blinked heavily, nodding my agreement.

"But first, you have to die." Her hands clasped my neck and with a sharp crack, the world as I knew it ended forever.

I was dragged back to my senses by a snapping of teeth. Sitting upright and pushing the hair from my eyes, I gazed across the cells to where Ignus and Ulvic Hund were standing, prodding at that damn wolf again.

"Finally," Ignus gasped. "How much of that stuff did you give him?" He rounded on Ulvic.

"You said you wanted him to remain this way for as long as possible."

"Yes, yes." Ignus waved a hand. "No matter. We can be sure it works now. But I'd like you to develop a quicker antidote."

Ulvic hesitated, then bowed his head. "As you wish." He shifted to the side and I craned my neck to see into the wolf's cage. "Forgive me, but why do you want him this way at all?"

Ignus grinned, the kind of evil smile that would make any normal person run for the hills. "I would like him obedient in both forms. There is much a wolf can't do, that a man can. And now that Varick has betrayed us, we'll need another monster on our side." He rapped his knuckles against the bars. "Hear that, wolf?"

"I have a name," a voice snarled from within the cage and my ears pricked up. I *knew* that voice.

Making my way to the edge of my cell, I tried to get a better look, my heart thundering in my ears. I must have been imagining it. It was impossible that he was here.

"Who cares?" Ignus marched away and Ulvic hurried to follow.

When they were out of sight, I hissed across the corridor, "*Hey!*"

Two hands took hold of the bars in the wolf's cell and a face came into view. His hair was overly long, but still hung in a loose plait down the back of his head. His light eyes found mine, eyes I never thought I'd see again.

I shook my head, trying to figure out if the Helsings' were

playing some twisted trick on me.

"Jameson?" I breathed in disbelief, blinking hard to try and shift the vision.

A hopeful smile curled up the corners of his mouth. "It's good to see you again, brother."

Did you enjoy V Games???

I like to think of each review I get on this book as a balloon lifting it up into the sky. If everyone adds a balloon, one day V Games will fly high among the stars!

Thank you for your support – I couldn't do it without you :)

- Love Caroline xcx

KEEP IN TOUCH!

Writing is a lonely job, and that's why it's so important for me to keep in touch with my fans. If you enjoyed V Games, please come and say hi and tell me what you liked about it!

www.carolinepeckham.com

If you'd like to stay updated about my upcoming releases then I'd love for you to join my VIP mailing list. And in return you'll receive THREE free books including Creeping Shadow (The Rise of Isaac, Book 1) and Falling Fire Parts 1 & 2 for **FREE!**

Printed in Great Britain
by Amazon

16169393R00237